**SELLING SIMON**

Copyright © 2026 Nichol Goldstein



ISBN 979-8-9915029-4-8 (ebook)
ISBN 979-8-9915029-3-1 (print)

*Dedicated to my husband,*
*who puts up with more of my crap than anyone should ever have to.*

# sick of this shit

. . .

THE SHARP *POP* is louder than she thought it would be, but the hole it blasts through his trousers is well worth it.

The blond john she was supposed to be servicing goes slack-jawed, gaping at his pants. They're not down around his ankles but scrunched between his upper thighs, the fabric now sporting a bullet hole right through the center of the stiff-stitched crotch.

While the man's junk remains hidden beneath a frumpy, saggy shirt, the hole screams its pristine circular presence to the room, showing the white of the hotel room door through the perfectly singed little tunnel. Angelica has always been a good shot.

She hinges her elbow, aiming the gun toward the ceiling as the heat of the barrel radiates against her cheek. Watching his brain's every tick and tock, she's curious as to what happens now, though she supposes she doesn't care either way.

At first, he doesn't say a word, but makes a high-pitched whine as he looks down. "W-why did you do that?"

"I'm not in the mood."

He swallows, eyes still glued to his pants. "And there wasn't a way to let me down easy?"

Angelica is silent. Dust motes cascade in flutters, visible for moments before disappearing out of the rays of light; they wink, glint, and glitter, twinkling the air with dirt.

Looking up with wide eyes, he starts to tremble. "I didn't do anything wrong. I didn't even touch you yet."

She blows out a rough breath. "You're at the tail end of a very bad day."

"Are you gonna shoot me?"

"Again?"

"Yeah, but like...me?" His gaze falls to whatever still lies hidden under his loosened jeans.

"Nah," Angelica says, scooting down in the bed but keeping the gun pointed straight up. "And I don't want your money either."

"I already paid Maxine," he murmurs, fixated on his pants. He pulls them up slowly, as if afraid the bullet hole will burn him.

"I recommend asking for a refund."

"From Max? You're fucking crazy, lady."

"You're not wrong."

Angelica pauses for a minute, watching this random man as he does up his belt in painfully drawn-out gestures. Put together again, he lifts his hands, palms out, and backs toward the door. "Not gonna shoot me?"

"Not gonna shoot you."

He whips around, tweaks the door handle, and launches himself into the drab, unremarkable hallway. Angelica can hear his racing foot-falls for a few short seconds before the door clicks shut, its locks engaging with an automatic whir.

Reaching down, she slips a pendant from beneath the collar of her lingerie, a pink frilly number the customer was supposed to like. The necklace chain is thin and dainty, the pendant an emerald-green stone she presses to her lips, emotionally numb and tired from her skin to her soul.

"Hey, Bee," she speaks to no one. "It's okay if I stop now, right?"

———

Simon gestures to the screen again, and again, as if the more times he flapped at it, the more likely it would be to turn into a pile a gold or something else awe inspiring. Something that would catch the eye and grab the imagination. Something that would shake trees and calm seas.

It doesn't seem to be working.

"Shut up." Though it's said with affection. "You can't be serious."

Simon scowls, looking at the presentation. "What do you mean? The numbers work perfectly."

Nando's arm drapes over the back of the all-too-firm office chair made of squeaking, creaking leather. The widescreen monitor between them displays data for Simon's most recent acquisition proposal, the lines of the revenue graph cascading in a series of squiggles one needs to be nose-close to decipher. His lips pull into an indulgent smile, one that comes from months of faithful practice. Simon's plans of late always seem to land the wrong way, and Nando's the only one who cares enough to give him a friendly warning. Or two. Many, perhaps. A plethora, one could say.

His accented voice scolds with love. "*Mio amico*, you show this to Lawrence, and he's gonna laugh in your face."

"For the tenth time, the numbers work."

"But the product lines, they don't." Nando snags the mouse from Simon and scrolls up a few slides. "It doesn't fit into our portfolio at all. How are we supposed to cross-sell this shit, eh?"

"We don't," Simon says, face angled to the mahogany desk. "It's a foothold into a new market."

Nando *pffts*. "Because experimentation works so well."

"How many times do I have to say it? Look at the financials they're putting up. They're pristine. We can even improve their bottom line by consolidating the common functions under our existing systems."

"Yeah, like IT and HR aren't already drowning in work."

Simon frowns, lifting his head up to narrow his eyes at his best friend. "They're going to have to figure it out. It will happen with any acquisition we do, not just this one."

"Which is why we shouldn't acquire things," Nando says, waving his hand in an eccentrically wafting, dismissive gesture.

Simon sags in his chair with a pathetic noise.

"Hey," Nando says, going to Simon's side and scruffling his hair into a mess. "You'll get there, eh? You're just not there right now. If Lawrence sees this,"—Nando lifts his shockingly green eyes to the screen, then drops them down to Simon again—"he's going to have thoughts. Career limiting ones, *sì*?"

"There's no way you're gonna get CEO before I do." Simon sulks, but Nando only musses his hair further.

"Yes, I will. But I'll be sure to give you a cushy new job in my organization."

"And you should run it, why? Javik International is my birthright, for Christ's sake."

"That's for Lawrence to decide. All we can do is keep our nose to the grindstone, hmm?"

Simon bats his friend away. "Yeah, yeah."

"Beers Sunday?"

"Mm."

Ninja chops rain on Simon's shoulders before Nando winds his way towards the door, tossing him a wink. "And relax this weekend, eh? You're going to kill yourself if you keep working this hard."

Simon grunts in response, leaning over his computer and turning the screen back in his direction. Closing the PowerPoint deck, he stares at the file icon for a long minute before dragging it from the desktop to the trash. He can't bring himself to empty that little pixelated bucket, but at least his latest failure can be out of sight, out of mind. He'll call the broker on Monday and let him know it's a no-go. No one wants to have that kind of call going into a weekend. Simon included.

———

This place has always been hard to find, though Angelica knows it's intentional. Necessary even. One doesn't run a prostitution ring in a sunny, open-concept office with an awning brightly stating,

*"Women for Sale! Discount rates available for used models!"*

Angelica quirks a smile, running her thumb over the smooth surface of her pendant as she works her way between rusted, salt-stained cars toward the building's front façade. When the unremarkable entryway comes into view, her amusement slinks away as if scolded, letting a more familiar dread seep in. No matter what she does, this conversation won't go well. Best to get that straight in her mind now so there are no false hopes flinging around in her overactive brain.

Taking a deep breath, she creaks open the heavy outside door, its NO SOLICITORS sign sagging and streaked with God-know-what. Inside and down the mangy hall, she approaches Maxine's dented office door and raps her knuckles against the faux wood surface, looking at the spy hole with what she hopes is fierce determination. Not a minute passes before Damion, that sadistic prick, opens up with a squeal of rusty hinges that grinds against her eardrums. His monstrous, lumbering body steps back, letting Angelica squeeze into a dimly lit room filled with smoke and malevolence.

"Sadie," Maxine purrs as she lights a cigarette. The Zippo snaps with flinty sparks before searing a red ember on the tobacco tip. Maxine's ageless mouth puckers around it, taking a single quick puff before stubbing it out. She must be trying to quit again. "I hear your most recent client was less than satisfied."

Of that, Angelica has no doubt.

"Did he do anything to warrant such behavior?" Max's face says she wouldn't care even if he did. She's known for letting girls get roughed up for a better price, but no scars or hits to the face or the client gets banned. No one wants to get banned.

"He didn't," Angelica says. "But you know who did."

"Well, boys will be boys." Max's eyes glint, her grin showing the points of her teeth. Damion chuckles, low and terrifying, and Angelica wants nothing more than to turn tail and run. This was a bad idea. But it's too late.

"I don't want to do this anymore," she manages, her voice husky with fear.

"So you've been saying for months."

"I mean it this time."

"And why should that matter to me? I own you, Sadie, body and soul, and I have for years."

The air prickles with danger as Damion looms behind her, taking up space like an oil tank and making the fine wisps at her nape stand on end. Angelica fists her hands, pulling her skin into pale nubs of knuckled bone as she stares at them. "If you don't let me go, I'll do it again. I'll come at every john you send my way and ruin your reputation. Either that, or maybe I start hacking pieces off myself to make sure I'm no longer useful."

As soon as she says it, her stomach flip-flops. Why put ideas in Maxine's head? One look at her says the thought has already sunk in well and deep. A reel of horror movies plays in Angelica's head, each more visceral than the last.

Max uses her long fingers to push her ashtray around the table without taking her eyes off Angelica. "You're affecting the morale of my girls, you know."

Like she gives two fucks about any of them.

The ashtray scrapes along the surface while Max stares at Angelica, but she refuses to wither even when she begins to tremble. Damion drifts closer, laying his meaty, spatulate hands on the curve of her shoulders and pinning her arms to her sides. His scent is like iron. Like blood. It's as if he bathed in it.

Maxine slides out of her high-winged chair and laces her fingers behind the small of her back, walking closer and closer until Angelica can smell the tang of her fancy perfume and the dank of her foul breath.

"I am a businesswoman above all else, Sadie. I can see when a deal can be made."

An undesirable, unasked-for, naïve hope flickers in Angelica's dead heart.

Maxine leans in, lips brushing her ear. "I want one hundred thousand dollars."

Angelica jerks back, but Damion pushes her close again as Maxine tucks long fingernails under her chin. "If you want to leave, Sadie, buy your way out."

"Where am I supposed to get that kind of money?"

Angelica's face gets tipped back and forth as Maxine scrutinizes her every freckle. "I don't know. Change careers. Sell your blood. Sell your organs. But I better not catch you selling that hot little cunt. Call it a conflict of interest. I'm sure you understand, being a smart girl." Max taps her cheek too hard, making it sting before she walks back behind her desk. "The price must be a heavy stretch goal, don't you think? Otherwise, all my girls might grow a sac and try to follow in your footsteps. Oh, and we need to discuss consequences."

Angelica's mouth goes dry.

"You can't walk away unscathed if you don't fulfill your end of the bargain." She leans back and toys with her ashtray again. If Angelica had the courage, she'd throw that damn thing against the wall. Instead, she bites her tongue as Maxine considers.

"If I don't have my money in, let's say, three months, Mr. Damion and his friends are going to find you. They'll track you like a dog, my dear, and then they'll cage you like one. Why take pieces out of yourself when these fine gentlemen can do it for you?"

Damion's hands are weighty, and she can actually hear the bastard smile behind her. She wants to throw up.

"As you can imagine, you're out of the house and out of my sight. But, Sadie, if you don't answer the phone whenever I call, the money is immediately due. If the tracker in your arm pings you even two miles out of the city, the consequences become reality. Understood?"

Angelica's throat is a desert when she swallows. "Let's do this."

She immediately regrets her decision.

———

A tiny chunk of concrete stutters down the sidewalk. Simon kicks it as he avoids the other pedestrians click-clacking by in their sensible heels and oxfords at a pace that says they have somewhere important to be. The crumbling rock's situation seems easier than Simon's. It boils down to one word: Exist. In Simon's world, existence comes with a tedium a rock can't feel. Simon is Sisyphus, rolling a stone up a high mountain peak only for it to roll back down again as soon as it hits the summit.

"Spare a dollar?" a voice rings out, startling him from his mire. A homeless man with salt-and-pepper hair and a rattail braid sits on the pavement against the wall of a building, a beanie stretched in front of him with a smattering of change and a few loose bills. Most people breeze by without even a polite shake of their heads, which is what Simon usually does. But not today. He's tired of being who he is.

Wordless, he whips out a fifty, the highest bill in his wallet, and plops it into the hat. Despite the man's slack-jawed expression, Simon feels a deep well of dissatisfaction drag his heart into his lungs.

It's not enough.

Opening his wallet again, he throws down two more twenties.

It's still not enough. The faded green bills barely cover the pennies flashing Abe Lincoln's worthless, copper, high-crested cheekbones. Angry for some reason despite his act of kindness, he starts tossing down every bill he has in little flutters, his face pulled into a grimace.

*Still* not enough. Hell, he feels like going to the ATM and emptying his bank account at this point.

The homeless man looks from his hat to Simon and back again, his brows drawing a straight line up his forehead. "Whoa now, boy. You mad at your money or something? This counterfeit?"

Simon blinks, dumbfounded. The man picks up the bills and holds them to the light of the late spring sun, squinting one eye.

"Why would I give you fake money?" Simon asks.

"Why would you give me real money?" is the reply.

"I—" Simon starts. "You need it."

"Oh, one hundred percent, but you're not doing this for me."

Simon wants to be offended, he really does, but he doesn't have it in him. He even fails at giving charity. How stupid is that?

"What's your name?" Simon asks.

The man stacks the money, keeping it separate from the rest that was tossed in his pile. Simon doesn't know how to feel about that.

"Ciel."

"Like…seal?"

The man snorts a laugh. "No. See-El. Kinda like Spanish for sky."

"You Spanish?"

"You Japanese?"

No, he's absolutely not. He's a white-collar white boy, paler than pale since he never goes outside longer than his commute requires. He runs a hand through his hair, watching his money get counted and inspected. "Look, it's real, I promise."

"Exactly what someone trying to get rid of fake cash would say."

Rolling his eyes, Simon sits down beside Ciel. He flings his stupidly large feet out to either side and slams his spine against the façade of whatever building they're in front of, tipping his head back and leaning against the brick.

"You're also willing to get grime and old gum on your nice suit," Ciel says. "Classy."

Simon looks at him askance. The people walking by are glossing over Ciel to look at Simon, the bigger anomaly. He sighs with a grimace before holding his hand out to the man sitting beside him. "If you don't want it, give it back."

But Ciel twists at the waist, holding the money at arm's length. "No take-backsies."

Scoffing, Simon crosses his feet at the ankles and hopes he doesn't trip anybody.

The homeless man gives him a once-over, top to bottom. "What's eating you?"

"I hate my job."

"You and everyone else."

"I hate my life," Simon adds, shutting his eyes to the world. "Everything is meaningless and empty. There's no reason to do anything. Everything I'm supposed to want, I don't. Everything I'm supposed to do is frustrating and fruitless. I'm living the same day over and over again, and it's not a good day."

"You're not about to jump off a roof or anything, are you?"

"What?"

"Sorry, people don't throw down all the cash in their wallet and spill their guts to a random stranger, never mind some bum on the street. This is more like a 'Goodbye, cruel world' kind of moment."

Crossing his arms, Simon scowls. "I'm not doing that."

"You got a woman?" Ciel asks.

With a sulking pout, Simon cinches his arms tighter. "No."

"Get one. In my experience, she'll either save your life or ruin it, but either way it's bound to be a hell of a ride."

That actually squeezes a huff of a laugh from Simon's otherwise dour mood. Sitting there, watching the sky, his belly rumbles, reminding him that life goes on no matter your angst. An echo comes from Ciel's middle too, as if answering the call for food.

"Wanna go get something to eat?" Simon asks, surprising himself.

"Nah. No place will take someone like me."

"I go to this one pub all the time. I'm pretty familiar with the bartender. If he tries to kick you out, I'll tell him I won't come back. Or that I'll open twenty fake review accounts to trash him online or something."

"And how are you gonna pay?" Ciel flops Simon's stack of money around. "I've got all your cash."

"Platinum card."

"You trynna make me rob you?"

This time, Simon gives a true chuckle. He flexes one arm, showing off the mediocrity that lives there. "I think I can take you."

It's Ciel's turn to laugh. "All right, Cruel World. Let's put that card to good use."

———

It's dark in the pub, which matches Angelica's mood perfectly. She sits at a shiny, overly waxed table and nurses her beer, the one she'll allow herself on her budget, which now consists of less than a hundred dollars. She's got no food. No clothes. No roof over her head. Max tossed her on the street and locked down the group apartment, ensuring Angelica had nothing to her name. Gwen and Kay are going to freak out, but they'll let her go easy enough. They never really got on, anyway. Kay's too young to be jaded and Gwen's too busy to care, in high demand with the fetishists willing to pay big bucks to be dominated. It suits her and her Amazon-esque stature. Angelica's pretty sure that woman wants to turn tricks until her vagina falls off.

The only way to have a warm bed tonight is to pick up a one-night stand. Even so, the guy's going to have to be really drunk to not oust her after the deed is done.

Angelica scans for candidates. Young businessmen in a booth laugh over a pint together, slapping each other's backs for successes unknown. Ladies with rainbow drinks chatter about this and that, completely enthralled by whatever the blonde one has to say. Angelica already hates her. She hates perky people who get attention for no reason other than the fact that they're alive.

"That's so unfair," a deep voice booms.

Angelica's gaze flits to two men hovering over the bar. One is bigger than a house in refined business battle gear, and the other is a shabby old guy who looks like he belongs on the street. The hulking stallion has black, longish hair which he can't seem to keep his hands out of—a sure sign of stress if there ever was one. He has a regal nose, his jaw a rare straight line cut from his ears to his chin, his Adam's apple prominent and masculine. His brows are furrowed into a straight line as his lush lips scowl. He's uniquely intimidating. Someone like him probably has a hard time getting women to approach him. He's too big, and he looks like he's been angry since birth.

Focused, he's zeroed in on the man to his side with what looks like a third shot in front of him. He inhales French fries and chews with his mouth open, unrefined despite his designer clothes.

"Bingo," Angelica murmurs to her pendant.

She fluffs her hair and reapplies the cherry lip gloss that is her pocket's constant companion. Standing as smoothly as possible, she slips her hands down her body to straighten any wrinkles in the only clothes she has left, and saunters to the bar where they sit wrapped up in their conversation. Well, the shabby guy sits. Her target is standing and slightly wobbling on his feet.

Easy pickings.

"Listen. Listen," Big Boy says. "I'm gonna give you a job."

Angelica hops up onto the barstool beside him and runs her fingers over the rim of her glass, hoping he'll notice her.

The old guy smirks. "Yeah? And what skills do you think I have?"

Angelica's only skill besides the one that lives between her legs is holding a gun, but Max was quick to take that right off her.

Big Boy waves his hand in front of his face as if the other man's comment doesn't matter and then throws down another shot. "I'mma find you something. I like find"—he holds in a hiccup—"finding things."

"Yeah, yeah. Eat before you fall down."

Obedient, the guy digs in. One bite takes down a solid third of the huge hamburger in his paw and Angelica cocks her eyebrow. Mouth full, Big Boy asks, "How'dya end up on da street anyway?"

"Same sob story as everyone, I suppose. Got home from doing my time in the service and was pretty screwed up. My saving grace was my wife. She was the one who held down a job and kept everything running." He heaves a heavy sigh, leaning one elbow on the bar top and sliding a fry through his ketchup as if he was going to draw pretty pictures with it. "I was a house husband, I guess you'd call it. She was everything to me. But then she died. Mugging went wrong. The pictures were…well, I don't want to think about those, but it set off something in my head, you know? I got shoved in the hospital and by the time I got out, there were eviction notices everywhere. I couldn't keep my head on straight and had my own 'Cruel World' moment. But she wouldn't have wanted… Wait. Are you seriously crying?"

Angelica's spine goes ramrod straight, and she looks at Big Boy's back. He's scrubbing at his face as he sniffs too loudly.

"You were lost without her. I totally get it." Another sniffle. "I wanna be like you. I want my first love to be my only love."

Shabby man's face squinches. "You've never been in love? At your age?"

In a mopey stage whisper, Big Boy admits, "I've never even had sex."

"You WHAT?" Angelica blurts.

Both men turn, and Big Boy's face immediately goes scarlet. "I'm drunk! Forget I said that! It was a lie!" But the way he's waving his hands while protesting reminds Angelica: enough shots of liquor and the truth will out.

The shabby man shakes his head and takes a sip of water. "Smooth."

"I went on a date once," Big Boy states, his words coming in rapid fire. "But it went bad, and I haven't had time since because my work is taxing and stressful and there's no need to get a woman tied up in all that. I wouldn't even know how if I tried." He throws his hands out as if to hold her at bay. "I mean, I know how. Maybe. I think. In theory. But I've got no game, you know? I'm a guy out of nowhere with nothing to say and my life is—"

Angelica puts a palm up to stop his painful ranting. Gulping the last of her beer, she slams the glass down and stands to her full height, small as it is, puts her hands on her hips and declares, "That's it. I'm teaching you how to date."

The man's face goes from pink to white.

"In exchange for room and board."

# say what?

· · ·

SIMON BLINKS at the beautiful stranger, his brain completely glitching. The wires in his head crackle and pop, ensuring his thoughts don't make a meaningful circuit. Her yellow dress hugs every part of her tiny figure, cutting off at mid-thigh and flashing the right amount of skin. Her model-long, jet black hair is curled at the ends and her lips look plush. Shiny and kissable. Her ice blue eyes are defiant, flashing as if challenging him. But to do what, again? What did she say?

Oh hell.

"I'm sorry, what?" he asks. "Are you…are you offering?" He gestures to his crotch.

Ciel coughs out his drink behind him, and Simon realizes what he said. It must be all the butterball shots, those creamy, tasty liquor bombs. He internally castrates himself and cringes. She doesn't seem offended. The lady in yellow only puffs out her chest, sporting those soft, soft curves, and tips up her chin.

"No. I'm going to teach you how to land other women."

"Land them?" Simon squawks. "LAND them?"

The whole place seems to be staring at him, and all he wants is to jump over the bar and hide under a mountain of glass bottles. Too bad the bartender is gawping with his mouth wide open.

Clearing his throat, Ciel stands. "Well, I better get going before they give away my bed for the night."

Whipping around, Simon yelps, "You can't leave me."

Ciel's smirk is wily, his eyes twinkling as he crams the last of his fries in his mouth. Grabbing Simon, he tugs him over and speaks low. "Do you want to make today different from yesterday? If so, this is your chance, right here."

Simon almost falls down. Ciel steadies him before dusting off his shoulders like a dad. His smile is devilish as he lifts his eyebrows high, and with that, he's out the door, his cash-filled hat pulled tight on his head and his rattail braid flowing behind him.

Simon turns to the woman, lost and way the hell out of his depth. His liquor-addled brain knows Ciel was right. Out of days of monotony, weeks and months and years, for the first time in far too long, this moment is different. It'll stand out. It's special.

Blindingly confident, the woman steps forward and pulls him straight, reaching around and plunging her hand into his back pocket. He *eeps*, but she takes no notice, rubbing against him and digging out his oversized wallet. It looks huge in her tiny hand.

She slips out his credit card with ease and waves it at the bartender who nearly jumps over to ring up the bill while Simon happily lets the petite, feisty, gorgeous stranger forge his signature.

His bleary mind latches onto her handwriting, which is so much better than his. She slips the card back into his wallet before cramming it in his pants, and all he can do is beg his drunken body not to get an erection.

Taking his hand in a clamped fist, she tugs him from the bar, nearly slamming him into the door on the way. Ciel is waiting for the light to turn at the crosswalk, and when he sees Simon, he twiddles his fingers, obviously uncaring that some random girl is dragging him down the street.

Until she stops and Simon nearly barrels into her. "Where do you live?" She says it like a command even though it's a question, and it does something to his insides.

Feebly, he points over his shoulder. "A...a...about two train stops that way."

With a huff, the woman spins him around and shoves him from behind. "Lead the way."

Feet flapping in front of him, he does what he's told, not sure why he's doing it. One thing's for sure, he's going to remember this day for the rest of his life.

————

Angelica is in a bathroom bigger than the size of the eat-in kitchen she shared with Gwen and Kay.

"Bee, look at this place," she says to her pendant, running her thumb along it as she makes a slow turn. It's all marble tile and rain-water shower heads.

The vanity has two sinks, one of which she's absolutely commandeering. It boasts a litany of pretty drawers down the side, all filigreed handles in deep brass. The space has an overwhelmingly creamy color, bright but not in the same way that her white linoleum and Formica countertops were. It's a warmer sort of place made for warmer sorts of people.

There is a knock at the door. Two soft little bumps, then a pause, then a stronger, sharper rap.

Geez, this man truly doesn't know what to do with himself.

Opening up the door, she notes his broad shoulders are hunched, losing him at least an inch or two to bad posture. A bundle of white fluff is held defensively in front of him as he stares at the floor. His ears are red and he's twitchy, which is hilarious. She's not even out of her clothes yet.

"I-I brought you a towel," he says.

"Thanks. Do you have any clothes I can wear?"

"What?" he meeps. Why does everything scare this man?

"Like boxers and a T-shirt," she says, rallying her patience.

"What?" he says again.

Angelica runs her hands over her face with a sigh. He has the most expressive, bourbon brown eyes, and they're filled with fear, as if she'd bite him at any minute. She might, if only to get the worst of it over with and shock some sense into him.

"Look, I'm not asking you to give me your wardrobe, I'm asking for a little help. A robe? Or do you want me to walk around naked and wet in a towel?"

He goes a million shades of red again. He's hopeless. She's definitely going to have to take charge with this one.

"Do you wear tighty whiteys?" she asks.

"No."

"Boxers?"

"Yes."

"And I assume you wear T-shirts?"

He nods rapidly.

"Then chop-chop, my fine friend."

He all but flees, shoving the towel into her hands. It's nice and soft, and smells like dryer sheets. Deeper into the room, which has an echo made for shower singing, Angelica hangs the fluffy masterpiece on a hook next to the nearly floor-to-ceiling glass shower door. A bathtub stands on its own beside the shower, a line of blue accent tiles swooping around the edges.

"Impressive," she murmurs to herself.

Almost at a run, the man comes back and plunges clothes into her hands before backing out of the door, clutching the frame and staring with his mouth cinched. There is a zip-up hoodie to go with what she asked. A nice touch. It's soft and looks almost new. The boxers are big enough to hit her knees, if they'll stick to her hips at all, but the T-shirt is so big, it will cover any accidentally exposed skin. If it doesn't, this man's brain might explode.

"It'll do. Thanks."

His "You're welcome" comes with a shy drop of his face. He seems suddenly fascinated by his shoes, shuffling them around on the plush carpet. "What's your name, if you don't mind my asking?"

Angelica's response is so rote, she doesn't have to think about it. "Sadie."

That soft mouth of his pulls up at the corners. "That's pretty. I'm Simon."

"Nice to meet you, Simon. Do you mind if I take my clothes off?"

He flees once more.

———

Sadie. Her name is Sadie.

She shuts the bathroom door behind her, and Simon thinks he's going to die. This isn't the same as a colleague from the office. This is a gorgeous stranger in his house, getting naked less than ten feet away. Getting in his shower. Into his clothes. He doesn't know whether to pass out or thank his lucky stars.

He bounces around his kitchen, touching this and that. Suddenly, the kitchen towels seem wrong. Not smoothed out or aligned like they're supposed to be. The colors don't even match one hundred percent. Black versus off-black. He never even considered off-black to be a thing until this moment.

His stovetop is speckled with grease, which seems unfathomable and untenable even though he's never noticed or cared before. His counters are cluttered with business books he has no intention of reading, has never had the intention of reading, but bought anyway because Lawrence and Nando said they were "enlightening." The only thing he reads is hardcore horror. Those gory gems sit by his bedside.

Wait. Will that make him look like a serial killer?

Focusing on his mess, he scrutinizes his kitchen table covered with junk mail he hasn't bothered to recycle in months. He huffs and then dives in, sweeping the décor magazines he never subscribed to into a little green bin. The letters offering tree trimming services when he lives in the damn city go in too, alongside the handfuls of pizza place coupons he struggles to part with, even when he religiously goes only to Tony's.

There. Tabletop = visible. Next question: Is she hungry?

He ransacks the fridge, finding cherries that have gone to smoosh, hashbrowns that boast a layer of green fuzz, and the unmistakable haze of barbeque sauce smell. Where is that even coming from?

Should he cook for her? Microwave something? What the hell does she like? Maybe she won't want to eat. Maybe she'll want to sleep.

Oh no. The bedroom.

He darts over to his guest bedroom, wondering when he last

changed the sheets. Busting in, listening intently to her humming in the bathroom across the hall, he sniffs the room for staleness.

Shit.

He ducks into his room and pulls out his cologne. With about twenty sprays, he eliminates the sealed-for-eighty-years stale air with fanning, swiping spritzes.

Double shit. Now it smells like him. Uncomfortably like him.

Flinging the bottle on the bed in a fit of pique, he wonders if the pillows are lumpy. In a blink, he finds himself picking them up and batting them against the wall, trying to loosen them up and get them fluffy.

If she saw him now, he'd look like a maniac.

But what about his room? Is there underwear on the floor? Not that it matters, she's going to be wearing his underwear after she's done running hot, soapy water over her perfect, naked body. Over that flat-looking belly. Over her soft breasts. Between those strong thighs.

Aaaaaand now his penis is standing up.

With a grunt, he lowers to his haunches and shoves his hands through his hair. How in the hell is he going to do this? What even is this? Why is this happening to him?

————

Angelica works shampoo slowly into her hair, taking her time, nails scraping over her scalp as she smiles to herself. It's all too simple, and too easy. Who is she to ignore a blessing when it falls directly into her lap?

It's not a conflict of interest if the piece of meat is male. Max doesn't deal in men, never has wanted to as far as Angelica could gather, but cougars will pay big bucks for virgin flesh. They like to be the ones to train them. Be the first notches in their belt. Hey, if they don't mind all the premature ejaculation, then that's good on them.

Bethany will help her.

Bethany aged out of the practice, but she still serves as something like a mentor to the girls. Hell, Bethany would probably want to go first. Take a turn on the wilting flower that is Big Boy Simon. It's not a bad deal for him. Bethany's still got her looks, and she's as patient as a saint.

Max got a couple grand a piece for new girls with their cherries intact. Sometimes more if they were particularly cute or didn't mind weird requests. Nothing too bad. Foot fetishes, planned voyeurism that becomes interactive, consensual non-con fantasies, fake somnophilia, stuff like that. All easy to negotiate from what Angelica's seen.

Simon couldn't handle anything like that. Not right out of the gate. But once he got a few rides around the track, maybe he'd be up for something more exotic.

The guy's not sex pot material, per se, but the potential is there. For now, he's imposing, but the minute he opens his mouth, he ruins it. For women looking to train the innocent, though, that's a tick in Angelica's favor. It will make him all the more endearing.

Then, after he's done with all his training, he'll be a force to be reckoned with. Gruff and sexy. That too would earn her a few dimes in the bank. It's definitely not going to be a hundred grand in three months though.

The thought sinks in Angelica's gut like a bag of rocks.

*I'll demand a consultant salary,* she decides. After all, she's offering her "dating" services and getting him laid. Looking around the posh bathroom she's enjoying, she's sure the man can afford it.

If she doesn't want to tip him off, she has to ask for something reasonable. And that means it still won't be enough.

She rinses out the shampoo that leaves her hair soft, even without conditioner. No wonder the guy's black mane looks so nice. She's used to hotel room toiletries which do their best to strip off every speck of bacteria known to man, even the good ones.

Looking around, she grabs another bottle, smoothing white conditioner into her hair and breathing in the unknown scent. It's not a smell she'd associate with a man, but it's relaxing. She could get used to this.

*Maybe if I can get at least half the money to Max, she'll give me leeway.*

Angelica groans, knowing that's as likely as crapping gold.

*This guy's libido is a factor too. It'll fuck everything up if he's not in this for an everyday sort of experience. He looks like he's in his near-thirties, so that's young enough to still be virile, right?*

After rinsing off she turns the shower knob and takes a deep breath. All she can do is move forward and hope her bravado doesn't land her in a coffin.

Picking up her necklace again, she presses it to her lips. "Bee, if you're really up there, please help me."

# the first date

. . .

SIMON'S COFFEE burns a trail down his throat. "Already? But it's only ten a.m."

Crossing her arms, Sadie's expression is haughty as she leans a hip against his tawny, marbled kitchen island. Her face says he's about to get scolded. He's quite used to seeing that expression on others.

"What do you think I've been doing since I woke up?" she says. "Making calls to every contact I have to see who would actually be willing to go out with someone like you."

The words ding his pride. "Aren't these things supposed to happen naturally? I go to a bar, buy someone a drink—?"

"Yeah, I've seen you at a bar. That is *not* where we're going to find success."

He grimaces. "I wasn't at my best. I had a really rough day yesterday."

"Me too. But did I let that ruin my professionalism?" She picks up an apple from the bowl on the counter and rubs it on the breast of his T-shirt. Seeing her wearing his clothes makes his insides feel funny, but he focuses on the conversation.

"No, it didn't."

She takes a bite, and the crunch fills the empty space between them as she stares.

He withers under her scrutiny, wondering what she sees when she looks at him. Someone pathetic, or someone who never made time for love?

He hopes she sees both.

Pathetic because maybe she'll be gentle, the rest because he wants her to know he can make this work if he applies himself. He has a good heart and he cares about people. Looks aside, isn't that what you need to make someone fall for you? Want to stay with you? Love you 'til the end, like his parents did for each other?

"Speaking of professionalism," she says, clearing her mouth. "I'm sure you understand there's a fee for my services."

He glances around his condo. "But I thought—"

"You think making me a roommate is enough to compensate me for the hours I'll be spending on you?" She takes another bite of her apple and resumes her stare.

"Then what is this?" He gestures a finger around his space where her shoes sit by the door, and yesterday's dress and underthings are strewn haphazardly over a chair.

Her swallow is audible. "It's a favor."

"A favor?"

"For a damsel in distress who has nowhere else to go."

This makes him tilt his head to the side. "Why?"

To this, she looks down, twirling the fruit in her hands. Round and round it goes as she avoids the bitten spots, and he doesn't know if he should regret asking the question.

"I'm trying to get out of a bad relationship," she says.

"Trying?"

She takes a rough breath and tosses her ebony hair over her shoulder. "It's not safe to go home. The good news? No one has any idea who you are, so I'll be safe here for a while. If I can make some money, I can get back on my feet and move on."

Concerned, he walks over and rests his hands on the other side of the counter. She fidgets, not even noticing the trail of apple juice trickling down her hand. Her eyes are glazed, looking at nothing, as if lost in her own thoughts. Whatever happened must've been drastic for her to take such measures.

Well, if she needs help, he'll be the one to do it. "How much do you normally make?"

She seems to snap back into herself and sucks the trail of juice from her arm. "Three grand a week," she states plainly, as if it's the most reasonable thing in the world. Simon's eyebrows hit the sky, but she only holds up a thin finger. "Let me remind you that you already have a lunch date set up. Day one, and I'm delivering. For the way I'm about to dedicate my life to you, I should ask for double."

"I definitely wouldn't pay double," he says. "I'm not even sure I want to pay three grand."

Ciel's words ring in his head. Despite his alcohol-induced haze at the time, Simon clearly remembers Ciel telling him this was his chance to make today different than yesterday.

"Fine," he says. What the hell is the point of having all that money in his bank account if he's lonely and miserable all the time?

She seems pleased with herself. And maybe with him. The idea makes him stand a little taller. "So, a lunch date?" he says.

"Yep. One o'clock. But first, take me to a store and give me your credit card. I'll spend part of my week's pay on some new clothes." He must be making a face because that scolding expression comes back. "Unless you want me to wander the world in yours."

With the way she looks in them, all adorable and swimming in the spaciousness, he'd be happy to let her float around in anything he owns. But early spring comes with frost in the morning, and while he'd like to keep her in his boxers, it's not the most gentlemanly thing to do.

"Fine," he says again.

"And while I do that, you should go to the gym."

"I'm not a member of—"

"Become one. Nonnegotiable."

She approaches with something predatory in her eyes, and it makes him back up against the pantry door with his hands up in surrender. Without a word, she lifts his shirt, and he squeaks. Who knew he could make such noises?

"Not too bad," she says, running her fingers over the center of him. He sucks in a breath as she regards him clinically, though the tingle in his skin is anything but. She hikes his shirt higher and spreads her fingers over his pecs, pressing down on the nothing that lives there. "Flex for me," she murmurs, and he unintentionally goes rigid, above and below.

She *tsks*, thankfully not noticing his budding erection as she squeezes his non-muscles. "You're big, but you're not toned. Soft. It's not bad, but it's not drop-dead gorgeous, either."

She keeps running her fingers over him and every touchpoint makes his skin burn. His face is hot all the way to his ears as she continues to pet him, nothing but contemplation on her face.

"Take off your shirt."

Before he has a chance to argue, she's yanking it over his head, giving him no choice but to comply. From there, she starts grabbing at his shoulders and squeezing, trailing her kneading hands down the tops of his arms, assessing him. Leaving her mark on him. Making him want her to touch him everywhere.

She strokes down to his hips, and that's when she notices how hard he is, tenting his pants.

His hands immediately fly to his crotch, cupping himself as he starts to blather apologies. "I'm so sorry. I swear I didn't mean—"

But she only pulls a frown and slaps the palm of her hand over his mouth.

"Stop being such a baby. Like I've never given anyone a hard-on before. Sheesh." Her eyes roll so hard, her head rocks to the side. Batting his hands away, she squeezes his hips again, and he has to bite his lip to keep from making another unfortunate noise.

"This is humiliating."

"This is necessary." Her fingers slide slightly under his boxers, following down the ridges of bone. His knees almost go weak when her thumbs swirl, grazing the top of his pubic hair before trailing up again. "At least you have the guy line."

"Huh?"

"That sexy line men get from their hips down. It's like an arrow leading a woman's eyes straight to your dick, and it's good that you have it."

Though he'd never have thought it possible, he blushes harder. It's crass, but also absolutely scorching. He wants to hear what else might be good about his body. What other sorts of words would she use if she kept touching him?

"When you're at the gym, I want you to focus on cardio. At least a half hour of the hardest run you can manage. We'll also get you on a good diet. For these," she runs her fingers up his abdomen again, "I want you to do sit-ups. But not the kind you'd think of. Lift your legs too. I want your elbows"—she taps them before sliding her hands down the sides of his thighs—"to touch your knees, you get me?"

"Uh-huh." He'd say anything at this point. Do anything. Hell, he's about to die at this point.

Her hands sweep up to his chest, her thumbs gliding over his nipples, though she seems to take no notice, her regard still assessing.

"For these, go to the machines and look for the ones that have the pecs shown as red on their instructions. Pick one and do as many as you can stand. Rest. Then do the same plus one. Keep doing that until you're trembling, yeah?"

The breathy word that sentence ends on keeps him raging hard, and he has no idea why she doesn't care. It's all he can think about at this point. He's going to forget every word falling from her soft lips since all his blood has left his brain.

"And with your arms, do the same. Find the machines that indicate your biceps and do a set, then switch to triceps, back and forth from one to the other. By then, you should be about ready to fall down. Then take a shower, dress in what I'll pick out from your closet, do up your hair real nice, and we'll go to lunch."

"We?"

"Of course. What, you think you can handle your first time out on your own? I'm gonna be there, walking you through everything you need."

"How? Are you going to be, like, at the table?"

"No." She smacks him lightly and he wants her to do it again. His skin is begging for any attention she'll give at this point. "While I'm out, I'll get us something so I can chat with you from a bit away. I'll be watching you and directing you through a little earpiece."

"Like James Bond?"

The smile she gives him almost melts him as much as her touch does, deep dimples blooming.

How did he not notice she had freckles until now?

"Exactly. I'll teach you what to say and how to say it to get her starry-eyed."

"Shouldn't she like me for me?"

Sadie snorts, handing him back his shirt. "Yeah, how's that been going for you so far? From the look of it, not well."

It's a kick to his ego, and he wilts in his pants. Nothing like shame to ruin a good time. She certainly knows how to pick at his soft spots.

He slings on his shirt with his eyes to the ground. "My friend Nando says I scare the girls away because I'm too serious-looking."

"Resting bitch face." She nods. "You had it when you first woke up. It was like you were already mad at the world."

He eyes her, and she points directly at him. "Oh. You're doing it now."

"Don't make fun. You don't know me, but I have a temper. Eventually. If you push me hard enough."

"Is that another thing that keeps the ladies away?" She's grinning again, teasing him. He hates it.

"That and my rank."

"And what might that be?"

"I'm a CEO candidate." He says it with no small amount of smugness and self-importance, but then the bitter taste of his situation taints the thought, and his good feelings go out the window. "My best friend and I are vying for top spot. I don't like going up against someone I care about for what's supposed to be my birthright, but my Uncle Lawrence can't be reasoned with. Mom and Dad wanted me to take over. Hell, they groomed me for it, whether I liked it or not, but my uncle keeps saying I'm not ready. He's pitting me and Nando against each other to keep us both motivated." He hesitates. "I want to win, I really do, but more and more I realize it's not because I want to be CEO. It's because I don't want to lose."

He scrubs his hands through his hair, feeling morose and vulnerable. Sadie observes him with her arms crossed, scrunching up the T-shirt's witty slogan between her breasts.

"You talk too much." She sounds blasé, bored even. His jaw drops a little. "And you're too honest. You can't go around spilling your guts to everyone you meet."

He feels the flush creep up his cheeks again, but for different reasons this time. He'd done that with Ciel too. What is he, desperate?

"Also, we shouldn't use your real name while you're dating."

"Why would I lie about something like that?"

"Believe me. We're not trying to find you a long-lasting relationship right now. We're trying to cram you full of experience. You're going to be making a lot of excruciating mistakes at first, and you don't want those tied to your name."

"Mistakes?"

"Yeah. Like coming after two strokes."

Simon chokes on his spit. "Excuse me? How could you even—? I absolutely will not."

Her lips quirk up at the side. "Wanna make a bet?"

"How much?"

"Another five grand."

Confident and—quite literally—cocksure, he declares, "Done."

———

Simon clears his throat. "Bethany, right? I, um, I'm Noah. Nice to meet you."

*"Say something nice about how she looks,"* Sadie's voice whispers in his ear. Even though he's sure his date can't hear his consultant's guidance, his nerves jangle, afraid to get caught with another woman dictating his every move. He's guessing that's somewhere on the list of a dating faux pas.

Simon takes in the woman before him. She looks older than he thought. Middle-aged, though still refined. Her makeup is doing a good job at making her look fresher, he supposes. Nice eyeliner or whatever.

"I like the way you painted your face," he says.

Sadie groans over his earpiece but, after a solid, uncomfortable beat, Bethany's eyes crinkle with a smile. "I suppose I've gotten good at it over the years. I think lips and lashes are the most important."

"Well, you've certainly made them very obvious."

*"Oh my literal god,"* Sadie whisper-yells. *"Have you never spoken to a woman before? Tell her she looks beautiful. Lovely. To die for. Say something dreamy, you asshole."*

He tries not to visibly wince under his consultant's verbal onslaught. Instead, he ducks around the table. He's not disappointed by Sadie's choice. The thin-stemmed crystal glassware and elegantly flourished cutlery handles are as one would expect from this high-rise's five-star restaurant. He stares hard at the finery for some semblance of comfort as he pulls out a chair for his date.

Gesturing to her, he takes her hand and leads to her seat. "I meant to say that you look lovely."

*Lovely.* That sounds so stupid. What is he, some archaic romance novel guy, swooning over a vapid and uninteresting main character? Not that this woman looks vapid. She looks sharp, gazing at him with a curve to her lips.

"Aren't you sitting?" she asks.

Oh. Damn it.

He ceases his dazed hovering and moves to his side of the table. "Yes. Sorry."

While pulling her chair out was all silent grace, handling his own causes a horrible squeaking scrape over the fine hardwood floor. Several other diners look at him and he smiles tightly before tucking his tie back against his chest and taking a seat.

*"You may not be able to see me right now, but I'm totally facepalming on your behalf,"* Sadie says.

Simon grits his teeth. He'd like to tell the woman Bluetoothing in his ear to shut right the hell up, please and thank you. She isn't making this easier.

He lifts his menu, words swimming in front of him. "What do you think? Does anything look good?"

With a broad smile, Bethany leans back and folds her hands together. "Why don't you order for me?"

He blinks. "But I don't know what you like."

She shrugs. "I like surprises."

"*This is tricky,*" Sadie says. "*Get her a salad and she'll think you think she's fat. Get her something too hefty and she'll think you think she's too thin.*"

So now he needs to think about what she thinks he thinks? Why does this have to be so complicated?

"Maybe we'll start with some wine?" he tries. "Do you drink this early in the day?"

"Oh, it's five o'clock somewhere. If one can have mimosas with brunch, why not?"

"Do you prefer whites or—?"

Again, she says, "Surprise me."

Sadie hums in what must be contemplation. "*She's certainly putting you through your paces today.*"

Simon deeply wishes this could be a two-way conversation so he could say a thing or two to his consultant. Specifically, "Get me out of here." Instead, he pastes on an inoffensive smile. "I don't know a lot about wine, but since you gave me carte blanche, you have no one to blame but yourself if you don't like what you get."

"*What the hell did you say?*" Sadie quietly screeches, but Bethany only laughs. It's strong and confident, like Simon wishes he was right now.

"I take full responsibility," Bethany says with her hands up. "You are absolved."

"Then let's do red."

He'd rather have another shot, to be honest. A strong one.

*I'll treat this professionally,* he thinks. *I've gone to business dinners with hundreds of women, and this doesn't have to be any different.*

Bethany rests her chin on the backs of her hands, elbows propped on the table as she takes him in.

Sadie voice is sly. "*Ohh, is she giving you vibes?*"

He has no idea what that means. Except, given the look on this woman's face, maybe he does. Context clues. Maybe he can't treat this like a work event after all.

"You're quite handsome, Noah. And I like that name. Strong. Manly. Like the rest of you."

Damn his red face. He signals to the waiter, if only to buy himself a moment as he orders their wine, casting a sideways glance at Bethany as he does. She's fixated on him, and it makes the corner of his left eye twitch.

"So, what do you do for work?"

Her foot traces along his inner calf and his leg jumps, ramming the underside of the table and making the glassware tinkle. Bethany bites her lip while smiling at him like a Cheshire cat. He must be the dormouse.

"Work? Um, I'm a…"

"*Lie,*" Sadie reminds, and his eye twitches again.

"…stockbroker?"

"How fascinating. What's that like?"

"Stressful," he assumes. "When you're playing with other people's money, there's a lot at stake. Not only your reputation, but the financial well-being of your clients."

There we go. Thinking on the fly. He might be good at this.

"I should ask you how to manage my portfolio," Bethany says. "I'm lost when it comes to dividends and short-term exchanges. Perhaps you can teach me all the ins and outs?"

Well, shit. He can't even find himself on the winning side of a 401(k).

"*Word of wisdom,*" Sadie says. "*Stop talking about yourself. Make it all about her.*" Makes sense. He can do that.

"What about you? What do you do for work?" The wine is delivered, and he takes a gulp that almost drowns him.

Bethany plays with her own, running a well-manicured fingertip over the rim of the glass and making it sing. "This and that. Sometimes, I mentor young women."

He perks up. "That seems nice."

"It is nice." Bethany smiles again. "I like doing it. Teaching people, I mean. I like seeing understanding settle into someone's eyes when they realize what they're supposed to do for the first time. It's amazing knowing that I gave that to them." She leans in and slides a hand over his. "Is there anything you'd like to learn, Noah?"

His knee bangs the table again.

*"Don't you dare pull away. Put your hand on hers."*

He does.

*"Smile."*

He tries.

*"Ugh. Like you mean it."*

He tries harder.

With her free hand, Bethany lifts her glass and knocks back the whole thing, all without taking her eyes off him. Setting it down, she licks the rose-colored stain on her lips and smirks. "What do you say we don't order lunch?"

Crap. Did he do this wrong? Did he offend her?

She slides her other hand over, trailing it up his arm. "There's something I'd much rather eat."

"M-McDonald's?"

Her confident laugh rings out again. "No, darling man." Her voice lowers an octave as she whispers, "You."

"Me?"

"Yes, you." She drops some money on the table and stands, pulling him with her and wrapping her arm around his. "I have a room upstairs. Sadie told me you need a teacher. And I think I'm going to enjoy this."

Simon whips around, looking for the woman who cursed him. He catches her black hair and freckles at the table behind him and she winks, giving a thumbs-up. He wants to let out a litany of swears. Is he about to lose his virginity? Now? To this random woman?

"Aren't we going a little too fast?"

She only tugs him along more firmly. "Come now, Noah. Not every woman needs a year of verbal foreplay before she knows she wants you."

"Wants me?" he squeaks.

Bethany casts a devilish grin over her shoulder as she takes him through the high-rise lobby and presses the elevator button. "Can't you tell?" She leans closer. "I'm positively wet for you."

Something in him tingles at the thought, his blood rushing south.

The elevator dings open and Bethany all but shoves him in. Alone, she presses her body against his, working her hand over his belly and down to his rising crotch. He can't help it. No woman has ever touched him this way, with those words on her lips and that look on her face.

Her grip tightens through his loose pants, and he whimpers.

*Oh my god.*

"You like this?" she asks. She clasps around his length and moves her hand sinfully up, squeezing him hard and shooting electricity up his spine.

*Ohmygod.*

She goes down this time, pulsing her grip over him.

*Ohmifuckinggawd.*

And on the upstroke, a lovely, never-ending upstroke…he comes in his goddamn pants.

His eyes go wide.

Her eyes go wide.

His mouth drops open and so does hers. They both look down at the blooming wet spot, and he wants to curl up like a shrimp and die.

*Sadie, I'm going to kill you. I swear it to the heavens above.*

Again, those apologies bud on his tongue, but like his consultant, Bethany silences his sputtering with a finger to his lips. She looks like she wants to devour him.

"Oh, sweet baby boy. How darling of you. You're so new. So cute." She places a peck on his mouth—his first kiss. "Why don't we see how long your refractory period is?"

For reasons unknown, Simon nods. He should be thinking about things, so many things, an ocean of things, a universe of things, but his entire mind is narrowed in on the fact that he now owes Sadie an extra five thousand dollars.

She was right.

He came in two strokes.

———

Mm, tomato basil, her favorite. Angelica breathes in deeply as her soup arrives, only moments after Bethany dragged CEO Simon out the door and into the lobby beyond. Removing the Bluetooth bud, she sets it down on the table before rubbing her ear. That thing's too big for her.

She snorts, wondering if Simon is too big for Bethany.

Not in his lifetime.

Still, she hopes Simon does his best and rallies up there.

The taste of hot soup blooms in her mouth, the perfect amount of salty and sweet, and she swirls it with her tongue, savoring the flecks of flavor as she does some quick math in her head. Twenty-five hundred left after shopping, five grand from Bethany, and four more for Simon's upcoming round two this evening.

Her phone lights up with a text message confirming the time and place, and she smiles to herself, spoon still placed between her lips.

Glancing up at the ceiling, she wonders how many rounds they'll go and if Simon will still have some pep in his step for the next "date" on his docket.

One thing's for sure, that man's cherry is definitely popped.

# the second date

. . .

"HOW YOU DOING THERE, TIGER?" Angelica sits beside Simon in the cab, rubbing his back. His elbows are on his knees and his face is locked in a scowl. He slides his bourbon gaze in her direction before opening and closing his mouth several times with no words.

"That good, huh? What happened?"

He groans, hiding his face between his knees and muffling his voice. "She made me—" The sentence becomes a slur of sounds. Muffle, bluffle, gruffle.

"Made you what?" Angelica asks.

He lifts his face slightly, cheeks aflame. "Made me finish three times."

"Oof." Angelica hands him a cool bottle of water from the cab's stash and he cracks the cap, leaning back and opening his throat to take the whole thing down in a few gulps. Impressive. That skill could be useful if he's into guys too.

Simon rests the bottle against his forehead, frowning so hard his chin puckers. "She did it with her hand. And then with her mouth. And then by talking to me."

The cab driver ticks his eyes up to the rearview mirror, but thankfully Simon doesn't see. "Talking to you?" Angelica asks. "You've gotta be kidding."

He shakes his head slowly side to side, eyes cinched. "She said nice things about my body and what she'd do to me, and what I should do to her, and what we could do if we were in a room of other girls and how all the body pieces would fit together and I—" He makes an explosion noise while his fingers flick out in a *boom* gesture.

"So, you didn't have sex?"

"I couldn't. I started crying."

"You what?"

Simon has the wherewithal to flinch. "A little. It was emotional for me."

"Oh god," Angelica says, feeling his humiliation secondhand. "Hey, you can make up for it. You still have tonight."

"What's tonight?" he asks, his eyes still closed and the plastic bottle still rammed against his forehead. The car halts at a red light and he shies away from the casual glances of those in the cars beside them, almost like he's hiding his face.

Angelica tries to rally him to the cause. "Tonight is date number two."

"Someone else?" He blanches, whipping his face in her direction. "I can't do that. Bethany asked me for another date to 'finish the job,' and I said yes. I have no idea why I said yes. I don't think I even like her like that. At the end she got scary and kept saying she was gonna bite me if I wasn't a good boy."

Angelica tilts her head side to side, considering. "Well, if she asked you for one more date, you can give it to her. But then we'll cut her off. Wouldn't want you to get too attached."

"I told you I don't like her. Can't you turn her down for me? Please?"

She scoffs. "You should be proud to spend time with Bethany. There's a lot you could learn from someone like her. Plus, your table talk needs work and you might be more comfortable with her a second time around. It will let you practice conversation that's less cringeworthy."

"She wrung me dry," he groans.

"But she also taught you a lot of tricks, I'd bet. Make sure to use what you learned for tonight's date."

"I can't be intimate with one woman and then switch to chatting up another in the same day. It's wrong."

It'd better be more than chatting, otherwise his date won't get what she paid for.

"Come on, what century do you live in? If both parties are into it and it's casual, that sort of thing doesn't matter. That's what I master in: casual."

He ignores her completely. "I'm dying. Between those stupid exercises and that acrobatic succubus, I need a bath, a nap, and about a hundred years of therapy to unpack my feelings about all this."

Concern tightens her chest, and she shoves him a little. "Don't exaggerate. You make it sound like you don't want this. You know I'd never make you do anything against your will. My job is to push you. Make you the best you can be. It can't have been all bad."

His eyes go wide as he looks off into space. "I didn't even think about condoms. Am I gonna get an STD? Can you even get an STD if you don't put it in?"

The driver looks at them again, and Angelica sighs.

"Everyone I recommend is clean. They get tested monthly. That's how this works."

"What works?"

*Max's empire* is what Angelica wants to say, but that won't do her any favors. "My dating service."

"Oh. But how do you know I don't have an STD?"

She narrows her eyes at him. "Do you?"

He puts his head between his knees again. "No." He almost sounds mopey about it. A bear paw of a hand comes to cradle his head as he sulks. "I know you're only doing your job, but I'm not sure casual is in my vocabulary. I want someone to love me. I'm tired of being alone."

Looking at him, Angelica's heart twinges, as does her conscience. Still, after watching his performance in the restaurant, he's not going to find what he's looking for whether she saddles him up or not. For better or worse, he needs practice.

Miserably, he says, "And I owe you an extra five thousand dollars."

The cab swerves for how hard Angelica laughs, face pointed to the sky as she curls her arms over her stomach, all breath lost. The part of his face she can see, a sliver between his folded arms, smiles a bit as well, self-deprecation likely getting the better of him.

She drapes herself over the wide expanse of his back and he stiffens. "Simon, you're adorable." He relaxes again. She starts scritch-scratching her nails through his dark hair, same color as hers, and enjoys the rhythmic motion. He actually hums a little bit as his tension lets go. "How about this, we'll do what you said. Let's get you a hot bath, then a nice nap, and a few protein-rich snacks."

He mumbles something inaudible.

"And after that's all done, you'll put on your big boy pants and go out on your second date."

His inaudible mutter sounds more irritated.

"And once you've leveled up enough and know how to treat a woman, both in and out of the bedroom, we'll find you someone you can fall in love with, okay?"

Still muffled, he mutters, "Really?"

She keeps petting his hair. It's incredibly soft. She likes the way it looks cascading through her fingers. "Really."

"You promise?"

"Cross my heart."

"You still going to be in my ear tonight?"

"Yup."

"And are you going to yell at me again?"

"Oh, undoubtedly."

He grunts and sags further, ramming his head against the cab driver's seat and making the man jump a little. They're going to owe this guy a big tip.

———

Simon's muscles ache. He didn't exercise anything in his back, but he feels like he's got a knot that starts somewhere above his coccyx and proceeds directly to the base of his skull.

"Her name is Satine," Sadie tells him, straightening his tie and pushing his hair behind his ear, making sure his ear bud is in before sweeping it back into place.

It's strangely intimate, and despite his multiple releases today, he finds he still wants her touch. She smells nice. As she concentrates on picking lint off him, her forehead is scrunched with a little line between her brows. She looks entirely grumpy and as nervous as he is, which is kind of cute.

Patting the lapel on his nice jacket, she blows out a puff of air. "You're as good as it gets."

He can't help the small smile that crosses his face as he checks the buttons on his vest. "Do you think she'll like me?"

"Depends on how much you open your mouth," Sadie says with a wink, and his smile turns into a petulant frown. "Just kidding. Calm down." She whaps his lapel again before checking her earpiece. "Go to the table and make sure you stand up when she gets there. Be a gentleman."

He nods, concentrating on what a gentleman might look like.

Someone like Fabio.

Yeah, he can pretend to be Fabio.

The restaurant is fancier than the one earlier today. More romantic. The lighting is dim and has a warm amber tone that offsets the chestnut wood. Never mind paying his consultant, this meal alone is going to set his bank account back a tick. The menu has a single group of items under a hundred dollars, but they're all side dishes. He never thought whipped mashed potatoes could cost over fifty dollars, but here we are.

"Noah?" a feminine voice calls out. It doesn't register.

"Noah?" comes the voice again.

*Shit. That's me.*

He stands up so fast, his chair almost topples behind him. An unknown person who was sauntering past takes the brunt of the weight in a nice knock to his elbow, and the uppity look of disdain he sends Simon's way does not go unnoticed.

Trying to stay cool, he stabilizes his chair and tries again. "Satine?"

Another middle-aged woman gleams at him, her teeth a dazzling white. She has blonde hair in a rough-cut bob and her figure is enhanced by her sleek black dress and the beaded pearl necklace tight around her throat. She waves happily and Simon strikes his best Fabio pose, one hand on his hip and his chin tilted slightly up before he remembers his manners and pulls out her chair for her.

"*What are you doing?*" Sadie asks. "*Was that a Superman pose?*"

Apparently, Simon needs to work on his Fabio.

"You look lovely," he says, tucking in Satine's chair and managing to get into his own without issue.

"Oh hush, this dress was the only one not at the dry cleaners," she says, looking everywhere but at him. She must be nervous too.

"*She's digging for compliments. Tell her more about how good she looks.*"

What? Why? He already said the stupid "lovely" word, didn't he? Fine.

"I'm glad you wore that dress." What was it Bethany told him? "You look good enough to eat."

"*Mrrrrow, Simon. Good job,*" Sadie tells him.

Satine blushes prettily and waves a hand at her pink face. "Is it hot in here?"

"Not as hot as you," Simon says.

"*Too much. Reel it in, lover boy.*"

"Sorry." He faux coughs into his hand. "It's definitely hot in here."

Tugging at his collar, he wishes he could take the damn thing off. At this time of night, he should be in front of the TV with his comfy pajamas on, watching something inane as he winds down for bed.

Wait. No, he shouldn't. That was his old life. His boring life. Now he's a sexpot or something.

No.

He is Fabio.

And the Fabio in him leans across the table, takes his date's hand, and says, "I suck at this."

"*Jesus Christ, Simon.*"

"But I'm going to do my best, I promise." Simon clasps the woman's strong hand in his. "I'm new to dating and I don't know what to do or say, but be patient with me and I'll try my best to make it a good night."

"*All right. That was uniquely charming.*"

Satine seems to think so, too. She clasps his hand in both of her own. "To tell you the truth, I don't have any idea what I'm doing either. This is my first time seeing someone like you."

"*First time using my service to meet men,*" Sadie jumps in. "*Make sure she doesn't regret it.*"

Simon smiles in earnest. "Well, then we'll figure it out together."

The waiter interrupts, and Simon turns to Satine. "Would you like me to order for you?"

She looks flustered. "Oh. I guess."

"I promise not to make you think I think you're fat or skinny based on what I pick, okay?"

Both Angelica and Satine blat out laughter, Angelica from a few tables over and Satine right to his face.

"I'll order for myself, it's okay," Satine says, wiping away tears of mirth. Locking on Simon's eyes with a twinkle in her own, she pauses for a second before saying, "Why don't I take a bourbon. I like looking at it. It's got such a pretty color."

Bourbon. That's the second time he's heard that word today. Sadie said he had pretty bourbon-colored eyes.

Why is Satine staring at him so hard?

Oh, wait! Is she complimenting his eyes in the weirdest way possible? If so, he should reciprocate such a sweet gesture, shouldn't he?

Simon nods at the waiter. "I'll take something blue or green or whatever her eye color is. It's too dark to tell."

His grin gets him nowhere as the waiter stares down at him. "I'm sorry, sir?"

Sadie seems to think fast. "*Tell him to have the bartender make you something with blue Curacao.*"

Simon repeats his instructions while the waiter regards him. Meanwhile, Satine is shaking with her fist over her mouth and her shoulders bobbing, trying to hold in her laughter. Oh well. At least she's not angry with him.

Sheepish, Simon repeats, "I told you I suck at this."

"It's cute. Don't blame me if I laugh at you. I'm super tense right now, but this is helping."

"I'm doing a good job?" Simon asks, wanting to wag his non-existent tail.

"So good. Thank you."

He preens.

*"Remember to ask her about herself. Make this all about her."*

Right. "Do you live around here?"

"Near the park. I get these great views in the fall when the leaves start to change. It's nice in the spring too. The cherry blossoms come out."

"Those are the pink ones, right?"

Her face falls a little. "Yeah."

The air between them changes. Where there were those vibes, there's now a tinge of sadness. "Is something wrong?"

Satine's smile has faded into a warbly line and her eyes swim. "My ex-husband picked that view before he up and left with a younger woman. After fifteen years, he went to go live the life of his dreams. The one I apparently held him back from. But hey, at least I got to keep the pretty view."

Simon feels weepy. Why does he do this? Nando is always scolding him for empathizing too hard. Feeling too much. He barely knows this woman, but feels terrible.

He takes her hand again. "That sounds hard. I can't even imagine." Clenching his jaw, he pictures the bastard in his mind as he slides his thumbs over the back of her hand. "If he were here, I'd knock him straight on his ass."

Something in Sabine's eyes goes starry.

*"Oh, Simon, you hit a goldmine. Even strong women want someone willing to protect her."*

Well, he could tap into that.

"The woman I fall in love with won't have to worry about anything like that," Simon says. "I'd never leave her. I'd want her young and old and fat and thin and every stage in between. I'd forgive her anything and annihilate anyone who wanted to hurt her. I'd take care of her in every way possible. I'd make her the center of my world, and she'd feel it right down to her core. I'd do anything to make sure she'd always have eyes only for me." His voice drops a gravely octave. "I may not look it, but I can be pretty possessive once I find something that's mine."

*"Bingo."*

The woman's eyes go from stars to supernovas.

*"Not for nothing, Simon, but even my panties are wet."*

Simon's face heats and his sudden smile is broad, his head shyly tipping toward the table. He's never said anything like that before, and Sadie's praise echoes through his body the same way her voice does. Warm and inviting. He thinks about those freckles and how he doesn't need a bright light to know the color of her eyes. Blue like Alaskan glaciers. They contrast so nicely with her ebony hair, freckles, and—

Reality sets in.

*You ass,* he scolds himself. *You mess around with the hellcat Bethany this afternoon, somehow ended up on a date with the emotionally sensitive Satine this evening, and yet you're sitting here thinking about Sadie who's technically your employee.*

"Do you want to get out of here?" Satine asks.

"But we haven't had dinner yet." And Simon hasn't had anything to eat other than granola bars and some orange juice today.

Satine bites her lip, her cheeks going pink. "I'm not hungry for food right now."

*Don't say it,* Simon pleads. *Please don't say it.*

"I'm hungry for you."

Simon stifles an exhausted groan.

*"Go to her, Simon. This is your chance to make up for earlier. Do you want to be a two-pump chump your whole life? Wanna pay me another five grand?"*

He breathes in deep through his nose and cinches his mouth. "Let's do this." Getting up, he snags Satine's hand and all but pulls her out behind him.

"Sir," the waiter calls. "Your drinks."

Simon takes a page from Bethany's book and slaps money into the waiter's hand without looking. He may have either grossly overpaid or grossly underpaid, but he supposes he'll never know, because he's yanking the lady of the hour out into the spring chill.

Wanting to slap his own forehead, he asks, "Did you bring a coat?"

She's looking at him like he's a miracle. "No. I wanted you to think I looked pretty."

Why wouldn't she be pretty with a coat on? What is wrong with women? "You are pretty," he says, but it comes out a bit too firm.

Even so, Satine leans up against his chest and whispers, "My car is in the garage." She points across the street to a three-tier lot.

"We're going to your place?" he asks, looking over his shoulder at the restaurant. He doesn't want to abandon Sadie. He thought maybe Satine had a nearby hotel room like Bethany did.

"No, silly," Satine says, her voice a low purr. "I said we're going to my car." He blinks at her, and she dances her fingertips over his tie. "Have you ever thought it might be exciting to get caught having sex?"

He wants to respond with, "I've never had sex," but his mind is clogging up.

She takes the initiative, grabbing his hand and dragging him to the crosswalk where the light is in their favor, letting her jog them to the garage.

"I've always wanted to do it in a public place. What makes it even more risky," she says, her too-high heels clacking on the pavement, "is that my car is on the first floor."

Simon's face pales. "We're not seriously gonna do this, are we?"

Turning, she grabs his shoulders, bites her lip, and looks him up and down. "Yeah, we are. I'm so lucky it's you, Noah. You're perfect. Be my fantasy. I want to scream your name."

He's at a loss for words. How did he get here? Simon Javik, a virgin yesterday, is about to have sex in a car in the most nerve-wracking, unromantic way possible, with a woman who doesn't even know his real name.

What would Fabio do?

*Sadie, give me strength,* he sends to the sky, taking out his earbud and shoving it in his pocket.

———

*He looks exhausted,* Angelica thinks. This Sunday morning he's on the couch wearing the softest pajama bottoms she's ever seen. He's flopped on his back with his legs up on the coffee table and a blue ice pack resting on his head. She'd feel bad, except that he's so damn adorable it's actually heartwarming. He'd had another little cry last night, but not because he was sad about finally managing sex—the whole one round Satine was able to squeeze out of him before they were found by a nuclear family with children in tow—but because he didn't get a chance to cuddle after. He was heartbroken. Angelica had cuddled him instead, letting him put his head in her lap while he sniffled. He really is like a big puppy.

Standing with the fridge door open, its light casting the bottom rack in shadow, she picks through what's available and adds it to what she went out and bought this morning. Simon needs to keep up his stamina, and has more than earned himself a deluxe spread for breakfast.

"What are you doing?" he grumbles, adjusting the ice pack and peeking at her out of one eye.

"Cooking."

"Oh." His stomach growls so loud they both look at it. With a groan, he rights himself and trudges to the kitchen, squeezing by, then taking a cereal box out of the pantry.

"What are you doing?"

"I'm hungry."

She slaps his hands away from the box. "I'm cooking for you, you dolt."

He seems confused. "Why?"

"Why wouldn't I?"

"No one's ever cooked for me before."

She shoves him back to the kitchen's entryway, shooing him to the couch, where he lands with a plop. "So, your parents let you starve?"

"Let me rephrase. No one's ever cooked for me unless they were paid to do it. Mom and Dad were always too busy, and I figured this isn't a line item on our nonexistent contract."

"Consider it a kindness, roommate to roommate. Besides, you did so well yesterday, you deserve a reward. I'm proud of you."

"I behaved like a neanderthal."

"And a weepy one at that."

He shoots her a scathing glare, which she promptly mirrors.

She lays a pan over the stovetop. While letting it heat up, she cracks a few eggs, then a few more for posterity. Given he's going to the gym again today, she'll make him pancakes, but there will be bacon over her dead body. The best he's getting out of her is cheese on his omelet.

"You like tomatoes? Onions? Peppers?"

"Ew, peppers."

She snickers as he watches her move around his kitchen, setting out bowls and chopping vegetables. After only two days, he's got a crush on her. It's not a record, but it's still pretty damn quick. It doesn't matter. She'll keep his wick so dipped, he won't even have time to think about her.

"I'm making lunch for us today," Simon declares, as if calling dibs.

"Only after we sit down and design you a meal plan."

He grumbles. "Whatever that means, I already hate it."

"Then you can do an extra hour of cardio to burn off whatever additional calories you cram into your body."

"I can't wait. It will be the highlight of my day."

She snorts. "If that's the truth, I'll have done you a disservice."

She presses a mug of coffee into his hands. He immediately sits up for and sips, that furrow in his brows smoothing out into bliss.

"What got you to start a dating service?" he asks.

Now what could she possibly say to that? "Necessity, I guess. You make the most of the skills you have."

"And what skills are those?"

There's another conversation she refuses to have. "I'm a people person. I can tell what they want, sometimes only by looking at them."

"Is your service exclusive?"

"I have a few members, but more seem to be joining of late." Specifically to jump Simon's bones. "It must be the residual blues after people see family for Easter and have no one special to drag to the table."

"Why is it so one-night-only, then? Why doesn't anyone want something more?"

Damnit. This conversation is full of plot holes. She didn't think this through from his perspective. Taking her necklace out from between her breasts, she rubs the green stone absently over her lips. *What can I tell him, Bee?*

It clicks. "I'm sure you noticed that both Bethany and Satine were older."

"Yeah, sorry to say, but can we pick someone in my age bracket next time?"

"Ingrate. Anyway, they're both singles looking to get back into the game," she lies. "Like you, they've got some acclimating to do. But you're a stud. You're dusting the cobwebs off their thighs and giving them a go."

He snorts down his coffee and hacks up his left lung in rapid succession. Angelica takes it as a win.

Whisking the eggs, she keeps herself busy as he hustles to the kitchen sink, washing his coffee-dribbled face and toweling off his nose. Leaning back against the counter, he sniffles, tipping his head back and letting that dark hair flow, revealing his too-round, too-big, totally charming ears.

"Well, that cleared my sinuses."

"I'll bet."

"What's that?" he asks, gesturing to her necklace.

Her hand flies up to touch it. Smoothing her thumb over the pendant, she tucks it back into her shirt. "Heirloom."

"It's nice. From your grandparents? Great-grandparents?"

"My Auntie Bee. She gave it to me before she passed away."

"Oh. Sorry for your loss."

He seems genuine and it makes her uncomfortable. "Yeah, well, it was a long time ago."

Thankfully, Simon drops it and watches her as she wanders around his kitchen, pouring batter onto a skillet and sprinkling cheese into the center of his omelet. It's kind of nice having someone around like this. Gwen never rose before three and Kay held down a day job. Angelica was often alone in the apartment they shared, even if there were bodies nearby.

Story of her life.

"Oh, by the way, have you ever eaten a girl out before?" The way he gapes at her speaks volumes. "I'll talk you through it. I know that tonight's date really likes it when you suck on her clit."

She likes how his face lights aflame.

"Jesus, Sadie, why? Just why? How do you even know such a thing?"

"Come on, Simon. By now you have to realize these women are as hard up as you are. And wouldn't your future wife like a husband who can suck her off?"

"Is that what you call it?"

Angelica shrugs. "Nah, but it's funny to teach you wrong." He narrows his eyes and presses his mouth into a flat line. "Future Mrs. Simon would like to be eaten out. Have her clit sucked. Have her pussy—"

"Please, don't say that word," he groans, putting his face in his hands.

"Would you prefer cunt?"

He visibly cringes. "Can't we say things like *there*? She wants you to touch her *there*."

Pivoting on the balls of her feet, Angelica approaches the big baby. "To lick her *there*. To make her ache *there*. To have you put yourself inside her *there*."

He's so red he's purple. "You're evil."

She pats him on the shoulder. "You'll get used to it. But tonight—"

"I can't do it tonight," he says.

"I promise, Simon, your penis will be fine. It will work again, and it will not break off, no matter what you say."

"It's not that. Well, it's also that. But mostly it's because I'm going out with my friend tonight. Remember Nando? I told you about him."

Vaguely, she remembers something. "Another lunch date, maybe? I'm sure she could rearrange her schedule and—"

"Can't I have the day off?"

Angelica's stomach tightens. This weekend earned her $16,500 so far, less than twenty percent of what she owes. But that extra five grand from Simon was a kicker she won't get again if last night was any indication. If he cries off for today, will this new client find someone else to "train" instead, deciding not to come take her turn with "Noah"?

Angelica has to capitalize on this moment. Rumors are already going around about the black stallion and his honest innocence, and most women are reaching out to Angelica to claw at any vestige of that sweetness before it fades away.

At best she has ten to eleven weeks before Max's hammer falls. She needs to make about $84,000. Playing it on the safe side, she'll need over $8k a week, but the more Simon goes out to play, the less he's worth.

Four dates a week, then. If she can average $2k each, she can make this work. That means Friday night, and at least three over the weekend. That's all they can squeeze in if his work is as busy as he says.

Maybe she can schedule a lunch quickie now and again.

"Sadie?"

Angelica snaps back to now. The pancakes are bubbling up at the sides and she's pretty sure the egg has singed. "Sorry. Got lost in my head there. I was wondering if the client would see you on another day instead."

"Well, if not, we can skip that one."

*Oh, you innocent fool.* His expression is the epitome of stubbornness, so all she can do is reluctantly give in. "Sure. I'll reschedule. Rest up today and have fun with your friend."

He's watching her again. She folds the egg over and plates it before flipping one pancake after the other.

"Do you wanna come with me tonight?" he asks, soft and sweet. "Hang out with us?"

Oh yeah. He's absolutely into her. "Not a chance. Remember, business partners and roommates, that's all. We're not friends."

His hopeful expression dies.

*Don't worry, CEO Simon, my hope is dying right along with you.*

———

Nando has never been one for subtlety. Sitting at the pub booth, he drops his mouth open, his pulled-pork clearly visible in his cheek. "A dating service?"

Simon sinks in his chair, his food untouched. He debates whether his fried chicken is worth the extra calories and another gym visit. Stupid Sadie. Lucky for her he's too damn obedient for his own good. He already hates meal plans.

"Yeah. The opportunity sort of came out of the blue. A right time, right place sort of thing." He doesn't have to say he was drunk. Or that she was otherwise homeless. Or that she has worn his underthings to bed twice.

Cheek puffed up with food, Nando says, "How long has this been going on?"

"I started yesterday. I've already been on two dates."

"That's fast. Your coordinator must be pretty good. Anyone bangable?"

What a horrible word. Simon fiddles his thumbs around each other. "You could say that."

"Scale of one to ten."

"I guess I'd have to say ten."

"They're that hot?"

"No, but I bang..." He drops his voice to a whisper. "I banged them."

Nando's jade green eyes are wide as dinner plates. He sputters, "*Them*? As in *both* of them?"

Simon waves his hands to hush his friend before leaning in closer, his cheeks burning. "Well, one of them. The other one didn't get me that far. Though she also did. Sorta. Kinda."

Nando couldn't look more flabbergasted if he tried.

"Am I kiss-and-telling?" Simon thumps his head off the table. "Shit, I'm kissing-and-telling."

Nando sets down his sandwich in a splatter of barbeque sauce. Steepling his hands in front of his face, he breathes in deeply and closes his eyes as if in meditation. "Do you mean to tell me you're finally not a virgin anymore?"

Though he wishes it happened in a better way, he says, "Yeah, I guess."

Nando throws his hands in the air and shouts, *"Wah-hoo!"*

Simon jumps up to grab at his friend's pinwheeling arms. He manages to get his grip around Nando's wrists and thump them back down onto the tabletop with a bang. "Hush, for Christ's sake."

"Why should I? This is like a party. I've got to meet these girls."

"Women," Simon corrects before shaking his head and flopping into his seat again. "And you're missing the underlying problem."

"What problem? All I see is that baby Simi is a man now."

"No, he's a plaything."

"Play*boy*. There's a difference, eh? Two women in one day. Whew. When you blossom you fuckin' poof open, don't you?" Nando grabs his beer and does a cheers gesture, his grin wide.

What Simon leaves out is those women were at least two decades his senior, he was scared out of his mind, he came way too fast on all four counts, and he may have been casually thinking about his consultant when he finally…did the deed.

He consoles himself with the fact that he'll never see these women again.

Except for maybe Bethany. But the way she talked about group sex, she'd probably let Sadie join in.

The thought makes him shift in the padded booth seat.

"But you're being careful, yeah? No glove, no love?"

"My consultant says all her pairings are clean and the women are on the pill." Or have gone through menopause, maybe. Jesus, what is he doing?

Nando tsks. "I don't trust it. Remember that time I had a pregnancy scare after the office Christmas party?"

"What was that, five years ago?"

Nodding sharply, Nando takes another drink. "I should've known better, but I wasn't thinking with the right brain. When I got that call, I think my anus clenched so hard it retracted to my teeth."

"Charming."

"Did I ever tell you who it was?"

"Did I ever ask you who it was?"

"If you're gonna kiss-and-tell, so am I. Her name—"

"Nando, I don't wanna know."

"—is—"

"Don't be such a dick."

"—Sophia."

Simon's brain skitters to a stop. "Sophia? As in my assistant Sophia? How did I not know this?"

Nando picks up his beer and takes another sip, a smug smile playing on his lips.

"You know she's a single mother now, right?"

Nando snorts. "I'm not surprised. She must be loose."

Simon crosses his arms. "Apparently, I'm loose too."

Ticking up a finger in Simon's face, Nando repeats, "Playboy. *Non dimenticare la cosa più importante*, Simi. The rules are different for men and women."

"That's the stupidest thing I've ever heard."

"I don't dictate the ways of the world, my friend. I'm a mere mortal who lives among the masses."

With that, Simon's asshole best friend digs back into his meal, still casting mischievous upward glances at him while he stares at his food, thinking of poor Sophia. Nando shouldn't talk about her like she doesn't matter. Who cares if it was a one-night stand. She's a good person and, from what Simon can tell, an amazing mother. She deserves respect.

In fact, the people he was with deserve his respect. Bethany and her enthusiasm for all his childishness. Satine and her sense of (arrestable) adventure. He wishes them both happiness. Success. And love. In the end of all this, once they're ready, isn't that what they're looking for? And once Sadie says he's ready, it will be Simon's chance to find his future.

Whoever the love of his life will be, she'll help him look back on this time and smile, knowing it was all in preparation for her. She'll know that's how much she meant to him, before he even knew her. How he dreamt of being worthy of a lover, a best friend, and a partner all rolled into one.

Nando fades into the background as Simon smiles at his hands. He's going to do the best he can with his training. It's all for his future angel, after all. No matter who she is, she's already worth everything.

He knows she's out there. And the best part is, he knows she's waiting for him.

"We should go to the cat shelter again," Nando says through food-filled cheeks, breaking Simon's thoughts in half. "They got a few new litters in and they're looking for people to foster."

Simon chuckles softly. "That's your thing, not mine."

"You know I can't bear to have cuteness go uncared for! Besides, you can help me pick."

"I always get you saddled with the runts."

Nando shakes his head sagely. "Doesn't bother me. You have a good cat radar, eh? Look at these!" He tugs out his phone and fiddles for a second, bringing up a ginger tabby cat and a wrinkled, hairless Sphinx. Simon had picked that one purely because it was so ugly. They both wear black, respectable cat-sized bow ties and look a million times better than they had when Nando took them in, healthy and happy. "How can you not adore them, Simi? So cute!"

"They've both been adopted?"

"Yes, but those pricks changed their names. What's wrong with Millie and Cuddles?"

"Aren't they both boys? Why'd you give them girl names?"

"Pfft! So narrow minded," which is a statement of pure hypocrisy. He tucks his phone away and tosses Simon a lascivious glance. "So, speaking of animals, may I venture to guess you'll be letting these sex kittens nurse you for the rest of your life? Or will you decide to adopt one?"

"Adopt?" Simon squeaks, turning red from his navel to his neck. Though the thought of his amorphous future beloved fills his mind again, strengthening him. She's his dream for the future. His someday sweetheart. He swallows and gathers his courage. "I don't like the way you put it, but I guess yeah, that's the plan."

"Well, keep me in the loop," Nando says. "You can kiss-and-tell all you want with me, eh? That's what I'm here for. I'll even tell you some tricks of the trade if you get me drunk enough." He lifts his glass with a smirk. "*Saluti.* May your life be long and your libido be strong. Until then, try not to get herpes."

# your effect on me

. . .

ANGELICA LIES ON THE FLOOR, lifting her legs up and down in scissor kicks as her muscles burn. Grinding her teeth, she forces herself through it, ignoring the quaking tremor in her thighs, exactly like she ignores a whole lot of things in life.

She doesn't have access to Max's gym anymore, so no personal trainer. No one to harass her into pushing out one more set, only her own stubbornness to keep her on top of her game. Years of staying tight for work have ingrained the need for exercise, and she finds herself twitchy without the physical outlet. Abstaining from aerobic sex is one thing, but locking herself in this high-rise with no kick-boxing or spin class is another. She needs to do something or she's going to split at the seams.

"What do you think, Bee?" she asks, puffing out her cheeks and feeling a bead of sweat run through her hair. "Should I get a day job? What could I do? Waitress at a high-end restaurant during lunch?"

She considers for a moment. "No. People might recognize me." Hoity-toity people used to request her all the time, fond of her dimpled smile and short stature. (Size kink truly is a thing.) She's guessing any new potential managers wouldn't be pleased with her previous employment if it came to light.

She plants her heels on the floor and starts clenching her ass, pushing her pelvis up in undulating strokes, keeping her belly clenched.

"What about stripping?" she wonders aloud, then huffs, breathless and amused as she shakes her head. "No. Too close to home turf. Better to avoid running into Damion and his goons."

Her amusement dies, and she represses a shudder. She wouldn't be surprised if he decided to rough her up on sight to keep her on her toes. Not that they can't find her if they wanted to. The tracker they stuck in her arm long ago pings her location on request.

Angelica presses her lips together and keeps pivoting. She clamps down her pelvic floor with each upward thrust, Kegels her forever-friend. *What earns the most money with the least amount of skill?*

She doesn't even have her GED. Life had other plans in store for the skinny twig down Avenue Q.

She goes still. Her father's beady eyes and thick jowls swim behind the blackness of her lids, his dark voice an everlasting threat.

*But Bee saved me,* Angelica reminds herself. *He can't hurt me anymore. No one can.*

Except for fucking Maxine.

Angelica grunts, flinging her hands to her sides and bearing down as she resumes her rocking motion, feeling her muscles flutter. She tried to get Simon to pick up dates during the week, but his side-eyed looks of irritation sank her into her gut with worry.

She has to tread lightly or he's going to sense something's up. He's always so on edge after he comes back from work. Tightly wound. Defensive, almost. Her CEO Simon goes from being a puppy to being an emo teenager. He even has dark hair long enough to flip out of his eyes. It makes her want to coddle him, which is stupid. She should be riding him hard, like Max would do for her. But Simon won't respond to that. He needs a gentle hand. Angelica can be gentle.

She sits up and hides her face between her knees. "Go ahead, Bee. Tell me I'm an idiot and get it over with."

She hears the sound of the key in the lock and throws herself onto the floor, turning her back to the entryway as she does side leg lifts, ensuring she's tightening her ass when he comes in the door.

"Welcome home," she chirps, not looking at him.

"Yeah, than—" He breaks off, likely catching a good view of her rear. "Thanks."

"Hungry? I was about to make dinner."

"You didn't eat? It's almost ten."

She flops onto her back, letting her hair splay out in a halo around her head as she arches her spine, pressing her breasts up, watching his gaze fix on them. "I was waiting for you."

Obviously exhausted with bags under his eyes, Simon blushes. "You don't need to do that."

"Oh hush," she scolds, standing up and chasing him into the kitchen, where he sets down his laptop bag. "I'm the one who does the cooking around here."

"Not in our contract," he reminds her while undoing his tie.

"Our unwritten, completely malleable contract."

He throws himself into the kitchen chair with a sigh. His hair is disheveled, as if he's been pulling at it for hours. He eyes her narrowly. "You're only trying to make sure I stick to the meal plan."

*Tch.* He got her. "I'm making it easy for you to stick to the meal plan. Did you do the gym during lunch, like I told you?"

He pops the top buttons of his collar open, revealing the slope of his Adam's apple. "Yeah, yeah."

"And you're drinking more water?"

"I had to pee no less than twenty times today."

"A gallon a day is good for you. Cleans out all those toxins. Believe me, you hate it now, but it's gonna make you feel so much better in the long run. More energy. Better skin." She starts digging in the fridge, bending over to keep the curve of her ass in his sights. She can tell he's looking. Maybe if she can get his blood up enough, he'll want to take out his sexual frustration on a willing candidate.

"What's wrong with my skin?" he asks.

"Water helps with early aging."

"I'm only twenty-nine."

"Yet you look a decade older."

He harrumphs and spreads his feet wide, crossing his arms, his fancy shoes not matching his bratty posture.

She takes out the marinating chicken. "And don't forget to masturbate before bed."

He groans. "Sadie…"

"The endorphins are good for you. Plus, it will help you sleep," she insists. "It'll also help with your Grumpy Gus attitude and your puffy, baggy eyes." She beeps the oven's buttons, getting it to pre-heat. A mischievous smile spreads across her face and she turns on her heel, giving Simon her most award-winning smile. "Unless you want me to bring you a hook-up kind of date instead. No wine and dine, just sex. I've got people in my roster looking for those."

He's still in bitch-face mode. "Who would pay you for that? That's what Tinder is for."

She draws a finger up Simon's shirt, getting his attention and softening him up. "But the people I sponsor are clean, caring, and kind." She helps him pop open one more button and he blushes. "You're kind, aren't you, Noah?"

A slight tremor runs through his body. God, he's so easy.

Standing in front of him, making no effort to remove her cleavage from his view, she starts squeezing the muscles between his neck and shoulders, feeling the knots of tension there. "Come on. Trust me. I'm here to take care of you, aren't I?"

He's starting to get hard for her again. Perfect. He shifts and closes his thighs, but she holds her tongue. Let him pretend she doesn't see it.

Her fingers dig into the meat of him, and he starts to sag in the chair as his eyes close. "You like this?" she asks.

His head drifts back. "Yeah. I get massages sometimes. Helps relieve the stress."

"So does sex," she tries again, but he only peeks at her with one eye, that stubbornness falling over his face again. Tamping down her annoyance, she squeezes harder, leaning in and angling her hands further around the curve of his neck. She's so close she could straddle him. She *should* straddle him. It certainly would make the goddamn angle easier. She's about to lose her balance and teach him how to motorboat by mistake.

"Have you ever gotten a massage?" he asks.

"No."

He peeks at her again. "I could give you one."

Oh yeah, his hormones are ripening right up. "Who's paying who here?" she asks with a wink. At that, she does straddle him, landing right in his lap with a plunk and ignoring the hard heat she finds there. His lips part slightly, and she feels nothing but smug.

"So, can I get you a wham-bam date for tonight?" she asks. "A nightcap before bed."

"I don't want to leave the house," he murmurs, his chest starting to rise and fall a little quicker, his pulse fluttering under his skin. His hands rest on her hips gently, and that's a step too far.

She pulls back with a snap and returns to cooking, putting the chicken in a pan with some root veggies she'd prepared ahead of time. She doesn't need to look at him to know he's probably at a loss right now, wondering if he did something wrong.

She has to redirect him and do it fast, or she'll lose him. "I have a person in mind. You'll like her. She'll come to you."

"But… C'mon. I can't do it with you in the next bedroom over."

"Oh please. It's not as if I've never heard anyone having sex before." She feigns a few good moans and hissed curses. "Besides, maybe I can give you pointers through the wall."

This time, she does spare him a glance and he is positively glowing siren-red. She doesn't know whether he looks terrified or seduced. Maybe a little of both.

"I'm kidding. I'll go out and snag a late-night snack at the all-night diner."

"You won't let me have snacks," he says.

"I'm seriously about to put a woman in your bed. What better kind of snack is there?"

There's a pause during which she shoves the tray in the oven, bending over for him again and dusting her hands over the curve of her backside before closing the door.

"Okay," he says, sounding utterly distracted. "I'll do it."

Cha-ching.

———

*At least my penis is doing its job,* Simon thinks. It's been a week, Saturday to Saturday, and he's had sex no less than five times, finishing at least twice that. Part of him is proud of his accomplishments. The other part is irritated he only gets matched with older women. He's going to develop an Oedipal complex if he keeps this up. The idea makes the corner of his eye twitch.

It's been a long day.

"And what do you do with the clit?" Sadie grills him over a late-night glass of wine.

He swigs, still hating these explicit terms for lady parts. "Clockwise, flicks, then write the alphabet." His face burns even though he's given this specific task his best try twice now, with varying degrees of success. He's grateful for patient, forgiving women.

"What can you use to do it with?"

He takes another gulp. "Fingers, tongue, toys, and a little teeth, if I'm gentle."

"Good boy."

He warms somewhere beside his cheeks. He has no idea why he reacts to Sadie like this. He should be sexed out, down for the count, wrung dry, and yet the slightest attention from this woman always gets him going again. He's never felt like this about anyone.

It's probably just because she likes wearing his underwear, which she is absolutely doing, her creamy thighs visible almost all the way to the top. If she asked him to go on another date right now, he'd refuse without a shadow of a doubt, but if she were to purr at him with that sultry voice, he'd put his hands on her in a second. He wants to even without her taunts. And maybe, after all his practice, he'd actually do a good job. It took him a half hour, but he managed to give that last date an orgasm.

He smirks smugly to himself.

"What else can you do with your teeth?" she asks.

He looks at her, appreciating her freckled skin and wondering what it would be like to touch her instead of these strangers. To count the sprinkles of brown specks on her nose and shoulders. To see where else he might find them. Along her back? On the curve of her bottom? Perhaps that sweet belly, the one he catches glimpses of when she's wearing a short shirt and lifts her arms too high. That strip of skin he fantasizes about.

A possessive flare lights him up. Oh yes, his motor is definitely running again. Snapping out of his imagination, he says, "I can nip them basically anywhere."

"But where should your focus be?"

He thinks back to this morning and sighs through his nose, trying to parse out when the punk rock, green-haired Hera had made those whining noises. "Between the neck and the shoulder. Maybe the inner thighs?"

Sadie clucks her tongue at him, waggling her finger. "You keep forgetting the nipples."

He sulks. "Can't we call them something else? Like peaks or something?"

"This isn't a romance novel, Noah. This is an anatomy lesson."

Sinking deeper in his chair, he frowns. "Don't call me that. I don't even like it when they call me that."

Sadie uncrosses and recrosses her legs, and he watches every inch of her movement. "Ah, but your stage name is your power. It's your mask to hide behind. It keeps you safe from vulnerability. Noah will do things Simon never could."

He doesn't know how he feels about that.

She sips her own wine. "So, you'll practice on tomorrow's date, right?"

"Stop. You're making me a man-whore. Slow it down. Scale back to just one a week."

She goes wide-eyed, as if he'd scared her somehow. Looking away, her hand flies to her omnipresent necklace and fiddles with it, rubbing her thumb against the stone and pressing it to her lips. Her knees pull up as she drinks her wine, going to that space in her mind she seems to retreat to sometimes. Every time she does, it fills him with concern.

*What happened to you, Sadie?* he wonders. *Did your "bad relationship" include getting in trouble if you did the wrong thing? If you annoyed the wrong person?*

The possibility makes his jaw clench. He thinks about it all the time, why she had to run away and entrust herself to a total stranger. Why she's excited to drain him of every dollar she can. Why she never talks about herself and dodges when he asks. What is it she's trying to escape from?

The terrible thoughts circling his head are maddening.

"Why do you always look so upset when I tell you no?" he asks.

Something in her shifts, her back going rigid and her eyes blanking. "I'm not upset."

It hurts to hear her lie.

Tucking her necklace under the collar of his T-shirt of the night—one that hangs on her more loosely than the others, drooping over her shoulder—she says, "I'm just a hard worker. I feel like I'm not doing my job if you're not out on the social scene." She tries to give him a smile, but it's fake. Too wide. Almost brittle.

"How about a bonus in exchange for a day off?" he asks, testing her reaction.

That smile becomes more real. "What about one for good behavior and you still let me send you out on the town anyway?"

He narrows his eyes.

"Fine," she says, lifting her free hand and waggling it jazz style. "I'll give you tomorrow off. But I have a roster lined up for you next week that I refuse to reschedule. You promised me you'd squeeze in a lunch date too, don't forget."

"Anyone my own age?" he asks for the millionth time.

That hand goes to her hip this time, and she flashes him a stunning grin, her ice blue eyes like a pale summer sky. "Her name is Jessika and she's your Saturday night."

"Uh-huh. And how many are lined up before that? Any grannies I should be aware of?"

"You should only be so lucky. They're easy to wear out."

Tipping his glass in her direction, he says, "Isn't your job to set me up with people I'm compatible with?"

"It's my job to set you up with women who don't mind putting up with an awkward, cringeworthy, near-virgin newbie."

He visibly deflates. This woman cuts him right to the quick sometimes.

"Be grateful. At least I'm vetting them all to make sure they're pretty," she says.

He purses his lips. It makes sense, but it's also terribly shallow. Is that how Sadie always operates? What if his someday-wife isn't conventionally beautiful? Would Sadie glaze over his soul mate, accidentally robbing him of the opportunity for true love?

*Once training is over, I'll ask to see anyone she has in her little black book,* he decides. If they're interested in him, he'll be interested in them. His future angel doesn't have to be beautiful to everyone, she only has to be beautiful to him. And she will be. He feels it in his bones.

———

The vibrating buzz of his damn phone makes Simon peek open one eye. He's cradling his spare pillow like it's the world's squishiest teddy bear and a drool spot darkens the blackish fabric. He fumbles for the electronic rectangle of doom and stubs his finger on the screen, trying to light it up so he can see who's calling at the ungodly hour of…ten a.m.? How the hell is it already ten a.m.?

Looking at the caller ID, he grunts.

Lawrence.

With a frown, he swipes right and opens the call with, "It's Sunday. Go to church."

"Not in the mood," Lawrence says, gruff on the other side of the line.

"You're always in the mood."

"Not when my nephew keeps unsending the emails he sends to me. It's like I see it in my inbox and then, poof, it's gone."

Simon buries his face in the pillow with a stifled groan. Too much wine made him brave last night, and at one in the morning, he'd decided it would be a good idea to send his latest draft proposal to his uncle. He had pressed "send," seriously doubted his sanity, felt his bowels clench, and immediately rooted around in his mailbox's functionality to recall the damning piece of evidence.

"You shouldn't be up that late at night," Simon says. "It's bad for your skin." As Sadie keeps telling him.

Lawrence snorts. "What did you send, anyway?"

"Work."

"I'd assumed. Unless you want to send me more YouTube clips of irreverent, curse-riddled musicals."

"That was for Nando," Simon groans. He'll never live that down.

"What if I liked it?"

"The musical?"

"The work, Simon," his uncle says drily. "What you almost regaled me with."

Rolling onto his back, phone pressed to his enormous ear, Simon runs his fingers through his hair and tugs for comfort. "It's just another half-considered idea. You know how I am about numbers making sense, but I haven't dug into their infrastructure or corporate culture."

"So?" Lawrence asks.

"So, there's a lot more to an acquisition than just sewing a company onto your bottom line like a benevolent tumor."

"Now there's an image I won't get out of my head."

Sitting up, Simon gusts air through his nose. "Look, I'm sorry. I know I'm screwing this up."

"No one said that."

"I am, though," Simon insists. "Mom would have bought three companies by now. Four. And they would have been perfect fits, every one of them." A bubble of anger makes him clench his teeth. She shouldn't have brought him into this company in the first place. Shouldn't have put him in a position to vie for CEO. If he could let go of his pride, he'd cut ties and just give the job to Nando. Or better yet, let his uncle keep it. He's doing a better job than Simon ever could.

"Are you spiraling over there?" Lawrence asks.

Yes.

"No," Simon says. "I'm just tired of telling you I'm sorry."

"You know, if you'd actually leave your emails in my inbox, I might be able to look at these with you and help you strategize."

"You gonna do that for Nando too?"

"I work with Armando all the time. The only difference is that he takes my advice."

"I'm supposed to be able to do this by myself. I'm not supposed to rely on some master to show me the light. I don't need a teacher."

"Everyone does. And new things take time to grow into. You just need practice."

*That's me in a nutshell,* Simon thinks. *Need to practice with women even though I'm almost thirty and should know better. Need to practice at my job despite the fact that my mother tried to groom me the minute my voice changed.*

"And so what if this deal doesn't work?" Lawrence says. "There's always something interesting on the horizon, as long as you don't stop looking."

Simon sits in sullen silence.

"Send me your proposal, kid."

"I deleted it."

"Well, un-delete it."

Simon pauses, tugging his hair again and taking in the popcorn pattern on his ceiling. Sadie comes to mind, unbidden. She guides him on what to change. What to say and do until he can manage it on his own. And, even when he pretends, some flavor of him still makes it into the mix. Something that's not Fabio or Noah. Something that's all Simon. And sometimes, that's what seems to make his dates the most charmed. The most vibey. He may need guidance, but there's hope that being himself may just be the spice in the stew that makes it work. Maybe it could be that way with his job too.

"Okay. I'll send you what I've got," Simon says.

Lawrence's grin is audible.

"Actually, I've got more than one."

"Oh?"

"Yeah..." He calculates. "There are at least three companies that haven't been sold yet. The rest are lost or under contract, but these could still be bid for. I don't have any hope, but—"

"Horizons," Lawrence repeats. "If not now, then soon."

The thought brings a small smile to Simon's face. "I'll email you Monday morning. Let me give them another once-over."

"I'm holding you to this. Feet to the fire."

"Yeah, yeah."

"Well, if that's all settled, maybe I'll go to church after all. See ya 'round, kid."

"See you."

Simon only just thumbs the red button when there's a knock on his door. Sadie. A welcome intruder in his empty home. How strange life is.

*I've known her for a week, and she's changed my life.* Sadie with her freckles and dimples. With her crass mouth and sweet touches. With her ultimate belief in his potential.

"You using the shower today or what?" she calls, her voice dulled by the wood between them.

"Eventually."

"You going to get up off your ass anytime soon?"

He chuckles. "Eventually."

She lets out something that's a cross between a snort and a growl. Knocking on his door again in rhythmic, unending, slightly annoying thumps, she says, "I made you breakfast, and you need to go to the gym."

The gym. He hates the goddamn gym. Though maybe it would be more fun if…

"You want to come with me?" he asks, completely prepared for her to tell him no, just like she does every other time he invites her to do anything other than live in his space.

"Hm," she says, the knocking continuing. "Do they have spin class?"

He blanks. "Honestly, I have no idea."

"You paying my way?"

His lips press into a flat line as he huffs. "Fine."

The knocking stops. She lets out something that sounds suspiciously like a *yippee* and he stifles a giggle. It may be the first time he's made her happy like that. The grin on his face must be idiotic, he thinks, for as giddy as that makes him. Maybe he'll do more nice things for her. Hell, if it feels this good, maybe he'll do a lot. And he has just the thing in mind…

———

She's sweating and gross and possibly smells bad, but God it's the best she's felt in days. Familiar self-inflicted exhaustion makes her wobbly as she pads along the black, pressed foam floor. Her spin class was exactly what she needed to relieve the pressure. If Simon gets her a membership, she'll come here every goddamned day.

Speaking of CEO Simon, he's off looking miserable on the bench press. He's not even trying. A man of his size should have at least twice the weight on the bar, but he's milking his newbie status with a mere fifteen pounds on each side.

Going behind him, Angelica wraps her hands over the metal rail and pops her head over. "Hullo, Simon."

His eyes fly wide, making a strangled cry as he tries his best not to drop the weight on his own neck. He would, if not for Angelica's firm grip keeping him safe from thirty pounds of strangulation.

"Jesus, Sadie, what the actual hell?"

She grins. He's adorable when he's annoyed. Which is good because he gets annoyed a lot. He seems to flip-flop between that and utterly awkward, and it's the most endearing thing she's ever seen.

"You're so cute," she says, receiving a look of confusion at the non sequitur. She nods toward his clothes. "And prudish. Most men wear tight shorts and skimpy tank tops here. You are in what looks like a floppy bathing suit and a shirt for a man twice your size."

"It's comfortable," he gripes.

"It's silly," she says with another smile. She bops her fingertip on the tip of his nose, and he flushes pink, just like he does every time she touches him. Another check mark in the sweet-as-pie column. "We should get you some new clothes."

"You're going to bleed me dry of cash, you know."

"But I'm worth every penny."

He makes a grumpy noise and hooks the weights back into the holster. "Are we done for the day?"

Hands on her hips, she leans closer to his face. He looks both nervous and entranced, and there is a heady power imbalance to it. "Did you do your cardio?"

He nods, staring at her lips.

"And did you do all the reps?"

"I even added legs," he murmurs, still staring.

"Good." She stands up straight. "Friends never let friends skip leg day."

"What?"

She waves him off. "Never mind. I'm going to hit the showers. Wanna come?"

He sits up faster than a rocket, his mouth dropping open. "Like, into the ladies—?"

"The men's shower, Simon. The locker rooms are right next to each other if you haven't noticed. Must you hit on me every chance you get?"

She's teasing, but he doesn't seem to realize. His hands lift and he shakes them back and forth with his jaw dropped. "I didn't mean… I just…"

Rolling her eyes, she snickers. He puts his face in his hands and mutters un-hearable things, his broad shoulders hunching.

"Are you sure I can't pop you into the shower and get you in some nice girl's arms tonight? You're looking kind of alluring right now."

He peeks at her through his thick fingers. "Me?"

She smirks and lifts her eyebrows up, walking her fingers over his deltoid. "Your work is already paying off. I know you canceled for the night, but are you sure you wouldn't like someone's legs wrapped around you?"

He shakes his head. "Can't. I have something…special planned."

*Special?* Concern weaves a spiderweb in her chest. Special. What the hell does that mean? "Simon," she *tsks*, trying to keep her cool, "are you seeing women without me?"

*Moreover, are you robbing me of money to dally on your own time? Are you cutting me out of what's rightfully mine? Are you fucking me over?*

She sounds like Maxine. A fact that makes her stomach queasy, acid churning in waves.

"No women," Simon says, a little smile tugging the corners of his lips up. "I'm going to get a massage."

Thank Christ. "You seem to have a thing for those."

"I get a lot of anxiety. It helps. Plus, it just feels good, you know? Having someone touch you in, like, a nice way."

"Oh my God, Simon…" Angelica grins like a fool. She cups a hand beside her mouth, lowering her voice so the other dude-bros don't hear. "Do you have a massage kink?"

"Kink?" he squawks, echoing in the expanse of mirrors and machines. "I don't even know what makes something a kink."

"Lower your voice," she scolds in a harsh whisper, slapping her hands over his mouth. Men and women pause all around them, staring at Simon. The man of the hour brushes her off, flings his head side to side to look at his audience with a glower…and flips them all off.

Now that's something.

"Is that the temper you talked about?" Angelica asks with one eyebrow cocked.

His bitch face reigns supreme. "No. You'll know when my trigger gets pulled."

"Fair enough." She plops onto the bench beside him, nudging him with her hip. Leaning until her head is almost resting on his shoulder, she whispers, "A kink is something that turns you on beyond reason. Something off the beaten path. For example, some people want to be slapped or spit on. Some people have a thing for anal sex. Some want to pretend you're asleep when they fuck you."

"I don't want anything like that," he hisses as if offended.

"It could also be something as mild as excessive praise," she murmurs. "Someone telling you what a good boy you are. How sexy. How much they want you. How they'll never get enough of you. How good you feel inside them. So hard and big and strong."

His eyes dance over hers. Ah, there's that familiar erection he's trying to hide. He crosses his legs and clears his throat.

Mercilessly, she asks in a low voice, "What's your kink, Noah? What makes you so hard it hurts?"

Face on fire, he fiddles with his hands. "I don't even know…but maybe I like sounds."

"When they moan for you?" she asks through a grin.

"Or just talk to me," he says. He might as well be a neon sign for how his cheeks glow.

Patting him on the shoulder, Angelica's about to stand up when Simon coughs up the courage to ask, "Do you have a kink?"

She laughs, she can't help it. "Yeah, mine is when a man keeps his pants buttoned."

Simon goes from red to white. "Jesus. And still stick it out? Like, from the hole? Wouldn't that get caught in the zipper?"

Angelica's wide-eyed blinks are rapid and long lasting until she breaks into guffaws. She pictures it, and it's just too much. A little wee-wee poking from beneath the cinched button of a pair of blue jeans, looking sad and flaccid and stuck in a zipper.

She's open-mouthed, head thrown back as she laughs, hitting him on the chest as images of that zipped-up penis sag in her mind. Unable to breathe, tears of mirth fill her eyes and dapple her lashes. Talk about a sad sac.

Her stomach hurts for how long she's rolling, slapping her knee outright and not caring how many people watch her. Every time it seems to have stopped, another man with a helpless prick pops into her mind's eye, and she's going to burst for how hard she's letting go.

Trying to settle, Angelica takes a deep breath and looks at Simon once more. His face is still agape as he worries about chafing, and she's off in gales again.

He tries to mope and turn away like the ball of angst he is, but her laughter is bringing a smile to his face, nonetheless. He turns that expression on her with a softness to his eyes, something that looks way too sweet and far beyond intimate. "You know, I think moments like this are better than sex with strangers."

Those words sink into Angelica's head like melting ice, quelling her amusement in cold wet stripes.

Is his crush on her getting stronger? If so, she's one hundred percent to blame. She's been stoking his fire to make him take out his sexual desire on other women, but she should have known the romantic in him would rear its ugly head sooner or later.

Shit.

"But it's getting better every time, right?" she asks quietly. "You're enjoying it more and more?"

"I guess so," he says, waggling his feet, pointing his toes and flexing them again. He takes no notice of her discomfort, biting the inside of his cheek. "But I don't want to talk about that."

Neither does she.

"I'm taking you to the massage parlor with me, by the way," he tells her. "You said you've never had one before, right? And no saying no. I'm paying for you, so you can't complain."

And now he's giving presents? Shit, shit, double shit.

"Consider it a business team building event," he says. "They do it in Russia all the time. Go to saunas and bathhouses and stuff."

"There's no way I'm getting in a bath with you," she chokes out.

His grin only widens. Her hand flies to her necklace, fiddling as she curses herself.

"Hey," Simon says, staring at his sneakers. "I've been thinking. Do you think those women like how inexperienced I am?"

Of course, they do. That's exactly what they're paying for.

"If so, I wonder, do you think that someone could love me as I am now? Without any more training, I mean."

Why would he ask this?

Is he asking about her? If she could love him?

The look on his face as he turns to take her in solidifies that thought into utter truth in her mind. His crush is turning into something deeper. The softness and vulnerability in his gaze sinks into her, and her pulse picks up. What is she supposed to do now?

Feeling like a villain for the first time, Angelica says, "I think anyone looking for something serious would be put off by you. You're too flawed."

The sweet smile on his face disappears slowly, like a dream dying as you wake up in the morning. "You don't think I add anything special? Some sort of naive charm? Or do I need to just be 'Noah' and nothing else?"

Angelica's heart hurts watching him as he clasps his hands together in his lap, leaning over his knees, his eyebrows knit so hard they nearly touch. Why is she hurting this poor, sweet man?

Because her life is on the line.

Because it's either keep him on the street or she'll die.

Her hand swipes over the tracker in her arm, feeling the tiny rise of it under her skin. "Just be Noah. Simon needs to grow up first."

# spoiled

. . .

"BEE, what the hell have I gotten myself into?" Angelica says aloud, pinching her necklace so hard, it's bound to leave imprints on her flesh for days.

She can barely see through the gray steam fogging up this hot, low-lit room, the tiles radiating searing warmth against her tufty spa-robed rear. The smell in this place is the same as Simon's shampoo—eucalyptus, it said on the doorframe—and the strength of it clears every inch of her sinuses, leaving her brain floating somewhere in space.

She's dripping with sweat, but as much water as her skin is letting go, the ceiling is doing it more, raining on her in essential oil drops. Her hair is still wrapped in her gym ponytail, but it sags uncomfortably against her scalp, and she finally gives up and yanks the thing down.

Another hush of steam rushes her, sapping away all the oxygen in a four-foot radius. Angelica has to remind herself to breathe slowly. That's what that uptight, stick-up-her-ass woman at the front desk had told her anyway. She also said not to stay in too long, and to leave if she felt nauseous. But screw that. That sort of copping out is for pussies. Simon said he makes it up to twenty minutes in these things, and goddamnit, there's no way he's beating her.

Another woman walks into Angelica's dark, head-floating cave. The opened door lets in a brisk gust of air that Angelica wants to fling her body toward, the crisp wisp like salvation.

Regarding her with wary eyes, the youngish, chubby-cheeked stranger with short brown hair and almond eyes says, "Wow, should you be in here?"

Well, that was blunt. What a bitch. As if Angelica doesn't look like she belongs. She's just as spa-worthy as any of the mix of multigenerational women wading naked in a pool together the next room over. Angelica should take a page from the book of Simon and flip off this random rubbernecker.

"Get bent," Angelica says. As soon as the words leave, she starts panting, trying to bring the little air she expelled back into her lungs. Still, she won't be cowed. She won't give up. It's her versus hot air, and who the hell loses to air? Not her. Not this ex-prostitute. Never in life.

"No, seriously," the woman says, walking closer. "You shouldn't be in here. You look like you're about to…"

And Angelica passes right the fuck out on the hot stone floor.

———

Angelica's eyes blink open, her body strewn over a lounge chair. Simon and the stick-up-her-ass woman stand over her with eyes too wide and mouths too pursed. Hair dripping wet, Simon is patting a frigid cloth on her forehead as stick-ass woman holds out a glass of ice water. When Angelica sits up, her head swims, but she rallies, grabbing the ice water and gulping it down in exactly four swallows.

Simon puts the cloth on her face again, gently caressing her cheeks and hairline. "Hey, you okay?"

"What happened?" Angelica manages, blinking slowly.

The stick-ass woman *tsks* her. "You stayed in the sauna too long, I'm afraid." Angelica would tell her to fuck off, but she doesn't have the energy.

A strong arm wraps around her back as Simon helps her sit straighter, cradling her and asking for another glass of water.

"I'm okay," Angelica says, waving off both his arm and his concern. "How long was I out for?"

Stick-Ass says, "It took us about ten minutes and three women to lift you into the co-ed area."

*Three?* What does she mean three? Angelica should have taken two at the most.

"Do you want to go home?" Simon asks, those puppy-dog eyes shining. Blargh. Why is he so adorable?

"Weren't you the one saying you needed this place because you were riddled with anxiety?"

"Yeah, well, no offense, but this didn't exactly bring my blood pressure down." He looks like that's the God's honest truth. He's got a vein sticking out in his forehead when he clenches his jaw, his fingers twined into knots.

"I'm okay, Simon, it's all right."

"Did you hit your head?" Probably. "Because we'll go to the hospital if you hit your head."

"I'll hit *you* in the head if you don't calm down," Angelica says.

Strangely enough, that snark seems to settle him, and his lips quirk up at one corner. "All right. Come on, I'll take you home."

He looks so disappointed—which shouldn't matter. Angelica knows this was a bad idea. She should just let him take her back to the apartment. She can go to bed and forget all about this stupid man with his stupid presents and his stupid crush and his stupid face.

But she doesn't because she's an idiot.

"Don't give me that," she says. "This was supposed to be your special night. Plus, I've never had a massage before, remember?"

Stick-Ass chimes in. "Well, we're ready for both of you if you're staying."

Simon rubs Angelica's back. "You sure?"

Nodding, she curses herself and her weak will. "Just help me up."

Stick-Ass seems pleased. Whether it's about Angelica's recovery or the fact they're not being sued for giving her heat stroke, she's not sure. "If you both don't mind following me, I'll take you to your room."

"Room?" Simon asks, his voice too high. "Singular?"

"Yes." Stick-Ass blinks. "For your couple's massage."

If Simon's intention was to help Angelica up, he drops her pretty damn fast. His hands start waving wildly. "No, no. We're not a couple. We're just fr—"

"Employee and employer," Angelica cuts in.

Stick-Ass looks truly concerned. "Oh. I'm so sorry. There must have been a mix-up. We don't have any additional rooms available. We're fully booked."

Simon groans, his hands flopping to his sides with heavy claps as he tips his head to the ceiling.

"Don't worry about it," Angelica says. "So we're not a couple. So what? They're just gonna rub our backs, right?"

Stick-Ass checks her sheet. "Full body. And I believe Mr. Javik especially enjoys his glutes."

The grin that takes over Angelica's face is outright sinister. "Oh Simon. But you said this wasn't a sex thing."

His cheeks skip all other DEFCONs, skyrocketing directly to one. With her canines showing in a face-splitting grin, Angelica takes his arm and tugs him after the tightly wound woman who suddenly tries her best not to look Simon in the eyes.

"Why do you do this to me?" he whisper-hisses.

"Because it's the most fun I've had all day," she whispers back.

He makes his now-patented mutters of general displeasure and allows himself to be dragged after Stick-Ass.

The hallway is lined with fake bamboo and the space is dimly lit. Soft music plays in the background that reminds Angelica of hippie yoga and meditation crap. This seems like the kind of place where no one is supposed to talk, like the weirdest, most pretentious library in existence, all sage greens and paintings with monochromatic splashes of pastel color.

"Here we are," Stick-Ass says, a polite smile on her face as she gestures to the room with a small bow.

Dropping Simon's arm, Angelica dips inside. What looks like two hospital examination beds with soft beige sheets lay side by side, about four feet between them. The room is warm, but not too warm, and that Zen music is louder. The heavy shadow of Simon floating behind her makes the room seem tight. Claustrophobic. He fills up the doorway with his sullen frown, robed shoulders, and bear-paw hands dug into his pockets.

Stick-Ass pops in her head. "Go ahead and take off your clothes to your level of comfort and place the sheets over you. Best to start face down, please." And with that, she closes the door softly behind her.

"We get naked?" Angelica asks, more than a little surprised.

Simon slaps his hands over his face. "You don't have to. I won't look. We don't even have to do this at all."

"Is it better if you're naked?"

He mlurfs. "They can get better access to—"

"My vagina?"

"Your muscles," Simon squawks, his gaze slamming to hers. "What do you think I do in here?"

"Ever heard of a rub and tug?" His blank look says it all. "Whatever, just close your eyes while I do this."

Simon does her one better. He turns to face the wall and wraps his arms over his head like a little kid playing hide-and-seek. She half expects him to start counting. Biting her lip to stifle a giggle, Angelica drops her robe entirely. Not thinking twice and feeling mischievous, she walks over and drapes the terry cloth wrap over Simon's shoulder, only to hear him do his angry mumble-grumble again.

"Sadie, for the love of God, just get on the bed."

"Ooh. Now, now, Noah. Don't be so demanding."

He almost whips around to scold her. Almost. As soon as his head bolts from the haven of his arms, he goes rigid, and plunges back into the safety of his blinders.

She does giggle this time, lifting the warm sheets and scooting under. "Your turn."

He turns so slowly, it's comical. When he sees her, his cheeks heat and he fiddles with his robe. "You're supposed to lie face down."

She turns and sees a round cradle pillow with a hole in the middle. "I put my face in this?" Before he says anything, she dives, tucking in her face and wiggling her hips around until she's comfortable. Behind her, Simon clears his throat.

"Don't peek?" he asks instead of tells.

"Why would I peek?"

She considers. Why wouldn't she peek?

The rustle of fabric makes her do just that. From her vantage point, Simon is facing away, showing the straight line that runs directly down his back to a flat little man-butt. It's a cute man- butt. Grabbable. Biteable.

It dawns on Angelica that she hasn't had sex in a long time. At least, a long time for her. She shoves her face back down before Simon can catch her in her act of transgression.

A sharp knock raps on the door, making Angelica twitch. She doesn't really know what happens now.

"Come in," Simon says, his warm baritone almost too loud in this confined, insulated space. The door creaks. All Angelica can see is the texture of the carpet as she stares straight down.

Discomfort tenses her from her toes to her forehead. She can't see what's happening. She's vulnerable. She could even be unsafe. She always stares down anyone who might touch her body until she deems them acceptable. She has no idea who the hell these people are.

But Simon's here. Simon wouldn't be here if this was a bad place. Right?

It doesn't stop the sudden knot in her stomach.

A soft voice says, "Mr. and Mrs. Javik?"

"Not his wife," Angelica pipes up. Simon groans again.

"Oh?" the voice says. "Well, my name is Brandon. Miss Dani and I will be taking care of you today. Do either of you have a preference for a male or female therapist?"

Both she and Simon say "female" simultaneously. Simon grumps. Letting her win, as he so often does, he says, "Sadie can take Miss Dani."

"Sure thing, sir."

It's very weird to be unable to see the bodies as they shift around them, ruffling and shuffling, moving and grooving for all Angelica knows. Interpretive dance to the tune of Zen and zithers. Angelica's body is a stone, rigid and uncrackable. Even her jaw is tight as this strange woman floats around her, fluffing her sheet and hiking it a little higher before folding it down, exposing her spine all the way to the crack of her ass.

"No glutes," Angelica muffles out.

"Glutes are the best part," Simon muffles back.

Miss Dani takes pity. "Whatever you like. This is for you. Just let me know if you want the pressure harder or softer."

"You too, Mr. Javik," Brandon adds.

Angelica hears something wet squelch. Like lube. Why the fuck are they using lube? She's outright thrumming with anxiousness as she hears the slippery slide of hand over hand before the stranger's palms come to rest on her back.

She jumps. She can't help it. People can only touch her in ways she's in complete control of. Preplanned boundaries. If they went off-script, spanking or biting, Angelica would lose her mind. It was too much like her father. Red light. Hard limit.

Angelica's breath hitches.

Miss Dani's voice is a soft murmur over Angelica's ear, too quiet for Simon to hear. "Since this is your first massage, I'll be very gentle. If you need me to stop at any time, I absolutely will. Okay?"

Tucked into her face cradle, Angelica takes a deep breath and nods.

Hands come to rest on her again. They sit there for a minute, just seeming to acclimate her to their presence before the pressure increases. Angelica knows what a frigging massage is. Hell, she's given them. But getting one?

Unexpectedly, the sensation of those hands sliding up and down her back pulls a soft sigh from her lips. The lotion warms as those fingers glide out toward her ribs and back again, long strokes leaving bliss in their wake. Thumbs come into play next, swirling in circles over Angelica's skin and digging in slightly. Not too deep, but just deep enough.

Her hair is swept to the side over her shoulder so those fingers can work their way to her neck. The chain of her necklace shifts, and Angelica thinks of her Auntie Bee. Bee was the only one who would touch her so gently. She was old even when Angelica was young, and her wrinkles were like a map of happiness and strife. Her eyes were gray, but she loved the earthy colors of nature, always wanting to take them to green places. But there was no money in green places. Money only came when Angelica was old enough to be legal. Then people touched her with a different purpose as she visited the dark alleyways of the city. That is, until she found the infamous Madam Maxine, and her clientele became of higher caliber.

Nights were long, but Bee was always there when she got home, holding her and letting silence say everything Angelica wouldn't. Her sullenness never put Bee off, though. Angelica had always been mopey, from five right on up. Why wouldn't she be, given that life was what it was? Still, Bee didn't mind. She loved her for her. She would run her fingers through Angelica's hair, crown to ends, so soothing it would make her eyes prick with hot tears she would never let fall. Just like what's happening now.

No one ever touches Angelica for Angelica's benefit anymore. Not until this moment. And it hurts as much as it feels good.

Her arms are being lifted and stretched, flexing her tendons in ways unfamiliar and causing happy pops and crackles. Miss Dani runs her fingers through Angelica's and squeezes, pulling the tension from all ten tips. Her calves are tighter than she ever would have thought, but the attention softens them, relaxing her even as her mind dips into sadness. Melancholy.

She sniffles hard, but Miss Dani only squeezes her feet in comfort. It's getting to be too much.

Angelica needs this as much as she hates it. As much as she loves it. As much as she—

Simon snores. Not a soft snore, but a loud *SNARF* followed by a shocked gasp.

His snore was so loud, he woke himself up.

Something in Angelica snaps, some wire holding her together, and she bursts into laughter.

For the second time today, Simon Javik has put Angelica into belly laughs.

She raises her head from its cradle to look at him. He whips his head toward her, eyes wide and lips pressed together so hard, his nostrils flare. He looks completely, utterly stupid.

And she's off again.

———

Feelings are complicated things.

Simon sits at his desk, playing with his bottom lip as he twirls his swivel chair in two full rotations before landing with his face pointed at his office's panoramic window. The sun glitters off the mirrored surfaces of buildings, thousands of people he'll never know struggling to earn a day's wage. Their numbers alone should make him feel something, some sense of awe or smallness, but it doesn't. He lives in a singular world where spreadsheets, ladder climbing, and inadequacy are all that is on his mind.

Only that's a lie. Sadie has changed everything, cascading a kaleidoscope through his world of gray, giving him embarrassment, encouragement, humiliation, happiness. When she laughs, something in his heart clenches, making him want to hear that boisterous sound over and over again, even when it's at his own expense—and, let's face it, it's usually at his own expense.

Last night after the massage, she'd been too giddy to take home. Almost lighthearted, which seemed new for her. Simon wanted to keep that going for as long as he could, a hopeful beat thrumming like a bass through his rib cage, so he decided to take her somewhere else. Simon loves records, so off to the record store they went, taking Sadie by surprise. She tried to act surly, but when he told her to pick out some vinyl for his collection, she perked up. Faking begrudging-ness, she picked through the sleeves with the focus of an ancient mathematician on an abacus, eyes glued to cover after cover. It made him giddy too.

She handed him a load of junk, telling him he was either old or a hipster to have something as archaic as a record player, but he only smiled at her. She'd gotten this soft look on her face, then turned tail, and almost left in the taxi without him.

When they got home, he put on something random she'd picked. Pop-techno-dancey crap. He was doomed at the first note because Sadie had said the next way to level up the Noah inside him was to teach him how to dance. It was painful. Not in a physical sense—though he might have strained something in his lower back—but in the "Why are my arms waving like a moron and why the hell won't you let me put them back down again" sort of way.

After four frenetic songs in a row came something slower. Sultry. Sadie had stopped jamming her feet in patterns unknown and instead was undulating, circling her hips while slipping her hands up her body and running her fingers through her hair, tangling it in the sexiest of ways. Wearing that devilish look she gets from time to time, she sauntered toward him, telling him it was time for another lesson.

Turning her back to him, she slipped his hand over her stomach and asked him to pull her tight. It was a fantasy come true without him ever having imagined it before. She told him, her voice lilting to the song, that he should sway his hips with hers. That if she were someone else, he should drag his lips over the arch of her neck. That he should keep his pressure on her lower belly firm.

His heartbeat picked up at the sound of her. He was right. If he had a kink, it was voices. Sadie, low and soft, telling him what to do, how to please someone, had him straining in his pants. She never seemed to notice, and he didn't know why. The round of her ass brushed against him until he was biting his lip.

She turned around in his arms, facing front and slowly rocking her hips, sinking down to a coiled squat before lifting herself up, rear first, her face right in line with his trousers. He wanted to be Noah in that moment more than ever before, and he wanted Sadie to be his woman of the evening with a fire that burned him from the inside out.

Reaching around the small of her back, he caught her and dragged her close, lifting his thigh between her legs and using his grip to pull her hips down. Her cry of shock was like a symphony, drowning out all other sound. She was half-lidded when she looked at him and, wonder of wonders, she pivoted her hips, rubbing against him. She did it once, her eyes glazing. Twice, her lips parting. Then she froze. The Noah in him cupped her cheek and leaned forward, whispering the words "Let's practice" over her lips.

And that's when he lost her. She'd danced away with a manic smile, making him cringe when she outright scratched the record to turn it off. Then, with a flick of her hand in salute, she dove into her bedroom, leaving Simon hungry for more.

He assured himself he was just doing what he was told when he shut off the lights in the apartment, finally tossing himself in his own bed and shucking off his clothes. She'd told him to touch himself before bed every night, and goddamnit, after that, why wouldn't he?

Something rang out in the stillness of the air. He didn't know if it was wishful thinking at first, but he swore he heard her voice on the other side of the wall. High-pitched. A whimper, maybe.

Was she touching herself too?

He cursed under his breath and got his hand to work, his rhythm hard and fast. Thinking of her writhing against him in the living room finished him all too quickly and he sat in disappointment, his lust unslaked. Whatever she had been doing in the other room, she hadn't stopped, and her sweet cries could be heard every now and then, sporadic and surprising, as if she was holding them back. He pictured her with one hand between her legs and the other over her mouth, stifling her sounds. It was enough to get him semi-hard again, full mast not far away.

He wondered what Noah would do.

Noah would slink over and knock on the door before opening it without permission. He'd ask if he could watch. He'd promise not to touch, and he'd tell her how sexy she was. How hot she made him. Before waiting for her to respond, he'd be at her bedside, hiking his knee onto the comforter and praising every inch of her body. He'd lie beside her and beg her to keep going. To be good for him.

And Simon was a rock again. This time, he was slow with himself, feeling the silk of his own skin as he let his imagination fly.

Sadie's ice blue eyes would sparkle even in the dark, he thinks. Her breasts, small and perky, would point right to the sky. He'd want to touch them, but he'd keep his promise, hovering his hand only close enough for her to feel his warmth. He would tell her how soft she'd be, and how nice he'd be to her. Enthralled, she'd arch her back, and he'd pull away, teasing her with his own vow. Teasing himself.

In his own bed, outside his fantasy, Simon's fist was a tight slide as he gripped himself, pressing his lips together as he heard one more of Sadie's muffled cries. It kept his imagination at full power.

Noah would move his hand down, hovering over Sadie's belly and begging to touch her. To taste her. Would Sadie please let him? Would she open those sweet lips and tell him yes? Let him dip between her legs and eat her alive?

In real life, Sadie let out one last sound, more of a feral grunt, and Simon went electric. His fantasy was far from over, but that guttural sound from his feisty girl's throat was enough to tear him over the edge, his deep groan matching hers.

Simon had stilled, panting. Had she heard him too? That should be a secret neither of them should dare speak of in the morning. Though, knowing Sadie, she might lord it over him for life.

The idea of being teased about it made him feel a fluttery mix of shame and excitement. Part of him, the Noah part, wanted to grab her hand, rest it on his crotch, and say, "See what you do to me? What you've always done to me?" Then he'd kiss her. And he'd tell her to get every other woman off his schedule because he wanted her. Just her. In his imagination, she swooned, but in real life, he knew she'd probably smack him. It didn't matter. In real life, he wouldn't have had the balls to do such a thing in the first place.

One thing was true last night that remains true today. He wants her. Not just for sex, but for teasing and giving things to and making her laugh. Sadie with her freckles and guffaws and filthy mouth. Every piece of stupidity he'd shown her makes her laugh so hard she might wet herself, and it makes him feel excited to embarrass himself again. And again. He'd bend over backward to keep that smile on her face, her joy makes him feel that good.

But she hurts him too. Words from her cut.

"You're too flawed," she'd said. "Simon needs to grow up." He's unlovable as he is. He'd always thought that, if he just dedicated the time, he could find someone. Hearing from an expert that his future angel wouldn't see him as worthy pulls his mood into sullenness, crushed by that idea that his special someone wouldn't want him. Just like Sadie wouldn't want him.

He tugs his lip a little too hard.

"Simon?" A knock sounds on the door, dragging him directly from his mired thoughts. His uncle Lawrence pokes his head in with a serious look on his face. "Are you sick?"

Simon's eyebrows knit. "No…"

Lawrence strides in and hovers by Simon's heavy, executive-style desk, not sitting, just resting his hands in his pockets. "I'd assumed you must have been, since you never sent the proposals."

Ah. That. Shit. He'd been too distracted.

"You promised me Monday morning," Lawrence continues. "Here it is Monday afternoon." Simon takes a deep breath, opening his mouth to speak, but his uncle cuts him off, eyes hard. "Do you even want to be here?"

The words bring Simon up short. "What?"

"Because if you do, you sure don't act like it."

Simon opens his mouth to apologize, but Lawrence lifts his hand to keep his words at bay. "Take family out of it," Lawrence says. "Take legacy out of it. If you're an employee and I'm your employer, the bottom line is that you're not meeting your goals or deadlines. If you were anyone else, you'd be put on warning. Instead, I'm offering to mentor you, but you won't open your books to me because of your pride."

*Or my insecurities*, Simon thinks.

"I want to help you," his uncle continues. "I want to teach you. I want you to be successful. But I can't do anything if you keep this up."

Simon withers. He deserves this talk. After all, he fires people who perform like he does. Business is business, and you have to pull your own weight.

Lawrence shakes his head, lifting his eyes to the ceiling. "I don't know what else to do other than threaten you. I talk, I cajole, I encourage. So again, I'm going to ask, do you want to be here?"

Winding them together, Simon stares at his hands so hard his pores should melt. The pressure of his palms against each other is the only thing holding him together. "Yes."

"You took too long to answer," Lawrence says. "It should have been immediate. Why wasn't it?"

Simon leans his elbows on his knees and slumps. "I don't know."

"Well, you should. Your parents wanted you here. I want you here. So be here."

Simon nods softly.

"And send me those damned files."

With that, his uncle turns on his heels and walks out of the office. He doesn't hustle, he walks with his head held high. Simon wants to do that. Simon wants to be that.

Maybe he does need to grow up.

The files are up on his screen in record time, and he picks through anything that's not numbers. He's been over those time and again and knows they're correct, right down to the decimal. It's the rest he needs to look at. Why they might or might not jive with the rest of the portfolio. What their marketing presence is like. Analyst placements in magic quadrants. He hates this part.

There is another knock that startles him. Nando this time. His lips are twisted to the side in a grimace as he comes in and shuts the door behind him.

"You got a meeting?" he asks.

Simon flicks his eyes to the calendar. "Not for an hour or so. What's up?"

Flopping into the chair opposite, Nando leans back and closes his eyes. "*Che palle*, did Lawrence ream you out?"

"Why? Did he do it to you?"

"And then some." Nando sighs. "I think he's anxious for us to end all this."

"Yeah, well, we've been at it for years."

"Almost three," he agrees. "We must suck."

"We bring great value to the company with every project we complete," Simon parrots his uncle.

"Bullshit. He keeps throwing us at stuff out of our wheelhouse, telling us we need to be 'well rounded,' eh? Well, I'd like to see him do the shit he puts us up to."

"He has. He's like some God-level savant without the downsides."

Nando puts his feet up on Simon's desk, something he hates but never bothers complaining about. "I can't figure out this damned realignment. There are too many pieces to the puzzle and way too many politics."

"You're a political science major."

"Which means I can see it and understand the roots of it. I just don't always have the social capital to work around it."

"Brute force. You're a CEO candidate."

"Yeah, and then watch everyone quit. We have a labor shortage as it is. We don't even have enough people in entry-level roles. Our recruiters apparently have their heads up their asses. They can find me a replacement for myself before they can find me a temporary junior accountant."

"I'd like to be a temporary junior accountant," Simon says.

"Right?" Nando agrees, eyes wide on Simon before he shutters them and flops his head down again. Seems they've both got it tough.

"Did you ever get your kittens?"

"No." Nando sulks, serving up a manly pout, if such a thing is possible. "You didn't want to come pick them out, so I let it go. I just sent over something like twenty bags of cat food and a handful of little blankets instead."

"No bowties?"

"Those are reserved for those who keep me company."

"Ever the altruist."

He snorts. "Shut up, Simi."

"Why don't you ever adopt one? It's not like you have a lot else going on."

"Call it 'commitment issues.'"

"That tracks."

"I told you to shut it." Nando's frown brokers no room for argument. With a huff, Simon does what he was told, turning to fiddle with his computer instead.

Another knock sounds on the door, but Nando doesn't bother taking his feet down. Sophia, Simon's executive assistant, pokes her head in the room, a notepad clenched to her chest. Nando peeks at her, deems her safe, and shuts his eyes again. She, however, stares at him for a beat or two too long.

"Simon, I'm getting lunch for the team today. Can I order you anything?"

"No, thank you." He's still on the friggin' meal plan.

Nando blindly lifts an arm in the air. "I'll take roast beef with those pickled red onions they have. So good."

His "so" came out as a low growl, and Sophia's face pinks.

How did Simon never notice this before? He'd always thought Nando intimidated her, but after seeing this look on so many faces at this point, he can call it out in a millisecond. She likes him. Maybe she has ever since that one-night stand Nando told him about. Maybe since before, because she's always been like this around him.

That won't end well. Commitment issues, indeed. He'd be a nightmare. Nando is a womanizer, and Sophia deserves someone devoted. A forever love. Someone who'd be a good father for her kid.

If there's anyone in the world she should avoid, it's Simon's bastard best friend.

———

Angelica scolds over text, her scowl unending.

> You promised a lunch date.

> And then work got busy. I'm sorry. I'll keep my weekend dates, but I don't think I can ever promise anything during the week.

> Everything's too unpredictable, and now that my uncle is all over me, I've got no wiggle room.

Angelica clenches her phone.

> Do you even want to do this anymore? Aren't you committed to this process?

There is a long pause. Then longer. Then longer.

> I wish I was just good enough as I am.

Angelica's heart wrenches. What the hell is she going to do?

Got any more guy friends who need dates?
Maybe I need new clients.

There is another long pause where bubbles start and stop. Then start and stop.

I'm committed.

I just can't lose my job over this.

I need money, or else I can't afford you, right?

Shit. Even over text message, he sounds like a puppy dog.

Give me two more months. Then I'll release you into the wild.

Because she'll either be dead or be free.

You think I'll be good enough by then?

He's good enough now. When he rode her over his thigh, she'd almost fucking melted in his arms. He's perfect. Fucking perfect. But Angelica doesn't deserve perfect, and she sure as hell can't afford it.

You're a quick learner. I believe in you.

It's the least she can say.

Really?

Really.

Now get back to work, or else I'll think you're not busy after all.

Roger that.

Pfft. What a stupid way to sign off. So why the hell is she smiling?

Another text pings, and Angelica's eyes fly to her screen, ready to scold even as she grins… but then her stomach sinks, and the fine hairs on her forearms prickle.

It's an unknown number.

Tick-tock.

One month down, two to go.

A hurricane whirls through Angelica's belly, working its way up her throat. It's Max. Must be. She said Angelica had to text back or the money was automatically due. Panicking, her thumbs fly.

I can pay in installments if that's what you want.

All or nothing.

The phone rings. That same unknown number. The muscles under Angelica's skin go into overdrive, trembling from her deepest pit to her topmost cells. She picks up, and Max's voice is as smooth as Swedish chocolate.

"I don't think I've ever had this much fun, Sadie. I don't know if I want you to win or lose."

Angelica's throat is bone dry when she swallows. Keeping up her tough act, she asks, "Why is that?"

"Sometimes I imagine you winning, and I'm almost rooting for you. Someone to finally beat the system and be reborn. Other times, I imagine you losing and my men tearing you to shreds. I'd like to show the other girls your destroyed body, so everyone knows exactly what happens when you fuck with Madam Maxine.

"I've heard about your hustle, Sadie, and I must say I'm both proud and disappointed. You seem to be gathering up quite the list of clientele, but you really stuck to what you know, didn't you? I thought you might become a vigilante or a cyber hacker, but no. You just traded out your pussy's hard work for a cock on call."

Angelica winces.

"What will you do if you win?" Maxine asks. "Are you going to become me, Sadie, whoring people out for top dollar? Is that who you are? I would have thought differently of you. Who knew you admired me so much."

A vicious scream writhes, trapped in Angelica's throat.

"Who is it, I wonder? Are you living with him? I don't know which apartment yet, but I know what building you rest your little head in. Advance notice, I'm going to post some men outside to follow you in. You should give them a tour of your new not-so-humble abode."

She chokes out, "That's not our agreement."

"Afraid we'll fuck up your piece of man meat? Don't worry. If he lives in an expensive place like that, he's probably not worth the trouble. But if you disappear from his life, I'm sure he'll get over it fairly quickly. Unless you're sleeping with him, that is."

"I'm not," she says through her teeth.

"Good girl. Don't shit where you eat."

Maxine lets the silence drag. Angelica's eyes lock on the whir of the kitchen fan, letting her eyes blur as it flickers the overhead light in her pupils. She's holding her phone so tight it might crack. Every part of her is a live-wire nerve, jolts of fear running from toes to crown, burning up her fingers and toes, leaving sizzles in vein-shaped lines over the pallor of her complexion.

"Well, Sadie, I wish you good luck. I'll keep praying for you and cursing you in the same breath, if you don't mind. Remember, keep your phone on and always answer, or we're going to have a problem."

Her voice is strained. "I will."

Max hangs up without another word, the call going dead in Angelica's hands. A buzz from the machine makes Angelica let out a yelp, and a new text reminds her:

Tick-tock.

# the cat's out of the bag

. . .

ANGELICA DRAGS her duffel out from underneath Simon's guest bedroom in a flash. Her fingers pinch so tightly on the zipper that the thin white crescent of a butter-soft fingernail rips when she pulls down the slider. The dusky camo-green canvas opens to reveal her horde of dollar bills, twenties, and hundreds wrapped in band after band, faces of bland dead men staring blankly from their crisp linen rectangles.

She's pulling in air so fast her lips go numb as she dives in and counts, again and again, even though she already knows the number. A measly $42k. She's almost halfway there, but even if she rides Simon hard, his worth decreases every day he steps farther from being an untainted innocent. His novelty is wearing off. He's only worth a grand a hit at this point, and he refuses more than three dates a week, crippling his earning potential.

Calculating quickly, Angelica knows there's no way she'll even hit $85k by the end, never mind the full hundred Max demands. That's fifteen fucking thousand dollars short.

Which means she's going to die.

Little black spots form at the corners of her eyes as she curls over, head nearly in her lap as she cradles her money. Money that's basically worthless.

No. No, she won't let that be the end of it. Rearing up, Angelica storms from one end of her room to the other, raking her hands through her hair and gnawing on her lip. She's bored all day, waiting for Simon to get home. There has to be something she can do to make up the difference.

Her mind scours math. Minimum wage at forty hours a week minus taxes would only earn her another three grand in two months. $3,500 tops. She'd have to make $50 an hour under the table to have it matter. Where the fuck is she going to get that kind of money without turning tricks? Because if she does fall back on her old ways, and Max finds out…

She shudders. Her left hand lifts absently to her throat, rubbing her green pendant for solace that won't come.

*Think, damnit, THINK. What can you do to earn cash like that?*

Maybe she could pick up another guy to sell. But who? Simon's friend maybe? But no, he might figure it out. Simon's too naïve to know any better, but any sane man would wonder what the hell she's doing. They'd complain that their dates are nearly twice their age, possibly even be rude to them, and that would ruin Angelica's standing with the rest of her network.

No, that's a non-starter.

*Drugs. I'm going to have to sell drugs.* The very idea makes her sick. She's seen way too many people lost, if not physically, then mentally, to white lines and needles. Not only that, but if she can't even escape sex work, how could she ever get out of dealing? At least if she'd stayed with Maxine, she'd have aged out. With drugs, she never would.

"I'm fucked," she whispers, her voice hoarse and ragged.

Knees turning to water, Angelica hits the floor. Her arms curl absently over her roiling stomach as the tears finally come. Tears for herself as an unwanted child, as a neglected, angry girl, as an aimless young woman, and as someone who finally found her courage, only to doom herself in the process. Why did she think she could do this?

Rocking slowly, her weeping becomes sobs. Becomes wails. Becomes heavy, breathless keens as she heaves and hiccups and gasps. It lasts until her guts have boiled. Until her throat has run red. Until her eyes have burst into useless smears. Then, and only then, Angelica goes numb. Slowly but surely, her heart slows and her sniveling ebbs. Her face burns from acid tears, but she can't feel the sting anymore.

All she can do is keep trying. She'll level up Simon's skill. Right now, he's gone from being an expensive new ride to a broken-in good time, but if she could make him dream-worthy, a fantasy lover, his price will rise again, she just knows it.

It's the only card she's got to play.

————

Some lighthearted thing Simon's already seen a few times is on the TV, but the familiar characters and cheesy dialogue are soothing. Maybe he should watch something new, but at the end of the day, his brain power has dropped to nil. If he tried to take in anything with a plot, he's pretty sure his head would burst.

Uncle Lawrence, to his credit, is doing exactly what he promised, mentoring Simon every day. He's a wellspring of information and ideas. He's helped narrow Simon's focus on what matters up front in an acquisition instead of getting caught up with what has to be integrated slowly over time. It's opened their options substantially. That doesn't change the fact that Simon hates looking at these companies with a fine-tooth comb, but it does stop him from trashing every other idea that comes to mind.

In the muted light of the low-watt living room lamps, Sadie is perched on the puffy chair diagonal from him, eyes locked on the TV even though she never smiles at the jokes. He wonders if she's even paying attention. She's a little red around the eyes, sleepy-looking and blinking at odd intervals.

"Hey," he says softly, and she startles, turning pale blue doe eyes in his direction. "If you want to go to sleep, you don't have to stay up with me." No matter how heartwarming it is.

Scrubbing her face with the back of her hands, she hisses in air through her nose and shakes her head. "I'm fine."

He tips his chin toward the TV. "It's almost over anyway."

She shakes her head. "Doesn't matter. I'm waiting to talk to you."

That's new. He clicks the TV off, leaving the room silent. She's still staring at the blank screen though, and he narrows his eyes in concern. "Sadie?"

"How do you use your fingers?" she says suddenly.

"My what?"

"During sex. What can you do with them?"

He sighs. This again. She's like a drill sergeant. "I put in two and"—he points his fingers out and looks at them, trying to articulate his thoughts—"crook them?"

"Right. Pads of your fingers only. No one wants cat claws digging into their insides. Now tell me some nice things you can say to her."

Warmth spreads on his face as he tries to shove down the embarrassment that still rears its head at this topic. He's numb to most of Sadie's instruction by now, but he still struggles with this part. He thinks he knows what he should say, but getting the words out is something else entirely. Especially in front of her.

Thinking of his fantasies from the other night, he remembers what fell from imaginary Noah's lips as he seduced imaginary Sadie. He still wants to make that a reality. Perhaps this is his safe place to practice. The biggest risk is no reaction. But if he says the right thing, will she make a face like she did when he dragged her core over his thigh? If he lowers the tone of his voice, will she cross her legs tight, flashing him the creamy part of her skin that exists right under the cuff of his boxers she always wears?

She has a prissy, haughty look on her face that he finds adorable, but he'd like to see it melt. "I can tell her she feels good," he says.

Sadie snorts and rolls her eyes. "That's a start, I guess."

His mind is in the devil's clouds wondering if she'd let him kiss her if he says the right things. Can he turn her on again? Make her touch herself so he can hear? The idea is heady and powerful.

"I could tell her I can't wait to be inside her," he says, never taking his eyes off the freckled, lithe, exasperating woman before him. "I could say I want to put my mouth on her. Anywhere. Everywhere. Then I can ask if she'd like that."

"And don't wait for her reaction. Just do it. It would be a perfect shock to her system. Such a turn-on. She'd be dripping for you."

He bites his bottom lip. Is it possible she's telling him her own desires? That she's projecting them onto these other women? Is this what Sadie wants? Would she be dripping for him?

He's getting hard in his pants but feels no shame. She never notices and he sees no reason why she would start now. What would she do if he started palming himself in front of her? Oh, how that thought only gets him harder. "And what should she do to me?"

It's a bold question. He wants her to say these kinds of things back. Help him imagine her touch. Let her seduce him with that velvety voice.

Instead, she says, "Just feel lucky they're letting you sleep with them at all. Worry about your own satisfaction when you're alone."

A surprised huff coughs from his lungs. "Seriously? Shouldn't there be some sort of, I dunno, give-and-take?"

"Do you want to be a good lover?" she asks, one thin eyebrow arched. "Then take pleasure in her pleasure. There are people who build entire sexual play scenes based on only touching their partner and refusing any gratification for themselves. Think of that. Think of how to make her beg for you, and then give her exactly what she wants."

"Is that what you want?" It falls out without him meaning it to.

Her expression shuts down into something cold. "It doesn't matter what I want."

Their conversation wisps away into nothing as Sadie unfolds her body and gets up, heading to her room and closing the door without saying good night. He sits up quick, watching her go with words on his tongue that burn him, unable to come out. Things like, "What happened to you to make you act this way?" "What can I do to help you?"

And "Why do you look so sad?"

———

A hotel bar this time, Simon notes, looking around. It's upscale—the Ritz—and all the décor is tastefully out of date. Overly white, curved loveseats offer a modicum of privacy in a room full of strangers. Sheer hanging drapes separate the space from the main lobby, and there are pop colors on the wall behind the bar offsetting the bottles of mild poison one can ingest for just twenty dollars a glass. And that's if you're being cheap.

"Are you Noah?"

His head snaps around, used to this name now even if he doesn't really care for it. His mouth nearly drops open. "Katie?"

The woman before him smiles warmly, black hair just like Sadie's, a similar dusting of freckles on her nose. Her eyes are a deep brown versus Sadie's ice blue, and her build is a bit taller and stockier, but they could be sisters. She wears a red cocktail dress with skimpy spaghetti straps, showing a sky of speckled dot-shaped stars along her shoulders. Her freckles are a bit more on the red side, sprinkled on rosy skin, but they do something to him.

Best of all, she looks like she's actually his age.

"Can I offer you a seat?" He gestures to the couch made for two, pulling his smile into that one that Sadie calls "dreamy." Sitting her down, he perches beside her, just staring.

*"Got you a nice one this time, didn't I, killer? You ready for a good time?"*

Sadie's voice in Simon's ear only makes him smile wider. He takes his date's hand and kisses the back, a little slower and lingering longer than he would if he were a prince on a white horse. Katie's shy glance to the side and quick clench of her thighs means she doesn't mind.

"What can I get you to drink?" he murmurs. Sadie says that women like low voices, so he sticks to his bottom register.

"I, um, what do you recommend?" she asks. What is he, a waiter?

*"Offer something fruity,"* Sadie says. *"Think of the cocktail list."*

He'd studied that for way longer than he should have. Making a show of thinking, he tips his body back and forth, side to side as if observing her from every angle. She squirms with a giggle.

"Hmm. I'd say you look like either a white sangria or a raspberry champagne kind of girl. What do you think?"

The sweet curve of her cheeks turns her eyes to half-moons when she smiles. "I love raspberries."

He leans in close and confesses, "So do I."

*"Smooth. Good boy."*

Sadie's praise never ceases to please him, and he nips his bottom lip in shy satisfaction. He really would do anything for her, wouldn't he?

He channels his inner sex god and runs a hand over his date's knee, making sure to spread his fingers and show how he can envelop her from one side to the other. Apparently, women also like big hands. With a sideways smirk, he asks, "Wait for me?"

"Of course," she says, breathy little thing.

He's on his feet and over to the crowded bar. This place is a bit farther away from his apartment than he'd like, the cost of the cab ride a small fortune, but Sadie said it would be worth his while. She didn't mention she'd be handing him her lookalike on a silver platter.

*"You like her?"* she asks, as if she didn't know.

Simon's answer is a silent smirk as he peeks at Sadie. She's sitting at the end of the bar, sipping an appletini, one that she's sure to bill to him. It's all he can do not to go to her and take a taste of her drink. He imagines sauntering up from behind, circling his arm around her waist, and leaning over her shoulder to do so. He'd feel bad for thinking about someone other than his date, except for that these women make it very clear from the beginning they want nothing from him more than a night, so he nurtures his budding feelings without remorse.

The bartender is young, floppy holes in his ears made for absent piercings. He's shaking something up for an older gentleman at the bar whose clothes are business-y and his face exhausted. Simon wonders if that will be him in ten years.

"What can I get you?" the bartender asks.

"Raspberry champagne and a grateful dead."

"What's that?"

"Think Long Island iced tea, but you take out that Coke and put in Chambord."

The bartender smirks. "That's, like, almost a hundred percent alcohol."

Simon ticks his eyebrows up. "Exactly."

With a nod the man starts to make his drinks, flourishing and tossing silver cups in the air, catching them with ease. He adds nothing short of a million maraschino cherries to Simon's drink, which he is not sad about, and hands them over.

He's about to turn when a thought catches him. Speaking quietly to the bartender he adds, "And give that lady on the end another drink from me. Put whatever she orders on my tab."

The bartender tosses a look at Simon's date in the white rounded chair before flicking his gaze at Sadie, but says nothing, pocketing the ten-dollar tip Simon sets on the bar top. Amused with himself, Simon strides back to the stranger of the day and slips beside her, handing the cool flute over and ensuring their hips touch.

Sadie reminds, *"Put your hand behind her."*

So he does.

*"And thank you for my new drink, Noah."*

He lets out a happy hum that Katie applies to herself. As she takes a sip, the bubbles sparkle in her glass and her eyes sparkle along with them, hiding a half smile as she keeps her gaze trained on him.

"What do you do for work?" he asks, tucking a strand of hair behind her ear and making her blush.

"Nothing much. I like to arrange parties. Well, more than that. Charity balls and masquerades."

"With costumes? They still do that?"

"Oh sure. But you have to play in the right circles."

Simon summons to mind the image of Sadie in a low-backed dress, her hair coiffed high, and an elegant gold mask bringing out the deep ocean flecks in her eyes.

"I bet you'd look good in a tux and a something that frames those eyebrows of yours," Katie says.

He rubs his fingertips through the wiry hairs. "Why? What's wrong with them?"

*"You insecure dork,"* Sadie groans.

"Nothing." Katie giggles, reaching up and smoothing out what he ruffled. "But you're so expressive. It would be sexy to hide it and pass you off as a stoic villain type."

Oh, he knows what he's supposed to do now. He leans into her touch and lets his eyes drift closed. "Is that what you want? A villain ready to burn down the world for you?"

"*Absolutely masterful*," Sadie encourages, and Simon's heart races.

*Keep talking to me*, he thinks. *Tell me what to do and how to do it. I'll practice on them and turn it on you. I'll make you feel this way, I swear.*

Katie's hand drifts down his cheek and her voice is husky when she says, "You're very handsome."

He blushes, ducking away from her and offering his thanks. Swigging the drink at hand, he already feels it in his head, making him light and airy. Two of these and he's done for the night.

"*Say something back*," Sadie urges.

"So are you," he says before stumbling over himself a little. "Beautiful, I mean. I mean, you're not a guy so you wouldn't be handsome but—"

"*I thought we were past this.*"

Simon recovers, grabbing Katie's hand. "Sorry. You fluster me. I haven't really dated anyone as pretty as you before." And it's the God's honest truth.

Katie surprises him and tucks herself into his side, resting her head against his shoulder as she sips her drink.

"*Well, this is new*," Sadie says.

No kidding. Simon flings his eyes in her direction, and she just shrugs, waving him on with her hands and then cheering him. The sensible thing to do is wrap his arm around his date, so that's what he does.

"Um, are you comfortable?"

Katie sighs happily and takes a sip of her drink. "I like your voice. I feel like I could listen to it for hours and never get tired of it. It gets me a little excited if I'm honest. I'm into noises."

*Like me.*

"Are you now?" he asks. "What other things are you into?"

Katie's chuckle is suggestive. "Just wait. I'll show you."

He pets her shoulder, forcing an awkward smile. "You may need to teach me. I'm still a little new at this."

"Oh, I'm sure you'll figure it out. Maybe if I talk you through it." Like Sadie does. A little thrill runs up his spine. "We could go now if you want to. I have a room upstairs."

Why don't they ever want to talk to him for very long? "Don't you want to finish our drinks?"

She leans back, taking the little skewer that pins the raspberries to the rim and holding it in one dainty hand. With the other, she tips her champagne flute up and flashes her throat as she swallows. The berries go in next, her provocative tongue swiveling around them before she takes them in her mouth. If Sadie did that for him, he'd probably die a little death. Hell, with the buzz this drink will give him when he finishes, he could probably pretend she *is* Sadie.

The idea licks him with sinful heat.

"Well, all right then," he says, lifting his own drink and doing his best to take it like a shot. She watches him, sliding a thumb across her bottom lip as if wiping away a kiss. One he suddenly wants to give her. "Let me settle up at the bar."

He's up and to the nearest barstool, signaling the aspiring mixologist and making the universal gesture for the check. At the curve of the bar top, Sadie gives him a knowing smirk, sipping her drink with mirth dancing in her eyes.

*Oh, if you only knew,* Simon thinks. He should feel guilty taking a woman to bed while thinking of another, but he doesn't. Instead, he embeds Sadie's face in his mind. Her and her raucous laughter. Her nightly bland, but lovely meals. Watching her sit near him as they watch whatever trash TV is on at night. Her huffing at him when he's not at the gym yet. Her buttoning his buttons when he hasn't gotten his clothes on fast enough. Her serious face when her mind drifts far away. The one that makes him wonder about her every nook and cranny. Her vulnerable face, so rare, so precious, which makes him want to protect her above all else.

He's got it bad, and he knows it. If he does have an angel waiting for him, he wants it to be her. His dark angel. One with sexy taunts, a sweet voice, and gorgeous eyes.

The bartender pops up with a check, and Simon barely looks before setting his card down, keeping Sadie in his periphery. He's going to do everything right tonight. He's going to unlock every box in this new woman's arsenal. If he's going to practice, let him do it, but let him do it with one woman in mind.

———

Katie coils in on herself suddenly, letting out a sharp cry of pleasure that he was completely responsible for. Again. He's done it to her three times now, and every muscle in her is quaking.

"More?" he asks.

She shakes her head, gasping. "You'll kill me."

"But what a way to go," he purrs.

The grin on his date's face is never ending at first but fades into a pout. "I can't. I've got to go home."

Simon frowns. He didn't get to finish even once. "Oh?"

She sits up, flinging herself onto his lap. "It's not fair. I don't wanna go home."

With his erection bouncing off her chin, he kind of doesn't want her to go home either. It doesn't seem to matter. She's up on her knees in a flash, smashing a peck on his mouth before darting up to put her clothes on.

"You were soooo good," she moans. "I can't even believe it."

*Then why are you leaving?* he thinks.

Shimmying into the red fabric of her dress, she reaches for her purse. "Now don't tell." With a sly grin, she undoes the latch and digs in. "I know I'm supposed to give this directly to Sadie, but I know how these things go. Your pimp keeps all your money." Her head shoots up. "Is that what they call it when a woman…? Never mind." She ducks back down and pulls out a wad of cash wrapped in stacks. Why would she…?

Diving close again, she mauls him in another kiss before dropping the money in his lap. "It's the grand, but I threw in an extra five hundred for you. Don't tell her about that part. It's a tip. I heard you were good, but you were so much more than that."

Simon's brain is on high alert as she kisses him one last time.

"I'll ask for you again next time my husband is away," she says, winking at him. "Don't forget about me, okay?"

She ruffles his hair and looks at him with a fond, wistful sigh. With that, she's out of the room in a flurry, reapplying lipstick on the way. The same lipstick that's, no doubt, smeared along his mouth.

The walls swim. Simon's head pounds. Lips parting, he looks at the wad of money in his lap. The dates. The sex. Older women. One-night stands. So many, and all so fast.

Is he…a prostitute?

# confrontation

. . .

DARKNESS HAS FALLEN on the city, but smog covers all signs of
the stars. A sliver of the moon hangs with a hazy halo Angelica catches
glimpses of when they pass by smaller buildings, making her remember
the green places. The only sound is the rumbling hum of the cab's engine
as it trundles along through the mellow, streetlamp-lit night. The cabbie
seems satisfied to leave his words unsaid, as does Simon, it seems. His
standard resting bitch face has blossomed into something that looks like
pure anger, and his gaze burns a hole in the seat in front of him.

Tension threads through Angelica as she looks at him at an utter
loss. Usually, after his dates, he's tired but pleasant enough, chatting
about what he thought his final score for the night would be. She calls
it his Naughty Noah Rut Rank, even though it makes him roll his eyes.
But there is no eye-rolling tonight. Only a thickness that seems to suck
the air from the space around them.

Angelica's skin prickles. She should say *something* but is too afraid
to say the *wrong* thing. The moment seems to seesaw on a tipping
point. Why is he so upset? What can she do to fix it? She needs Simon
now more than ever, and the thought of him tapping out makes her
want to break into pieces again. But she won't. Not in front of him.

Her hands clench into her skirt, the fabric stretchy and soft. Trying to catch his eyes, she asks, "Was Katie mean to you?" She'd never paid Angelica. She'll have to follow up or ban her in the community. She can only pray the woman was in a rush and forgot to meet her at the bar. Maybe things went wrong somehow?

Simon gives no response other than to clench his jaw tighter. She swears she can hear his bones creak. Softer, she tries again. "I got you a younger one this time. I thought you'd be happy."

"Happy." He repeats it as a sentence, not a question, his voice toneless as he grimaces.

Something is definitely wrong. "Noah?"

"Don't call me that," he spits, blaring his side eye toward the door beyond her, not looking her directly in the face.

Dread seeps in.

The cab's brakes screech to a whiny stop outside Simon's apartment, and he's out and slamming the door before Angelica has a chance to say another word. He didn't even pay. Mouth drawn down at the corners, Angelica digs into her clutch, praying she brought enough. Fumbling around for a few agonizing moments, she manages to cram rumpled bills into the cabbie's awaiting hand; meanwhile, Simon has already flown through the double doors of the apartment building. The weighted glass shifts shut again as she watches his long strides take him farther and farther away.

*What happened?*

Not bothering to give any pleasantries, Angelica jumps out, nearly twisting her ankle on her fancy high heels in the process. Fumbling with her keys, she chases after him, wrenching open the doors only to find him ramming the elevator button closed. The glare he points at the ground is vicious and his eyebrows are jammed so close together, they become one. Seeing him, Angelica's throat tightens, a monster wrapping around her lungs.

*What the hell happened?*

She doesn't get there in time. The elevator doors close in her face and leave Simon flying up, up, and away. It's her turn to ram the button, stabbing her fingers in until the tips hurt. She hits it over and over, as if that would make it come faster, but the wait is painful as she watches the unmoving sealed doors.

*What happened? What happened? What happened?*

When she hears the *ping* of the elevator, she pivots her body inside, pushing the round number fourteen like it's her enemy. "Come on, you sonofabitch," she curses through her teeth, willing the doors closed. There's an eerie, muffled silence, and it locks her bones tight, waiting for a jump scare that's not coming.

Floors slip past unnoticed until the reflective silver panels finally part, and Angelica all but flings herself out of the damn machine. She bolts to Simon's door, wrenching the knob and finding it locked. Panic sweat starts to bead on her forehead. Her shaking hand nearly drops her keys as she works them in, but even though she twists with a click, the door still won't open.

He threw the fucking deadbolt.

Her insides are turning to mush as she trembles. Metallic clacks rattle against the top golden lock as she works to insert her key, the edge bumping and thumping as it tries, and fails, to go in. Her brain rams her with questions, but in her heart, she already knows the answers.

Something goes *snik*, the lock sliding clear, and the door swings wide open. She slams it behind her and presses her back against it, finding him in the blink of an eye. He's pacing. His hands rake through his hair, disheveling it into haggard clumps, and his steps are heavy slaps on the hardwood as he wears a trench through the floor.

"What's going—"

"Are you selling me?" he hisses.

Her stomach drops to her ankles. "What?"

Whipping around, he finally looks her in the eyes, manic and furious. "ARE YOU *SELLING* ME?"

Words don't come. Her mouth opens and she tries to make sound, but it comes out strangled, mangled, and useless. "I can explain."

He scoffs a derisive, nasty noise as he shakes his head. Twirling around, he stalks to his bedroom, nearly snapping the wooden frame when he slams the door shut.

Angelica isn't in control of her body as she dashes to the barrier between them. She pounds. "Let me try to explain. Come out. Talk to me."

It's barely a moment before he rockets the door open again. She almost loses her footing but gains it back right quick when he advances on her, fists balled at his sides.

His voice is satin with fury. "All this time, all this training, and here I was, convincing myself I could use it on you. I thought I could make you mine. I told myself that you could want me if I could only…" He winces at his own words. Rushing his hands to his face, he covers it with his palms and lets out a horrible, anguished cry. "How could I be so stupid?"

Her back hits the living room chair hard enough to scrape it over the floor with a grinding squeak. The noise makes his hands drop and eyes snap to hers.

"Did you make enough money off me, do you think?"

He advances again. He's enormous. She's always known he was big, but he looms like a nightmare.

"Do you want me to show you the fruits of your labor?" he asks. "What a good little slut you've made me?"

A thin thread in her snaps, anger flaring from a well of familiar pain. "How dare you use that filthy fucking word? You don't know anything. This is legitimate work that people dive into every day. For some people, it's the only way to get by. How dare you insult us with that holier-than-thou—"

"Us?" he cuts in with a terrible baritone. "Does that mean you're a whore too?"

She goes to backhand him, but he catches her wrist, drawing her close enough to feel his heat. "You are, aren't you? Tell me, is deceiving people one of the qualifications for this 'legitimate work' you do? How did you get this job? Did you choose it for yourself?" He narrows his venomous eyes. "Or were you tricked, fooled, and used like me?"

She tries to yank away, but he's like a vise. "You had a golden deal. If you never knew, you would have—"

"I never asked for this," he yells, his voice a trembling mess. "All I wanted was someone to love me."

Something mean and vicious crawls its way into Angelica's belly.

"And you thought it could be me?" She scoffs. "You must be stupider than I thought."

He goes cold then. The spark in his eyes, that flare of cruel anger, snuffs out into something much worse. It hurts her to see it. It shouldn't, but it does. She wants him to smile. To blush. To get flustered. To get shy and fidgety because she's too close.

This isn't her Simon.

And she has no one to blame but herself.

She lowers her eyes as her lip trembles. "Someone like me doesn't deserve someone like you."

That does something to him. His posture changes, shoulders dropping as he releases her wrist, tossing her hand away as if throwing a crumbled bit of trash into a wastebasket.

"What if I pay you?" he says, his voice detached. "You like money, right? Why don't you teach me my last lesson yourself."

Tears don't come, but her eyes burn anyway. She knows exactly what he's doing but decides she doesn't care. If she's going to ruin this, let her ruin it all the way. "How much?"

His smirk is cold and mirthless. "How much are you worth?"

*Nothing,* her mind whispers.

Without finesse, she reaches behind her, unzipping her dress. She drops it to her feet, shimmying out of her underwear, never taking her eyes off his. He doesn't look down. He doesn't take her in, he just locks his glare on hers, relentless and unwavering.

"Get in the bedroom," he says.

And silently, Angelica does as she's told.

———

The light is muted, something that always annoyed him, though it sets a tone now. Not a soft or romantic one. One that seems almost ominous.

That doesn't stop him from undoing his belt with a slithering whip sound and tossing it onto the floor. The belt buckle chimes, and Sadie looks over her shoulder at him. He still refuses to drop his line of sight past her shoulders, instead digging into his pocket and bringing out three wrapped stacks of twenty-dollar bills. Five hundred, a thousand, fifteen hundred, all hitting his bureau with a dull *thwack, thwack, thwack.*

Sadie's smirk is wry. "She tipped you." It's so easy how the puzzle pieces snap together in her mind.

He matches her expression, note for note. "Apparently, I was worth it."

"Is that what you're paying me, then?" she asks, twisting a blade in his heart.

He doesn't answer. Instead, he ticks his chin in the direction of the bed and watches her turn to lie down. This time, his gaze catches the back of her, a swooping line that leads to two dimples to the left and right of her lower spine. Her rump is round and perfect, like he knew it would be, and the skin is smooth, without her mottling of freckles, which is somehow disappointing. He'd wanted her coated in them on every curve, though that doesn't change how beautiful she is. How sad this is.

Simon has a temper, and he's always known it. He has every right to be furious. To yell. To blame. He would never hurt her...or would he? Isn't this moment its own kind of punishment?

He wants her to cry. To apologize. He'd forgive her the world if only those pretty lips would say, "I'm sorry." But they don't. They press together in a thin line as she turns onto her back, breasts on display as she looks placidly at the ceiling.

He needs to change that expression on her face. Right now.

He stalks until he's standing beside her, working his buttons open slowly like she taught him, looking down at her as if she's a meal and he's starving. Her gaze doesn't move, locked on a spot above her, and it's as if he's not there at all.

"Look at me," he murmurs, and her eyes slide to the side, her neck arching to follow. He rolls his shoulders, the fabric sliding from him as he bares his chest, the one he's been working so hard, hoping for her to praise him. Instead, she assesses him. There is no emotion in her eyes, and it's as heartbreaking as it is infuriating.

*Feel something,* he scolds her silently.

She's completely naked, so he gets that way too. When he'd

thought of being with her, seeing her body like this, he imagined himself as diamond hard, ready to claim her at a moment's notice. Now, it's like his body isn't even paying attention, and fuck him if she doesn't assess that too. Still, no disappointment or rebuke reflects in her eyes. Not a single thing.

*Feel something*, he urges.

He moves to the bottom of the bed and her knees lift, curling as if to hide herself from him, but he's going to see every part of her tonight, every span of skin, every pucker, every curve, whether he wants to or not. It's too late to stop this now.

He gets on his knees, reaching up to grab her hips and tug her bottom toward the edge of the bed, feeling the smoothness of her skin. "Open your legs for me."

They part like a gate, and he lets his gaze fall. She's not bare but trimmed neatly, the rest of her pink and plush. Her scent is what gets him in the end. A sweet musk that takes over his senses as he breathes in, and his body finally responds.

He wants to say, "Will you let me taste you?" or even "I'm going to make you come on my tongue," but her response, or lack thereof, petrifies him, so instead he nuzzles and waits for any sign of resistance. Any flinch or cringe. She makes none, only spreading her legs slightly wider, and that will have to be enough.

She tastes like she smells. Perfect. He remembers her previous instructions, how his face burned with embarrassment, but in the absence of her voice now, that memory is all he can hold on to. She'd told him how to use his tongue. Flat and slick, toying around her entrance and dipping in, his nose caressing that bundle of nerves at the center before he slides up and takes it in his mouth, flicking its pearly hardness before suckling. Her memory leading him on, he presses his fingers inside her and curls them while his mouth does its magic. He works her, strokes her, coaxes her.

Other women would have gasped and squirmed, but there is nothing save the slight tang of her wetness.

*Feel something. Please.*

He's getting hard. He wants her. Wants their bodies to connect.

Wants their hearts to bridge the gap. Wants their words to soothe the sting and make this all better again.

Tears prick his eyes as he works his kisses up her body, pressing gentle lips to the crests of her hip bones as his heat seeks for home. Her breasts in his hands, in his mouth, feel so wonderfully soft and inviting. He can feel her intake of breath, and if he closes his eyes, he can pretend it's quickening. That she's a silent but invested lover. But he's lying to himself. Stealing a glance at her face, she looks almost bored.

His anger flares.

*Fucking* feel *something.*

He presses his crown against her entrance, swiveling his hips to rock just barely inside her. He nudges in little arcs, going in centimeters at a time. She's fire-hot and slick as spit, and her body grabs him like a fist when he bottoms out with a groan.

Nothing on her face. Nothing in her body. Anger flips to rage.

His laugh is breathy and low. "If this is your job, you think you'd be better at it."

That gets a reaction. Her eyes pivot to his, something burning in them. She locks her sight until it seems like he's all there is in this world and her legs coil around him, clenching muscular thighs and pulling him in deeper.

This time, she gasps, her eyes fluttering closed and her rouge lips dropping open. She says the word "yes" in a dreamy sigh, and his nerves short out. Her hands plunge into his hair and grab the nape of his neck, dragging him into a kiss that dreams are made of, her tongue laving against his until his body trembles. She's lifting her hips and grinding against him, letting out tiny whimpers as she clenches her insides, milking him in slow strokes.

He moans into her mouth even as his mind spins. Her sudden reactions, her turn on a dime…

This woman is terrifying.

She cries out and bucks into him. Reaching around, she clenches his backside and digs her nails in before pulling him hard, slamming him into her. She reverses direction, pushing out his hips then dragging him in again.

"Faster," she whines, her voice an airy whisper. "Please."

That word is like silken sin. His sounds are guttural whimpers as he sits up, hiking her hips high and giving her everything he's worth. The sight of her splayed beneath him would be more than enough, but she snakes a hand down and starts toying with herself, her other hand fondling and pinching her nipple while she bites her lower lip. She's going to kill him. So sexy. So perfect.

But not his.

He rams into her, driving deep and rocking her body in rough waves, pushing her up the bed as he goes to his hands and knees, caging her with his effort. He's going to come soon, the telltale signs are there, but he wants her to go first. He needs her to go first.

"Come for me, Sadie," he begs. "Be a good girl for me. Show me what it feels like to have you fall apart around me."

Her speed picks up, he can feel it press against his groin as her fingers dance. She's panting now, her little mewls reminding him of when he heard her touching herself before, back when everything was filled with hope and potential.

She makes that same rough grunt, her teeth bared as she finishes, clamping down on him so tight his hips stutter. Her insides undulate against him in squeezes that break his restraint, and he dives in to maul her. Merciless pounds, hands pinning her wrists, and his mouth on hers. Everything is sweat and slick and him suckling any part of her he can reach, from the crests of her collarbone to the curve of her neck to the shell of her ear. Kissing her cheeks. Her lips. He's breaking inside and he can't hold it in anymore.

He goes to pull out, but she slams him in again, unrelenting.

"Come inside me," she demands. The woman who always tells him what to do. The one he obeys blindly.

And Simon does what he was made for.

His cry is soft even to his own ears, but the sound turns him on, even so. He rides out his aftermath in slow strokes as her fingers card through his hair.

He loves this. He wants this.

But it's all fake.

His trembling muscles let go, collapsing him over her pale body as their breath evens and the seconds spool. He pretends this is real, even though his heart knows otherwise. He sits in this feeling of frayed nerves and afterglow, hoping, praying for that apology to make it all better. For her to wrap her arms around him and beg forgiveness.

Instead, the moment breaks when she utters the words, "Are you satisfied?" and something in him shatters.

She presses his shoulder gently and he rolls off her, obedient as always. When she gets up, the cool air of the room freezes him, and he curls in on himself.

She's naked. She's beautiful.

She's leaving.

In the doorway, she pauses, looking at him over her shoulder. "Whatever this is, it isn't love."

With that, she takes her money and walks into her room. He can hear the closet door open and shut. Drawers are scraped out. A bag is zipped. Still, Simon can't move. He's curled in and cursing her. Cursing himself. Metal hits the little plate by the door, a familiar jingling clatter as she leaves her keys behind. When she escapes, she doesn't slam the door in a final stroke of anguish, she just closes it gently.

This was all so wrong. So fast. So undeniable.

She's left him.

Their moratorium is over.

# all alone

. . .

SPRING IS STILL FUCKING cold in Angelica's opinion. Anyone who moves straight to wearing T-shirts in the lingering frost should be shot on sight.

She shivers, hiking up her duffel bag and pulling Simon's hoodie tighter, no less than three long-sleeve shirts on underneath. She's glad to have stolen his clothes. She was miserly about spending any money on her own, leaving her with an inadequate number of bras, undies, jammies, and anything made for colder weather. She'd focused on dinner dresses with pockets, sneakers that didn't tear up her Achilles tendons, and jeans that fit without the cuffs going past her toes.

She walks faster than she needs to. It's the only thing keeping her warm at this point. She spent last night in their apartment's alleyway, half praying Simon would run after her. In her epic fantasy, she had the courage to tell him the truth and he'd offered to keep working—work even harder—to help get her the money she needs. In her wildest imaginings, he picked her up like a knight in shining armor and flew her off to Tahiti, a place that's warm, serene, and safe. Almost magical. It was hard to come back to reality after that.

Her phone is running out of battery, which is terrifying. She needs to find a coffee shop that will let her squat for the day. If Maxine texts or, god forbid, calls, Angelica needs to be available. In the meantime, all she can do is look at the last words Max sent her.

Tick-tock.

She presses the button to darken her screen once more, her head throbbing with last night's dreams. Who needs them? They're useless. That bitch could follow her to Tahiti, anyway.

Angelica passes a hand over the soft fabric on her arm and throws mental curses at the tracker. She should slice and dice and get it out, but she doesn't know how deep it is. Given that her goal is not to die, it seems prudent not to dig among her delicate veins for gold. Another dead end for salvation.

Her shivering upgrades to shudders, eyes misting as she wanders another narrow alleyway. Like a broken record, her mind asks what she can possibly do without Simon. Right now, she should be making him something to eat and prodding him to go to the gym. He should be waving her off and asking for five more minutes. Ten more minutes. Sixty. He should be sleepy-eyed and tousle-haired and grumpy.

Why does she give a shit about him? He's a body, nothing more.

But even thinking that lie makes her tears fall. Other than Bee, no one had ever been so kind to her. So sweet.

But fuck him. And fuck her if she can't stop crying about him. Last night's memory is ripping through her, and she's going to burst at the seams. He wanted her. He'd longed for her. But she used it against him. She didn't give him a choice in anything he did. She made him do things that could have ruined his life and reputation. Hers is already destroyed, but his…

Her mental walls fall, the inner maelstrom finally crashing down and making her lose her balance. She scuffs off the rough red brick of the building beside her, cradling her bag as detestable sobs scrape rusted nails up her insides. Unsuccessfully, she does her best to catch her mourning behind a cupped palm as her legs collapse beneath her, and with the weight of life and death on her shoulders, she sags, lost in her grief, extinguished hope, and fatalistic fear.

*I'm going to die. There's no way around it. It's going to happen.*

*And they're going to make it hurt when it does.*

Her mind spirals over gruesome possibilities. Limbs and bones and flesh. What will Gwen and Kay say when they see what's left of her? Will they pity her or think she got what she deserved for doing something so stupid?

Her hands shake as she presses her palms against her eyes, keening softly, wanting to stay hidden forever. Wanting to disappear. Wanting—

"Hey," a voice calls out. "Don't I know you?"

Angelica flinches and topples back onto her rear, eyes shooting wide.

Run. She has to run. But her feet can't get under her in time as a man jogs up, trying to shush her as she stumbles.

"Whoa, girlie. I don't know what you're running from, but it doesn't have to be me."

"Said like a creep I should kick in the balls," she bites out.

"I'd honestly prefer you didn't."

Managing to get her legs under her, she lunges away, but he calls out one more time. "You're the girl at the bar with Simon, right?"

It brings her up short. She looks over her shoulder, clutching her duffel and sniveling wetly, tears staining her face. "Simon who?"

The man cocks his eyebrow. He's older with brown hair at the top, but salty roots coming in at his temples and nape. He has a long rat-tail braid that falls over his shoulder, and he fiddles with it when she doesn't respond. "Big guy? Black hair? Drunk off his ass?"

She still says nothing.

"You were gonna teach him how to date or something. End his virginity." The man cracks a grin.

*Not so virgin anymore,* she thinks bitterly. "What do you want?"

"I want to see why this girl I met one time is losing her shit in an alleyway." He narrows his eyes. "Simon didn't hurt you, did he?"

"No." she says, a little too vehemently for her liking. Clearing her throat and scrubbing an arm under her leaking nose, she says, "He took care of me. He...he worried about me. He th-thought about me and he..."

She's off in tears again. Why does it matter so much? He's just a john. He's not even a john. But still, her heart is breaking. One way or another, whether he knew it or not, he was supposed to save her. Now there's no one…

She can't help it. She breaks. Her breath hitches and her voice rasps with a dry, high hysteria as another sob wracks her. Why can't she hold this in? Maybe because it's poison and her body is purging it, every secret she's ever had on the tip of her tongue. Every promise, threat, and sin.

"It's too much," she bawls. "I can't do it anymore. There's no one I can turn to, nowhere I can go. I can't run, I can't hide, and I just… just…" Her words devolve into nothing but inarticulate sound. She's shaking so hard her teeth chatter. Her mind is on fire. What is she supposed to do? There's no way she can fix this.

She barely feels it when the man wraps around her. He's warm and smells a little like sweat, but his kindness is the last straw. She drops her bag, collapsing against him and clinging for dear life. Her fingers dig into his shoulders as he cradles her, making hushing sounds she can barely hear over the volume of her weeping. She bleats, "I'm sorry. I'm so sorry." But who is she saying it to? To herself? To Bee, who made her promise she'd be smart? To Maxine for fucking everything up in the first place?

To Simon for breaking his heart?

Her hair is swept off her forehead as the stranger rocks her. "Hey now. Hey, little one, it's okay."

"Don't call me that," she manages.

He only chuckles. Holding her, he tips side to side until her breathing finally settles into little hiccups instead of heaving gasps. Leaning her back on her feet, he asks, "You sure he didn't hurt you?"

"He didn't." In a whisper she can't hold back, she adds, "He almost saved me."

There is a long pause where the distant cars roll by, making muted rushing sounds as the man holds her gaze, looking from one eye to the other. His face is laced with concern. "Can I ask what's going on?"

She shakes her head.

"Can I do anything to help?" he tries again.

She mumbles the word "No…"

The older man pulls her in for another short hug, brief but tight, before letting out a heavy sigh. "Okay." Leaning her back again, he pats her upper arms as if dusting off hair or makeup. "Have you eaten? I know a food kitchen for women. I can't go there, obviously, but I can get you over in that direction."

"Do they have a place to charge my phone?" she asks miserably.

"Only if you get there early enough. If not, you still look good enough to get into a coffeehouse. They won't feed you though."

She shakes her head. "Doesn't matter."

"'Course it does. My wife used to tell me the world is worse on an empty stomach, and Jesus, do I believe her now."

A slight smile pulls onto Angelica's face.

"Word of advice from someone who learned the hard way. When you go, keep your bag on you at all times. Sit on it if you have to. Zipper always pointed at your chest, your lap, or flat on the chair. Yeah?"

She nods, running her sleeve under her nose again.

"You ever gone to one before?" he asks.

"Not since I was a teenager."

He doesn't pity her, which is welcome. He just nods curtly, picking up the hood of her sweater and pulling it over her hair. "They take no shit in there from what I hear, so I bet no one will mess with you, but they do close down between meals. If it's anything like the co-ed kitchen, you've got until ten or so before they kick you out to flip for lunch, but then you just get right back in the minute doors open. Same thing when they close to prep for dinner. Yeah?"

Since she has no idea what to do at the moment, she'll say yes to anything. He brushes her cheek in a fatherly way, then nods to the mouth of the alley. "Let's get out of here. That is, if you don't mind walking with a distinguished gentleman such as myself."

She snorts a pathetic little laugh. "I'm guessing you look better than I do."

He turns her around to face the street, walking beside her instead of in front or behind. "The way you look right now, all puffy and blotchy, I better drop you off a few blocks away or women will fly from Timbuktu to hammer spikes into my dick."

She rubs at the offending parts of her face. "Sounds like a rough crowd."

"Well, who doesn't need a good spiking now and then?" He winks, patting the crest of her back and leading her on her bleary way. "It's gonna be okay, you know?"

Cynicism drips from her voice. "And why is that?"

"I get a feeling about stuff like this sometimes. I think you and I were destined to meet again, or some shit."

"Are you hitting on me?"

"Consoling, if such a thing is possible. I don't know what you're in for, but I'm going to help you, all right? Us shelter kids gotta stick together."

Despite all odds, Angelica warms inside. "Thank you."

He slings an arm over her shoulder. "You're very welcome."

———

Simon's eyes barely open, crusted and swollen as he peeks through them, the light too bright. Saturday morning usually brings Sadie and her fussing, bustling, and harassing him to get ready. For what?

To be sold, that's what.

He hates her. He misses her. Everything is so hard to pick apart. He'd been told that a woman would either save or ruin him. Is this what it feels like to be ruined? Work beats him down, exhausts him and tanks his self-esteem, bores him and makes him itch for more, but it doesn't hurt. Not like this.

When he sits up, his head pounds. Too much drinking and self-hatred got the better of him last night. His apartment seemed so empty, and it was the first time it ever felt that way. Lonely. Sad. It went along with his mood perfectly.

She said she didn't deserve him, and if this is the person she is, she's right. Not because of her job, but because of her deception. Her cruelty.

But she was also kind, funny, and sweet. She took care of him. She made him laugh and smile. For better or worse, she made him happy. Challenged him without being intimidated by his title or put off by his sulky, irritated, childish sides. Was it because he mattered to her as a person? Or was it because he was a piece of meat?

He shoves his hands over his face, curling into a ball again. He can't do this. He can't just sit around and wallow or he's going to lose his mind. The office might be empty, but he's got the codes to get in after hours. If he went there, it would at least be a change of scenery. He wouldn't have to lie in the bed where he tried to give her pleasure…and where she didn't even care. Not until she faked it for him.

He wants to burn this mattress.

Shoving himself up, he puts himself in the shower, going through the motions blindly, picking through her actions and motivations. Why did she come to him? She chose him because he was naïve and stupid, obviously, but why did she need to do it in the first place? Is this her thing? Does she traipse from house to house, finding the blindly willing? Hell, teenagers have more experience than him, and they live with their parents, so it's not like she'd crash with them. That means he was a last resort. A Hail Mary. She'd get these dark, faraway looks, especially when he'd refuse to go out with one of her…what? Customers? He was losing her money. She charged him through the nose for her "services" too. She needed liquid cash. But why?

Every road he travels down leads him to that word. Why? Is she just evil? Is this her business model? Does she need to buy something expensive? Is she in debt? Is she being blackmailed?

The more his brain circles, the more his heart spirals. She didn't seem evil, but what the hell does he know? All the women he experienced either raised him, grew up hating him, work for him now, or—thanks to Sadie—have had their way with him. He doesn't know what makes someone good or bad, just easy to deal with or hard. She was easy. She fit. It was natural. Maybe that's why he was falling in love with—

No. It wasn't real. Her kindness was calculated.

But it couldn't have been. Not always.

Growling, he scrubs shampoo through his hair way too hard, not caring if it gets in his eyes. Screw his eyes. The ones that watched her lying naked beneath him, her expression cold and unwavering, something he'll never unsee until the day he dies.

He slams a flat palm on the tiled wall. The slap echoes in the steam-filled room, everything so hot it makes it hard to breathe. He can't stay here.

He rinses and tweaks off the dial before stomping to his room and slinging on clothes without toweling off, his wet hair running rivulets down his back and sopping the fabric of his sweater.

He barely notices, let alone cares. Taking his keys from the little dish by the door, he pauses long enough to look at hers, lying there as if all was right with the world. Innocent, innocuous, and infuriating.

He picks them up and launches them against the wall with a satisfying, shattering crash. Fuck her.

Outside, Simon walks as if he's furious at the concrete, scuffing his feet and kicking anything in his way. Crumpled paper bag? Boot. Abandoned coffee cup? Smash, the bottom of his shoes be damned. His face hurts from his furrowed expression, but he can't make it stop. He must look like a demon. Anyone who crosses paths with him flick their eyes to his but drop them to the ground in a flash. Good.

A male voice calls out from behind him. "Simon?"

He ignores it. Assumes whoever it is must be talking to someone else. It's only when his elbow gets snagged that he whips around, puffing his chest wide and ready to beat the shit out of anyone who messes with him.

It's...that guy. The homeless one he'd taken out to dinner. The one who gave him the quip about "women and ruin" that's been slamming his brain with a sledgehammer.

The man takes one look at Simon and throws his palms out in self-defense, his eyes dinner plate circles. "Whoa, boy. Stand down. Too early in the day to get my ass handed to me."

Simon's brows knit harder.

Drawing his gaze from Simon's shoes to his still-wet hair, the man says, "You look like hell."

"Is this where I thank you?" Simon grinds his teeth, the pressure in his jaw making his head ache. He sounds like an asshole, even to himself. Taking a deep breath, he forces himself to deflate. "Sorry. Bad day."

"I'll bet." The man takes that at face value and uncringes, relaxing his gently lined face and tucking his hands into his overlarge coat, layers and layers on underneath it. At least he's warm. Simon still hates to think about this man, and others like him, walking around the city without a place to stay.

The man tips his head to the side with a smirk. "Not sure if you remember me. You were kind of cocked the last time I saw you."

As if he could forget. And he wasn't that cocked.

"Ciel, right?" Simon says. "You wouldn't take my money." Which is ironic, considering.

"I should thank you for convincing me otherwise. I didn't get arrested for using it either, so that's a plus." Ciel gestures at the façade of the building beside them. "I've been waiting for you. Hoped you'd come by here again."

Looking up, it's the bar Simon walks by on the way home, its awning green and proud. This is the one he comes to with Nando. The one he brought Ciel to. The one where he first met Sadie.

He wants to burn this place too.

"You need something?" Simon says, pressing his fingers to the bridge of his nose, wanting nothing more than to leave.

"Yeah, I thought you'd want to know about that girl."

"What girl?"

"Little raven-haired chickie? Offered to help you date?" He puffs out a harsh breath, rocking on the balls of his feet. "Today seems to suck for both of you."

*Putting it mildly,* Simon supposes.

Wait.

Simon's eyes snap up to Ciel's. How would he know? Where did Sadie go after she left the apartment? Did she have some place to crash? She never seemed to have anyone else in her life…but maybe Ciel is one of her clients?

*No, that's impossible. He doesn't have enough money,* Simon thinks bitterly. "Where is she?"

The man gestures west. "Showed her where the women's food kitchen is. She looked terrible." Simon's eyes cast in the direction of Ciel's pointing finger. "First time I saw her, she kinda declared she was living at your house and dragged you home," Ciel says. "I don't know what's going on now, but I guarantee she's in trouble."

The protective bone in Simon tingles. "Why? Did she say something?"

"All I can tell you is that I found her a wreck. She was bone cold, so I'm pretty sure she slept outside. I know what that's like and how it sinks into you. She was hysterical—more than just tears. I'm talking full-out breakdown."

Discomfort makes Simon's nerves pulse.

"Honestly, I asked if you hit her or something."

Simon flinches. "I'd never—"

Ciel holds his hands up again. "Believe me, kid, she came to your defense right quick. But the way she talked about you…let's just say I think you're her safety net."

"Me?"

"Hence why I've been sitting here for hours hoping to catch a glimpse of your"—he gestures—"tallness. I'm hoping you can go get her."

"What am I supposed to do?"

"Be there for her? Feed her? I don't know, keep her on your couch? A girl that pretty should absolutely not be sleeping outside alone. Hell, she shouldn't be sleeping outside at all."

Simon looks toward the west again, fighting with himself. Should he help her? Should he not? His heart already knows the answer.

"Can you give me the address?" Simon asks.

"Sort of. I can tell you what the cross streets are."

Simon whips out his phone and thumbs it on. "Good enough."

---

Lunch is a selection of sandwiches Angelica doesn't like, a soupy-looking coleslaw, and an actually soupy tomato basil with oyster crackers. She sticks to that, careful not to get any on Simon's hoodie. She doesn't know why, she isn't what she'd consider a neat freak, but decides it's because she doesn't want to walk around with an orange glob oozing down her chest for the unforeseeable future.

With her puffy eyes and cagey demeanor, it seems to be the general assumption that Angelica was abused. She doesn't bother to correct them. When they talk to her, all she does is look down and hold her duffel closer. It has more money in it than these people have seen in years, and Angelica can only imagine the free-for-all that would go down if anyone snuck so much as a peek inside.

They all seem to know each other, either joining together at shabby, graffitied tables or actively avoiding one another with scowls and white-knuckle-clasped spoons. Angelica keeps her mouth shut. No one seems to blame her for it, and after a while, all the curious looks stop. She becomes just another new girl in what must be a lifetime of new girls.

"Okay, time's up, ladies," one of the kitchen staff shouts. She's Latina with a chubby tummy and a mole under her right eye that looks like a teardrop. She waves her hands in a shooing motion but with a sympathetic smile on her face that she turns on each and every one of them in turn, making sure each one is seen. "You know the drill. Open again at five. *Ándele*, out, out."

Angelica expects people to groan or grumble, but they surprise her. They pat each other on the back—or glare, to each their own—and work their way out. Angelica follows, wide-eyed and lost, not knowing what to do now. Between breakfast and lunch, she'd loitered outside the place, and the cops almost picked her up. One noted that she was new, and her partner took pity. They explained things to Angelica like she was an idiot. A simple "you can't stay here" would have sufficed, but they lectured her about keeping moving, not squatting in any empty buildings, and no panhandling near the park. Again, Angelica thought about her money and how she could blow everybody's minds, instead she wallowed in the fact that, no matter how much it was, it still wasn't enough.

Making her way back outside, the weather is milder and the sun is high. People mill around as she wonders where the hell to go. Her phone is at ten percent battery, so she needs to find a Wi- Fi café. She could maybe spring for a crappy latte and nurse the damn thing while her phone charges.

Looking around, she figures the closest one is down a few sets of quiet side streets onto the next main drag. The other women seem to be dispersing in different directions, which would give her at least some modicum of privacy. If they catch her ordering seven-dollar beverages, they probably won't let her back into the food kitchen, and God knows she needs somewhere to go.

She clears her throat, hanging back around the corner, waiting for the street to be empty enough…until she hears footsteps behind her.

"Sadie, Sadie, Sadie. Fallen on hard times, have we?"

Angelica's body goes rigid.

It's Damion.

Voice unsteady, she doesn't look around. "What do you want?"

There is a rough slapping sound, like a bat into a palm. She turns, preparing herself to scream if she has to. "I still have two months."

"One month and twenty-five days," he corrects. Damion's face is flabby, his cheeks puffy, and his nose pug-like. He indeed has a weapon, but it's not a bat. It's a billy club, like the cops used to carry. The straight black baton hits his hand with a hollow *thwack* every time it swings down. Behind him are two others she doesn't recognize. One is rail thin, but wiry and scrappy-looking. The other is thick all over, like Damion, but seems nimbler.

"Why are you here?" Angelica asks, mouth sticky with drying spit.

"Miss Maxine pinged your tracker and you seemed to be out of your standard radius. She was concerned. We've been keeping an eye on you, and this part of town," he *tsks*, "it's not a good place for someone like you."

"I'm not selling myself, if that's what you're asking. Max says that voids our agreement."

"Oh yes," Damion agrees, his thugs happy to let him talk. "And then I get to play with you."

Angelica's spine freezes in a zipping line, making her limbs feel numb. "I've got almost half."

"Give it to me," he says with a slimy grin.

She ticks her head side to side. "Max said all or nothing." Angelica will be damned if these goons take her money and fuck off with it. "I need money to make money, understand?"

The heavy one chuckles. "You gamblin', darlin'? What's your game? You don' look like you got a poker face."

"That's the truth," says the skinny one, his voice almost silky. He'd be attractive if not for a thick scar that draws a purple line over his cheek. "Maybe she's more of a blackjack player." He tosses her a wink that makes her shudder.

"I don't give a shit if she's betting on horses or riding sixes," Damion growls. "I care that she has a hundred thousand dollars." His glare narrows in on her. "And I'm guessing what she's got so far is in that bag."

Angelica clutches it tighter. "This is against the rules," she hisses. "You'll piss Maxine off."

"Madam Maxine," the skinny one adds. "Mind your manners, lovely."

For some reason, that endearment scares her more than any threat. She turns to bolt, but Damion grabs her by the hair, dragging her deeper into the side street. She drops her bag with a *thump* and tries to scream, but he's one step ahead of her, slamming her against the wall, ramming the billy club in a slashing line against her throat and clamping a hand over her mouth. All that comes out is muffled, quiet croaks as she struggles, grabbing at his hands with hers. He's immovable, like a nightmare sculpture of tempered steel.

"Hey! I'm calling the police," someone calls out.

Angelica struggles to point her eyes at the sound, but she'd know that voice anywhere. Simon is standing at the abandoned intersection, phone to his ear.

"Fuck you," Damion growls, but Simon just shouts:

"911? Yeah, I'm on the corner of Vine and Ash and there are three men assaulting a young woman. One is heavy, has blue eyes, and a T-shirt with a stupid American eagle and flames on it. Another is skinny with a scar on his right cheek—"

"Shit," skinny guy says, grabbing at Damion's shoulders. "We've gotta go."

"The other one is fatter than Buddha with brown hair and brown eyes," Simon continues, "Looks like he never showers and has the kind of face that's made for radio."

"What da fuck?" Heavy Guy says, but with a laugh in his throat. "Dis' guy got a death wish."

"No," Simon says into the phone, his eyes manic and body poised to fight. "No. I don't promise that, so, yes, send an ambulance." He watches the crowd behind Angelica. "The sooner the better."

In a flash, Simon tosses his phone to the side. It barely has time to clatter on the ground before he barrels forward, plunging into the skinny guy first, knocking his ass on the ground and getting a good few pounds in before Heavy Guy snags him. Angelica struggles again, but Damion's grip is painful now as he spits a "SHH" at her.

Two arms wrap up and under Simon's, dragging him upright, but he throws his arms straight, slipping from Heavy's grip before whipping around and taking his feet out from under him. Heavy lands on his back so hard, Angelica hopes his teeth shatter.

Damion lets her go, turning her hard and scraping her face against the wall, scuffing up her cheek. Her hand flies up to touch it and comes back dappled with red.

Everything is a blur of motion as Skinny tries to come at Simon from behind, but he throws his head back, bashing his assailant in the face. All Angelica can hear is a crunch and a cry.

"Fuck this motherfucker," Damion says, lifting his weapon high and diving in, bringing it down on Simon's shoulder. Angelica screams, but it does no good. Another crack sounds off Simon's ribs. Heavy takes advantage and pounces, driving a balled fist into his face.

A siren wails nearby, and everything goes still. "Shit," Heavy pants.

Damion jumps to the side and grabs Skinny, lurching him to his feet. Turning to Angelica, he growls. "One month and twenty-five days. All or fucking nothing. And I pray to God it's nothing."

With that, the three haul ass as the wail of the police car nears, an iconic whoop that splits the air. Angelica's head is light, like she might pass out, her throat throbbing from where Damion had her pinned. Voice hoarse, she says, "Simon, we've gotta run."

Facing away and curled on his side, he lets out a pained huff. "We didn't"—he coughs—"do anything wrong." Her brain doesn't process. "Or did you?" Simon asks.

"No," she chokes out.

"Good," he says with a groan, trying to sit up and failing.

Angelica rushes to his side, touching him gingerly. He gasps and curses under his breath, his teeth grit and his eyes slammed shut. Angelica's heart hammers the words: *They hurt him. They Hurt Him. THEY HURT HIM.*

"Jesus fucking Christ, Simon. Why would you do that? They could have killed you."

He groans, eyes cinched. "Don't I at least get h-hero points or something?"

Her heart wrenches. No one ever protects her. Never ever. No matter what she does, other than Bee, the world is against her.

Angelica's eyes flood with tears that spill over as she whacks his arm. "Stupid. You're so stupid. Moron. Bastard. Asshole." Every insult is marked by a slap, and he winces every time, just taking it like the idiot he is. "What if they cracked your ribs, huh? What if they dislocated your shoulder? What if they broke your eye bones or something?"

"Then I should be glad I asked for an ambulance," he manages.

The cop car screeches nearby, doors slamming as red and blue flickers in the alleyway. Guns point around the corner and, instinctively, Angelica's hands fly straight up, straining her shoulders. Simon, however, just lies there like a lump. Angelica wants to kick him. Beat him up more. Hold him in her arms. Fucking grow magic powers and heal him. What the hell is wrong with her? With him? With the world?

"He's hurt," she yells as best she can through her swollen throat, hands still to the sky.

One of the policemen talks into a radio on his shoulder, something unintelligible Angelica can't hear. The other lowers their gun and walks closer.

"The ambulance is coming, ma'am. They'll take good care of him. They'll see to your face too."

Her fingers reach up to touch her cheek again. She hadn't even thought about it, but the contact stings. Simon rolls over onto his back, finally opening his eyes to look at her. His gaze locks on her face and throat before darkening into nothing but rage.

"Those sons of bitches," he grinds out, reaching up to hover over her bleeding wound. She flinches away.

"It's fine."

"It's absolutely not."

Another siren wails up and another screech is heard. Doors slam as medics bring out a stretcher. There are metallic clacks as its locks engage, and the cart rumbles over the uneven and potholed street. Simon glances to the emergency crew before his sight falls back on Angelica. He looks so sweet. So soft. So hurt.

"Come with me?" he asks.

And how could she possibly say no?

# make it work

. . .

SIMON AND ANGELICA sit in a little private room with pastel curtains blocking their view of the rest of the ER. Needlessly, Simon is hooked to little oxygen and heart monitors he plucks at periodically with an irritated grimace while Angelica stares at her hands, her knuckles slowly whitening as she tries to make diamonds out of coal with her grip. The air between them is fraught, and why wouldn't it be? He'd asked her to come with him so nicely, but the pain seems to have gotten worse since his adrenaline wore off and he's been shoved into X-ray machine after X-ray machine. Now his sour mood is enough to make lemons pucker.

"Explain," he says, his voice rigid as he picks at the oxygen clip on the tip of his finger.

"What?"

He turns toward her, one of his eyes a bloody, mottled purple, puffy from his brow to his cheek. "Last night when you almost pounded my door in, you said to let you explain. So…" He gestures outward, as if giving her a grand introduction at an upscale venue. He favors his left shoulder, which isn't broken or dislocated, but bruised to be damned.

"Do your ribs hurt?" she asks.

"Sadie." His entire body reads no-nonsense. "Either talk or get out. I just took a hell of a beating for you, and I deserve to know why."

Somehow, her grip gets harder as her back curves toward her knees. She's afraid to say it. Afraid of what his reaction will be. Afraid of the repercussions.

Afraid he'll hate her.

His voice softens. "How's your throat?"

She touches the tender skin where Damion pinned her. "Just a bruise. It'll be fine."

"Your face?"

"Okay. Doctor said I might get a scar though."

She swears she hears Simon growl *motherfuckers*, but she can't be sure.

He looks at her expectantly. Pleasantries over, it seems it's time to confess, but where can she start? What can she say?

"I don't know how to talk about myself," she admits. "I never have. I don't know if I can find the words."

Unexpectedly, his hand lands on her head with kindness, a thumb stroking her hair. Its weight is like a steady anchor in her internal storm. "Start by telling me why those guys were after you."

She hesitates. "They work for my…previous employer."

"Previous?"

Angelica feels the rawness of her throat. "I didn't want to do it anymore."

"So, you made me do it instead?" he says, resentment soaking his tone. His hand lifts and she feels its loss like an ache.

Steeling herself, Angelica says, "She told me I have to buy myself out. I have…a time limit."

"One month, twenty-five days," he echoes eerily. "Is that what that bastard meant?"

She nods.

"What happens if you don't meet the deadline?"

She pauses, a heavy tear rolling down her face. It stings as it dissolves into the gauze on her cheek.

Simon shifts, lifting her chin until she's face-to-face with his bourbon-brown eyes. "What happens?" he urges.

It comes out in a pained whisper. "They're going to kill me."

Simon's eyes go wide. He tips her chin higher, looking from one iris to the other, likely judging her honesty, speechless as he stares.

"They want to set an example," she says.

His voice is pitchy. "For what?"

"So the other girls won't try to leave." Another tear rolls down her unmarred cheek, leaving a track that starts hot but cools as it drips from her chin. "I'm afraid, Simon."

Something in him seems to shift. He pulls back and lifts his good arm, shoving a hand through his hair as he folds his knees to his chest, straining his poor ribs. The blankets shift with a shushing sound and Angelica knows this is when he leaves her for good. She's dangerous. She's not worth it.

"How much?" he asks.

She shakes her head slightly, not sure what he's asking.

"How much buys you out?"

Angelica wraps her arms around herself in Simon's hoodie, trying to find comfort. She smells the acrid, antiseptic hospital air and watches the scuffed linoleum gaze back at her with memories of others who were wheeled into this room. She squeezes her vocal cords into shapes. "A hundred thousand dollars."

Simon gapes at her, pity stitched onto his face in fine lines of horror. "Oh Sadie. Jesus."

"Angelica," she corrects. "My name is Angelica."

His eyes lock on her for a long time, though he says nothing. His hand still rakes through his longish hair, black strands sticking through his pale fingers. "Can you run?"

She shakes her head and lifts her right bicep, rolling up the sleeve past her elbow and poking the meat of her forearm. "They put trackers in all the girls. They said it was to help if we ever got kidnapped—in this line of work, you never know—but now…" She shrugs.

"Can you get it taken out?"

"With what? My medical degree?"

Scowling, Simon leans back and pushes his button to call the nurse. It flickers a red light above his head and makes a chiming *bong* sound that barely echoes.

A gust of frustrated wind pulls from Angelica's lungs, and she slumps in her chair. "What are you gonna do, Simon? Get some random nurse to whip out a scalpel and start fucking tooling around in my arm?"

"Almost," he says.

"You think someone like me has insurance? The people I work for know I'm here, anyway. They probably have a crew ready to take me the minute I walk out the door."

His hands grip into fists and the tendons in his temples pulse. Retreating inward again, he lets his gaze flit around the room as he thinks. "How much money did you sell me for? How much do you have?"

Angelica kicks her bag too hard, and it skids across the floor, zipper down and scraping. "A little less than half."

He scolds her with a harsh look. "Is this where you tell me I should have gone on more dates?"

"This is where I tell you I'm completely fucked."

Simon's acid glare shoots to Angelica's duffel. "What if I gave you the rest?"

Her sarcastic laugh fills the small room. "And why the hell would you do that?"

"Because I care about you," he says through his teeth, glaring at her in a way incongruous to his words. There is another painful beat. Finally, he clears his throat and adds, "I'm imagining the police are out of the question or you would have gone to them already."

She snorts. "I wouldn't be surprised if they handed me directly to her."

"Her?"

Sinking deeper in her chair, Angelica hugs herself again. "For your sake, let's just call her the Big Bad Guy."

The nurses call sign bongs again.

As they sit in strained silence, Angelica's mind digs through its pink crinkles, looking to fill the quiet space. "I wanted to earn it myself, you know. The money."

He scoffs.

"I mean it. I wanted to do what I could to make this work. I made this a business. It mattered to me. I needed to prove I was worth something on my own, so I just stuck to what I know. I can still do it now. If I could just—"

"If you ask me to sell myself again, I'm going to throttle you." But it's said without malice. Exhaustion more than anything. There goes that idea.

"Let me give you the rest," he repeats softly. "But let's make it a loan. You'll prove your worth by paying me back."

"How?"

"We'll figure it out. That part doesn't matter."

"And where am I going to live, huh? Where am I going to stay?"

"With me." He looks at her like it's a question instead of a statement, as if asking for her permission. He adjusts his body with a quiet grunt. "Can you trust that they'll let you go?"

Angelica nods. "Of all the horrible things there are to say about that woman, the one saving grace is that she makes good on her deals. But they know I live with you. If she changes her mind…"

"Then let's hide you."

"How?"

His eyes drift to her arm. "Take that thing out and put it on a plane that flies far away."

"Now we're back to the medical degree problem."

That's when a nurse finally comes in, shutting off Simon's chime and not even bothering to spackle a perfunctory smile on her face. "What is it, Mr. Javik?"

"I'd like to speak with Dr. Knight, please. He's an old friend of mine and I'd like to see him before discharge."

"He's doing rounds, I'm afraid."

"I figured as much. Just tell him I'm here and see if he can make himself available." Simon's voice is smooth and executive. A firm "do what I want" sort of tone without being harsh. His body posture has changed too. Even with his ribs bruised to high hell, his chest is puffed out a little and his back is straighter.

Ruffling her scrubs—drab, dusky pink things—the nurse nods. "No promises," she says, waggling a finger as if Simon were a bad child.

"I won't hold you accountable," he replies with a slight quirk to his lips. Confident-him is kind of sexy. As much as Angelica loves—likes! —Simon's fumbling, bumbling side, this one has a definite appeal.

The nurse nods sharply and leaves, clearly annoyed by the extra task. Angelica doesn't know a lot about doctors or nurses, but assumes with all the hypochondriacs out there, they must be busy people.

Left alone, Simon twiddles his oxygen clip again, flicking his eyes to the screen that reads somewhere between ninety-eight and one hundred percent. His heart rate picks up suddenly, the beep, beep spiking a little higher. When he looks at her, pink flushes his cheeks with familiar brushstrokes.

"Last night, you said someone like you doesn't deserve someone like me." His voice drops to the gentlest thing she's ever heard. "Does that mean you want to deserve me?"

That heart rate spikes higher. Fixed on her, his lips move in sweet sweeps. "If you want me, then earn me."

Her face gets raging hot, blood rushing to match the monitor, spike for narrowed spike. "What did you say?"

His gaze doesn't drop. "You heard me."

Both their blood pressures skyrocket. If they keep this up, that pissy nurse will come back, thinking Simon's in cardiac arrest. Angelica needs to find her words. She needs to say something. Anything. And what comes out is: "I think that's the hottest thing you've ever said."

He freezes for a moment before throwing himself back on the bed, groaning and hissing a wince before whining, "Oh, thank God, because I almost died when I said it."

The tension breaks in an instant. Oh. And there it is. Despite the day, despite the pain from her face and the fear in her gut, her mouth purses into a cinch as she sputters, spraying the air around her.

Simon watches with a steady smile as Angelica leans back in her chair, clutches her belly, and laughs her fucking ass off.

———

Pain medicine is one of life's true miracles. A few little pills and his body has wound down to a tolerable level of *ow*. With his current company, he's been unable to sit still, although he definitely should, and so has been tweaking his abused muscles in all sorts of ways. But what's a little pain when another person's life is in danger? God help him, he wants to believe her story. If she's telling the truth, this little experiment will both benefit her and put him on the road toward forgiveness. He wants that. As much as he wants her words not to be her reality, he prays she's not lying again. His heart can only break so hard.

It's been a long time since Simon has seen the marvelous Dr. Knight, and he's not disappointed to see him again.

"Still bald?" Simon asks.

"Still a jerk?" Tyler replies before clasping Simon's hand and making him cry out a little when he moves his bad shoulder. His child-hood-friend-turned-medical-professional grimaces on his behalf.

"Got the crap kicked out of you, huh?"

"I gave as good as I got," he lies. Glancing at Sadie—no, Angelica—he sees the small smirk on her face but she doesn't call him out for his fib.

Simon feels like he's looking into the past as he takes in his friend's familiar poised posture and amused expression, a careworn crinkle now in the corners of his eyes. He sends a quick plea to the heavens and says, "I'll be honest, Ty, I need a favor."

The man stuffs his hands in his pockets. "What? No foreplay? I haven't seen you in over a decade and you just jump right into demands? That's the most Javik thing I've ever seen."

Simon would shrug, except it would suck to do so. "What can I say, I'm a time saver." Knowing the drill after years together, Tyler moves to slide the room's door shut, glancing at Sa... no, *Angelica*.

"No offense, miss, but you might want to step out of the room."

"She stays," Simon says.

Tyler shoots him a wary look.

"She's the reason I need you."

There's not a single moment that passes before Tyler groans, sliding the door shut with a click. "God, Simon, what illegal thing are you going to make me do now?"

"Illegal?" Angelica chirps.

"Oh yeah," Tyler says. "Simon here used to get into all sorts of crap, and I would have to hide him in my basement so the cops wouldn't find him. He had a temper and a penchant for lighting things on fire."

Angelica's jaw drops, her lips curving up. "No way."

"I was a little dark in school," Simon deadpans. It's putting it mildly.

"Could have destroyed the whole campus if he set his mind to it." Tyler clasps his hands behind his back with a wistful smile. "But I always believed in him. He might have been a prick, but he was my prick."

"Don't start." Simon scowls.

"What? Unrequited love looks good on me."

There's a grumble in him somewhere, but he can't be bothered to dig it out. Instead, he nods to the lady of the hour. "This is Angelica."

"Girlfriend?" Tyler asks.

*It's complicated*, sits on Simon's tongue but he holds it back. "Ex-employee, but a close friend."

She flicks her eyes down and looks shy—the first time he's ever seen an expression like that on her face. He'd like to see it again. He'd actually like to see it about twenty-four thousand times, and he doesn't know if that makes him tragic or stupid.

His head aches. His everything aches.

"Permission to speak freely," he asks no one in particular. Both potential parties give him some sort of nod or shrug. "Evil people put an evil thing in her arm, and I want you to cut it out."

Angelica facepalms while Tyler balks with a "Say what now?" Weirdly, it warms Simon's heart. He missed this guy.

Tyler looks at Angelica like she's nothing but trouble before turning an exasperated face toward Simon. "Okay. We're looking at x-rays, local anesthetic, lots of bits and bobs, stitches—"

"All of which you'll pretend are mine and charge to my insurance."

Tyler tosses his hands in the air. "Insurance fraud? That's what you're making me do?"

"And you can get Val in here to help you."

"Only if whatever 'evil thing' lives just under the surface of her skin. We don't do surgery here, Simon, we have experts for that.

Besides, Val hates you. When she talks about you, it's only to vow to avenge her honor and kick you in the face."

"So, tell her she can kick me in the face. Or that I'll owe her one. Or that I'll lick her goddamned ballet slippers, I dunno."

Tyler slaps his palms to his face and whines, stomping like a toddler. "Whyyyy, Saiiiiii?"

He points at Angelica. "Because she's in trouble if we don't do this."

Giving her the side-eye, Tyler pouts. "What are we removing, oh complicated one? A bone? A tendon? A subcutaneous gang tattoo? A GPS tracker?"

"That's the one," Simon says, and Tyler blanches. His head snaps to Angelica in horror.

"That's not real, that's spy stuff. Are you a spy?"

"If I was, I'd have a special ops med guy to do my bidding and a super-buff extraction team," she says, resting her chin on the heel of her hand.

Tyler says, "So, you're running away from prison or something?"

"That would mean an ankle bracelet," she corrects. "Keep with the times."

Tyler flips his arms in the air again. "This is helpful. Really helpful. I feel enlightened. I feel one with God."

"Ty," Simon interrupts, putting on his most pleading, dewy-eyed, childhood-friend face. The pain is coming back in a blooming crescendo, so it's not hard to milk it. "You're our only hope."

The man looks back and forth between Angelica and Simon, then tosses a decidedly scathing look at Angelica, then a desperate glance at Simon. Then he snags Angelica's arm and palpates it, his thumb hitting a place a few inches below her elbow that makes her frown. He frowns in return.

Throwing his head back, he grunts. "Fine. God help me, Javik, you better be best friends with me again after this."

"Only if you promise not to grab my crotch."

"That was one time."

Simon lifts an eyebrow.

"Okay, maybe three times."

Simon lifts both eyebrows.

"Okay, maybe enough for you not to be friends with me anymore, but still." Dropping Angelica's arm, he puts his hands on his hips, muttering things like "insurance fraud" and "owe me" and "why the hell" before opening the door and stomping back into the ER bustle.

———

I hear you had a run-in with the boys.

Angelica's heart picks up. Her eyes fly first to the tightly wound bandage on her arm and then to the tiny bottle that holds the extricated tracker. It sits on the end table, too paltry-looking for its sinister purpose. Her arm throbs, but it's worth it, and by carrying the damn electronic thing around with her, it'll ensure Max doesn't know what she's done.

Your man-meat had your way with them, it seems. Does he know he's your whore yet?

She swallows down her self-hatred.

Yes.

Would you defend me like that, I wonder.

Angelica doesn't answer.

Are you fucking him?

Scowling, Angelica's thumbs slap down three times. Tap, tap, tap.

No.

Last night doesn't count.

For him to play hero, he must want to fuck you.

> Makes sense. You've got a grade A snatch,
> decent ass, and pretty lips.
>
> Without the holes in your body, though, you're
> not worth much. He'll figure that out.

Angelica clutches her phone, wanting to bury it in sand. Drown it in the ocean. Instead, she takes a breath and tries to steady her shaking hands.

> You said part of you was rooting for me.
> Maybe you should be a bit nicer.

There is a pause and Angelica's stomach sours. Every time she opens her mouth, she pulls the noose tighter around her neck.

> I'd almost forgotten. It must be my age.
>
> I suppose it doesn't matter. Lose, win, one way
> or another, I'll see you soon.
>
> Remember, dear, time is ever our enemy.
>
> Tick-tock.

Angelica stares at her screen, waiting for more dots from Maxine's typing, but none come. Instead, from the bathroom she hears a growled "Goddamnit," likely as Simon tries to get a shirt back on after his shower. She told him to stick to button-ups, but he only rolled his eyes. He seems to pendulum between sweetness, utter petulance, and sizzling bitterness. Angelica, for her part, is just trying to keep her head down. She sits in her standard chair, making her body small and trying to disappear. She wants to lock herself in her old room, but it hasn't been re-offered yet and she doesn't want to step out of line. She does, however, contemplate burying her face in her nearby duffel like an ostrich. Instead, she sits, suffering in this penthouse purgatory with her foot jittering against the hardwood floor. Thumbing her necklace, she takes what comfort she can from the familiar little ridges and valleys that hold the green jewel in place.

The bathroom door opens, and a grumpy, damp Simon works his

way into the kitchen, slowly ducking down and yanking the bottom freezer drawer out with way too much force. Out comes one ice pack that he tosses unceremoniously onto the counter, then another, then a large bag of frozen peas. Angelica looks at him over the edge of her chair, but as soon as his eyes pin her, she sinks down again.

Muttering unintelligibly to himself, he comes over and eases onto the couch, gingerly clamping one ice pack between his arm and ribs and slinging another over his shoulder. With a groan, he leans back and rests the peas over his swollen black eye with great care.

"Ground rules," he says.

At this point, Angelica doesn't feel like she has a right to say anything. She twines her fingers together, wondering what terrible things are on their way.

"I am never doing the meal plan again," he says.

Angelica cocks her head to the side. Of all the things to start with.

"And I'm quitting the gym."

"But you were doing so good."

His one-eyed glare shuts her right up. "There is no dating, there are no women, whatever black market you have me on, get me off immediately."

Angelica nods.

After a pause, his uncovered eye narrows. "How did you advertise me, anyway?"

She hikes up her knees and twiddles her toes. "I called you an unridden, raven-haired stallion, ready to be broken in and—"

"God no. Jesus. I mean, like, how do you even find these women?"

"Bethany," she explains. "She helped me get on a list where you put up offerings. I've known her for a while. She helps train the new girls sometimes. Gives us tips for safety. How-tos. Examples."

"I don't even want to imagine what that looks like."

"Kind of like what I did for you."

That glare comes back. "Was she always touching you? Sitting on your lap? Picking at you?" He leans back again. "Making you feel like you're worthless as you are."

*No*, Angelica thinks. *That was Max's job.* "You're not worthless," she says quietly.

"Just stupid."

Her heart aches. "I can leave. We don't have to do this. I can just go figure something else out. Now that the tracker's gone, maybe I can—"

"Hush." He deflates, nestling in. "Just give me a bit to process this. I have every right to be pissed and hurt and whatever the hell else, but it doesn't change anything. I said I'd help you, and I will. Besides, you said that the Big Bad Guy—or woman, or whatever—knows where we are. It's dangerous for you to leave, tracker or not. The best thing to do is give her what she wants, as long as you really trust she'll go away."

"I do," Angelica says.

"Then I'll go to the bank on Monday. Just sit tight until then."

Her lower lip stings for how hard she's biting it. Angelica hates this. Sure, selling Simon didn't work out, but at least she was doing something. Making connections, reviewing candidates, motivating Simon. She wasn't just sitting on her ass waiting for a handout. This is charity. Angelica doesn't take charity.

She sets her jaw. "I'm going to pay you back. I guarantee it. When I get a job, you can expect part of every paycheck and I'll even slap something extra on the top. I'll calculate monthly compounding interest at six percent. That will make this more than worth your while. A better investment than cash just sitting in a savings account."

Simon's one eye sparkles like a kid who just found a barrel of candy. "You can calculate compound interest?"

She shrugs a little. "Yeah."

"In your head? Not, like, with an app or a website?"

"Yeah."

That one-eyed twinkle turns into an outright gleam. He sits up carefully, peas still slapped over his face. "You like math?"

She picks her fingernails. "It was the one thing I was good at in school. English was stupid, I couldn't relate to a single one of those books, history pissed me off because why do I care about dead people, but math…math doesn't make you try to feel anything."

"It just tells the truth," Simon adds.

A half smile pulls Angelica's lips. "Yeah. I like that. I can do a lot in my head, but I like writing some out on paper too. Calculators are okay, but they suck for higher math."

"Did you study it in college?" he asks, seeming truly interested.

"*Pfft*. I didn't go to college. I didn't even graduate high school."

"GED?"

She sulks. "Not that either."

"Why?"

She tucks her chin to her bent knees, her toes scrunching into the puffiness of the chair. It feels grounding, soft and cushy. She suddenly wishes the world existed of only her and this one point of contact.

"Another ground rule," Simon says. "Stop hiding things. No hiding, no lying, no tricking."

"There's a difference between hiding things and not talking about them," she says with a frown, looking at him askance. He drops the bag from his bad eye, showing off the bruised purple.

"Not to me. Not anymore."

Mulish, her mouth becomes a straight line. "I don't know how to talk about myself," she repeats.

"Fine," he says. "I'll keep it simple and ask yes or no questions. Did you flunk out?"

"No." She sulks.

"Did you drop out?"

Discomfort prickles the nerves under her skin. "It's not that simple."

His tongue clucks. "Did you run away?"

"Sort of…"

"We'll start there." He waves a hand at her in a flourish again. "Extrapolate."

She snorts at that. "Has anyone ever told you you're bossy?"

He huffs. "Well, I do happen to be this close to running a global company," he holds up pinched fingers. "I manage entire teams of people. Business units, even. Why do you think I work such insane hours?"

She'd never thought of that. "To me, you've always just been mopey, kinda dopey, sulky Simon."

"A title I will shed immediately."

Trying to hold in her sarcasm, she gives a little two-finger salute.

Her silent tone is still heard loud and clear, and his lips purse in irritation.

Uttering a quiet curse, he shifts, putting the peas back over his swollen skin. "Anyway,"—he waves his hand as if conducting music—"extrapolate."

As irritated as she wants to be, the feeling doesn't come. Instead, she breathes in Simon's diffusing eucalyptus shampoo and sighs. "My Auntie Bee took me away."

"The one who gave you that necklace," he states with a nod.

"You remember?"

"You'd be surprised what I remember about you. Go on." He adjusts his shoulder pack and snuggles down.

She considers. "My father was…a monster. She saved me."

Simon lifts up his bag of peas again, seeing her with both eyes. She focuses on a ball of lint on the arm of the chair.

"He'd hit…but worse than that, he'd bite." She grimaces. "Never where anyone would see, but there would be these horrible bruises. I hid them at all costs, you know, but if kids at school patted my back or my arms, they'd always hit one by accident. I hated them for that. Auntie Bee realized what was happening. She had no legal rights to step in and I had no proof it was him, so we ran. I don't think he ever even bothered looking for us."

"Where did you go?"

A little smile perches on her face. "We hid in what we called 'the green places.' Cabins in the woods. We'd take care of people's vacation homes off-season…but then the season came, and we had nowhere to go. I tried being a waitress for a while. A guy came on to me and offered money. I wanted it, he wanted me, so I took him up on it." She shouldn't have said that, maybe. But now that her tongue is moving, it doesn't seem to want to stop. "It wasn't horrible, it was fun even, so I did it again. By then Bee got sick, and I needed more money, but there was only so much time in a day and the stakes were high if you got caught. The 'Big Bad Guy'"—Angelica snorts at the nickname, wondering what Max would think of it—"found me and offered a higher caliber of clientele, better pay, plus room and board for my aunt and me, so it was a no-brainer.

"My money helped buy what I could for Bee, but she still needed more. Medicines, surgeries, nurses. We had no insurance, nothing to sell but me, no help from the state, so I…" Angelica finds herself having to blink back tears. Her voice shudders, and she lets it. "I just had to watch her die. She got so weak. So frail. She was in so much pain, but she tried not to let it show." Wringing her hands, Angelica feels small, like she's a little girl again, flailing at nothing without aim or control. "She was always so strong, waiting up at night for me to come home, just in case I needed her… And when she died…I saw it all. Every second."

Bee had withered, wheezed, and choked on nothing until she turned a shade beyond blue. Angelica had panicked. Angelica had screamed. She'd called for help while her straight arms plunged against Bee's frail chest, begging for her heart to start again. It wouldn't, and Angelica couldn't do anything about it. No matter how long or how hard she tried, she was useless. Powerless. Pointless.

Her words tumble, fall out, and crash. "I shouldn't have let her take me away in the first place. It took away her job and security. It ruined her life. I may as well have killed her myself." She rakes in a breath. "And then I went numb. I just did whatever I was told, which is exactly how they liked it. I did that for years, just letting the days blur by without giving one shit, but then a client…he…" Angelica grinds her teeth, remembering it with white-hot fury. "He fucking bit me. Even though it's a hard limit, even though it's a red light, even though it's written all over my fucking paperwork. And nobody cared. I never realized it before, but I was just a thing to them." She remembers Max's words and growls, "A series of holes for men to stuff themselves into. No one gave a fuck about me or my life, only Bee, and Bee is gone. Now I'm lost. I have fucking nothing and I'm all alone."

"You're not though," he says gently, interrupting her hurricane.

Her chest saws in and out, tears streaming down her face as clenched hands leave fingernail crescents in her palms. Her stitched-up arm aches as her muscles twitch and tremble. Embarrassment swallows her whole, but it's too late to take her words back.

When she works up the courage to look at Simon, his good arm is held high, making an open space against him. "Sit with me?"

Angelica stares at the empty place for too long, but he doesn't move. He just looks at her, not offering pity or meaningless platitudes, just comfort.

Like an animal on the verge of spooking, she edges from her chair and takes a single step.

What's happening right now? Is this really okay? Is she going to make this worse somehow?

He just lifts his arm higher. "C'mere."

He doesn't say "it's okay" or "you must be so strong" or "I can't believe all that happened to you" or any of those stupid things people say. He's just there, cheeks not pink at all, in executive mode. Confident and competent mode. Maybe that's why she finally moves and tucks into his good side. His arm wraps over her and he says nothing, just existing beside her. He's warm and smells like the soap they use, a balsam something or other that reminds her of Christmas trees.

"You're not alone," he says again. "You have me. We're friends now."

She lets out a gusty, pathetic laugh. "Is that what we are?"

He tucks her in closer. "Yeah."

An exhaustion grabs at Angelica's ankles and pulls. "Today sucks."

"Yesterday sucked too," he adds.

He's not wrong. Tentatively, she rests her hand to the right of his breastbone, feeling his warmth and the thump of his heart. She suddenly wants hers to meet his rhythm. She wants their breath to sync. She wants her skin to melt into his.

"I'm sorry," she whispers, the ache of it filling her secret hollow spots.

His heavy inhale lifts her as his fingers thread through her hair, stroking from root to tip, just like Bee used to. He rests his temple against the top of her head. "I forgive you. And I'm here with you. You don't have to do this all by yourself."

She snuffles hard, her tears spilling onto his shirt and wicking away.

"Let's start over." He clears his throat. "Hello. My name is Simon. I'm a grump who works too hard with absolutely no results. I'm terrible with women, but my heart is in the right place, even if everything that comes out of my mouth is trash. I'm a terrible, weepy drunk and likely have horrible self-esteem. I hate the gym with a passion, have been craving carbs for weeks, and may refuse to eat a vegetable ever again. Nice to meet you. Will you be my friend?"

With a giggle, Angelica tucks closer. "My name is Angelica. I'm nothing but trouble and there's no reason to keep me around, but if you really want to be friends, I think I'd like that very much."

He pets her hair again. "Then there we go."

———

"What man at your age gets the shit kicked out of him like this, eh?" Nando asks, lifting his coffee mug to his lips.

Simon's headache is level eleven out of ten, and he regrets not hiding under his covers all day. "Only ones who are falling in love with someone very complicated."

Nando doesn't even spit his drink. His jaw drops and it just Niagara Falls into his lap, skewing his words with burbles. "I'm sorry, what?" With a grimace, he starts looking at the trail he'd left down his expensive shirt, and Simon hands him a tissue. "I thought you were doing wham-bam one-night stands. Who in hell did you fall in love with?"

What to call her at this point? Probably better to stick to her lie. "My consultant."

Nando slaps a scolding hand on the table. "We don't date the staff, Simon."

"Tell me that again, considering you've had sex with my EA."

"She's not *my* staff." Pursing his lips, Nando glowers. "How would you know what love is anyway, eh? *Col cavolo*, Simi, you've had zero girlfriends."

"What else do you call it when your eyes follow a woman everywhere she goes, watching every flit of body language for clues to who she is and what she needs? Where she makes every inch of you want to protect her and stop those beautiful tears? When she crushes your heart like it's nothing before making it feel such an aching worry it could never leave her? When she heals it again with two simple words?"

"What words?"

"'I'm sorry.'"

"Ah, the perfect start to a relationship," he deadpans. "Sounds like a short road to long years of therapy."

Simon would laugh, but that would split his head like a grapefruit.

"How often do you see this woman, anyway?" Nando asks.

"Every day. She lives with me."

This time, Nando spits out his drink with incredible force, and Simon gets fitzed upon. He icks over the spray on his desk and the spatter on his hands.

"How did I not know about this?" Nando gapes. "For how long?"

"From the beginning, actually."

"Why didn't you tell me, huh?"

"Because I thought you would tell me I'm stupid."

"You *are* stupid. You were born stupid, and you'll die stupid, but this is next level."

Simon's sigh is next level, that's what.

"Aren't I supposed to be your best friend?" Nando asks, mopping up Simon's desk with what's left of the tissue, leaving little dissolved pieces behind in sopping flakes. "What the hell good is that if you don't tell me anything, eh? What if she murdered you in your sleep?"

"Something tells me she prefers paychecks to prison."

Nando mutters something in Italian that reminds Simon of his own bad habit of cussing as quietly as possible.

A knock turns Simon's head toward the door as Sophia steps in. "I made the executive decision to cancel your afternoon...oh." She catches sight of Nando and immediately stands straighter. And...did she just suck in her tummy? Simon's done that at the gym, wanting to see what was so damn sexy about it, but didn't get the concave appeal. Sophia seems to think there is one, God knows why. "Mr. Ferrante, um, I didn't know you were in here."

He turns a highbrow stare at her. "Did you forget my first name, Miss Yang?"

She blushes to high heaven, her mouth working. "Sorry, Arman—"

"Nando, is fine, thank you." He turns his back on her, and she instantly deflates. How does he not see how she reacts to him? Simon wonders if he'd ever been this dumb. Probably.

"A-anyway," she stammers, looking at Simon again. "You should go home. I cleared tomorrow too."

"My uncle will have a fit," Simon reminds.

She only shrugs. "That's what laptops are for. You can work just as well in bed with pillows fluffed all around you as you can in that horrible chair."

She's right. It is horrible. Even on the best of days, it makes his ass hurt.

She sets a hand on her hip, "So no buts. If you can't be responsible for yourself, I'll be responsible for you."

"And that's why you're getting a raise," Simon tells her. She responds with a grin that makes her almond eyes crinkle.

"I'll hold you to that."

"Let's get lunch before I leave though, okay? That way I don't have to grab something on the way home. I want eight gallons of pasta and meatballs. Get whatever you want. Splurge. I'm feeling generous today."

With a thick envelope of over sixty thousand dollars sitting in his drawer, that's putting it mildly. Now that was an adventure. More than ten pages of explanatory bank paperwork, a caution that the vault may not be carrying enough, and a darkly issued threat from Simon that he was more than happy to take his portfolio of business elsewhere. They even pulled him aside and, based on his face and general gait that screamed "I just took a beating," they asked if he was being blackmailed or if someone he loved was being held at ransom. They hovered their hands over the phone to summon police on his behalf, and it was all he could do to say he just wanted to buy a goddamned piece of fine art in a private sale. A lie, a very blatant one, but it was his own goddamned money and they shouldn't give a shit if he flushed it.

Sophia's grin turns devilish. "So, can I get mac and cheese with barbecue pulled pork?"

His fingers snap. "Excellent choice."

Nando jumps in. "Ooh, if we're doing food comas, let's go in together." Turning toward Sophia as if she was a waitress, he waves his hand—the ass. "Make that two."

Sophia seems to not know whether to frown or smile, her face making a weird combination of both one after another before she scoots out.

When Nando turns back, Simon cocks an eyebrow. "What do you think of her?"

He shrugs. "I have vague memories of her making sexy faces. She also had very strong thighs."

"Never tell me that again. I mean her personality."

Crossing his arms and leaning back, Nando huffs. "Can't say I have an opinion."

"Well, you're about to get one. I'm inviting her to eat with us."

The face Nando makes is confused, irritated, and priceless. Maybe Simon can be a matchmaker. He'd thought Sophia was better and more deserving than Nando, but when oil and vinegar mix, sometimes it makes a salad. Would Nando change if the right woman was in his life?

Simon looks through his office's long panel of side glass to see Sophia sitting forward in her chair with the phone pressed against her ear and wonders what love can do.

———

Angelica twiddles her fingers, the TV on with an intense drama that would normally have her on the edge of her seat, the sound of gunshots and explosions barreling through the apartment.

Instead of biting her inner cheek in suspense, though, she's staring at her phone. Simon said he's coming home early, and she doesn't know how to act anymore. What does "friends" look like? Is it friends with benefits? She doesn't want that. But she doesn't want to lose the comfort of his arms either.

She thrusts her hands through her hair. This is all so fucked up. Her heart's been dead for years and suddenly this weird gigantic man with personality swings is growing little sprigs from her ashes. Little green hopes she should stomp on.

For the first time, she doesn't want to stomp on them.

The door clatters as Simon puts his keys in the handle, jiggling them around since the damn thing sticks sometimes. Angelica flies to the door for reasons unknown, hands straight down beside her as if greeting some military officer. What the fuck is next? Does she salute?

When he ducks in, his hair is all out of place and his gait is stilted. At least the swelling in his eye has gone down. Now it's just mottled red, yellow, and purple with flecks of unfortunate blue. He toes off his shoes before he finds her waiting, and when he does, the look on his face is priceless.

"Hello?" he says tentatively, looking around. "And you're greeting me at the door why?"

Shit. Double shit. "I just wanted to make sure you're okay. Did you get in trouble at work for looking so…" She gestures up and down.

"Suave?" he tries.

Setting down his laptop bag and shrugging off his business jacket, he makes a face, scowling, and Angelica jumps in to help him. This feels so weird. Why is she making this so weird?

"I got the money, if that's what you're worried about," he says grumpily.

"That's not why I'm doing this. It's because…" Why the hell *is* she doing this? "Because this is all my fault."

He glances at her over his shoulder before turning and setting that reassuring hand on her head again, petting her hair. It should be insulting, belittling, but it's not. It's a connection of touch that isn't taking, only giving, asking nothing in return.

"I'll heal. Believe it or not, this isn't the first time I've come home black and blue."

"All that pyromania as a kid came with a violent streak?"

"You have no idea," he says with a self-deprecating smirk. He works himself to the couch, easing down as he has since Saturday, and Angelica finds herself rushing to get him his ice packs. When she zips back to stand in front of him, he only cocks an eyebrow.

"You're acting weird."

"Am I?"

She is.

Settling the ice packs around himself, he says, "Shouldn't you be telling me to toughen up or get over it or that I'm an idiot and I shouldn't have stuck my nose in?"

She tumbles into her chair with a *fwump*, legs splaying out to either side. "I'm sorry."

He smiles at her again. His eyes squint with the strength of it and cute dimples etch themselves into his face. "I'll be fine," he says. "Oh, and I found a way for you to pay me back."

That perks her up.

"We need an accounting intern. You like crunching numbers, we need numbers crunched."

She looks at him like he's crazy. "With what degree am I going to land that gig?"

"With nepotism. You've got to pull your weight though. I'll put you under my EA, Sophia. She'll help you out."

"Don't I need to know how to do, like, spreadsheets and stuff?"

"Do you know how to use Google?"

She shoots him a look.

"Then you'll figure it out," he says. "If eight-year-olds can learn how to hot-wire a car, you'll figure out how to add things in a spread-sheet. Besides, businesswomen like you should have no problem diving headfirst into something they have familiarity with. This comes with lots of algebra."

Her eyes light up.

"Idiot math too, like addition and subtraction, so don't get your hopes up, but you might be able to make some graphical models that help tell stories with numbers. I like those the best."

"Why would you need me? Don't you have a trillion applicants?"

He shrugs with his good shoulder. "Nando says our recruiters suck. Our job descriptions are all screwed up too. They want an entry-level customer service rep to have a bachelor's degree. The job can be done by a sophomore in high school, and they get paid with that in mind, so why the hell are we asking for a sixty-thousand—or more—dollar degree for these people?"

Angelica doesn't know anything about that. What she does know is cause enough for concern. "What if they find out about me? About my previous job."

Simon seems to not have thought about that. "Well, you went by the name Sadie, right?"

"Yeah, but I have the same face, Simon. If anyone hired me—"

He scoffs. "Who would have hired you?"

Coolly, she crosses her legs and folds her arms. "You'd be surprised."

He gives in quickly with a nod and a gesture of peace. "Sorry. I guess we'll just have to cross that bridge when we come to it."

Suddenly the TV catches her attention again, even though she's not really watching it. It's just something to look at that's not CEO Simon in executive mode. "Wouldn't you get in trouble for giving me the job?"

If he'd answered right away, she wouldn't have believed him. Instead, he thinks about it long and slow. "It would be a ding to my reputation for sure. They might ask me to fire you."

"And then what?"

"I don't know. If you're doing your job and doing it well, what should it matter? People can be terrible though. They might be mean to you."

A bitter tang fills her mouth. Picking at the gauze over her arm's healing incision, she lets herself feel the throb in her still-patched cheek. "Any worse than being roughed up and operating under the threat of death?"

Simon looks at her with sympathy and blows his hair out of his eyes. "Touché."

"But people do suck," she agrees.

"They do. So, let's just do what we can to keep you as Angelica… what's your last name?"

"Hart."

"Angelica Hart. Very respectable. Who wouldn't want to employ an Angelica Hart?"

She tosses a pillow at him, making him grunt when he flinches.

"One thing though," he says.

"Another ground rule?"

"No, nothing like that." She looks at him expectantly as he turns that familiar pink again, more like her normal, fidgety Simon. "I'd still like to offer free room and board," he says shyly.

Those sprigs of green in her heart grow an inch taller as warm sunlight fills her insides. "Really?"

"Yeah."

It's Angelica's turn to flare up, pink to red, and Simon sees every shade. "Does that mean you want to stay?" he asks.

She has no words, so she only nods.

With a smile as soft as butter, Simon says, "Then welcome home, Angelica Hart. Now we just need to find where I threw your keys..."

# inspiration

. . .

NO MATTER how much concealer she puts on, Angelica's cheek still looks scabby. Simon told her not to worry about it, but of course he'd say that. He looks like a blueberry smashed itself into his face. At least he's walking better. And lifting his arm better. Not that Angelica is watching or anything.

"Stop picking at it," he murmurs in the elevator. The one to his floor. His office floor. His goddamned office floor where people walk around with paperwork and laptops and shit.

Angelica's hand drops from her cheek and she bites her lower lip, staring at her brass reflection in the elevator doors.

"Don't be so tense," Simon says, looking pretty tense himself. "This is just a working interview. We'll get you in the door, get you at a desk with stuff to do, and see how the day goes."

"Still don't see why I can't just bartend. I can learn how to make a pink-tini or whatever the hell else."

"And you're gonna pay me back on that salary?"

Not with the interest rate she'd promised him. Apparently, it doesn't matter who she's with, Angelica can't help but set herself up for failure. Simon's face is smarmy, and she'd deck him, except that the doors ding open.

He stomps out with a purpose, Angelica trailing in his wake. This is CEO Simon Land, the mythical place he goes every day before coming back more pissed off than he was when he left. The landscape is made of gray partitions, giving the business villagers privacy even when stacked one on top of the other. A crowd of desks are almost chest high, made for standing up, and the people hovering around them look like a pack of yuppies. That's all right. Angelica is good with yuppies. Each workstation has two—or more—monitors, as if people can't bear not having every inch of their peripheral vision full of emails and files and whatever the hell else. She doesn't belong here. She belongs in a bar with a skimpy dress and shiny lip gloss, ready to smile at someone she doesn't know. Though, perhaps, that's exactly what she's going to do now—minus the skimpy dress. Instead, she has a fitted pin skirt, a camisole that looks way too adult somehow, and a reasonably priced sweater that hangs long on her hips. That and some low heels qualify as Angelica's new battle gear.

Here there be dragons.

"Morning, Simon," chirps a feminine voice as they round a corner.

He lifts a hand and escorts Angelica over, gesturing to—what Angelica is guessing—is her mentor for the day. "Sophia, this is Angelica. Angelica, Sophia."

"I know you."

Angelica's attention snaps up from her shoes. Shit. Is the jig already up?

Across a desk strewn with fidget toys and stress balls, a petite, compact Asian woman points at her with a jabbing finger and a squinted eye. "You're the sauna lady."

Angelica cocks her head to the side.

"Do you know how heavy you are?" Sophia says. "You're either solid muscle or you packed in a good dinner that night."

"What night?" Simon looks just as lost as Angelica feels.

Huffing, Sophia sets her fists on her hips. "I was at Elementals for a massage and went into their steam room. There was this woman who looked like she was about to pass out. She was rude for about four seconds, and then she *did* pass out."

Oh God. Of all the stupid things to haunt her.

"Me and two other women had to haul you into the lounge." Sophia says. "You were dead to the world."

Simon's face pulls into a wince as he gives Angelica a sympathetic glance, likely remembering having to nurse her awake with ice water and cool towels.

"Ah…um…" Collecting herself as best she can, Angelica holds out a hand to the feisty chick in front of her. "Sorry for that. Thank you for helping me."

Sophia tips her face to the side, narrowing her thin eyes and pursing her lips as she judges her.

After a beat, she sticks out her hand to shake. "And you're our interviewee, hmm?"

"It's a small world," Simon says, obviously wanting nothing more than to duck out of this conversation. Angelica's guessing it would be taboo to say Simon had brought her there in the first place, got naked in the same room as her, and snored so hard he almost made her piss herself laughing.

Sophia waves her hands in little shooing gestures. "Go on, Simon, you have an eight-thirty. Remember to say hello and ask how people are, Europeans actually pretend to care about each other."

Simon gives his standard under-his-breath mutters. "You don't have to remind me how bluntly American I am."

"Yes, I do."

He concedes. "Yes, you do. Good luck, Angelica. I'm sure Sophie will take good care of you."

When Simon's wide door clicks shut, Angelica's vision tunnels. She's at a desk. A desk for work. Work that she has no idea how to do. What the hell is she doing here?

"I feel like I should call you Sleeping Beauty," Sophia says, moving things around to make room. She seems completely oblivious to Angelica's existential crisis. "I love that place as much as anyone, but why didn't you leave if you were getting sick?"

Why does everyone want to make her talk about herself? Conversations revolve around the client, only and always, though she guesses she better broaden her horizons. "I'd never been in one before. I wanted to prove I could do it."

"Do what?"

"Withstand."

A boisterous laugh finds its way out of Sophia's mouth. "You know, most people think it's relaxing."

"That medieval torture?"

"It's more like pore cleansing." She caresses her smooth, flawless face. "Speaking of which, what happened to your cheek, if you don't mind me asking?"

*I mind.*

Angelica reminds herself to play nice. "I hit a wall. And not in that 'I'm secretly being abused by my husband' kind of way, I actually hit a wall."

Sophia blinks at her as if she's just said something bad.

Oh no.

Jesus, she's like Simon. Her words are trash words. Awkward, idiot, make-you-uncomfortable trash words.

To her credit, Sophia takes it in stride. Little snowflakes of torn paper are whisked into the nearby trash, and she pulls a second chair flush to her own like two squashed, gray, blasé twins, patting it for Angelica to take a seat. Sophia's workstation is a private corner where her desk makes an L shape, her back to a window showing the morning sunlight. There's a sunscreen down, drawing a black film over the outside world, and Angelica can only assume it's for the glare.

Tucking her skirt under her rump, she sits as daintily as she can. "So, what do we do now?"

Sophia pulls open a lower drawer with an ancient rumble, taking out a laptop that's bulky enough to be from the nineties. Setting it down doesn't come with a clatter, but a chonky *thunk* that's too heavy to echo. Angelica can only gape. For a woman used to thumb-pecking her phone and fiddling with Simon's sleek, modern, hyper-thin machine, this thing is a monstrosity. At least it has a full calculator keypad instead of a row of numbers that trails across the top of the keyboard.

"And this is…?" Angelica asks.

"Agatha."

She frowns. "It looks more like a Bubba to me."

Sophia presses a button to turn it on, and Windows 95 loads. "Bubba implies a certain level of strength. Agatha is frail, older than God, and should really be either retired or dead." She gapes suddenly, whipping to Angelica. "You don't know anyone named Agatha, do you?"

She shakes her head, and Sophia places a hand on her heart with a relieved huff. Pulling out milky white, unlined paper, she hands Angelica a few scribbled-on sheets, the letters octopussing their way across the page.

"Data entry," Sophia states. "Take Simon's notes, decipher them, and type them in."

"Into Agatha? Isn't Alzheimer's one of her upcoming problems?"

"No doubt, but this is just to make sure you can both type and read his finger seizures. He handwrites a lot of his math, so if you can't read his alien language, we might not have a fit."

That rat bastard. Simon told her data entry, but she'd assumed random customer forms and legibility. He could have at least written her a note so she could practice or something.

She glares at his door.

It is nice that he writes out math by hand like her, though. They're starting to pile up things they have in common. The idea makes her feel uncomfortably gooey.

"Just get me started. What letter is this?" Angelica points down to the first erratic symbol on the page.

It's not without pity Sophia says, "That would be an A."

———

"How's Agatha treating you?"

Angelica startles. Simon stands next to Sophia's desk with his hands in his pockets and his perma-frown on his face.

"She only blue-screen-of-deathed once."

Sophia, working kitty-corner with her back to Angelica, snorts in amusement. "Give her time."

Angelica leans back a little, blinking her hazy eyes. Staring at Simon's notes is blinding, but she's getting the hang of it. Enough to make assumptions anyway. If something says ch—ce, she can use context clues to fill in the blanks. It's usually "chance," which is a word Simon shakes like salt across his pages, as if he's not sure of anything except his numbers. "There's a chance that we could…" "Chances are that it…" "If we took a chance…" all paired with math and graphs and what Sophia called trend lines. She'd looked at Angelica weird when she'd asked what they were, as if she should have already known, and it made Angelica's face burn hot.

"What time is it?" Angelica asks the room at large, rubbing her eyes.

"Ten," Sophia chimes in, spinning around. "Time to start on turning those notes into tables. Let's see if Excel won't crash this stupid thing." She wheels closer and tugs Agatha over, clicking around with dull tapping sounds.

Spreadsheets. Angelica can do spreadsheets. Simon warned her about this, and she spent the better part of Tuesday through Thursday watching every online tutorial she could. Simon even let her practice on his laptop at night. This one's in the bag.

"Stay until lunch today," Simon says. "We'll bring something in, hang around as a team, and see how it goes. If Sophie likes you, you can start on Monday."

A lick of jealousy whips its way up Angelica's backbone. She raises an eyebrow at the woman who's watching the program load.

"Oh, I'm sure we'll get along fine," Sophia says. "You know me. I'm easygoing."

"Is this where you say, 'otherwise I wouldn't put up with your crap, Simon'?" he asks with a slight pull to his lips that makes Angelica's random jealousy burn brighter.

"I put up with you for the paycheck, but I work hard because you're a good boss."

Simon's smile grows wider, and Sophia's to match. Is there an office romance here? Why does Angelica even care? She doesn't. Not at all. Nope. Well, maybe. Yup. Godfuckingdamnit.

Simon's hand comes to rest on Angelica's head again, giving her unacceptable tingles. "I'll see you in a bit." Breezing by in his natural habitat, he winds through the gray jungle of cubicles into the wild office yonder.

Sophia's smile is sly. "What's going on with you two?" Angelica's back goes ramrod straight.

"We're friends."

"Yeah, no, Simon only has one friend. How did you guys meet?"

She and Simon discussed this. What she can say. What she can't say. Who she can say it to. "We met in a bar. I was kind of stuck with nowhere to live, and he's letting me stay in his guest room."

Agatha blue screens again.

Sophia leans in and whispers, "Be careful who you tell that to. A lot of people want to get close to Simon…and *work under him* if you get my meaning. The cats will come at you with their claws out if they think you guys are dating."

"We're not dating," Angelica squeaks, but then she double takes. "Wait. People want to be with Simon?"

"Of course," Sophia says, absently starting up Agatha as if she's used to this insolent behavior. "He's in a position of power, and that alone inspires wannabe groupies. I think they like how stern he looks all the time. He brings out all their boss fantasies."

"Do you have a boss fantasy?" It's out of Angelica's mouth without her permission, and she bites the inside of her cheek.

"God no. That wouldn't be a good mix. Besides, I've got to focus on my daughter right now. She's four and she's a handful."

Angelica hasn't seen a kid since she was one. As if through some psychic connection, Sophia turns and rummages through her purse, a simple, non-flashy thing, and brings out her phone. After a few taps, she turns it in Angelica's direction with a grin. "This is Ginger."

That's a name for a cat.

Angelica takes the proffered phone and scrolls through a few pictures. She's…adorable. Her hair isn't dark brown like Sophia's, it's lighter, more like chestnut than chocolate. It's swept up in a wispy ponytail at the crown of her head that feathers out at the top, wrapped in a hair tie that sports little kittens. Her face is pudgy and sweet, but you can tell she's mixed race. Her eyes are doe round, and they sparkle a stunning green.

"She's gorgeous," Angelica admits. "She must have her dad's eyes."

Sophia pulls the phone back with the most loving smile Angelica has ever seen. She stares at the picture of her little one and pets the screen's glassy surface, flicking through a few other photos. "She does."

"Is he hot? Do you have any pictures of him?"

Sophia's face falls a little. "No. We're not together. I did something stupid and—boom—earned myself a Ginger. I wouldn't change it for the world, though."

Watching Sophia talk makes Angelica wonder about her own mother. She never really spares her much thought. She died giving birth and that was that, but if she hadn't, would she have loved Angelica like this?

An unknown feeling rolls through her stomach.

Agatha fully booted and Excel loaded, Sophia pushes the decrepit thing back in Angelica's direction. "I like you," she says. "You might be a little old for an intern, but I get being down on your luck. You gotta take what you can get, sometimes." She pats Simon's stupid pages again. "Get through this, and you're as good as on the team. Us ladies have got to stick together."

As a rule, Angelica generally doesn't like women. They're competition at best, conniving cunts at the worst. But Sophia seems...nice. Maybe her fangs will come out later, but for now, Angelica will give her the benefit of the doubt.

She grabs the computer, clicks cell A-1, and gets to work.

———

"We've been getting lunch a lot lately, eh?" Nando says, picking through the catering bag. "If you're trying to impress me, you should try doing something grander."

Simon's mouth becomes a flat line as he looks at his friend. *If you're gonna be a brat about it, maybe you shouldn't come.* Not that Simon would say it out loud.

Sophia brings Angelica in, the woman's sight set ever on Nando even though his back is to her as he rummages. Angelica's gaze is glued to the floor as she edges in, looking out of place in his sterile work bubble.

"There it is." Nando finds his food on the bottom and brings it up, not bothering to empty the bag for the rest of the team. Instead, he plunks down across from Simon, nestles in, and puts his feet up on his desk again. Simon's frown pulls deeper. He really does hate that.

Sophia, however, seems to be charmed, the side of her mouth ticking up as she does the right thing and brings out the contents for all. Rather than sitting like an asshole behind his desk, Simon comes over to his mini-conference table with everyone else. Without thinking about it, his date-training kicks in, and he pulls the chair out for Angelica in a smooth slide.

"Have a seat?" he offers in a Noah-deep purr before blanching. Angelica's face turns as pink as petals, and she basically tumbles down as if she'd lost her footing. Sophia and Nando are staring at him hard, and he clears his throat. "What did you get?" he tosses in as casually as possible.

"Oh, I don't normally eat lunch," she says, fidgety.

Huh? That's not meal plan. Sadie… Angelica…would go on about Starvation Mode and his body hoarding calories to congeal into fat unless he grazed like a goddamn animal. She's painfully meticulous about food, so why would she…?

Nerves. She's nervous. He's an idiot; one look would have said as much.

Sophia unwraps a generous steak and cheese. It's ooey-gooey provolone strings out in long lines when she takes a bite, and her moan is nothing but endearing. "This is so good." She waves at her mouth as if it's too hot. "Simon. Sit."

Oh. Right.

Tucking his tie back, he sits next to Angelica, hyperaware of her. Maybe it's because he's pulling out something that's absolutely fried and carb heavy, but it's more likely because she's existing in his space. This is more nerve-wracking than home, and since her leg bounces like an NBA basketball, he's inclined to think she agrees.

"So, who are you?" Nando asks, looking curious in an off-putting way. His smirk says he likes her. Of course he does. She's beautiful, and that's all it takes to be his type.

All of a sudden, Simon wants to punch him.

"I'm Angelica. I'm here for a working interview. I kind of suck at this, but I'm praying they give me the job anyway. I promise I'm not a moron or anything."

Simon's head twitches in her direction, and she shrinks.

Having mercy, Sophia slides a bottle of water over. "Don't worry about her, she's just feeling a little awkward in an office environment."

Awkward? Her? She's the overconfident one! She should be ranting about crotches and erections and French kissing—specifically while randomly touching him in places that make him tingle. Who is this person, and what has she done with his loudmouth, bossy consultant?

Nando lets out a salacious hum that sets Simon's teeth on edge. "Well, if you need anyone to walk you around the floor, I offer my services."

All three of them turn to face the man. He simply tucks a fry into his mouth and happily holds their stares.

"Be nice," Sophia scolds, a little sharper than she usually scolds Simon.

"I am being nice," Nando says. He looks at Angelica with a conspiratorial wink. "Assuming you've gotten the job, of course. But if you've made it to lunch, chances are Simi will take you in. Stay on your toes if you don't want to get eaten alive by the office hoard when they find out you 'kind of suck at this,' though, eh? Wouldn't want to make him look bad. He already makes enough poor business decisions."

Angelica flicks her eyes in Simon's direction, and he offers a mild shrug. Nando treats everyone like this. He's the prick-ish gift that keeps on giving.

Her gaze hardens and snaps back in Nando's direction. "Actually, I think he makes very good decisions. Looking at his notes today, I thought they were really put together and insightful. I feel like I learned a lot."

If Simon could glow, he would.

"Ah. An ass-kisser, eh?" Nando says, making Simon's protective bone tickle again. Still, if he says anything, Nando will just make it worse.

A tightness appears on Angelica's face that Simon has never seen before. A sort of set to her jaw. "If I was an ass-kisser, I'd get your job instead of an intern's."

The room goes silent, and Angelica only ticks her chin higher.

*There she is. Welcome to the table, Miss Hart.*

Nando's face goes from self-amused to a cold, calculating stare. This isn't going to go well. "Angelica, hmm? I think Simon told me about you. I guess the consulting business must be slow nowadays for you to be getting a job here. Was he your only client?"

"Nando," Simon warns.

"No, I'm seriously asking. If she was any good at her job, I'd imagine she'd keep it."

"I was good at it," Angelica says, her head still held high. "I was in high demand and lots of people requested me. I had several clients that came back time and again. The job might have been fun at first, but it gets old, and I got tired. You know what that's like. That's what the old man bags under your eyes say, anyway. Do you hate your job too? Maybe you should quit and be an intern, like me. If you could get the job, that is."

Sophia chokes on her food, but Simon can't hide his grin. Some deep dark part of him is enthralled. Entranced. Turned on, even.

*Yes. Put him in his place. I've been wanting to do that for years.*

"Simi, you're not seriously going to hire her, are you?"

*Oh, I definitely am.*

"She passed all the tests we set up for her, and based on the last two minutes, I'd also say she'll be able to hold her own against the office horde."

Nando's scowl is chiseled. "This is a mistake. Let it be known that I think this is going to go badly." He gathers up his things, tossing his sandwich back into its container where it cascades apart. "Count me out for lunch next time. And prepare to get your ass handed to you over beers this Sunday."

Simon grimaces, he can't help it. A Nando on a rampage is one he prefers to avoid. He expects it when the heavy door slams shut, but still groans when it happens. That thing's hinges have seen better days.

Angelica stands up and brushes off her skirt. "He's right, this was a mistake."

"No," Sophia murmurs. "It was brilliant."

Both Simon and Angelica look in her direction.

"He thinks too much of himself. He's rude and he's selfish. Maybe it would do him good to have someone knock him down a peg."

God knows Simon hasn't been able to. Not when they met in college, and not now. But watching that little show made his younger self burn. The part of him that would gladly get into fights, scrape matches into glowing ribbons and flick them into trash cans. The angry kid whose parents never paid attention unless he caused trouble. The one whose spirit they tried to quash with tutors and grooming and salaries that weren't worth giving up. He morphed from angst to cowardice, a man so afraid of losing his golden life he became a loser.

"Come on," Simon says. "I'll walk you out. You can go home for the day."

There is a lilting tone to Sophia's voice. "Oooh that's right, you two live together." He can basically hear the smirk emoji in her words.

"Hush," he says. "And don't spread that around."

Hand to her heart, Sophia confirms, "I would never." Simon can only pray. Lawrence would never let him hear the end of it.

Opening the door for her, Angelica ducks through, a defeated look on her face. "I screwed this all up."

Moving her along, Simon nods slightly at Harrison—who still owes him a goddamned report, by the way—before turning his attention back to his new intern. "If Sophia can say it was a good thing, it definitely was."

"Why?"

He leans closer as they walk, dropping his voice. "Didn't you catch it?"

"Catch what?"

"The vibes," he says. "I swear, ever since you taught me that word, it's all I see when I look at them."

"That man wouldn't vibe with anything but a mirror."

He can't help his snicker, and it draws Maryann's attention. She waves at him, and he nods back. She owes him work too.

"I agree with you, but Sophia? She seems to…" He lets his words drift off.

"May God have mercy on her soul. That's a recipe for disaster."

"You might be right." He presses the button for the elevator. "But he's my friend. I'd like to see him happy. I'd like to see both of them happy."

"How can you be friends with that?" She fakes a shudder.

"That…is a very good question." The empty elevator dings open, and he places a hand on the small of her back to lead her inside. Damnit. That's another date move. This is most certainly not a date. If it were, though…

"I liked that doctor guy better," she says.

"Tyler? Yeah, he's a good person. I forgot how funny he is."

"If he stops touching your penis, maybe you can be friends again."

About four office faces snap in their direction before the elevator doors slip shut. Angelica doesn't seem to notice, but Simon has to hide his face in his hands.

"Hang out with him," she says. "If you're not going out on dates, you might as well be making better friends."

"Are you counting yourself in that equation?" he mutters through his fingers.

"Maybe. I'd hang out with that guy. He's gay, so he won't come on to me. Did you see how that Nando asshole was looking me up and down?"

Yes, he most certainly did. It boils him.

"I don't put up with shit like that unless it comes with a paycheck." She pauses. "Fuck, this does come with a paycheck."

The doors slide open, and he holds the panel back, letting her scoot out in front of him. "No, we have rules in place for that. On Monday, you're going to have to do a ton of HR training. Sexual harassment isn't an allowable thing."

"Tell that to your friend."

He absolutely should. "See you at home?"

"Maybe. I might go to see The Big Bad Guy."

His heart stops and he stumbles out of the elevator, only just avoiding getting his foot pinched. "You're doing what?"

She strides away, heels clacking on the marbled floor. "If I'm getting the job and can start paying you back, I don't see a reason to put it off any longer."

"Simple, I'm not there with you." Trailing after her, he runs a hand through his hair, tugging at the roots. This woman is going to kill him. "Go this weekend. I'll come. I told you, you don't have to do this alone."

"And I told you, I'm only letting you get so involved. These are not safe people, Simon, and there is no reason for them to know any more about you than they already do. You want another black eye?"

"I can take it," he says with more gusto than he feels. His ribs still ache and are an unfortunate shade of purple, yellow, and green.

"Well, I can't." She wheels on him, one hand on her hip, the other gesturing in staccato jabs. "Do you know how I felt watching them hurt you? It was like I could hear parts of you breaking. Didn't you hear me scream? I was terrified. I thought they might kill you. No one has ever done anything like that for me before and I couldn't bear it if —" Her words falter, and her lips pinch shut.

"Hey." Instinct makes him reach out and run his hand over her hair again. Her eyes are wet, and it sparks something in his soul. Some need to soothe her. Coddle her. It doesn't help that she always looks so vibey every time he does it. He slides his fingers through her softness, all the way down to the slight curls she weaved into the bottom.

"Why do you do that?" she asks, not shooing him away.

*Because I want to do so much more.*

"You'll get mad if I tell you."

This time she does shrug him off. People mill around the building's lobby, but Simon barely takes them in. This moment is filled with just two people. Him and her. The rest can fade into mist.

"That doesn't sound promising," she gripes.

He puts his hands in his pockets and rocks on the balls of his feet. "When I was young, I had this adopted dog."

"I already hate where this story is going."

Simon chuckles. "She was skittish. She'd only really come out to eat, so we assumed she wasn't treated well by her previous owners. She wouldn't let anyone close. I started by putting her food near me and just letting her get used to my existence. Then, I would feed her treats from my hand. Then, she finally let me pat her head."

"So, I'm a dog in this scenario."

He shakes his head, a smile on his face. "I realized that it made both of us feel better. It made us trust each other. I started to trust that she wouldn't bite me, and she started to trust that I wouldn't hurt her." Looking at those heavy-lashed, ice-blue eyes and still fascinated by her freckles, he says, "I'm not going to hurt you, Angelica. So please don't hurt me either."

Looking to the side, she blinks back the vestiges of tears. "That's why I'm trying to keep you away."

"You think I won't be hurt if you come home beat up and I could have been there to stop it? Or worse, what if you never come home at all?" He hasn't let himself think about it, but the sudden reality of it falls on him like a heavy curtain. If this goes wrong, he might never see her again. His chest tightens into a painful knot.

"This is something I have to do on my own," she says, walking backward in her new professional wear. She looks just as good as she does dressed up for all the fancy places she's taken him to.

Is he stupid? Is he a fool to be so invested? How could a month with a stranger matter so much?

It's not just because he was lonely. It's just because of her. His special someone. His angel. Covered in clouds that shroud her wings, but something that gives him hope, nonetheless.

"Not tonight. Please. Let's think this through together. I care about you," he says for the second time, this one more heart-aching than the last. "I really do."

"I know," she says with a shy smile.

"And you care about me too, right?"

God help him, she lets out a soft giggle that has him mooning. Her backward footsteps don't stop, and he's overcome by the feeling that she is his Cinderella, running away before the ball is over. He wants to chase. He wants to clasp her hand in his and walk her home. He wants to stay there with her. He wants to hear more of her sad stories and share his own. He wants to hold her...and so, so much more.

Instead, he stays put and hears her say, "I'll see you tonight."

"Promise?"

She nods. "I promise."

———

I ate already. You should get your own dinner or eat what I have in the fridge. I'm going to the gym.

Simon's lungs fill with way too much air, stretching his painful ribs before he shoves a sharp breath out through his nose. Angelica's text makes his palms sweat. She said she wouldn't do anything rash until they talked, but can he trust her? As petty as it sounds, she is known to lie.

What time will you be back?

I have spin then hot yoga. Two hours? Be back around ten?

How anyone could bear two hours at the gym is beyond him. Just thinking of it makes his biceps ache with a trauma response. A "please never do that to me again" whine.

I don't know whether to admire you or stage an intervention.

Just appreciate that I look hot.

Well, that's putting it mildly. Should he text that? Is that too forward? She didn't like it when Nando hit on her; would he be put in the same lecherous boat?

He sighs again, no idea how, when, or if to try to move their relationship forward. She needs a friend. He can be a friend. But, damnit, he doesn't want to *be* a friend.

Fine. I appreciate it.

There. Not cringeworthy. Maybe? What would Satine have thought? Bethany? Jessika? Katie?

God, why can't he remember the other names?

He runs his hands through his hair again, ignoring the fact that she hasn't texted him back while simultaneously obsessing over it. The evening is still bright at seven o'clock, summer edging ever closer, and the streets are miserable with people as he walks home. Looking down, he realizes his shoes are in need of a polish. The ground is in need of a sweeping. The concrete is in need of patching. The man in the brown beanie is panhandling for money.

Wait.

"Ciel?" Simon asks, stopping short and getting bumped into by an irate woman behind him. He shrugs his apologies, twinging his shoulder, and looks down again to see…a stranger staring up at him.

The man points at himself, completely white-haired with deeply lined, clear blue eyes. "Me? I'm Joe. How do you know Ciel?"

Simon points too. "That's his hat."

"Until I won it off him." Joe's grin is smarmy, but he sounds like a preacher, all sonorous tones, clear diction, and wide vowels. "Now it's mine. Spare a dollar?"

Sliding his wallet from his back pocket, Simon drops two twenties into a small bag of sorts. "Is he anywhere around here? I owe him a thank you." If not for him, Angelica would have been in that alleyway all alone. Who knows what could have happened then?

Greedy fingers pluck up Simon's forty dollars. Joe looks left and right before shoving the money into his interior coat pocket, leaving only single dollars in his hat. Peeking up at Simon, he cocks his head a little, his shoulders pulsing up and down. "Trick of the trade. If people saw me sporting twenties, I wouldn't see another cent for the rest of the night."

"Oh. Sorry, I don't have smaller bills."

A light chuckle works his way out of the man. "Are you apologizing for giving me money?" In hindsight that is kind of stupid. "But no, I haven't seen Ciel. He's still pissed at me for winning." The man adjusts his beanie with no small amount of smugness. Simon vows to buy Ciel a new hat.

"Do you know where I might find him?"

"Dunno. He hasn't been to the shelter the past few days." He shrugs. "Nights have been mild, though, so he's probably doing all right."

Running his hand through his hair again, and again, likely ruining it, Simon considers. Worrying about whether Angelica is telling the truth or not is going to drive him crazy. He doesn't want to be alone right now. "Do you want me to take you to dinner? I'll throw in an extra twenty for what you won't make from spending time out here."

The guy scoffs.

"Okay, forty," Simon says.

This time, he sputters.

"Sixty, but that's my final offer, because that's all the cash I've got."

There is a long, awkward moment where all Mr. Panhandler does is stare at him. "You're weird."

He may have heard that before.

The old man narrows his eyes. "You're not a serial killer or anything, are you?"

Though he loves reading books about them, he says, "No, I'm not. And the place I go is close by and public. I took Ciel there too."

"They let in people like me?"

Simon ticks up his eyebrows with a smirk. "When I make them."

That earns him another laugh. Like the tin man with rusted joints, Joe stands up with all manner of cracks, pops, and grunts, slinging a heavy-looking backpack over his shoulders. "Never get old, my friend," he says through his teeth.

Leaning down, Simon picks up the little sack Joe was gathering money in and hands it over, earning himself a Southern-sounding, "Much obliged."

"You from below the Mason-Dixon Line?" Simon asks, guiding the man along at a slow enough gait that he can keep up, yet speedy enough so as to not irritate the other commuters.

"I'm from all over. I was army, so I went anywhere they sent me."

"Ciel's a veteran too."

"Yeah, but he's Marines, the prick."

"Sorry, I should know the difference, but I don't really."

"They have harder basic training and they never let you forget it. They're usually first on the ground when things go sideways too. He holds it over my head, but I know he hated it. Me? I liked it. But you either move up, age out, or get hurt. I was in for nineteen years before my back went. Nineteen. You get retirement benefits if you hit twenty or more. I was so close, it hurt. Literally and figuratively. I imagine God just wanted to give me a good kick in the teeth for all the trouble I caused."

"Why did you go into the service?"

"Meh. I tried college first. Community college, you know, nothing fancy. Joined up at twenty-two when I realized an English degree was gonna get me jack for a job. At least I know how to decipher poetry."

"You're one up on me. I only read fiction. Horrors, mostly."

"Believe me, I'll take it where I can get it. I've got all of two books in my backpack. One is on self-actualization and the other is a trashy, smutty romance. If my johnson still worked, I might like it better."

Simon chokes on his spit.

"Now it's just a reminder of a time long since passed." Joe looks wistful, as if remembering something from once upon a time.

Looking to recover from his red cheeks, Simon says, "If you want to stop by my house, I can give you some spare books."

"Nope." Joe pops his P. "You might be a serial killer."

"I swear, I'm not."

"That's just what a serial killer would say."

This is becoming a pattern. Ciel accused him of being a counterfeiter, a suicide risk, and now he might be a murderer? What the hell happens to these people to make them so suspicious?

They come up on the pub with its familiar green awning, and Simon holds open the door for his new friend. It's much warmer in here, and though the bartender tosses him a look and rolls his eyes, he doesn't say anything.

"Can I buy you a drink?" Simon asks.

Palm flat, Joe holds up his hand. "Nah. I need to stay sober or they won't let me keep my bed at the shelter. Was hard enough to get them to let me in in the first place. I'll take some food though."

"I'll even send you back with leftovers, how's that?"

That palm claps Simon off the back hard enough to make him grunt. He needs to heal up before anyone else wallops him, please and thank you.

Sitting down, Simon signals the waitress. She goes as far as to curl her lip at Joe, but if he sees it, he doesn't react. Simon sees it though. He's going to cut this woman's tip right in half.

"How many people are at the shelter?" Simon asks. "Maybe we can get enough food for all of them."

Joe waves his hand absently. "Nah. There's forty of us on a good night. They squeeze in fifty on a bad one. That's occupancy limit though. After that, we're a fire hazard or something."

"Do you have anyplace else to stay?"

"In the summer, a lot of us tend to sleep under the stars if it's not raining, as long as we can find a place where the police aren't being asses."

"Why sleep outside?"

"Short answer? We stink. You try smelling rosy fresh when you get a bathroom sink wash-up every few days in the swelter of city summer."

The waitress comes over with waters and a scowl that looks like they stepped on her babies. Forget half, Simon's cutting her tip into a quarter. Not a quarter of the standard amount, literally twenty-five cents.

Her face sounds stuffed with bubble gum. "What can I get you?"

"Bacon cheeseburger for me," Simon says, "with sweet potato fries. Joe?"

Joe doesn't even pick up the menu. "Same. Thank you. And about four more waters, please." The waitress doesn't even bother nodding. Never mind. Her tip is zero.

Simon plays with his fingers, picking some dirt out from beneath the nails. "This might be a landmine, but can't some of you get jobs? Even you. If you wanted one, I could get you a job." If he could do it for Angelica, why not more people? They need a slew of entry-level bodies.

Joe snorts. "Never mind my age; looking at you, I'm going to guess your office is out of my league. Besides, I know you mean well, but you assume none of us have tried. Sure, a lot of us bottomed out and are resigned to staying there, but some of us tried to battle back uphill too. The cards are stacked against us. Number one, I have no clothes. What you see is what I got. Number two, I have no address for all the application forms. They don't let you use shelters. Number three, I don't have a computer to fill out the online job applications. Even if I use the library, what the hell am I supposed to do if I get an interview? Maybe you'd hire me—and, trust me, it's strange that you even offered —but I'd bet my new hat that no one else would be so generous. Even if you dressed me up and scrubbed me down, what do I have to give?"

"I'm betting a lot," Simon says, and he means it. People like Joe have perspective. Worldly wisdom. Tenacity. Grit. Skills can be learned, but perseverance is unteachable.

Simon's whole brain lights up, wires firing on all coils.

That's it. That's his merger. That's the company in his portfolio of potentials. That's how he builds something worthwhile that benefits the company. It's quick, slick, easy, and ripe for the taking. All he has to do is make one phone call. One, and his uncle will finally see his worth. The pressure will be off. The battle will be won.

This is his chance.

"Joe…you just gave me a fantastic idea."

The only bad part is, Nando is going to hate it.

# closing a chapter

. . .

"THAT'S A PERFECT IDEA," Angelica says, squeegeeing her hair in a towel of white fluff, another wrapped around her wet body.

Simon sits on the couch with one leg strewn over the other, his ankle tapping to a silent tune. It shakes his entire lower body as he plays with his lip, gaze far away but with that same glint he gets when he talks about math. "You think so?"

"I just spent half the day squinting at your notes until my eyes bled. Everything I read was dry and boring—"

"You said you learned a lot."

"I learned that your job is tedious as shit. And everything was so wishy-washy. There was no 'we will do this,' it was all 'could we possibly somehow maybe hopefully someday do this?'"

He grunts, his eyebrows pulling low and crinkling the bridge of his nose. "All acquisitions are like that. You make educated guesses, and then you pray."

"Don't get defensive." She pulls the towel from her hair and uses it to whip-crack him in the leg before coming to rest on the arm of his couch. He eyes the towel clenched against her bosom before scooting away.

Angelica continues, "All I'm saying is that it lacked excitement.

Passion. But look at you now, you're like a nerd in a gaming store with a thousand dollars smashed in his sweaty fist."

He grins, and it's such a dazzling thing Angelica has to look away lest she go blind. Instead, she leans left and plops down in the cranny between him and the arm rest, her towel likely hiking up a tad too far and showing too much thigh, but whatever. Nakedness is half of Angelica's life. Plus, she just worked these bitches into trembling, so they deserve their chance in the sun. Simon's neon red face says otherwise though.

Mind drifting back in time, all Angelica can hear is his baritone saying, "If you want me, then earn me." Her face ignites as well. She tucks her towel under her ass and moves to her chair, careful to keep her legs crossed and not flash him her lady bits. "Look, I'm just saying you care about it this time, so ignore the 'ifs' and just make it happen."

He seems to snap out of a daydream after staring at her bare calves. "Huh? Make what happen?"

She ticks up an eyebrow. "The merger?"

His back bows as he uncrosses his legs and rests his elbows on his knees. "I'm not sure I can. Nando will hate this—which might be a small part of why I like it—but he'll try to squash this idea like a bug. He always sees the flaws in my plans and rubs my nose in them."

"I thought you were equals. Is he the one who makes the decisions?"

He sinks back, weaving his arms together like ivy vines. "No, that's my Uncle Lawrence."

"Then why does it matter what Asshole says?"

"He's my sounding board. I show him all my ideas first. If I can't convince him, how will I convince my uncle?"

"Aren't you two vying for the same spot? Did it ever occur to you that he just might be making you doubt yourself on purpose so he could get ahead of you?"

Simon's jaw ticks to the side. "He wouldn't do that."

"Why the hell not?"

"Because he's my friend." He emphasizes the last word a little too hard.

"Is he though? He's kind of a dick to you. I saw him for all of five minutes and I wanted to punch him on your behalf. Putting him in his place was the highlight of my day."

That brings a sly smile to Simon's face. "If I were English, I'd say you were bloody brilliant."

"Well, then do the accent and say it again. I have a thing for accents."

He sulks, pouting slightly as holds himself tighter. Is he grumpy he doesn't have an accent? God, why is he so cute? She just wants to jump on him and squish his huge face until he either bursts into laughter or she does. And the fact she has that urge makes her want to cover herself in honey up to her neck until the bees buzz in.

"Anyway, enough about me." He clears his throat. "Let's talk about your situation. What's the plan?"

"Simple. Go. Bring money. Give money. Leave. Die years from now instead of months."

If unimpressed stares could be registered on a thermometer, Simon's is somewhere around one hundred degrees. Celsius. "It can't be that simple. You need leverage to make sure they won't try to extort you for more."

She *pffts*. "I told you, the Big Bad made a promise."

"Now who's naïve?"

Angelica's eyes narrow to slits. Their roles seem to have reversed today with her being the bottom, and that's not how she likes it. Gripping her lower towel in a twisted whorl, she launches up and exits the conversation. Too bad for her, he follows, bumbling on his own two feet. It's his own fault for being enormous everywhere.

"Look, just let me come with you. I can offer some protection."

"With what? You think your good looks are going to get us off easy?"

He doesn't pick up the sarcasm, halting and asking, "You think I have good looks?"

"Of course you do, you idiot. Women were literally paying money for you."

He scowls at the reference to their mutual landmine.

"It doesn't matter," she says. "I already told you no. Stop asking."

She slams her door in his stupid face. Whipping off her towel, she chucks it to the side, nakedly rummaging through her drawers for anything to jam on her body, more focused on the desire to jam her finger into this man's eye. "There's no way I'm bringing you. You're a liability. They take one step toward you, and they've got me over a fire. They promised me out, no one ever said a goddamned thing about you."

He bats at her door. "I can hold my own."

She slings on an oversize T-shirt—one of Simon's—and stomps out, finding him leaning against the wall with his hands in his hair, like always. "And what if they have more clubs? Or knives? Or guns? You ever think of that?"

He hadn't. It's clear all over his face.

She shoves her way past him. "Thought not."

He's following her again, yapping about "not being alone" and "being smart" and "thinking it through," but when he dares utter the words, "What would Bee say?" she whirls on him.

"Don't you fucking dare." She points her finger right at his nose. "Don't you turn that on me."

But he's uncowed. He only grabs her hand and lowers it, leaning into her space. "You didn't answer my question."

Angelica tries to pull back, but he holds her tight.

He fills her space with furious words. "Would a woman who took a teenage girl from a bad situation want to throw her into another one without thinking it through? Would a woman who's only wish in life was to keep you safe want you in danger? Would a woman who loved you want to see you get hurt? Or killed? Or worse?" With every sentence, his voice gets higher, until he's pleading with her. "Angelica, if these are bad people, you can't trust them. You should just let me deliver the money for you."

Her heart drops into her stomach, her anger fleeing. Simon against Damion with no one in his corner? Over her dead body. "Never."

She tries to pull away again, but he holds her tight. "Please, if they hurt you—"

"They're not going to."

"You can't know that!"

"You're being so stupid right now."

"And you're being a stubborn little *brat.*"

Out of breath, they sit there in the moment. Angelica's chest heaves as her thoughts go back to Bee and how she'd tease her about the same thing when she was young. Her bullheadedness. Her habit of digging her heels in, immovable and angry. The memory is soft, even with its hard edges. It makes her remember Bee's smile when she would say it, her expression filled with a love Angelica always wanted for herself. She remembers the green places and sitting under the trees, watching the sunlight filter through the pine needles as the birds twittered in and out of them. It was their safe space. Their haven. A place where no one could touch them. That's where their mother-daughter relationship bloomed. Even once they'd moved on, Bee would kiss her on the cheek every night, telling her to be safe. Be flexible. Be smart.

She's not being smart, and she knows it.

She snaps to attention when Simon's hand lifts, plucking her necklace up and running his thumb over it. He stares with intensity as he studies its uninspiring, chipped green surface. Costume jewelry. Having someone like him look at a cheap piece like this makes a well of insecurity open up in her. She doesn't belong in his world. His office. His life.

Bringing her pendant up higher, Simon leans close. His forehead nearly brushes hers as he presses his full lips against it in a kiss one would give a rosary cross while kneeling in a stained-glass church. "Bee, please make her understand."

Angelica's eyes mist, clouding Simon as he lowers her most precious treasure. Reverently, he sets it back down, letting it slip between her clothed breasts before resting a gentle palm against her face. He swipes beneath her eye, wiping away a tear she didn't know had fallen.

"Don't shut down," he tells her. "And don't run away from me. I negotiate for a living. I have something to offer here." His hand runs through her hair again, warm and sweet, so close he could take her lips in a moment. His eyes glisten with a wetness of their own. "Talk with me. Hear what I have to say. I told you that you're not alone."

She shakes her head, just a tick back and forth, even as her resolve crumbles.

"Come on, angel," he whispers. "Trust me."

She cants closer. She wants to wind around him like a tangle of red string, wrapping around all his nooks and crannies. He's so soft on her. He's always been soft on her. But now he's soft *to* her.

*Earn me*, he had said. For the first time, she wonders what that looks like.

She pulls back, and this time he lets her go. Watching her own toes, she backs up a step, and then another, putting a safety barrier of air between them before she does something she can't take back.

"Fine. I'll hear you out. No promises, not for anything, but I'll at least listen."

"Okay."

"But only with ice cream."

His eyes go wide for a short second before he cracks a grin. "Seriously? Miss Meal Plan is going to have ice cream?"

She scrubs her eyes and latches her hands together behind her back. "Last meal and all."

"Don't joke about that."

Breaking the tension, she dashes away, ducking into the lower part of the refrigerator to open the freezer drawer. As she bends, Simon lets out a sharp, high-pitched squawk that makes her startle, squeaking as her body jumps.

"Jesus, Simon, what the hell was that?" Rummaging, she turns over her shoulder to find Simon looking anywhere but her, his face on fire.

"Didn't you forget something?" he asks.

She shrugs as her fingertips pass over frostbitten, likely million-year-old things. "What?"

He buries his face in his hands. "Underwear."

And Angelica stands up quick, baffing the back of her skull off the refrigerator door handle. Her hands fly to her ass. Oh, shit, she absolutely did. He must have gotten a full-moon view…and who knows what else?

It's Angelica's turn to put her face in her hands.

---

Nichol Goldstein

*Ping.*

The text takes Simon by surprise, and he slides a snarky bookmark into his latest horror novel, *Dear John*, a story about someone who's been kidnapped and thrown in a well with two other dying men. If he can't get them out, they're all doomed. Simon huffs. He was just at a good part.

He considers ignoring the message, but it pings again. And again. And again.

> Yo, Pyro.
>
> Yo.
>
> Yoyoyoyoiyoyoyoyirhdj

Why is Dr. Tyler Knight, his erstwhile/current friend, slipping into his DMs. Is he drunk?

> The doctor is in the houuuuse letting off some steeeeeam. Do you ever go clubbing?

Yeah, he's drunk.

> I'm wound too tight for that.

> Shame. How's Trouble?

> You mean Angelica?

> How many other Troubles you got? How's her spy boo-boo?

> Healing.

> How's your cracked ribs?

> They weren't cracked. But they still ache like I was smashed with a bat.

> Because, you know, I was basically smashed with a bat.

Tyler adds a little LOL onto Simon's message.

We should hang out.

You hitting on me?

No. Maybe, but no. Bring Trouble. You like her, don't you?

Simon sits up with his face scrunched like a paper bag. His thumbs fly.

I never said that. I said she was my *friend*.

Yeah, well, remember that girl you were obsessed with in junior high?

I wasn't obsessed.

Yes, you were.

You make that same face at Trouble. If you're not in love or going in that way, I'll eat my doctorate.

That's not something you can eat.

Killjoy.

How are you?

Simon thinks about that for a moment. Tyler knows nothing about his adult, boring-as-dryer-lint self. Though it's not that way now. The past month has been more stimulating than the rest of the decade since he'd last seen his friend, filled with embarrassment, eroticism, idiocy, frustration, rage, heartbreak, hilarity, romanticism, and terror, all because of one woman and the whirlwind she brings. But tonight was something special. Tonight they schemed and plotted. Life. Business. Existential threats.

I feel like I added value today.

There is a pause before bubbles start.

Don't you add value every day?

Simon snorts.

Not in my ripe old age. I'm more of a curmudgeon.

Don't use big words, I have very few brain cells right now.

We should hang out.

You said that already.

But you didn't say yes, so you obviously didn't hear me.

And I can bring Angelica?

Trouble is always welcome. Tell her to show me how to throw a ninja star.

Spies don't do that. And she's not a spy.

Can I text you when you're sober? I'm sober?

One of us has to be sober.

Simon snickers, tossing his book on the side table.

Tomorrow is bad for me but call me Sunday if you want.

Deal.

Dealeeyo.

Dahliyo. Don't you thing Dahli was an awskomt pntr? He's like mid blowking.

I think your thumbs fell off. Go to sleep Doctor Knight.

Dam rite doctr Knight. Woo.

I like that. Residens should say it.

Nite, Pyro.

I'm happy we can be friends again.

Simon smiles.

Take aspirin when you wake up. And drink water.

What? I can't hear u dad lalalalallalala.

And Tyler adds a happy face, then an *oops*, then a correction made of a sleepy face with zzzs.

Simon gives it a thumbs-up and lays his phone to the side, grinning at it. That goofball.

He looks at his bedside clock and rubs his eyes, his body starting to drift into dream space. He needs to get up early to go with Angelica tomorrow, and he needs to be well rested and on his game. A lot rides on this. Too much.

But yes, he added value to their relationship today. And he's going to do it tomorrow too.

———

Angelica's nails dig into the taped gauze around the cut in her forearm. The stitches pull like fishhooks through cheeks, and she can't wait to get them out. Yanking her sleeve down, she hoists her duffel higher, sliding a hand over Simon's soft hoodie—borrowed, not stolen—and into its front belly pocket where her little glass vial sits, boasting the metallic chip that represents Maxine's stranglehold on Angelica's life. That ends today.

Simon and she plotted last night. Whispered and yelled and gave each other demands. Simon's refusals to "stay out of it" piggybacked by fervent requests to "just let me come" fell on deaf ears…other than his strategy. That stuck like brains to walls.

Angelica wishes she had her gun.

Before the sun graces the sky, she sneaks out of the apartment, toes feathering the floor in whispers as she bobs and weaves around furniture in the dark. Simon's room is quiet, and all for the better. The memory of Damion's club driving down against Simon's body, that hollow *thud* and *thwack,* is a brand on her soul that makes Angelica's insides turn to acid. She won't let them do that to him again.

She leaves her key in the little cup by the door. Its potential jingle is a threat, and the fact that Max may get her claws on it sets Angelica's mind wheeling into fear they'd come for Simon in the night. That the money won't be enough.

But Max promised. She *promised.*

And that means she put her reputation on the line. Business is business, for good or for ill. None of the other girls would try to pull in a hundred grand without using their bodies, especially in only three months, but Angelica's stupid ass did. But despite Bee and Simon's opinions, her bullheadedness is what gets her through life. If there is a decision to be made, she makes it, and damn the consequences.

Her decision today is to try to save herself while protecting Simon.

The door handle twists with agonizing slowness, and the creaks of the inner clockwork seem to shriek in this otherwise soundless moment. Clenching her jaw, Angelica begs the door not to squeal when she opens it, and then thanks the heavens when it blesses her with silence.

The hallway creaks are less worrisome, though Angelica still feels like her ass is clenched like hands in prayer. *Don't let him hear. Don't let him come. Don't let him find me. Keep him safe.*

The fact that she shouldn't care is out the window. Every time he looks at her with those puppy-dog eyes, a little pin in her lock gets picked. Every heavy hand passing over her hair unwinds a coil within her. She will not let that man be hurt. Not now. Not ever.

———

Simon's head is a muddled mess when he wakes up. He sits up with a yawn that squinches his face and a stretch that makes something pop in a good way. Looking at the sky, it's around dawn, and the green blink of five-thirty on his bedside clock makes him want to crash back down into his comfy pillows. Holding still, he listens to the quiet. If Angelica's still asleep, he can sleep too. He just wants to keep her from stepping out on her own, though even now, he knows that's a long shot.

A long shot…

A garrote pulls against his lungs.

Slinging off his sheets, he steps into a crumpled dark blob on the floor—his pajama pants—and hikes it over his hips. Not bothering to put on a shirt, he yanks open his door to rush at hers, planning to knock until she grumbles or mutters or even yells at him to leave her alone, but instead he sees two things on his threshold, laying innocuously by his feet.

One is her cell phone. Her fucking *cell phone*. It lays over a piece of paper folded so neatly he wants to rip it to pieces.

"Son of a bitch," peels from his mouth as he rears back, scouring his hands through his hair and sinking his teeth into his lower lip. He knew she would do this. He knew. "Fuck."

He storms to his dresser to get clothes on. But where would he go to find her? She never told him, no matter how much he begged.

"Fuck!" He slams his drawer shut and shoves heavy wood, a slow poison threading its way through his veins. His chest tightens, his hands clench, and he wants nothing more than to throw over this hunk of furniture and hack it to pieces.

Twisting around, he stoops to retrieve what she left behind. When he picks up her phone, the screen alights with a missed text from an unmarked number. It says, "See you soon."

His blood turns to ice and he drops to his knees. That stupid woman. That stupid, stupid woman. He rips her note from the ground and unfolds it with a grudge.

Simon,

You didn't think my reasons were good enough, but believe me, this will go better if it's just me and her. Remember, you *don't know this world. You don't know these people. This is my mess, and you're already doing enough to help me clean it up.*

*My phone has everything you need, just like we talked about.*

*I can do this.*

Her phone password is printed neatly at the bottom.

He crumples the pseudo-apology for abandoning him to go get herself killed into the smallest ball he can and launches it across the room. Before it tumbles to the floor, it *skritches* off the overly loved, dumpy, squashed living room chair. Her chair. Just like half his goddamn apartment is hers. He's given it freely, happy to have her exist in his space, eat from his fridge, take up half his bathroom and TV time, and now she's gone.

"Fuck," he says one more time, but it comes out soft. Defeated. Useless and impotent.

Plunking on his backside, he knows all he can do is sit here and wait…and it's the last thing he wants to do.

————

This place is as dingy as Angelica remembers. She's been hiding out at an early morning coffee shop nearby, awaiting her ten a.m. meeting time with Maxine. And Damion. And whoever the hell else is going to be greeting her this fine morning.

The walls in Max's "office building" are yellowed with either time or grunge, she can't tell. It's like a smoker breathed their cancerous lungs all over the walls, leaving nothing but tobacco and filth behind. It smells that way too. Like stale cigarettes and long-forgotten flickers of cheap lighters.

She's been here only a handful of times and hated every one of them. Those visits prickled her nerves, making her feel like bugs were doing pirouettes up her arms, but this time it's like an army of them are digging their pincers in, keeping her so hyper-alert, it's painful.

Her duffel is heavy and her shoulder aches from carrying it all over town. At the early hour she was tromping around, she's surprised she didn't get mugged in the dark, though she supposes even bad guys are in bed by three. Too bad she couldn't get in a nap at that coffee shop. She could have used one.

The door is a towering Frankenstein's monster, and Angelica looks at the shape of it for way too long. Her tightened fist hovers under the little, circular peephole, knowing it should knock, but unable to bring itself to do so.

*You're stronger than this. Or, even if you're not, you need to put on a hell of a show.*

Swallowing, she raps at the door.

One.

Two.

Within three seconds, Damion opens it. His eyes are predatory pinpricks as they look her up and down before scanning the hallway. His jowls tighten as he lords over her, making her want to quake. Instead, she stands taller and frowns at him, as if daring him to lay a finger on her. That only results in a smile on his fleshy face that shows too many teeth.

"Is that my Sadie?" Maxine calls from inside.

Stepping back, Damion gestures at her as if in welcome, inviting her in. The room is still its windowless, ominously dark self, and Maxine's ashtray is filled with stubbed-out, orange Marlboro filters. Apparently, she fell off the wagon when it came to her nicotine vice.

"Come, come," she says, standing and throwing her arms wide. "Don't lurk. Let me see you."

Keeping her sailor's legs as steady as she can, Angelica walks in with her head held high. Maxine and her heavily perfumed scent envelop her in an embrace that feels like needles. Pulling back, Maxine grabs her chin, tilting her face to the side as she *tsks* over Angelica's healing cheek.

"Damion, how many times have I told you not to mark up faces? This would take hundreds off her price."

Meaty shoulders rise and fall. "Sorry, Miss Maxine. Next time I have a go at her, I'll make sure to focus on other places." His voice drips with a sadistic glee that makes every survivalist instinct in Angelica start to scream.

"I have your money," she says, keeping her voice as steady as possible. "Every cent."

Maxine hums before flicking her eyes to Damion. He lets the weighted door swing shut with a bang before tugging the duffel from Angelica's shoulders, and bringing it to a credenza too fancy for a tomb like this. Unzipping it, bundles of bills come out, and Damion rifles through them all one by one, licking his fingers and thumbing them into new piles, hand to hand. Angelica's surprised he can count.

"So, now comes the end of our deal," Maxine says while Damion does his one, two, threes. "You know, the girls have been asking each other where you are."

Morbid curiosity wins her over. "What did you tell them?"

"That you got yourself into a bit of a predicament with me, and your fate was yet undecided."

A shiver hits Angelica, as if the room temperature dropped ten degrees. "It's decided today though, right?" She nods at the hulking monster behind Maxine. "Once his count is clear, you'll let me go?"

Maxine looks at her nails. They're black and fashionable with modest white flowers painted along the sides. Unchipped and shiny. Brand new. Her lips purse as she regards them, her eyes passing over each and every one. "Will I though?"

Angelica's heart hammers. "But you said—"

"What on earth would you do with yourself, anyway? How are you going to survive?" she asks as if she's truly concerned, but her saccharine sound drips with too much sugar.

"I have a job."

She snorts, rolling her eyes in wide circles. "Doing what?"

"Office work. Clerical stuff."

"My dear, I'm surprised you know the word."

Angelica watches Damion drop a bundle of her money and casually kick it under the credenza, losing it to the shadows. "Hey!" she snaps.

Maxine looks around and Damion freezes. That sweet voice turns to acid. "Now, now, are we playing fair, Mister Damion?"

The color in his cheeks pales slightly and he bends at the waist, reaching under and digging for the money he booted away. Drawing it out, he mutters his apologies and goes back to counting. Maxine sighs and leans her hip against her desk, turning to face Angelica.

"You know I'm going to tell them that I killed you."

Lungs constricting, Angelica nods. "Makes sense." That way, no one else will think of leaving.

"The question remains whether or not I'll really do it."

"I'm going by my real name now. No one is ever going to hear of Sadie again. They won't know I got out."

"Is that supposed to sway me one way or another?"

"You promised." It comes out childish and pleading, but Maxine's vicious grin tells her that Simon was right. Angelica was naive. But they planned for this. "Plus, I have leverage."

Maxine's perfectly plucked, steadily stenciled eyebrows pull high. "Oh?"

"I left him with information," Angelica says. "On you. On the girls. Your organization. Everything I know is in his pocket. If I don't get home to him, he'll—"

"What?" She scoffs. "Go to the police?"

"Go to the reporters."

That gives Maxine pause.

"He has our texts, which confirm our whole deal. He has this location. He has your name. Damion's. The boys. The police may let you go, but the reporters will dig and dig and dig, because that's what they do. They'll talk to previous johns and—"

"And what? Bring me to justice?"

"No," Angelica says. "Hit you in the pocket. Who will come to pick up one of the girls with investigators hot on your trail? With journalists snapping pictures of who they're taking into hotels? With men with microphones talking to their families?"

There is a heavy slap as Damion tosses the last bill stack down on the rest. Like a bullet, he bangs forward, grabbing Angelica by the wrist and tweaking it behind her back, raising it until it touches her shoulder blade. Her cry of shock and pain echoes in this dreary room, but she knows that, even if someone outside hears her scream, no one will come.

"He loves me," she calls out. "And because of that, he won't stop. He has money and lawyers and with enough pressure, eventually the police will roll on you. You're not the fucking mob. You're just a whorehouse with brainless muscle who gives those fat pigs free romps with pretty girls. Once reporters start looking into their potential connections to you, they'll drop you like a hot stone."

Damion wrenches her hand higher and pulls her hair hard, making her shout and exposing her throat. Simon had promised this would be the pivotal moment. He'd blushed to high heaven when he told her what to say, but he promised revenge and personal vendettas would speak to people like this.

Through her tears, Angelica can see the look on Maxine's face, and it tells her Simon was not wrong.

She sits there for a long time while Angelica writhes, trying to escape Damion's clutches only to have him tighten down. Her scalp is on fire and he's about three degrees from dislocating her fucking shoulder. It strains in the socket, begging for mercy.

"Did she have all the money?" Maxine asks, voice disinterested, even though Angelica knows she's anything but.

Damion's breath reeks of coffee and rotting bacon. "Yeah. All of it."

Angelica squirms once more and screeches when he twists her harder. He's going to do it. He's going to break her fucking arm.

Crisp and cold, Maxine says, "Enough."

Angelica is shoved to the floor, and her bare knees grate over the industrial carpet. The pain doesn't stop, but the howling does, and she cradles her arm like a baby.

Maxine stands over her, cast in shadow with the lamplight glowing from behind. "You know I can find you forever, right? Longer than he'll love you."

"Maybe," Angelica says, panting. "But I have hope."

The word makes Maxine throw her head back and laugh, a shrill cackle that seems to pull right from her belly. She works her way behind her desk and eases into her chair, trying to rein it in and wiping merry tears from her eyes. "Oh Sadie. Hope is for children."

*And for me.*

There is a long moment where Max plays with her ashtray again, sliding it back and forth over her desk while Angelica's knees bleed into the carpet. Finally, she looks up with a smirk. "Fine. Business is business, and a deal is a deal. But I know where you are, and if you cause a moment of trouble, I'm sure Mister Damion here will take great pleasure in eviscerating you. I think he likes taking the eyes the best."

"They pop like grapes," he agrees, and Angelica shudders, hugging her arm closer.

"See yourself out, Sadie." She plucks a cigarette from a nearby pack and taps it twice on the desktop. "May you be reborn in your new life."

Those last words have a quality that almost sound like an honest well wish, but Angelica won't stand around long enough to question it. Pushing up, she darts to the door, grabbing the handle and releasing herself into the greasy hallway, praying to never see it again. Like in a nightmare, the entryway leading outside seems to elongate as she barrels forward, needing to escape before her personal boogeyman changes her mind.

The spring chill has never felt so good as Angelica slams the door open. She has nothing to carry except the baggage in her heart, and it makes the going easier. The training she punishes her body with serves her well. Her feet pummel the street until she works her way to more crowded territory.

People walk with purpose as she skirts them, a stitch starting to burn in her side. She knows what she has to do; this is the last part. She only prays that it works.

Fleeing to the curb, she thrashes her hand back and forth, waving down a cab. When one pulls over, she yanks the door wide and leans in. It smells like a cloying, flowery air freshener.

"I'm writing a book on cab driving," she pants. "Do you guys park at your house or a depot?"

Her chest heaves as a chubby, older man turns over his shoulder to look at her. His expression is all wrinkles and knots as he says, "I ain't got parking at my place. We all use a lot over in Charlestown."

*Oh thank god.*

Angelica works her hand into her pocket. "How much to get to Tremont Street, do you think?"

The man considers. "We missed traffic, so maybe thirty bucks?"

Good. Angelica has sixty tucked into Simon's hoodie pocket. She jumps into the cab, slamming the door behind her. A prayer on her lips, she drops the vial holding her tracker on the floor, nudging it beneath the passenger seat with her sneakered toe. Her heart is slamming so hard she can't breathe, but this is the last step. If Simon is no longer her failsafe, if he abandons her to her fate, at least Maxine can't find her. She'll truly be free.

When the cab edges into the ebb and flow of cars, Angelica puts her face in her hands, and tries not to throw up.

It's over.

It's really over.

"Simon," she whispers, "I'm coming home."

# tenderness and commitment

. . .

SIMON SITS in front of the unchanging door frame, watching the entrance for any sign of her. A moody record plays in the background, bass-heavy and dirge-like, perfect for his outlook on life. His stomach roils, his jaw is tight enough to make his head pound, and his jittering nerves have him on the verge of running—potentially to wherever she is, or maybe far away from it all. Anywhere that isn't sitting here in this feeling of being left behind. Forgotten.

His parents forgot him once. He'd been doing his homework, waiting for them to come home, the only sound his eraser grinding the paper as it shredded into pink rubber castoffs. He'd been ten or so, and the maid had gone home for the day, leaving a roast in the oven for his parents to take out once they got home—but they never came.

Simon had startled when the fire alarm began to scream. Downstairs, a haze of smoke choked the air in misty white fists, making him clap his hands over his mouth. The oven trickled wafts of steam and the air reeked of something burning—a charred, charcoal smell that made him gag.

Running over, Simon remembered his mom's nightly routine and put on the special gloves. The thick ones that said "Kiss the Cook" and immediately made your palms sweaty when you crammed them on.

Opening the oven, a blare of heat plumed. Dinner was burned into a blackened log, but Simon didn't know what to do next. His mom would have taken it out, but his shorter arms couldn't reach right. Pawing, he tried to get a hold of the glass edge of the pan, but only managed to sizzle a piece of his arm on the oven's molten frame. He cried out, but the fire alarm cried with him, drowning him out as his eardrums split with sound.

"Come on," he growled, shaking himself off. He was a whole ten years old. He could do this. Reaching in again, his tummy clenched and his heart hammered. Where was his mom? His dad?

The alarm shrieked. *BEEP BEEP BEEP.*

With a grunt, he managed to tug the thing from the oven rack only for it to crash onto the floor with a ringing clatter. The ruined meat and singed vegetables scattered, and Simon seized. He was going to get in trouble. They were going to think he did this on purpose. That he was being bad again.

*BEEP BEEP BEEP.*

Using those mitts, he shoved the oven closed, but even on tippy-toes, he couldn't reach the oven's off button. His lower lip trembled as his mind wound into unbreakable knots. They were going to blame him. They never believed him when he said it wasn't his fault.

It was so hot, and the smoke burned his eyes. What could he possibly do?

*BEEP BEEP BEEP.*

Grinding his teeth, Simon threw the mitts off and grabbed a kitchen chair, dragging and scraping it over the marble kitchen tiles, *squeak, creak, rumble,* until he managed to get it next to the countertop. He climbed from the floor to the chair, then to the white marble top covered in serving spoons, knife blocks, and blenders for his mother's special morning shakes. The ones she said he was still too little for.

*BEEP BEEP BEEP.*

On his hands and knees, Simon edged his way along the thin counter, trying his hardest not to fall. The smoke was thicker up here, and he started to gasp, lungs looking for clean air while his eyes watered. Panting, he peeked over the counter's edge at the floor littered with blistering food.

He shouldn't be doing this. He wanted his parents. Glancing at the microwave display, it was seven thirty. They should have been home by now. Why do they always come home so late?

The top of the oven was just as hot as the bottom. The stovetop emitted an aura that seemed too dangerous to touch. Still, Simon leaned over it, reaching his hand out to push the off button while the alarm's high C notes threatened to shatter glass.

*BEEP BEEP BEEP.*

His finger jabbed, and something chimed. Off.

He did it.

His...his head felt light.

Coughing, he scooted back the way he came until he could slip his feet over the edge and onto the kitchen chair once more. At that point, he heard knocking on the front door. His head swam as he tried to go get it, but wooziness overtook him, and he went to his knees.

Whoever was at the front door started shouting, and the knocks became bangs. Became handle jiggles. His mom used to always tell him that the best part about a gated community is that you never have to lock your doors. That thought flitted through his brain as he lay down on the floor. It was cooler down there. Easier to breathe.

Before he could register what was happening, his neighbor had scooped him up and was dragging him outside as another shouted up the stairs for his parents.

"I'm alone," he said, squeezing out another cough.

When the neighbor dialed his parents' numbers—shared in case of emergencies—they didn't answer. And when the fire truck came, they still were nowhere to be found. Simon sat in his neighbor's house, watching the moon rise outside the unfamiliar window as he cried. He wrecked the food, he messed up the house, and now his parents were going to hate him and never come back.

It turned out that his mother had been in a terrible car crash. In the end, she'd only broken her arm and three ribs, but his father had run to her aid, destroyed at the idea of losing her. In his anguish, he never remembered to think about little Simon waiting for someone to come home.

Just like he's waiting now.

He curls tighter into himself, tucking his chin onto his knees.

The rhythmic strum of a bass guitar throbs in his ears, and he thumbs his remote to raise the volume, wanting to drown out these childish thoughts. His parents loved him, he knows it. Angelica cares about him too, she's just being stubborn because she's worried, just like he's sitting here, heart in his throat, worried about her. Her and those belly laughs, those crass conversations, her teasing, her wearing all his clothes constantly because she never used her money to buy enough of her own.

There is a jarring twitter of beeps that overrides his music. Eyes squinting, he thumbs his remote again, killing the latest heavy metal riff and leaving airy silence. After a beat, the twitter bleeps out again, longer this time, and he realizes it's his front door signal. No one has ever used it before.

Angelica. She left her keys behind.

He's on his feet and bolting in milliseconds, snagging his own from the little bowl by the door and jabbing the elevator button like he's trying to poke out its eye. Gritting his teeth, he cusses at the thing as the elevator rises all too slow, and when the doors part, he throws himself inside.

At the bottom, past the quartz-threaded marble tiles of the foyer, lay the double glass doors that lead to the street. There she stands, holding herself. After a second, she smashes her hand against his bell again with the grumpiest, most endearing expression. He sees her mouth the words, "Come on, Simon," and that's enough for him.

Launching open the door, he ignores her surprise and snags her, wrapping her in his embrace. She squawks, but he can't let her go, diving into her soft black hair and breathing her in. The scent of their shampoo tingles his nose. She's real, she's here, she's okay.

"Simon, you're hurting me…"

Shit. She's not okay.

Thoughts of Fabio and chivalry ring through his mind like a blaring horn, and he bends to pick her up princess-style. Her "EEP" gets her nowhere as he storms back through the door and to the elevator. He couldn't be her hero before, but he can do it now. He can…he can…

Jeez, she's heavy.

"Angelica, be a dear and push the elevator button," he says through his teeth, his arm muscles trembling.

"You idiot." She squirms and he has no choice but to relent, letting her wriggle down his body. Huffing, she holds her shoulder while shooting him a glare.

"Are you hurt?" he asks.

Her eyes flick to her shoulder before she lets it go and ticks up her chin. "No."

But he can see the difference in her posture. He had the same when they messed him up. A dark fury winds its way through Simon's soul. "What did they do?" She opens her mouth, but he reminds her, "No more lies."

Her bottom lip tucks in and she presses the elevator button. "I'm fine. He just got a little rough."

"Your knees!" Simon squeaks, regretting the high pitch, but too late to do anything about it.

They're scabbed, raw, and a trickle of blood has dried down her leg. "I told you I'm fine."

The elevator door opens, and he picks her up again, ignoring how she swears at him. Huffing, puffing, and doing his best to latch on to her despite her bucking and cursing, he manages to get her into the apartment and toss her down on her chair with a *thwump* and a loud "oomph."

He points a finger at her. "Stay."

Crossing her arms, she leans back and sulks, but makes no move to leave. In five steps, Simon is rummaging through his bathroom, tossing away spare rolls of toilet paper and bottles of cleaner until he finds what he's looking for. Tromping back out, he gets on his knees in front of her and pops open the first aid kit.

"What are you doing?"

"Hush. You won't let me keep you safe? Suffer through my after-care." He starts digging for gauze and antiseptic.

She sinks deeper into the cushions. "This is not what aftercare is. In BDSM—"

"Don't need a lecture right now, angel." He finds what he's looking for and pops open the cap.

It's going to sting, but he doesn't warn her, he just pours a river atop her boo-boo.

"*Motherfucker.*" She tries to kick out, but he holds her steady. "Your aftercare sucks."

His frown sinks deeper as he concentrates, mopping up and moving to the next knee. To her credit, she only hisses and jerks this time, but her face is still a storm.

"You want Frozen Band-Aids or the regular kind?"

"Why the hell do you have kids' Band-Aids?"

"Naughty girls who sneak out of bed at night don't get their questions answered."

Despite his brattiness, the snark breaks the proverbial ice, and she huffs an exasperated laugh. "Do you have Olaf?"

The slick paper crinkles as he rips open one—Ana—and then a second to find the singing ice cube. Aiming the gauze just so, he smooths the big-toothed Disney character over her skin. It takes ripping open another seven packages to find enough Olafs to cover her scrapes but adorning her with snowmen is somehow cathartic. He needed to do this. He needed to help her.

He's so in love, it fucking hurts.

She's looking at him softly, and he prays she feels it too. Maybe it's just a spark for her, but that's okay. He's going to do all he can to fan it to a flame.

"Everything's done then?" he asks. "You're safe?"

Angelica still favors her right shoulder, but nods. "Yeah."

"Did you need to use the plan?"

Her eyes drop and she sighs. "Yeah."

He holds back the "I told you so." Instead, he takes a deep breath and reaches up to run a hand through her hair. It's always so soft, so much better than threading his fingers through his own. "And the tracker?"

Leaning into his touch, she murmurs, "I put it in a cab. If they watch this place, they'll know better, but if I have to, I can run away. They won't be able to find me."

Though it hurts his heart to say it, he asks, "Do you want to run away now?"

Her hand comes up to rest on the back of his, pulling him closer to cup her bad cheek. "No."

"Good," he whispers across an exhale.

"But if your people find out about me, I'm fired. I'll have nothing."

"You'll have me," he insists. "As long as we're friends, I'll take care of you."

Her freckles are undertoned by a shade of pink, and Simon's sure his face is red to match. It burns all the way to his ears. Up on his feet again, he's in the kitchen in a flash. "Hungry? I think today you deserve something I'd make versus something you'd make."

"Ugh."

"Come on. I'll even go to the gym with you later. You can…ride… bikes…or whatever it is you do."

At this, she peeks over the back of the chair. "Can't. I'm hurt, remember?"

He facepalms. Recovering quickly, he opens and closes cabinet doors, snagging out one thing after another. "Well, I'm going to make pancakes, bacon, and omelets. If you don't eat anything, it will be a waste."

She gets a playful smirk. "Will you put peppers in my omelet?"

"Ew. Do I even have peppers?"

"You do."

"You contaminated my fridge?"

Pausing, she fiddles with the worn threads on the back of her seat. "It's my fridge too, right?"

Warmth like a blanket fresh from the dryer drapes over his soul. Slowing his flurry of motion, Simon turns to her with a quirk to his lips. "It absolutely is."

"Welcome home, me?"

He wishes he could kiss her. "Welcome home, you."

———

Simon struts around outside, enjoying the sunshine as it beats down on his too-white face. Angelica went for a much-deserved nap and so he's out on a much-needed walk. After all that tension, he needs to move his body and get out of that space where his fingers constantly itch to hold her. Now the budding outside warmth is relaxing that coiled wire within him, settling him back into his body and calming his mind.

His phone is pressed to his ear and his smile is unending as he continues his reconnection with his old friend.

"I think it's a good idea," Tyler chirps.

"You sure that's not the hangover talking?"

"How many people have you talked about it with?"

"Just you and Angelica."

"And what did Trouble say?"

Simon grins, looking at his shoes as he scuffs the toes off the sidewalk. "She liked it too. Truth be told, all the opportunities before this just didn't call to me, but this one does. I just need to check out one more thing before I try to tell Nando."

"Your friend?"

"Yeah, he'll give me his honest opinion. He's always got my best interest in mind." Simon hopes, though what Angelica said is stuck in his head. Could Nando possibly be holding him back on purpose?

He dismisses the idea.

"Well, then he'll see how important this is to you and help figure out how to make it work," Tyler says. "In business, if I remember my undergrad correctly, you can negotiate the terms in your favor. I'm sure these people aren't going to rake you over the coals or anything. You just have to pitch your uncle right."

"That's the problem. I roll over like a friggin' puppy dog when it comes to stuff like this."

"Since when?" Tyler scoffs. "Look, I don't know New Simon very well, but Old Simon took crap from no one. He believed what he believed, and if anyone bucked against it, he either made them see reason or told them to go pound sand. That or he may have beaten the snot out of them."

Simon chuckles. "Yeah, well, I can't go around doing that now."

"Hashtag adulting. When are we going out for beers? You and Trouble free on Friday?"

"I am, anyway." No more dates for him ever again. "I'll check with her."

"Then let's pretend to be teenagers for a night. Bring out Old Simon."

"If you try to bring me to a gay club—"

"I never."

"Or a straight club—"

"Fine. We'll do pool or darts or something. Mundane enough for you?"

"That actually sounds like fun." Since when has fun been in his vocabulary? "Think I can beat you?"

"Ah, and there's Competitive Simon. I missed him too. We'll see, though. I am a doctor. I'm very good at precision and pokey things."

"Is that a medical term?"

"Very. Are you still a weepy drunk?"

"That may or may not be how I met Trouble," Simon admits, earning laughter in return.

With a few repetitions of "Good*bye*, Ty," his old friend finally lets him off the phone to continue his saunter. He'd googled the address, but the winding streets and distance makes this place a pain to get to. No subway stops nearby, no bus stops. It's like they want these people to be out of sight, out of mind. It's depressing.

The homeless shelter comes into view, a squat building with graffiti tags up and down the side walls. Some are haphazard, but others are quite artful, bright pink swoops and spots. The colorful, wax-like drips over the rough brick add to the aesthetic of the pieces. Some of this isn't vandalism, but almost like an act of love. Love of art or love of this place, Simon supposes he'll never know.

Skrag grass pokes through the sidewalk tiles, yellow, dry, and withered. None of the season's magic seems to have come here. No little blooms. No trees to be spoken of. Just concrete. If Simon didn't know any better, this would look like a prison.

Unsure of where to start, he knocks on the front door, a thick, metal rectangle that sounds hollow inside.

"Hello?" Simon calls, cupping his hands and peering through the window beside the entrance. A face pops into view, an older Black gentleman with creases worn across his face. The door opens a crack, but Simon can see the lock chains keeping the inside protected from intruders.

The man narrows his eyes at Simon, giving him a slow and steady once-over. His accent is thick. "Ya'll don' look like da kinda guys we get comin' 'round 'ere. But either way, it's too early."

Simon flicks his wrist to look at his watch, pursing his lips as he tries to tell the analog time. He might be in his high twenties, but it still takes him too long to count the tick marks. "What time do people start coming back?"

Suspicion drips from the man's voice. "Why ya wanna know? Ya need a bed?"

"No, sorry. I'm looking for Ciel. Or Joe?"

Unchaining the door, the man opens it wide enough to lean against it, crossing his arms and jutting out his chin in a sharp jab. "Dey in trouble?"

"Huh?"

"Dey steal somethin'?"

"Not to my knowledge?"

"Den what ya lookin' for?"

Simon supposes mentioning he wants their ideas on a business proposal might sound odd. "They're my friends."

The other man's eyes glint. "Ah. Yer da one takin' 'em out to dinner and givin' 'em way too much money."

Simon frowns. "It's none of your business how much I give them."

Hands out, the man acquiesces. "'Ey, no harm. You might think of me as Grandpa to da grandpas, if you get me. I don' need no cash, so they don' mind tellin' me when dey get a good deal. Thought you were stupid at first. Not sure you're not stupid now."

Isn't this man pleasant. "I'll come back later. I was just hoping to catch them."

The old man points to the side. Down the road a ways is a bridge over an alley, derelict and seedy, like the rest of this place. "I ain't seen Ciel in a few days. Weather's nice, so some stay out to make room for da others. It's winter where they'll kick each other in da ass for a space.

Check down 'dere. Dey hole up sometimes and the police don't bother 'em none."

Simon flicks his eyes in that direction again. There's trash peppering out from beneath the arch of the bridge and more skrag grass—longer and reedy this time—pokes out. He tries to tell himself that it's like camping down there, tents and marshmallows, but he knows it's a lie.

His mood sinks. "Thanks."

The old man salutes him and wordlessly enters the shelter again, letting the heavy door slam shut and sliding the locks into place once more. Swallowing, Simon turns on his heels and works his way over. That jittery tension comes back. He knows these are just people, but what if he gets mugged? Beat up again? It's not like all homeless people are created equal. But maybe he's stereotyping? Maybe his bias is screwing him up? If he wants his idea to work, he's got to get over the hurdle of his knee-jerk reactions.

The closer he gets, the more chatter he hears, the tighter his jaw gets as he grinds his teeth.

His fists ball and he starts to sweat, trying to keep his steps soft. Maybe that's a mistake. Maybe he shouldn't surprise them.

Turning the corner, he sees a few patchy groups of people sitting on the ground, men and women with weathered backpacks and stuffed trash bags littered around them. There are a few dogs, matted and raggedy, but panting and looking happy to be amongst these people. Gazes turn toward him, and more than a few eyebrows raise, but that feeling of fear ebbs from his limbs, leaving only a disturbing sense that he doesn't belong here. He's intruding. It's like he walked, uninvited, into someone's home.

"You lost, bro?" someone asks, scratching his dog behind the ears. He has greasy hair that's a bit too long and grubby, pink, fingerless gloves. Even so, he looks friendly, if not a little confused.

"I'm looking for Ciel or Joe. You guys know either of them? I think they stay here sometimes."

Grubby-gloves points deeper under the bridge, down to where it's darker. Simon thanks him, but he's still on edge. The deeper in he goes, the danker it smells. There are fewer people here, but some are curled up and sleeping, their meager possessions clutched in their arms or pillowing their heads.

Coughing catches his attention, wet and phlegmy, and he hears someone hock a loogie against the wall. The spit makes a sick *splat* that makes Simon grimace. The dimly lit shape that coughed curls in on itself and shivers. It isn't until Simon can make out that rattail braid that he recognizes him.

"Ciel?"

The man looks up, his head lolling back. "Simon?"

Simon steps up, all discomfort whisked away. "Yeah, I came to…" but the feeling comes back as Ciel starts coughing again, his whole body clenching as his shoulders bunch. "Are you sick?"

He manages a smirk. "What gave it away?"

"Do you need a doctor?"

He shrugs, resting back and giving a little shiver when he does so. "It's probably just the flu."

"Even so." Simon leans forward and sets a hand on Ciel's forehead. It's pushed away—kindly, but quickly—but not before Simon feels the burning heat of fever.

"Don't say it," Ciel gripes.

"You're coming to my house."

"I said don't say it."

"What's wrong with my house?"

"I don't take charity," he says, coughing in a harsh fit again.

"You sound like Angelica."

"The little one? You guys make up?"

"Don't change the subject."

They eye each other for a short minute before Simon points a finger at him. "And you take charity every day you sit on the sidewalk." He holds a hand out, and Ciel looks at it for a hard minute before grumbling and taking it.

"Let me make this clear, I ain't stayin' long. You get me up and at 'em, and I'm out the door. Capiche?"

"The capichiest."

"There's a limit to how much I'm willing to take advantage of someone."

"Call it 'easing my conscience.'"

Ciel chuckles before snuffling back something wet. "You always give charity for your own sake?"

"I suppose it's better than not giving any at all."

At that, Simon ducks down and picks up Ciel's backpack. It smells a little like feet, but what are you gonna do?

———

Angelica pulls slowly from slumber, keeping her heavy eyes closed and enjoying the darkness behind her lids. Her dreams of late have all been nightmares, sweat beading her back when she'd jerk awake, escaping death by inches. Nothing much lingered except the panic and the dread, and long minutes would tick by before her breath and her mind steadied. This last trip to the land of nod wasn't anything like that, though. Nor was it dreamless. In it, every time some shadow lurked around a corner, there was Simon. He didn't always do something heroic, often it was something asinine and silly, but once he just took her hand, wound their fingers together, and walked alongside her. It's not fear that woke her up this time. It was the throb of her heart.

There's a rumbling cough from the living room, wet, like it pulls straight from the bottommost curve of someone's lungs. Rubbing her eyes, Angelica looks at the clock to find it's past six. She's slept away five hours of her free life. One where her body is her own, there's no fear of violence, and a friend is there to bring her world softness— though the pull in her chest isn't one of friendship. After all this time, after all his cute red faces and bumbling faux pas, she actually likes him back.

Damnit.

She scrubs at her eyes and sits up, throwing off her covers and kicking at their fluffy warmth like a toddler with a tantrum coming on. She doesn't want to have a crush. Especially not on someone who is now effectively her boss.

That cough comes back, more dry hacking this time, and it goes on for far longer than Angelica would like. She looks in the direction of the sound, her eyes falling on a benign Home Goods painting on the wall instead. Who the hell decorated this room, anyway?

Simon's voice murmurs and another voice comes back.

Shit. Did Max's people come for her? Have they come for Simon?

Her nerves riot, and an electrical pulse shoots her from the bed. Hiking Simon's overlarge T- shirt back over her shoulder, she slams open her door and stomps out, mouth open and ready to screech the house down, but only finds Simon blinking at her. Someone lies flat on his back on the couch, a thermometer tucked neatly between his puckered lips.

"You remember Ciel?" Simon gestures, only for the other man to salute. The coffee table is littered with twisted-up tissues and colorful bottles of what can only be cold medicine—acid oranges and viscous green blues. A bag of cough drops has let go of its contents, and they dapple the table in a diagonal scatter. "He's going to be staying with us for a while."

She gapes and looks back and forth between her "friend" and the poor bastard who looks like he's never slept before. "But there's only one extra bed."

The thermometer beeps and Ciel takes it out, eyeing the thing. "No worries, little lady. This couch is the best thing I've ever had."

Un-bloody-likely. Angelica looks at his feet hoisted up over the armrest, too tall for the thing. His holey socks reveal sneak peeks of his toes, and a new knit cap is pulled down over his ears, the price tag still on and smooshed against a fluffy pillow cradling the man's head.

Simon snags the thermometer before Ciel can wave it out and frowns. "Yeah, you're definitely grounded."

"A hundred isn't so bad."

"This is a hundred and one."

"That isn't so bad either."

"Go back to sleep or I'll hop you up so high on decongestant you'll never come back down again."

"Don't threaten me with a good time."

Snorting, Simon turns and works his way into the kitchen, stirring something. Keeping Ciel in her peripheral vision, Angelica asks, "What are you making?"

"Chicken soup for the soul, apparently," Ciel throws in, pulling up the heaviest blanket Angelica has ever seen and snuggling down before coughing pathetically again.

"Tyler's coming over to make sure he doesn't need antibiotics or anything," Simon says over his shoulder. "He said he wanted to check your stitches too."

Ah, the unforgettable Dr. Knight.

Angelica has no idea what to do with herself all of a sudden, and without looking at her, Simon seems to sense it. "Will you show him how to use the TV?"

"I know how," Ciel gripes. "You turn the knobs and adjust the antennae."

The younger generation stares at the older one and he offers nothing but a grin. "You two have no sense of humor."

The air smells of onion, celery salt, and brothy goodness as Angelica sits down on her chair, rummaging for the three remotes that normally sit in a pocket off to the side. She supposes they are a pain in the ass. She's always using the wrong one or turning the TV to the wrong input. "Ever heard of Netflix?"

"I'm homeless, not dead."

Simon snickers from the kitchen. "This feels weirdly cozy. I'm glad I keep picking up stray cats on the side of the road."

"Cats?" Angelica and Ciel shoot back in unison.

"Fine, nothing feral. Maybe you're more like cake—a dessert I can look forward to at the end of a long day." Simon sets down his wooden spoon with a clatter and turns to the island, chopping carrots with haphazard thwacks. "Ciel would be rum cake, because when I get a slice or two of him, I get silly drunk."

"Sloppy drunk," Ciel cuts in.

"Semantics." Simon keeps his hands busy but can't hide the way his face blooms pink. "And Angelica can be chocolate lava cake. A little firm on the outside, but soft and sweet once you dig in a little."

Ciel gives her a sly smile and her cheeks heat as well.

"What are you, big guy?" Ciel asks. Simon spreads his arm in a wide shrug.

"Angel food cake," Angelica says quietly, trying to look anywhere else, though her eyes keep finding Simon anyway.

His smile has gone lopsided and shy as he picks up his unevenly cut carrots and dumps them in a bowl. "I'll take it."

He gets back to work as poor Ciel begins to hack up another lung, his throat getting raspy. Flopping to his side, he cuddles up like a kid, just missing the stuffed animal, and regards Angelica in a way that should make her uncomfortable but doesn't. This man is fatherly, but not in the way that she's experienced. He's the kind of dad you see on Hallmark Christmas specials. The ones who are all sage advice, acceptance, and warm hugs. The way he helped her earlier, she's half on her way to asking for one of those hugs now, but the fear of whatever bug this guy's got keeps her at bay.

"You look much better," he says quietly so Simon won't hear. "I'm glad you two got back together. You seem good for each other."

"We're not together," she scoffs, keeping her voice down to match. "And I'm not good for anybody."

"My wife thought that too." He smiles, more to himself than to her. "She had a temper, swore like a sailor, and was the spitting image of 'hell hath no fury like,' if you get me. But she forgave as quick as she heated up, no matter what kind of shit I got myself into. She always said she never deserved me, but she was wrong. She was exactly what I needed."

He looks wistful and sad, his eyes glittering with moisture. Angelica's heart sinks on his behalf, wondering what happened but unwilling to ask. Some wounds are best left unpicked at.

Perking up a little, he says, "I heard Simon gave you a job."

Her mood sinks a little further. "Yeah. That. I barely have any idea of what I should be doing. I've been watching YouTube video tutorials all week, trying to figure out what the hell, but I've never even been in an office before two days ago. I don't know what to study. It's exhausting, honestly."

"But you have an open future now. Last time I saw you, you looked like you were doomed. Desperate, you know? I don't know what was going on, but if a bit of self-doubt is all that's got you now, you're doing just fine."

They share a little smile before he goes into another series of coughs. Angelica unravels him a yellow, honeyed throat drop in sympathy. From the kitchen, Simon calls, "Dinner," as if shouting to bring them in from the field after a long day of tilling, and it makes her grin.

He was right. Cozy is exactly the word for this.

---

For the first time, Simon looks at the green awning of his favorite pub with reluctance. If he could, he'd turn tail and head straight home. Tyler said Ciel has strep throat and Simon wants to make sure he's swallowing his antibiotics, eating enough, and taking care of himself. He seems bad at that, if Simon's required nagging is any indication. Angelica is home studying his past presentations so she understands what he's looking for at the office too. What if she has questions? Of all the places he could be right now, he doesn't want it to be here. He wants to be hanging around his once-empty apartment with people who make him feel good. Useful. Appreciated. Instead, he prepares for his biweekly dinner with his asshat best friend.

A hand claps off his back, taking the nape of his neck and shaking it amicably. "What are you doing standing out here, eh? You waiting for an invitation? *'Ndom.*" Nando grins at him and whaps him on the back a few more times before heading directly into the restaurant, not bothering to hold the door open behind him. Simon watches the man's dark head go right to the hostess and migrate toward a table while Simon still stands in the dusk's falling shadows.

With a sigh, he puts his hands in his pockets and heads in.

Sweeping off his jacket, he scoots into the table across from Nando as he finishes ordering himself a beer.

"You want something?" Nando tips his hand open to Simon in invitation.

He stuffs his coat into the booth beside him. "Screwdriver."

Nando's eyebrows lift as the waitress makes her way to put in the order. "Starting hardcore today, eh?"

"I'd like to say I had a bad weekend, but it was more of a roller coaster." Simon trails his hand up and down.

"Oh? Surprised you weren't on more meeting-and-humping-strangers dates. Done with the finer sex now that you're in love with a mistake?"

Simon bristles. "She's not a mistake."

"Well, hiring her definitely is. I'd be surprised if she makes it a week before charging you with sexual harassment or something to get a settlement, yeah? If she's hard up for cash— enough to take a shit job —then I'm guessing this is her plan to make bank."

The waitress delivers their drinks, setting a large pint of amber liquid in front of Nando and an orange juice-filled highball glass in front of Simon. Leaning her way, Simon says, "Make that two," and knocks back the first in three gulps.

Nando laughs through his nose. "Come on, Simi. You can't be that simple. A woman you just met suckers you into letting her live in your meager apartment, she puts you on dates with women less attractive than she is—which makes her seem extra desirable, by the way—and then she charges you through the nose for it. And yet somehow, you're still all starry-eyed. Let's face it, she's duped you. She's taking advantage of your feelings. The signs are all there."

Simon feels the sting of his words. He's not wrong. Not about the beginning of their relationship anyway. It's different now, though, he's sure of it. "We're friends."

Nando cheers his glass at him. "But you want it to be more. Who wouldn't? She's a sexy little *imbrogliona*."

A flush of irritation prickles his skin. He needs to change the subject. "Oh, I finally have an idea for our merger."

Nando watches Simon over the rim of his glass, taking a nice long sip. "Do tell."

"I'll go over it with you tomorrow. I want to get some slides ready. If I can get you onboard, I'll show it to my uncle. He's been hearing me out lately, mentoring me."

"Of course he is. He's tired of paying you to do nothing and figures imparting wisdom is better than firing you."

Again, he's not too far off. Still, Simon's eyebrow raises a tick. "He told me he's coaching you too."

Nando waves his hands as if wiping the sentiment away. "He thinks he is. He's just an old man looking to leave a legacy, eh? Indulging him looks good on my CV. I let him"—Nando makes mocking, tuba-like noises as he Pac-Mans his hand open and closed—"wah-wah-wah at me, I nod in the right places, and then I go about my happy business."

"He's smarter than you give him credit for."

"Old man's a pain in the ass, yeah?"

Running his finger around the rim of his glass, Simon corrects, "No, he's the key to our future."

"And so, we are made to suffer." With a dramatic sigh, Nando leans back in the booth, draping his head over the top.

Simon's second drink comes, and he downs that too, a light buzz making his head cloudy. "Why are you so negative all the time?" The moment the words fall from his lips, Simon's shoulders tense. He flicks his eyes in his friend's direction, but he hasn't even lifted his head.

"Says the man who mopes around day after day because he can't contribute anything."

Simon's head leans to the side as he scoffs. He'd like to say his friend has never spoken to him this way before, but this is par for the course, isn't it? This is what their relationship is. Banter in which Simon is the butt of all jokes, and he takes it with nothing more than a scowl on his face. Old Simon wouldn't have put up with this. Maybe New Simon shouldn't either.

"I don't like it when you talk to me like that."

Nando only waves his hand again. "Don't be a child, Simi." He sits up and snags his drink. "You know I'm only teasing."

"Do I? Because sometimes it doesn't feel like it."

If an eye roll could be measured in circumference, Nando does a full three-sixty.

"No, seriously," Simon says, "no one else treats me like you do."

"Because no one else knows you like I do."

"That's not true."

Nando takes a gulp instead of a sip, clacking his drink down a bit too hard. "What? You've got friends I don't know about? You think because a piece of ass is sucking up to you constantly, wheedling you out of house and home, that all that drivel she plies you with is real? I heard her in the office. She's 'learning a lot.' Bullshit. Even I can't make sense of your notes and I have a fucking MBA."

A mean smirk takes over Simon's face, twisting a corner of his lips. "Interesting that a piece of ass is smarter than you are. Maybe you should get your money back for that useless degree." He says it without thinking and has half a mind to clap his hands over his mouth. Only the thinnest of threads holds him back.

His friend's face falls into a familiar sarcastic smile. He clucks his tongue, ticking his head to the side. "Well, look at this. Our first fight as a couple. Over a woman, no less."

"If that's what you need to tell yourself." Simon's heart is in his throat. What the fuck is he doing? What. The fuck. Is he doing?

He digs in his wallet and drops cash on the table. Snagging his jacket, Simon is up and at 'em and ready to run. "See you at work, Nando. Enjoy your dinner."

And with those words and something akin to panicked glee skipping along his insides, Simon walks himself right out the door.

He barely spent ten minutes at the table, and he just screwed up the dynamic of his life. As he looks at the setting sun, a star streaks by in the twilight, and Simon makes a wish that it will all be for the best. Sometimes truths are hard truths, but they make things better, like he and Angelica. Nando will come around. After some cooling down and some thought, he'll understand Simon's point of view and change. After all, they've been best friends for years. One little fight isn't going to change that.

Right?

# secrets

. . .

ANGELICA SITS ON THE SIDELINES. As soon as Simon came home, he went immediately to fuss over their homeless friend, tucking him in over and over even though the man was dead asleep, mouth gaping as drool trickled from the corner of his lips like a glistening strand of goop. Cough syrup with codeine will do that to you. As soon as Ciel took it about an hour ago, he went into a la-la land Angelica couldn't help but envy.

She clicks a few buttons on Simon's laptop, flicking through what he calls PowerPoints, and adds that to the ever-growing list of stupid office things she needs to learn. At least she figured out how to type in high school.

He huffs, hands on his hips and his back in a steep S curve. His resting bitch face is prominent as he stares down at his friend.

"Dr. Knight said he'd be fine," she reminds him.

"Yeah, and he also said your stitches will fall out soon, but that doesn't mean it doesn't suck that you have them in the first place."

She'll give him that one. "Hey, I saw this chart I didn't understand on page sixty-four. Do you always have to make a million slides, by the way?"

Simon makes a snorting pig noise and comes in her direction, leaning over the back of her chair and partway over her shoulder. "Show me."

She hunts and pecks, her tongue shoved into her cheek. "This one. How the hell do you get all those graphics based off the Excel sheet this goes with?"

His face comes closer to hers, near enough she can feel his warmth. He's in CEO Simon mode now, so he doesn't see beyond his work, and Angelica is grateful. Her cheeks are so warm, it's like someone pushed a hot water bottle on her face for a full minute, leaving her to scald.

"You start with a pivot table," he says. His voice is a murmur in her ear that sends a thrill up her back. What is she? Some virgin middle-schooler? He leans back and pets her hair again, making her just about melt. Why does she like that so frigging much? Is she a dog? "You should google that. It's my favorite functionality."

She would grump, except that she can feel him standing behind her, his fingers still trailing through her hair, root to tip. After a moment, she asks, "Why are you doing that?"

His hand snaps away. "Sorry."

She peeks around at him. "I didn't say stop, I just said why? This is beyond just training a pet not to bite you."

He spreads his fingers and looks at his palm as if in a faraway memory. "My mom used to do it to me to calm me down. If you haven't noticed, I do it to myself, but all it does is make me look like I put my finger in an electric socket."

"Which shows off your big ears," she adds, earning herself a scowl.

"But yours," he plops a hand on her head again, "it relaxes me. It's soft."

"I must have good shampoo." She quirks her lips, knowing their eucalyptus product is all his doing.

He chuckles, watching his fingers trail through the curls at the ends. He seems almost reverent, his bourbon brown eyes deep and enthralling. "Do you not like it? I can stop."

She shakes her head. "It calms me down too."

His smile is brilliant, his white teeth glinting in the low light. His lips are plush even when stretched into a grin, pink and utterly kissable.

Shit, what the hell is she thinking?

Holding up the laptop, she breaks the moment. "Thanks for lending me this. I think I get it. I'll watch some videos on how to make these sorts of slides too. Keep 'em nice and pretty."

He seems disappointed as he takes the thin, titanium-coated machine from her. Their fingertips brush, and it's all she can think about for a moment. "We have templates at work, so you won't have to do any fancy design stuff. Just remember, there are millions of slides because no one wants to see too much on one page. If it becomes an eye chart, then everyone will be too busy reading the fine print to listen to me talk about it."

Ciel lets out an enormous, snot-riddled snore, and rolls over. Angelica takes that as her cue. Flitting to her door, she tosses a "Good night, Simon" over her shoulder, trying her best to ignore the look of longing on his face. Trying to ignore how she wants to make him smile again. Blush more. How she wants to put her hands on him like she used to, making him get hard for her.

Oof.

What is she going to do with herself?

————

"I'm so sorry," Sophia says, regret in her voice as she flutters around their now-shared office space. "I forgot she has her physical today and it's ridiculously hard to get in with her doctor."

Sophia is shuffling and stacking papers, rapping them on the surface of her desk and putting them in—what Angelica assumes is—a pile for her. More of Simon's notes to transcribe. His idea from this weekend. Boy, when he gets something in his mind, he sure moves quickly.

"Come on, Ginger, say hi to Miss Angelica."

Sophia's little girl looks up with round eyes, emerald and so unlike her mother's. Sophia's are so brown, they're almost black, but this kid glitters at her, all innocence with a little cupid's bow mouth.

"Hallo," she says, tucking her hands behind her back and twirling on her mini hips. Oh my God, how fucking adorable is that? "You help Mama?"

Angelica ducks down and rests on her haunches, her thick, respectable nylons riding up the crack of her ass. Why she can't wear thigh-highs is beyond her. Maybe it's because when she tried hiking them up this morning, lifting her skirt to do so, she's pretty sure Simon almost fell over.

She smiles a bit at the memory.

"Yeah. Your mom is teaching me how to do a good job."

"And then she's abandoning you on your first real day," Sophia whines, still snagging items from around their ample cube space. After flopping down some more scattered papers, she reaches into a drawer and sets down a sleek laptop, better than Agatha by a long shot. "This is yours. IT will connect it to a secondary screen in about"—she looks at the surface of her phone—"fifteen minutes. After that, they'll set up your email. HR probably already has a crap ton of stuff in your inbox to take care of but put that off for now. The most important thing"— she slaps her hand on Simon's notes—"are these. He texted me this morning all in a tizzy since I wouldn't be able to get these done in time. He remembered Ginger's appointment before I did." Sophia rests her face in her hands with a long, angry grunt.

"Anyway, he has a meeting with Mr. Javik at the end of the day. Remind Simon he has to go to his uncle's office for once. He can't expect the CEO to always hoof it over here.

"IT will also hook your calendar to his, so you can stalk him and get him to his meetings on time. He's usually good about it, but some-times he just drifts off in thought." She wafts her hand around like a butterfly. "In the meantime I—"

"Who do we have here?" a masculine voice coos.

It's that Nando bastard, Simon's so-called best friend. Angelica's irritation spikes. He's dressed perfectly with his Italian hair gelled into model style and his lips pulled into an honest grin.

"Who is this?" Nando says, ducking down and patting little Ginger on the head. "Now isn't she the cutest thing in the world. Hello, kitten."

Ginger looks down at her shoes, twiddling one cowboy-booted foot on the faded industrial carpet. Seriously, how is one child so goddamned adorable?

"Say hello to Mister Nando, sweetie."

"Hallo," she says again, playing with a bow on the front of her dress before snapping her eyes up in defiance. "Mama's takin' me to get a shot, but I don' wanna." She says it with a vehemence unbefitting a little tyke like her, but the man only laughs.

"Aww, they're not so bad, eh, *bella*? Just be sure to ask for a lollipop as a reward."

"A polylop?"

Angelica is about to die from the sunshine rays of perfection beaming from the child's face.

"We don't do a lot of sugar," Sophia says. "But I'll get you some strawberries."

The child claps her chubby hands so hard, her ponytail bobs. Nando reaches over and tugs at it with a wide smile. "Strawberries it is."

Sophia is tucking things into her bag, but her movement has changed from frantic to snail-slow as she stares down at the man fawning over her child. "You like kids? You look like you'd be a good dad."

Fiddling with Ginger's ponytail and making her giggle, Nando says, "Nooo, thank you. I'm a full-time bachelor. If I had kids," he gently bops Ginger's button nose, "I'd sell them. Wouldn't I?"

Ginger squirms with riotous laughter as Nando tickles her, and Sophia watches it all with a mix of tenderness and hurt on her face. Simon mentioned she had a crush on Nando—that he picked up on the vibes—and damned if he wasn't right.

Without another word, Nando dusts himself off and lets himself into Simon's office without knocking, shutting the door a little too hard behind him. Can he do that? She turns around to ask Sophia, but the woman's eyes are moist. Those frantic gestures have returned as she finishes cramming her bag and slings it over her shoulder.

"All right, Gigi, time to go." She sniffles a little and drags a finger under her eye.

"You okay?"

"Yeah. Allergies, I swear. This time of year always gets me." She sniffles once more and takes her daughter's hand. "Sorry again. I'll make it up to you."

Before Angelica can say anything else, Sophia hustles away, little Ginger's legs at a half-run to keep up.

That was…very weird.

———

Simon is mindlessly going over the emails that came in this weekend, defaulting to the delete key whenever possible. Usually, he comes in with an empty inbox, nothing better to do than pore over it every hour of every day. Now his life is…more.

He flinches when he hears the door slam, startled out of his reverie. The bronze man in front of him doesn't seem to notice. He does, however, look unsure of how to stand. As opposed to his usual casual grace, he shifts back and forth on his feet like he needs to go to the bathroom, arms crossed, mouth a perma-frown, and forehead crinkled like the discarded answer sheet for a failed pop quiz. He's upset…and it's probably Simon's fault for running his mouth.

"For what it's worth," Simon says, "I'm sorry about last night. I shouldn't have left like that."

Nando puts his hands on his hips and huffs. "Let's pretend you got bit by a stray dog and went rabid for a short minute. I take it you're ready to act like an adult now?"

Simon breathes through his nose, letting his frustrated lungs balloon. Apparently, Nando didn't get the message. Below the irritation is a hurt he normally ignores, a niggling that picks at his hidden soft spots, but today it's closer to the surface, crooking its nails into the sensitive underside of his skin. He finally had the courage to say something…and it changed nothing.

Dragging a chair behind Simon's desk, Nando plops down and stabs his elbows into his knees. Leaning forward, he peers at Simon's primary monitor with his mouth pulled into a thin line. "Go on."

"Go on what?"

"Show me." Nando gestures at the screen with an exasperated gust of air. "Let me see this idea of yours."

"You're too early, I don't have a deck yet."

Nando scoffs. "Simon Javik didn't stay up all night getting his shit together? Since when, eh?" He pauses for a few beats before shaking his head. "Since her."

"Don't start. I was up until one in the morning getting my notes down. Believe it or not, I do have things to do at home."

"Oh? *Scopare*?" He makes lewd gestures with his fingers, his pointer and middle sliding into a loose fist.

"For the twentieth time, we're not like that."

"Then what? Did you do your nails together, huh? Talk about the finer points of American history?"

"I have a sick friend at home. I've been taking care of him."

"I'm your only friend."

Simon grits his teeth. "Contrary to popular opinion, it is possible for other people to like me."

"Not with that face," Nando says lightly, as if it was all just a joke to him. He leans back with a sigh and winds his arms together. "All right then, if you can't show me, tell me. I've been curious all night. What's got you all crazy?"

That flare of excitement ignites in Simon's brain again, shifting his gear into drive and overtaking all else. Putting his qualms aside, he dives in. "One of the deals still on my desk is a talent organization. It focuses on recruitment—"

"We already have recruiters."

"Which you admit suck. Not only that, though, it has training programs to help single mothers get back into the workforce. It teaches them office skills so they can have a better salary than retail can give them. This place has got a day care, a GED program, something like a crash course in computer applications, basic accounting, and—believe it or not—event planning. They think that if their candidates bring something special to the table, it will give them a leg up."

Nando looks unimpressed, but Simon muscles on.

"We're lacking in entry-level candidates, another thing we both know. Seems like that's the case all over the city. The place has more job recs than they know how to fill. Enter us. I can top off their talent funnel. I have connections to some homeless people who are completely capable, life just hit them hard."

Nando sits up straighter. "You can't be serious."

"There's a facility they stay in. We're always looking to donate charity money, right? Investors are into that now. 'Corporate Social Responsibility.' We could renovate the space to include baths, then open up our HR requirements and let them use that address as a place of residence. Make it into more of a halfway house than just a shelter."

"Of all the stupid—"

"All we have to do is build an annex. With everyone my mom introduced me to on the city planning board, I know I can get the permits we need. The block they're on is basically empty. If we can upskill these people, get them some work-appropriate clothes—"

"Yes, by all means, let's hire the junkies and flunkies. Do you even hear yourself, huh? You think our employees, our *real* employees, are going to work alongside the needle-sticking, pill-popping masses?"

"Ciel said that too."

"Who?"

"But we can drug test. Believe it or not, a lot of them are clean. They're just regular people, Nando. Ones who deserve a chance."

"So, let's just alienate all our real talent. *Che stupido.*"

Simon turns toward his friend, squaring his jaw. "You don't under-stand the new generation entering the workforce. The long-timers may balk, but we'll get a flood of college grads who look for something in a company beyond a paycheck. They want to belong to something with a higher mission."

"And where's the profit in all this, may I ask?"

"This talent firm makes money hand over fist. They place high-value candidates too. A lot of people believe in their mission and will only work with them."

"And all this extra money goes to, I can't believe I'm even asking this, 'homeless halfway houses' while we're sinking current revenue down the hole?"

"That should be net neutral. We'll trim the fat around here to make up the difference. There are too many people in mid-range professional roles. The staffing is bloated. An upside down triangle."

Nando scoffs.

"Do you know I walked down a whole cube aisle of people playing video games the other day? Solitaire and Mahjong and Mario emulators."

"What the hell is an emulator?"

"And they didn't even care that I was behind them. Like this was just part of their job. If they were busy contributing, we wouldn't have stuff like that. There's your profit. Lean out the organization. You can probably cut half the managers too."

"We need those managers' oversight," Nando grumbles, his temper budding.

"No, we need employees we can trust to work hard and care about the company. But first, we need to be a company worth caring about. That's what my mother would want."

Nando stands, leaning into Simon's space. "How dare you throw that nepotistic babble in my face, eh? You don't know what your mother wants any more than I do. Know why?"

The "because she's dead" lingers, unsaid, in the air between them. Simon's heart is a sudden pit of hurt, the old, painful wound widening his eyes.

Pale, Nando seems to know he's gone too far. His best friend's mouth opens once, twice, before he turns on his heel and storms out, leaving Simon lurching in silence.

———

Angelica's not eavesdropping. She's not. Except for that she is. Maybe. Kind of. Okay, definitely. She can't really hear what's going on, though. The muffled voices are just low notes drawing long lines. One thing is for sure, they're talking fast. What could that bastard be ranting to Simon about for so long? Angelica has half a mind to—

The sound escalates to a shout…then silence. Then the door flings open and the dick in question slams into Angelica's unprepared frame, nearly bowling her over like the last pin before a spare. He catches her, then seems to realize who she is, scowling and dropping her like a lava stone. His green-eyed glare is pure loathing, but she refuses to shrink.

"Can I help you?" She might as well have told him to go fuck himself for the tone in her voice.

The man bites his tongue, holding back what he obviously wants to say—perhaps shout—at her. Instead, he brushes by without a second glance. His silence is more unnerving than any scathing retorts would have been. She follows his movement with her lips pursed, angry and suspicious. Was he yelling earlier or was Simon? And where would he be going in such a hurry? His feet make hard thumps on the carpeted floor, and the people around him give a wide berth, intimidated in a way Angelica refuses to be.

She shivers at the thought of him touching her with those smooth, uncalloused hands. What a vicious expression he gave her. What cold eyes he has.

…Eyes.

She looks at the empty space where Sophia sits, pieces falling into place in her mind.

That's who Sophia's baby looks like.

It's Nando.

---

The morning fades into late afternoon with Simon in a daze. He watches the sun travel to its apex out of his large window with nothing but sorrow on his mind. His mother was precious to him. She'd been the one who nipped his violent, wild ways in the bud, giving him a "higher purpose." His father helped too, teaching Simon other outlets for his frustration. Things like diving deep into numbers, those brush-strokes that tell honest truths about the things people try to obscure. Those graphic representations of the physics that rule the universe. The equations that break down life into the smallest of quarks.

The unstoppable Mrs. Lisa Javik-Audra took what was left of Simon after the angst was torn away and pulled him to her side, teaching him everything he knows and introducing him to anyone who'd bother setting eyes on him. And with her influence, that meant almost everyone in the city. Simon's old life faded away, another sliding into place. One of cocktail parties he was too young to drink at and remembering names of people he'd only just met and may never meet again. He hated it, but he loved her. He'd do anything for her, and having her finally give him the attention he'd craved his whole life only made him want to work harder. She loved her business as much as she loved her family, and he'd thought his new idea could benefit both. It would fulfill him, and it would do good for the legacy she left behind.

Simon wipes his face hard and puts the thought aside.

A tentative knock comes at his door. "You look depressed."

Simon spins around at his uncle's voice with a frown. "You're early. I was going to go down to you."

"Meh." Lawrence shrugs. "I needed the walk. What's eating you? You look like someone killed your puppy."

"That's terrible."

"That's how you look. Seems like you need a walk too. How 'bout we hit the big room?"

Simon gives a smile, weak but honest. Conference Room A takes up half the floor below, its exorbitant, stadium-style seating made for the really big presentations. Lawrence and Simon have snuck down there to watch movies with cafeteria popcorn balls in hand. It was only twice, but it mattered.

"Sure."

The two men saunter through the office floor. Simon can't help but notice, with no small amount of bitterness, how people seem to fret in Lawrence's presence, closing application windows and upsizing spreadsheets and Word documents, trying hard to look busy in a way they don't when Simon walks by.

His uncle doesn't make small talk, which is welcome. They just stride next to each other, and the warm sense of family is enough to make Simon feel a bit better. Uncle Lawrence believes in him, even if Nando doesn't.

High-ceilinged and cacophonous with whispering silence, Conference Room A is devoid of life. Almost. Much to Simon's chagrin, Nando sits in one of the chairs with his head down, not looking up when they enter. Instead, he plays with a sharp crease on the leg of his trousers, his face petulant and sad. Simon's heart twinges, but much less than it would have a month ago. Or even a week.

"Did someone kill your puppy too?" Lawrence asks, looking between them.

Unable to keep the grimace from his face, Simon says, "I told him my next acquisition plan, and he didn't like it very much."

"Oh?"

"Don't bother listening to it," Nando says with a rueful smile. "Simi's tender heart is getting the best of him, I think."

Tossing over a smirk, Lawrence says, "You have a tender heart? Since when?"

"Since I found something I care about."

Lawrence hums. "You have a presentation together?"

"Sophia is out, so my other admin is taking care of it. She's new to the role—her first day, actually— so it's just taking her a little time to get the hang of it."

"Because she's unqualified," Nando adds.

"Don't," Simon says sharply. "Just don't."

Lawrence ticks his eyes back and forth between the two of them, curiosity written all over his face.

"I'm getting you final numbers by tomorrow," Simon says, never more sure of anything in his life.

His uncle doesn't look convinced. "I've heard that before."

"I'm serious," Simon says. "Nando, since you're so keen on coming down on my work, why don't we review your plan at the same time?"

Nando snaps to attention. "Excuse me? I don't have time to pull together anyth—"

"Make it Friday, then," Simon says. "If you've been working as hard as you say, you've got to have something to show for it, right? We're CEO candidates, not our game-playing, half-assing employees. It's time we get out of our own way and end this. And I can't wait to see the look on your face when I win."

Eyes wide and jaw dropped, Nando starts to speak, but Simon has no patience for it. He jogs up the stairs of the auditorium, leaving the two other heads of the company gaping at him. He's tired of being looked down on. Tired of being second-guessed. This is his do-or-die moment. If he has what it takes to be CEO, so be it. If not, he's quitting this goddamned place and the stress of his family's gift to him. A forever job with more money than he knows what to do with isn't worth his happiness. Not by a long shot. He deserves to have more in his life than this.

And if they don't see it, then he doesn't need them.

———

The windows look lonely as Angelica peers up. One of them is Simon's, she just can't tell which. She stands outside with a palm hiding the glare of sunset as it ricochets off the building, wondering about why he was so blunt when he dismissed her, sending her to watch over Ciel on her own. He took her work and thanked her, but seemed a ball of fury otherwise, saying only that he'd be staying very, very, *very* late.

Insecurity wiggles its way into her mind. She hopes she did a good enough job to help him. She's used to saying pretty words, puckering her lips, and showing how acrobatic she can be in bed for four hours a night. This is exhausting in a whole new way. Her brain is fried. Her hips hurt from sitting in a chair for hours on end and her wrists are sore from typing. Still, her hourly rate kept her going, adding chunk by chunk together and knowing it was all hers, not Max's. She vows to buy pajamas with her first paycheck. Bottoms, anyway. She'll still wear Simon's T- shirts, but she'd like a pair of boy-cut shorts that show off her ass. That will make him drool.

Wait. Bad idea.

She sighs at the windows that are probably not his and reminds herself to behave. He's her shelter in a storm. She'd be stupid to screw that up no matter how much she wants to touch him. To have him touch her.

What exactly did his dates teach him?

A wave of jealousy that is incongruous with her life view rears its ugly head, and she puffs out an angsty breath.

"You," a voice growls behind her. Someone takes her arm in a tight fist and drags her closer to the building, out of the way of wandering pedestrians and almost into the prickled bushes that line the perimeter. It's Nando. Those cold eyes scan her like she's trash, his lips pulled into a sneer so deep it leaves creases in his face.

"You've changed him," he says. "And not for the better. What in God's name are you telling him, eh? What pretty lies got his head shoved so far up his ass?"

"Simon?"

"Of course, Simon," he spits, gesturing at the high-rise windows. "I thought I knew him, but in less than two months, you've completely fucked with his head. Now he's treating me like I'm not even his friend."

"You? A friend? Not that I've seen. I don't know how long you've been doing this for, but I guarantee you're doing it wrong."

His hands ball at the sides, the threads of his veins swelling underneath his olive skin. "You know nothing about this. I basically carted him through grad school. You think he's awkward now? You should have seen him when—"

"Spoken like someone who truly cares about him." Angelica pushes Nando back, getting him out of her face. "Tell me, have you ever thought about how miserable he's been? How lonely? If he grabbed on to me this hard, did you ever think it's because he had nobody else?"

And that's the truth, isn't it? The only reason he wants her is because he never had the chance to love anybody else.

Anger, hurt, and shame fill her like an empty cup.

"You make him feel like he's nothing," she says. "You take every thought in his head and make it useless. Friends make people stronger." Like he does for her. "Friends protect each other." Like she wants to do for him. "Friends don't cut you down every chance they get, like I've listened to you do. And if you don't get your shit together, you don't deserve him."

They sit in stone-cold silence, their eyes locked in a battle for dominance. Something in Nando's face changes, though, and Angelica's not sure she likes it. He looks her up and down, a mean-spirited smirk pulling his lips to the side as those green eyes shimmer with a predatorial gleam.

"I see. I know what you are now." He leans in closer. "You're a whore, aren't you?"

She rears back a hand to slap that smug fucking expression off his face, but he snags her arm, stopping it mere inches from busting his lip.

He *tsks*. "And I don't mean promiscuous, *tesora*, I mean you're an actual whore." His smile is like the cat that got the cream. "I know you, don't I?"

His face says he does.

Oh God…

# lines drawn

. . .

THERE'S a crackle of static between them, violent and electrifying. Angelica steels herself, trying not to tremble in the face of her adversary.

"I hired a hooker for my cousin's birthday once," Nando purrs. "For the price, I thought I'd get some strung-out meth addict, but in you walked, a pretty little thing, and when my sloshed *cugino* started puking and all I could do was laugh, you read me the riot act, ranting that I should care more. That I was a bad influence. That I should— what was it? Get the fuck off my ass? I see that attitude of yours hasn't changed. Still like to tell me off, do you? At least you have your clothes on this time."

Angelica struggles to free herself from his grip, but he's like iron.

"Leave Simon alone," he growls. "Leave the company, leave his house, leave his life. Otherwise, I'm more than happy to share your little secret."

Angelica ticks up her chin. "He already knows. He doesn't care."

There's a thick pause before he tosses her arm away. "Of course, he doesn't." He rubs his fingers into his eyes, skewing them sideways as he huffs out a breath of frustration. Or disappointment perhaps. "You're right. He must have been very lonely. Otherwise, he'd never lower himself to someone like you. Someone so dirty he could only be ashamed if others knew what you are."

Nando scours his fingers through his hair before shaking his head, his face sorrowful and wounded, as if she's acid and he's forever marred by her existence. "I've been his friend longer than anyone, and I refuse to watch him make mistake after mistake because he's being tainted by some stupid *troia*."

"Look, I'm not—"

"You are. You can try to convince yourself otherwise, you can try to convince *him*, but the fact wafts off you like a stink. You don't belong here. You never will. And it's only a matter of time before he sees that too."

Grimacing one last time, grinding his hate into her, he turns his back and walks away. Angelica has half a mind to chase him, to let loose her claws and attack, but the other half of her wants to curl into a ball and cry.

This is exactly what she was afraid of.

Simon is going to suffer because of her.

———

It's late. So late Angelica can barely keep her bleary eyes open. She scrubs them and slaps her cheeks, scrolling through her phone for things that piss her off, if only to keep her brain from falling into a foggy stupor.

She hears the crisp jingle of Simon's keys in the door and glances to the top of her screen. Eleven o'clock, later than he's ever come home before. She wonders if he's eaten. Ciel is passed out in the land of prescription cough syrup again, so perhaps, if she sneaked, she could whip him up something quick. Not that he'd want to eat carb-less.

She wants to hole up in her bed until she rots, weeds sprouting from her bones in pretty tangles, but there's no putting this off. "No more hiding things," he'd said.

These ground rules suck.

Bile in her throat, she tiptoes to her door, opening it just enough to poke her head out. The small space between the two bedrooms is dim, lit only by cast-off glow from the nearby bathroom. How is she supposed to have this conversation? She doesn't know where to begin. Even the thought of opening her mouth and letting these words fall out clamps her throat shut and sends dread tingling down to her toes.

"Hey," she hisses a whisper.

No response, but she can hear him quietly rattling around in the kitchen.

"*Psst*. Simon," she tries again, earning his head poking around the corner, dark circles under his half-closed eyes.

Shit. He's exhausted. That makes this so much worse. He should be taking care of himself, not dealing with her mess.

"Hey," he whispers back. "How'd he do tonight?"

Flicking her gaze left, she looks at their mutual acquaintance. Ciel lies flat on his back, tucked in tight with his wrists flung up over the arm of the sofa. He looks dead to the world. At least someone is having a good time.

She keeps her voice low. "He was still coughing his brains out, but his fever is gone. None today at all, he said. Though, knowing him, he could be lying through his ass."

"You mean through his teeth."

"Through an orifice, anyway."

"Surprised you're up. You seemed pretty tired earlier. Is something the matter?"

Here we go. The starting gun has fired. This is where the fight begins. This is when he kicks her out. This is when he tells her she's not worth the trouble.

This is when he breaks her heart.

She fingers her necklace. Why does this hurt so bad? Here she stands, eyes misting as she prepares to be ousted by the man who wormed his way through her defenses, digging past the thick wall surrounding her heart to find the whimpering shrivel left behind.

She opens her mouth to say something, anything, to stop this moment of silence from dragging out while his eyes flick back and forth between hers, concern etched on his face.

"Do you want to quit?" he asks. She can't answer. "You shouldn't.

You did a good job today. Everything was set up exactly the way I needed."

The shapes of words stick in her throat, choking her. How can she put this? Something along the lines of: "Your friend called me a whore in broad daylight and threatened to tell the world about me" maybe? "The person you're closest to is more than willing to drag me through the mud by my hair" perhaps? Ideas and apologies jumble in her head, overwhelming her until all she wants to do is throw down and scream.

Wonder of wonders, he smirks. "Still can't talk about yourself?"

She huffs a pathetic little laugh, but a tear skates down her cheek, even so. She scrubs it away with the back of her hand, praying he didn't see, but knowing he did.

His fingers flow through her hair again, strong and warm and heartbreaking. "Is this job too much for you?"

She sniffles. "It's not that."

"Did something happen? Was someone mean to you?"

Another tear falls.

His voice drops to a rumble. "Who was it?"

She doesn't want to say. Asshole or not, Nando is Simon's best friend. It would be like shooting herself in the gut if she were to try to go toe to toe with that man. Years by each other's sides creates a bond Angelica can never hope to break. Why would Simon choose her over him?

"Someone recognized me," she manages. "Told me a story I don't even remember about myself, but it was so in-character it can't have been a lie. They know what I am."

"What you were," he corrects, though his voice has taken on a detached quality. His hand pulls away to rake through his own night-shade tresses instead, knuckles whitening as his fist clamps down and tugs. "What did they say?"

Her hands wring so hard, she can hear the whisper sound as they pass over each other. "If I don't disappear, they'll tell."

"What does it matter? I already know."

"You're not the only one with ears, Simon."

And he seems to realize it too. A vein in his temple pulses as he grinds his jaw. "Who's doing this?" he asks more forcefully this time, his gaze pinning her down. At her continued hesitation, it seems to click. "Nando."

Two, three, four little droplets of hot moisture trace from her eyes to her chin. There's nothing she can do but hang her head. "I'm so sorry."

He doesn't say anything and he doesn't touch her. She's terrified to look him in the eye and see his rage boil. Digging her grave deeper, she asks, "What if he tells your uncle?"

There is a heavy pause. "Then I'm guessing CEO is off the table."

Angelica's heart crumbles into bits that rain down her body. "Why?"

"My…history with you…it would cause a scandal our investors wouldn't like very much."

Dizzy with overwhelm, she squats on her haunches, arms wrapped around herself. Her experiment with this new life has already failed. Why did she think it would be any different? Her existence is based on bouncing from one misery to the next, after all.

She shouldn't have bothered escaping Max. What was she hoping to become? Something else, sure, but what? A paragon of virtue? A doctor to the stars? A Wall Street tycoon?

Or maybe just Simon's?

Dreams she didn't even know she had are dying.

"I'll leave," she says. "You've worked too hard for too long for something stupid like this to fuck it all up. You don't need this drama. You don't need me. You never did."

He drops to his knees, arms cradling her back and cheek pressed against the top of her head. He's heavy and all-encompassing and perfect. "Shh. I didn't say that."

Her body couldn't ball into itself any tighter. Unbidden, the words seep out, "See? No matter what I do, I'll never deserve you."

It's an admission of wanting, as blatant as if she screamed her heart's desire in his face, blunt, raw, and tactless. Stupid. How fucking terribly ridiculous to confess to a man who should drop her down a well, never to be seen again.

He wraps himself more firmly around her, squeezing and sharing his heat. His heart beats in rabbit thumps, fast and hard and sweet as he nuzzles against her. "Don't be like him. Don't pretend you know what's best for me. Don't take my feelings and throw them away. If I believe in something, trust me to do what's right."

She sags, holding back a sob as he caresses the curve of her spine with the tips of his fingers. "Trust me," he whispers again. "Believe in me. If something happens, we'll figure it out together, just like before. I told you you're not alone." His voice hitches. "Please don't leave me alone either."

Her arms cling like ropes and she silently begs him to love her. To let this moment be real. To not let it break.

"Don't go." His fingers thread through her hair, clutching at the nape of her neck. "Please."

She can't talk. There's no sound that could pull from her throat right now that would make any sense. Her nails dig into his suit as she holds on to that broad back. She leans against him so hard, she nearly topples them, but he still won't let go.

His voice is a low song. "I'm sorry for what I did to you. When I found out about the money, the way I acted—"

"Don't." She presses her face into the crook of his neck, breathing him in. "That wasn't us. It was Noah and Sadie. We're not them anymore."

Simon uses his grip to pull her back, letting whisper-kisses pass over her cheeks to whisk her tears away. His gaze is hazy, half-lidded but unwavering. "He lives in me though. Maybe he always will. I feel like him right now. My mind is going a mile a minute, thinking about what I'm supposed to do. What I want to do."

His tug on her hair lifts her chin and makes her ache inside, her body waking up to his presence. His attention. His touch.

"I want to hold you." He's a hair's breadth away from sliding those soft lips over hers. "Kiss you until you can't breathe." His fingers flex, sliding down her sensitive ribs to the swell of her hips. "Touch you everywhere you'll let me." She can taste the sweetness of his breath as her lashes flutter closed. "I want to go slow, take my time, and completely, utterly seduce—"

"Children!" There is a harsh *clap, clap* from the living room as Ciel glares from the couch. "There are two bedrooms behind you. I suggest you pick one."

Simon couldn't launch away faster. He lands on his rump, legs sprawled and face like a burst cherry.

Ciel, stuffed in his puffy blanket, holds his hands up, palms out. "Look, sorry to cockblock, but you're literally right in front of me."

"Cockblock?" Simon squeals. His eyes shoot to hers. "What's a cockblock?"

Ciel groans and rubs his temples. "Context clues, Simon. It's a compound word."

Angelica sees the exact moment it sinks in, and Simon lets out a sound like a damsel about to faint. "I didn't…! I wasn't…!"

"You were." Ciel smirks, clearing his throat and letting out a weak cough. "Now man up and drag her into your room."

Which seems to have the exact opposite effect. Simon scrambles up like a foal trying to run and darts to his door, calling "G'NITE" all too loudly.

He slams himself away, and Angelica is left stunned on the carpet, eyes like circles and her jaw dropped. With her drying tears, she's run the gamut of emotions this evening, but she's clearly not done yet. Looking at Simon's door, she sees the back of his heels through the gap as he stands stock-still on the other side. Angelica can picture him with his palms slapped over his face as the hard-on she likely gave him deflates. In her mind, it makes a cartoonish droop sound.

She bursts into laughter, slapping her hand on her knee and snorting hard, giggles rolling through her. She wishes she could see his face right now. How red would he be? How deep would his scowl pull?

Her guffaws seem endless as she pictures him in all his humiliated glory. There is no one better than this sweet, innocent, unforgettable man. Not by a long shot.

So fuck Nando. If he can dish it out, they can take it, she'll make goddamned sure. If Simon wants her as bad as she wants him, the rest of the world can burn.

———

"This is nice," Sophia says, sipping a cup of tea. "I don't usually get to work with anyone so closely. Being a direct line to the higher-ups usually makes people either want to suck up to you or stay as far away as possible. Be ready for brown-nosing or snub nosing, depending on people's risk tolerance."

Angelica rolls her eyes, unprepared for office politics. It always comes down to jockeying for power. That will probably pop up between her and Sophia as well. She likes her, but she's waiting for the other shoe to drop. She'll do something wrong, and this woman will turn on her, getting all prickly and bitchy. Until that happens, though, Angelica will allow herself to just enjoy it. Sophia isn't like any other woman she's met. Being with her comes naturally, like floating on a raft down the river. Wouldn't it be great if that feeling could last?

Angelica's foolish optimism makes her smile softly. It comes too easily to her sometimes, and usually gets her in trouble.

"Thanks for holding down the fort yesterday. Gigi did well. She didn't even scream when she got her shot, which was a real surprise. She seems like an angel, but she can wail the house down with the best of them. She's a bit of a tyrant."

*Like her father*, Angelica thinks, lifting her own mug and taking a sip. It's apple cinnamon spice, like drinking the scent of a Thanksgiving pie. Pure decadence. They have reign of a small conference room they commandeered for "teatime." Sophia brought in cookies—actual, homemade cookies—as an apology for making Angelica spend her first day alone. She's never had a snickerdoodle before, but it's more than worth the calories.

Sophia rests her head on the blonde, wooden, oval-shaped table, sweeping aside a tangle of cords that go to god-knows-what. "Don't you think Nando did good with her yesterday? He'd never seen her before, but they seemed to like each other."

Nando. What a stupid nickname. Then again, it's not like Armando was a gift to begin with.

Angelica scoffs into her drink. "Who would have thought?"

"He gave you a bad impression the first time you met, I know, but there's more to him than meets the eye." Her mentor fiddles with her cup. "He's deeper than people give him credit for. I just can't think of him as a bad person. I know he's arrogant but—"

"But he's Ginger's father." The words drop before she has a chance to consider them. "So you'd rather give him the benefit of the oh-so-obvious doubt."

Sophia's round face goes pale. "I never said that. Why would you think that?"

…Shit. Well now she's done it. Open mouth, insert demurely heeled foot. There goes her optimism.

Clearing her throat, Angelica taps a finger high on her cheek. "Her eyes. They're exactly the same."

Sophia's fingers clench. "You won't say anything, will you?"

She *pffts*. "I wouldn't tell that man if his head was on fire."

The thought doesn't seem to reassure Sophia in the slightest. She slides the filigreed tray of cookies away and clasps her hands together under her chin. Her face is one big wince, agonized and devastated. "If you figured it out, then it's only a matter of time until the rest of the world does."

Angelica's regret goes all the way to the bottom of her. "It was a guess. I wouldn't have thought it just by looking at them, but you were —I don't know—flustered and dreamy once he showed up. And the way you watched them together…? I'm good at reading people, and it seemed like there was something more there, that's all. I shouldn't have said anything, I'm sorry."

"I should have known I couldn't keep my cool. Not that I'm very chill in the first place." When Sophia picks up her drink again, her movements are sluggish and slow, her lips pulled into the tiniest hint of a sad smile. "I have this fantasy that, if I keep bringing her to the office, he'll fall in love with her. And maybe, because of that, he'll fall in love with me too."

What a terrifying thought. "Some men aren't worth the effort."

A sigh, long and heavy-hearted, gusts out in a puff, Sophia's chest rising and falling as if a bellows had blown her up and squeezed her out again. "Being a single mother is hard. Even harder when the solution looks at you every day without really seeing you. Thank God for Simon. He's always letting me duck out to get her at school if she needs me, letting her play in his office when I need to bring her to work for whatever reason. He's been really good to me."

Angelica's heart warms. "He's good to me too."

"If he didn't have such a mad face all the time, women would throw themselves at him."

"Thank baby Jesus for resting bitch face." Angelica giggles.

It's Sophia's turn to speak uncomfortable truths. "You two like each other, don't you? Are you together?"

Angelica almost chokes on her tea. "No. I mean…not yet. Not that I don't want to. I just…I don't know how to be with someone like that and…why would he even…" Ah, damnit, she's rambling like Simon does. He must be sprinkling his personality on her. Firming her chin, she nods. "I just want to deserve him."

"Why wouldn't you?" Sophia asks. "Spa steam rooms aside, you seem like a nice person. And you make him happy, I can tell. Plus, you're doing a great job for never having done office work before."

Pride fizzes in tiny bubbles, bringing a smile to her face. She's been working hard in her off hours to make sure she isn't a drag or a burden. Having it pay off means everything to her. "You think you can train a bunch of entry-level staff like me? If Simon gets his way, we'll have a lot of people who need some hand-holding."

"Ohhhh, I read his plan," Sophia says, a dreamy look in her eyes. "I was so sad when he was going to pass on that talent agency, but this is an amazing way to fold it in. Sometimes he has these strokes of brilliance he doesn't give himself credit for. That's why people like us have to look out for him. We have to remind him how bright his star can shine."

"I can get behind that," Angelica says. Because he's the brightest star in the fucking sky. Picking up a cookie, Sophia holds it out as if to cheers with her, so Angelica follows suit.

They clunk their treats together, dusting crumbs all over the table. "To Simon?" Sophia asks.

"To Simon."

———

Thursdays are the best. Simon called a single "no meeting day" per week, so his team can focus on getting work done as opposed to meeting after meeting, *talking* about getting work done. He, himself, is in the weeds, his inbox piled up with documents and contracts to review. Letters of intent to buy a business are heavy reading, and Simon's eyes blur as he scans for the key, understandable bits, praying that the legal team does their job to dig through the unintelligible rest.

Leaning back into a stretch, he peeks out the doorframe window of his office to where Angelica and Sophia sit with their heads down, hammering out work. Angelica has been a godsend to his over-whelmed EA, taking on the grunt work so Sophia can focus on more complicated things. Better work-life balance all around. He couldn't be happier he hired her.

She swore to Ciel last night that half of her first paycheck was going to Simon. He wasn't supposed to hear it, futzing around with his hair in the bathroom as he was, but she had a long rant about responsibility and turning a new leaf and taking it seriously. If he wasn't falling hard for her before, he's definitely doing it now.

With a stupid smirk on his face that probably screams "lovesick," he refocuses on his work, tappa tappa-ing out in-line comments and edits to benefit their position. The world drifts away into his monitor as his mind swirls through the opportunity, believing in it more and more with every typed line.

"Call it off," comes from his entryway, startling him. The door shuts in that familiar, too-hard way, and Nando walks in. He is a kalei-doscope of things that are out of character. His shoulders are hunched, his hands thrust into his pockets. His always-perfect hair is disheveled and his face is pinched as his green eyes search Simon's with an inscrutable expression. "I can't do it tomorrow."

"Do what?"

"The presentation. I'm not ready. I need you to delay your proposal."

Confusion mixed with irritation interrupts Simon's normal programming. "Impossible. Never mind that Lawrence has been hounding me for days, but this opportunity isn't going to just sit here. I can only—"

"See, that's the thing. *I. I* can only. But for me, I have to get a team of people onboard. HR is dragging its ass and I need to coordinate with ten other departments globally. It's not fair. You're fucking me over with this, and you know it."

Simon hardens. "How is this my fault? I've been working on plan after plan for months. Sure, none of them have passed the Nando Test, but at least I've been trying. What have you been doing all this time?"

"Thinking," Nando says through his teeth. "This isn't something we should take lightly. It's a huge disruption to business and it affects our stock price."

"So do acquisitions."

"But one sets the company up for growth, the other looks like we're cutting costs to make up for bad sales and overall failure."

"They see our quarterly financials. They know better."

"See?" Nando scoffs. "You don't care what you're doing to me. You're justifying advancing your agenda because you want to screw me. We're supposed to be friends."

*Supposed to* being the phrase that sticks in Simon's mind. He clucks his tongue against the roof of his mouth, anger burning in his belly. "Angelica was right. You're holding me back on purpose."

His "friend" groans, putting his fingers to his temples. "That fucking woman. She sees me dig in on you once and thinks she knows everything."

"This isn't new. You always find a way to shoot me down, whether telling me my plans are trash or just making me feel small. Even though I'm always giving you ideas, you've never done a single thing to help me."

Nando advances, flailing at the door. "Because she says so? What the fuck do you tell her about me?"

"The truth."

"The truth that you're utterly alone without me? Huh? The truth that no one else wants to be anywhere near you? How your attitude turns everyone off? How I'm the only one who bothers to—"

"So I'm a charity case. Not someone you actually like, just someone you feel bad enough for."

It's like he slapped him. Eyes hurt, Nando steps back, shaking his head. "I didn't say that."

"No." Simon glowers. "You just act like it."

"We had no problems before her. Don't you see? She's trying to isolate you. Twist you against the people who care about you. If not for me, who's going to warn you about that cunt and her fucking schemes?"

Simon stands to his full height, shoving his chair behind him with a stuttering roll. "Say another word and I want nothing to do with you."

Another cut to Nando's sensibilities. His face falls, and everything about him dims from a fire to a flicker. "Over a woman?"

"Over that woman."

"You're not even fucking her."

Simon sneers. "This is about more than just that. If there's anything she taught me, it's that sex can be mindless and meaningless. I'd rather talk to her for an hour than sleep with her for ten."

Something in Nando's expression changes. There is a tension in his eyes as the corner of his mouth pulls into a smirk. "Don't worry, Simi. A whore like her? I'm sure there's a world full of customers who can tell you exactly what you're missing."

A tight fist forms at Simon's side, clenching so hard his knuckles strain. For the first time in a long time, he needs to hold back from knocking someone's teeth out. Who would have thought it would be his best friend that made him want to explode?

Nando's face is nothing but smug satisfaction. "Since you have no sense of decency, I guess I'll see you for our presentations tomorrow, eh? If we're done, let it be fucking done."

With that, he shakes his head as if in pity and turns on his heels. The door is opened and slammed before Simon can blink, and it's all for the better. There are no more slicing words to fling at each other. Without saying much, they already said it all. The only thing left is to let their rage fly and beat each other into the dirt...but Simon would prefer to win in other ways.

Let it be done, indeed.

# actions and consequences

. . .

ANGELICA'S and Sophia's heads swivel as Simon's door slams shut…again. What the fuck is wrong with this Nando guy and why can't he close the door like a normal person? It's louder than the first time, shaking the frame with a clatter.

The man looks ready to kill. Angelica, specifically.

A prickle of fear pebbles her skin. This is different than when Damion looked at her. He wanted to indiscriminately pounce, tear, and shred. This man looks like he hates her down to her every cell and sinew.

"Is something the matter?" Sophia asks.

Nando flicks his eyes to her in the most absent of ways before turning his regard back to Angelica, who feels like she's about to become the victim of a screaming match. One she's not so sure she can win. Instead, he scoffs with narrowed eyes, shaking his head and stomping off. He goes so fast, the sides of his suit jacket billow open behind him, his body bouncing with temper tantrum steps.

"Is this an everyday thing for him or…?" Angelica says, turning toward her counterpart.

Blinking, Sophia stands to look around the corner and watch him melt into the distance. "Do you think something happened?"

Angelica snorts. "Simon probably told him off."

"You do know who we're talking about, right? Simon would never."

"Well, if he didn't, he should." Angelica goes back to clicking around her HR training, which she is only now getting into. It's been a busy few days, but now that she's started, she's inhaling nothing but video upon video about corporate corruption, anti-harassment, and privacy laws in Europe of all things.

Sophia plops down into her chair with a *fwump*, staring after the brown-haired menace. "I've never seen him upset like that before. Usually, he leaves with a smile on his face."

"You mean a sadistic smirk. He probably gets a hard-on from driving Simon crazy."

Sophia hisses a shush to her, and Angelica remembers that sexual misconduct blurb from a few screens ago. "Sorry."

Turning toward the corner once more, Sophia lifts to peek around again. "Something must be wrong. This isn't like him. I should do something."

"When someone rages against the machine that hard, steer clear, lest you become the innocent victim of their outburst."

"He didn't outburst. He…non-burst. But he looked like he wanted to rip the world apart."

Angelica tips back in her chair to look at her colleague. Sophia is biting her lower lip, slumped over with her skirted knees open too wide. Thank goodness their desk has a privacy panel.

"You really care about him, don't you?"

Sophia doesn't answer, only puffs out a breath.

"You deserve better than pining over a man who isn't worth it."

"Don't say that," Sophia murmurs softly. "Gigi deserves to know her father someday. She deserves a family." She leans back farther. "And he should know the truth about all this. Do you think I should tell him?"

"Now? Absolutely not."

"But I've been thinking about it ever since you and I talked. I've gone over and over it in my head. What I want to say, what I want him to say back. What he might say instead. I can't sleep because of this."

"Bad timing. Warning. Danger."

Sophia tosses her a sarcastic look, making it quite clear Angelica's banter is undesirable. "He deserves to know. I never gave him the chance to choose. What would you do if you found out there was a child out there you could love with your whole being who's been denied you all this time? One you saw for only a moment, and your heart skipped a beat. You saw how he reacted to her. How she reacted to him. It was so natural, it was adorable."

"He also said he didn't want kids."

"But he didn't say he didn't want *her*." Sophia's eyes flash with her rising temper, shutting down any other words in Angelica's arsenal. "She deserves a dad. Didn't you have a dad?"

Not one who loved her. There's no guarantee parents will want their children.

"If he's this upset, maybe he needs to know that there's a chance for happiness in his life. Some hope. Something to love and care about. Some*one*." Sophia stands up, smoothing her skirt and straightening her blouse, and an unexpected fear clamps down on Angelica's heart, taking her blood pressure from the ground to the moon.

"You're not seriously going to do this…"

When she looks at Angelica, Sophia's eyes have gone from nettled to nervous. She knits her fingers together, twiddling them as she asks, "Will you come with me? Like, for moral support?"

"He hates me."

"But I don't."

Sophia's eyes are made of glass and something in Angelica melts like butter on a hot summer day, savory goodness running through her in sweet and salty drops. The woman in front of her seems so vulnerable, so in need of a friend. Angelica wonders, if she'd ever let herself look like that, would something have been different? Is that what she looked like to Bee? Because all of a sudden, Angelica wants nothing more than to protect this person. Stand up for this person. Be what they need when they need it.

"Okay," she finds herself saying. "What do you want me to do?"

———

The trek to Nando's office is filled with tense silence. Employees are typing away on their computers, looking blank-faced and bored. Angelica passes a glance at one of the strangers, thinking she's looking at the beginnings of a blog post, but catches a few words, realizing the person is writing smutty fanfiction. She scoffs at the audacity but follows Sophia without slowing.

Timid, the woman of the hour loops a small hand through Angelica's arm, looking back and forth as if a monster is about to come out and bite her. Every aisle, every hallway, every cube seems to make her tense, her fingers digging deeper into Angelica's bicep. Unsure of what else to do, Angelica rests a hand over the other woman's, trying to offer courage and strength.

"If this is what you want to do, I'm here, okay?"

"Just listen at the door," she whispers. "If I need to dissect everything after, it will be easier if you already know what went down."

"Went down." Angelica snorts. "Do people even talk like that anymore?" To which, Sophia offers her a pinch. "Where the hell is this place, anyway?"

"He tucks himself away like a turtle, I swear. All his meetings happen in his office, except when he comes to see Simon. He used to have an EA too, but she quit, and he never rehired anyone. I think he just doesn't know how to be close to people."

"He's definitely lacking in the charisma department." She gets another pinch.

Sophia puts a fingertip to her lips as they near a corner office door. Cubes still surround, but they're all empty, their gray walls facing Nando's door, leaving him with ultimate privacy. It looks sterile compared to Simon's lively space, cluttered and filled with people and chatter, kitchens and elevators.

If they keep walking, they'll crash right through a wide exterior window. High up, it faces the sunset, getting the sting of the afternoon glare and casting long shadows. Peeking into the glass panel next to Nando's door, he's on the receiving end of it, making his office look uncomfortable to exist in.

The furniture seems sparse, but only because the space is so big. Bigger than Simon's by at least half. He has no picture on his walls, only what looks like degrees written with curlicues and flourishes. He sits at his desk with his back to them, head in his hands and his computer screen dark and abandoned. This is absolutely not the time to have this conversation, but Sophia squeezes her arm for comfort, and Angelica squeezes back.

She mouths, "Are you sure?"

Sophia shakes her head at first, but then breathes in deeply and nods.

She shoos Angelica to the far side near the huge window and puts her finger to her lips again before ducking inside.

It gives Angelica the shivers. Her nerves are buzzing. Why is she so afraid? She barely knows this woman, but her heart is in her throat. He could either make Sophia the happiest she's ever been or crush the fantasies she's been building since before her daughter was born. Angelica thinks of Ginger's big emerald eyes and feels relieved that this is happening nowhere near her. She knows what it's like to be on the wrong side of adult conversations. How fucked up it can be when people talk about you like you're a thing.

Her stomach knots up when she hears Sophia speak, wishing she could see inside. Sophia sounds like a mouse as she knocks on his door with soft raps. "Nando?"

"Not the time," he says. Angelica would feel vindicated for being right, except that she's hooked to a tether, tugged into this moment.

"Sorry to be a bother, but I really need to talk to you."

He scoffs. "Tell your boss I said to go fuck himself." Angelica bristles.

"Um...this doesn't have anything to do with Simon."

There is a metallic creak and a sound like leather sliding against something soft. "And what else could be so important that you'd grace my door at such an unfortunate hour?"

There are soft footsteps as Sophia walks deeper into the room. "It's about...well, I guess you could say it's about us."

"Tired of working for that man? Prefer to come over to the dark side and handle me instead?"

"Handle? No—no, not at all. Listen, do you remember when we..." She trails off.

"We what?"

"A few Christmases ago. At the party…"

Angelica imagines an awkward gesture, Sophia's hands waving forward in little circles, begging him to fill in the blanks.

There is a rough, angry sigh. "Why would you bring that up now? In the mood for a rematch?"

God, this guy's a dick.

"Not that either." Sophia sounds small, not her normal, boisterous self. "Remember when we thought I might be pregnant?"

There is dead silence.

"When I said it was just a scare…well…I lied."

That silence continues, painfully long. The seconds spool out slowly, as if pulled by a snail. "You *what*?" he hisses.

"Do you remember Ginger? You, um, you met her the other day before I took her to her doctor's appointment. Brown hair? Green eyes? What am I talking about, of course you remember her." She laughs nervously. "I… Nando, I've been dying to tell you for years, I just didn't know how. But, after seeing you two together, I thought maybe it would be okay. You just seemed to like her so much. Ginger…see… she's…well she's your—"

"Don't say it. Please don't say what I think you're going to say."

"She's your daughter."

There is a slam, as if something sharp hit the table. Angelica tenses, almost rushing in, but manages to hold back. Nando wouldn't hit Sophia. She won't give him credit for much, but she'll give him credit for that.

Another creak, and wheels rolling along the wooden floor all too fast. A hard *thwack* rings out as something hits something else.

"Why would you lie?" he growls.

Sophia's voice goes up in pitch. "Because you told me to get rid of it. You offered me money. You said—"

"Then why tell me now?"

She sounds on the verge of tears. "Because you liked her. You saw her and you melted for her, and she's yours. I told you what I did to protect myself and our baby, but now, the way you treated her, I wanted to come clean."

More silence. Then what sounds like a sheaf of paper flutters across the room.

"I've barely looked at you this whole time. We've barely spoken. You hid all this from me?" His voice is low, strained, as if he's trying his hardest not to shout. "How dare you look me in the face every day and lie to me?"

Sophia hisses in a breath. "I owe you nothing. You made your stance clear, and I've done this all on my own. You have no idea how hard it is. How other moms ask me about my nonexistent divorce, and she hears them. She's too little to know that her parents just had a fling and her father forgot about it. But me? I never forgot. Not for one minute. And if you'd bother looking around you, you'd see how hard I try to make you notice me."

"Stop. You don't get to lecture me. You don't get to hide and scheme, spring this on me and make me the bad guy. I'm not the fucking bad guy. What do you want from me? Money?"

"No."

"Then what?"

"I want you to love your daughter," Sophia yells, much louder than she should.

Her spine straight with fear, Angelica's head swivels to see if anyone's heads are poking over their desks, but no one's is. This area is truly lonely. All for the better.

"Why are you doing this to me?" Nando asks, high and pathetic.

Another one of those silences passes before Sophia lets out a heavy sniffle. "I thought it would make you happy."

Angelica's head whips around as Sophia runs through the door, breezing by her at full tilt.

"Wait," Nando tries. It's only seconds until he's out too, grabbing onto the door frame and pivoting to watch her run. His hands are in his hair and his breaths come all too quickly as Angelica watches his back. She tries her best to fade into the wall. She doesn't want to be here. She wants to be with Sophia.

He turns to go inside, his face a desperate twist of anxiety...until he locks eyes with her. "What are you doing here?" His voice is black coal, harsh and jagged. Eyes like ice, his bottom lip trembles. "Did you bring her here?"

Angelica backs up, keeping her shoulder to the wall. He has her pinned.

"You are single-handedly ruining everything. Putting my career at risk, taking away my only friend, upending my whole fucking life."

Breathing in through her nose, she tries to keep strong. This man's wrath is nothing.

Pulling away from the wall, she stands taller. "All I do is listen to people, make them feel like they matter. I want them to have self-compassion and self-respect. If being there for them gave them the courage to stand up for themselves, then I'm glad. But everything you're blaming me for is your own shit coming back to bite you. This isn't me. Take some fucking responsibility."

Wonder of wonders, his eyes are moist. Gritting his teeth, he cinches them shut and growls a sound of utter frustration before turning in the direction Sophia ran and darting after her. Angelica watches him pass by the hollow emptiness of this space with a different feeling in her heart. One she didn't expect.

Pity.

———

Last night was spent with a book of matches, something Simon hadn't done for a long time. Sparks flew as he slashed the sulfur heads across their little black matchbox strips, watching them burn until his fingertips singed. Waving them out, he dropped them on his chest, no doubt leaving little black marks on his sweater, but he didn't care. No one was around to see him anyway.

He avoided his found family like the plague, needing the space to sulk in silence. Nothing but the scrape and quiet *fwoosh-sizzle* as little flames danced. He should have been over this, but he wasn't. Self-soothing with destruction has ever been Simon's modus operandi, and that doesn't seem to have changed with age. Tyler would either be disappointed or amused, Simon supposed, not sure he cared much about that either.

He ran over his presentation as yellow and hot blue danced before his eyes. Over and over again, he muttered the words and imagined the slides that went with them. If he didn't get this right, he knew everything would be over. His chance at winning. His rivalry. Maybe even his job. His golden parachute would disappear, and he'd have to look for someone else to take in the failure that is him. He'd disappoint the people he'd excited with the opportunity for something more. Angelica would easily be booted from the company, and no one else would give her the chance she so rightly deserved.

He should have been furious. He should have been afraid. It didn't matter. Right then, Simon was numb.

But he's not numb now.

Standing in front of the LCD screen showing his favorite growth chart, Simon closes his speech. "And this is only the beginning. There are untapped, untrained resources throughout the city. Think of urban schools with kids who can't afford higher education. They might not test well, but if they have ambition, they can make it work in practice. Learn by doing. Other companies who want Good Will written all over their annual reports are going to jump all over this, and every placed job position is money in the bank. I believe in this, heart and soul, and I think the company should too."

Lawrence is resting with his elbows on the conference table, his aging eyes squinting as he reviews the TV screen. "This is way outside our portfolio, Simon."

Walking over, he takes his seat across from Nando, who refuses to look him in the eye, the same way he stubbornly refused to tune in to Simon's spiel. "And that's why it's going to work. It supplements and diversifies us. Software is competitive and we have to constantly be churning out new releases. The real estate market is declining for corporate setups and our tenants are reducing their footprints. Gas prices are too high for the travel industry to boom. And yes, this is out of our portfolio, but when has that stopped us?" His last flourish is, "This is what Mom would do."

Screw Nando's downplay of that. As the company's founder, her vision is the tenet they live by. He won't let that go simply because she's gone.

Lawrence considers, flipping through the printouts of Simon's deck, notes strewn across them in neat handwriting, so unlike Simon's —prim, proper, and straitlaced. Simon doesn't know his uncle's risk aversion level, but he can only pray the feedback he's gotten in his mentorship sessions is an indication. Lawrence himself gives no visible sign of approval or disapproval. He merely looks at Nando and says, "You're up."

Simon brings up Nando's deck and slides over the laptop, handing over the remote control to advance the presentation. His jaw ticks to the side when Nando still doesn't bother to look at him, slipping the remote away without even a nod.

The man's eyes are red, as if he didn't sleep. When he stands straighter, his tie is crooked and little lines show at the corners of his mouth. What has gotten into him? It can't be over a stupid fight, no matter how big it was. Nando is beyond feeling remorse over that, Simon tells himself, refusing to take the blame for the man's current state. Nando's head is likely too far up his ass to care about their exchange, anyway, but there's something. Simon can't put his finger on it, but his "friend" looks utterly wrecked.

Clearing his throat, Nando thumbs the remote. "Reorganizing the business units isn't the only place we're going to find success." He brings up an org chart. "This higher-level management chain is over-staffed. There are too few direct reports underneath them, and too few one level down, as well. Call me crazy, but only two direct reports per manager seems bloated."

That's the word Simon had used.

"Not only that,"—Nando clicks, and red slashes go across the little boxes representing certain staff members—"these people have low scores on their annual reviews and didn't qualify for raises last year." Another click results in black circles. "And these are on performance review plans. We need to cull the underperforming staff and redis-tribute the workload. Restructure the management chains and lay off those who are redun—"

"This is my idea," Simon cuts in. "You just took everything I told you and threw it up on a slide." Lawrence flicks his eyes back and forth between them.

Shrinking, Nando fiddles with the remote. "CEOs listen to all people's ideas and don't let their ego get in the way of implementing the good ones. If they aren't open to feedback and suggestions, they shouldn't be given the role."

The utter betrayal singes Simon's soul, blackening it to a darkness he hasn't felt in a long while.

"The severance packages will hit our P&L too hard," Lawrence says.

Simon grits out, "You cut the ones who aren't performing without severance. This is an at-will company, our contracts in every country say so, and we have a paper trail so they can't sue. If we do it all as a mass culling, all the better for optics. Don't backfill them. Then we stagger the redundancy layoffs. Give people warning. Three-month stints, six months, one year. Anyone with half a brain will go for job security and find something new before they're at the end of their tenure, forfeiting their severance. Then—"

"Simon can't be CEO," Nando blurts. All eyes turn to him as he stares fixedly at his feet, a deep frown reigning over his paling face. "He doesn't listen to reason. He has poor judgment. He's out of his depth and he's grasping at straws, completely emotionally unstable. He starts fights over nothing, ranting about things that don't matter and coming up with these crazy, irresponsible schemes. More than that, he's dating, living with, and even *employed* a prostitute!"

There is a harsh intake of breath as loud as shattering glass.

Lawrence—religious and righteous, church-going and charitable— lets his jaw drop, his round eyes flying to Simon's with a stinging disgust.

And that's it. That's all it takes.

This is all over.

# giving up and giving in

. . .

"WHAT DID YOU JUST SAY?" Lawrence asks, appalled.

"She works for him. She worked for him before this company too. A dating consultant if you can believe it. And now she's under his EA, completely unqualified—"

"She is capable of every bit of the work assigned to her," Simon growls. "Sophia even says she's over-performing."

"So, you're not denying it?" Lawrence asks. "This woman sells herself for money?"

"*Sold*," Simon corrects, slamming his hand on the tabletop, his voice low and dangerous. "And her past has nothing to do with her competence."

Nando lets out a hollow laugh. "See? Completely emotionally unstable. Head over heels for a whore. *Che schifo*. Who knows how many men she's been with—"

Simon seethes. "What does it matter?"

"—what diseases she has?"

Simon rears up and Lawrence pushes back from the table.

Nando's ranting doesn't stop. "Is she going to pick up the trade again when people in the office come on to her, eh? She looks like she's up for a party, doesn't she, Simi? How much does she sell herself for, do you think? A woman like her's got to be worth, what? Fifty bucks? A hundred? Who could have respect for someone who does such a thing? Takes advantage of the weakness of others. Treats their own body like a dirty drug to be sold to the low and the lonely. It's disgusting. Disgraceful. It's—"

"*I sold myself too!*" Simon bellows. He may not have meant to, but it's the truth.

In the space between seconds, everything about Nando drops. His shoulders, his hands, his face. He gapes. "You've got to be shitting me."

"And I was worth *thousands*. Does that change my competence? Is everything I've done for the company a lie? All my projects before acquisitions were huge successes, that's why I got this job in the first place. This idea is good," Simon insists, his teeth bared and his hands clenching the back of his chair. He's stiff to the point of breaking, body starting to sweat. Indignant, furious, and steadfast, he turns to both flabbergasted men. "It's good, it's profitable, it's moral. And I hope that, whoever becomes CEO, they will act on it."

He thrusts his chair forward, colliding it with the table. Tossing a last look at his once-friend, he scowls, shaking his head. "I hope you burn for this."

And right now, in this moment, he means every word.

Storming out, Simon trembles with unleashed anger. He needs to leave, but he needs to grab Angelica first. The last thing she needs is the third degree from any monster in that room. If he can't protect himself, at least he can protect her.

He loves her.

And he's failed her.

———

His hallway has never seemed so gloomy as he walks Angelica home, his hand on the small of her back as he leads her forward. She might be in shock for as quiet as she is, lips pressed together and feet dragging. The story is all told, and the truth hangs heavy, all secrets out. The ground rule of "not hiding things" goes both ways, he'd reminded her, but he's not sure she appreciated what fell out of his mouth straight after. Now the silence wraps around them like cotton, muffling their footsteps as they drudge toward his door. Their door.

Opening it, Ciel is straightening out the living room, gathering up tissues like they're toxic waste, pinching them with only the tips of his fingers. His backpack is no longer lonely in the corner, but open on the couch, getting the random odds and ends chucked into it. Throat drops? In. Box of Kleenex? In. New blue knit hat? Tucked in by hand. He doesn't see them walk in, too focused on what he's doing, traipsing around with the small bathroom trash can as he cleans up his mess.

"Hey," Simon says, his voice raw.

Ciel startles, almost dropping the little wastebasket, which would be a shame. No one wants that moist content spattered all over the living room floor. "Yo. You're home early."

Simon scans the space, seeing Ciel's puffy blanket folded—military crisp—next to the window. The TV remotes he's been clinging to for days are back in their pocket hidey-hole, innocuous and abandoned.

"Are you leaving?"

"Ah, crap." Ciel leans back, popping something in his spine. "Was gonna leave you a note."

"A note?"

He shrugs. "I suck at goodbyes."

"But...you're still sick." Simon says. "You haven't finished the antibiotics yet. It's ten days you're supposed to be stuck with me, not six."

"Pfft. Tell that to my body. I feel better than I have in a long while. Penicillin is apparently a cure-all for whatever the hell other shit's been living inside me."

Simon's at a loss, and Angelica is no better.

"Why do you guys always look like your house is falling down?" Ciel asks. "You're not gonna cry or anything, are you? You knew I wasn't staying."

"It's not that," Simon says, then he corrects himself. "It's part that, but everything today just went to hell."

"Putting it mildly," Angelica mutters. "I want to kill that man."

"What man?" Ciel asks.

Simon tosses himself on the sofa next to Ciel's bag, sinking in and letting his petulance rule him. "My friend has royally screwed us both."

"Next time I see him, I'll fucking tear him apart." Angelica crooks her fingers, snarling.

"Don't bother," Simon says. "It's not worth it."

"Why wouldn't you want to throw him in a trash compactor?" Angelica asks. "One that squishes slowly."

"I do but… There's something about how he looked. Acted. It's not like him. Something's wrong. I don't know what it is, but it goes way beyond us wanting to wring each other's necks. Maybe the pressure got to him? Maybe he cracked?"

Angelica goes from feral to furtive, her eyes skirting to the side. She leans over the back of her puffy chair, resting her elbows and letting her arms dangle. "Do you know anything about Sophia's kid?"

Simon and Ciel both cock an eyebrow.

"She has a daughter. Ginger. You ever really look at her eyes? They're her father's, one hundred percent. I kind of called Sophia out on it because I recognized them. It made her go all squirrelly and think she needed to confess to the dad."

"Confess what?"

"That he was the father. It was a secret. He didn't know."

"Who's the father?" Simon asks, not following. "I've known her for years, and all she's said is that it was a fling."

Angelica's fingers twiddle. "It was…but the dad saw the girl at the office and really liked her, so Sophia just figured…"

"What does any of this have to do with Nando?"

He must be the world's biggest idiot for how she looks at him. "He's the father."

Pieces snap together in his brain like a puzzle.

"You guys had your fight," Angelica continues, "and I told her the timing was bad, but she couldn't hold it in, I guess. We followed him and she confessed. He did *not* take it well. She ran out and he followed, but then he spotted me and…I think he wanted someone to blame other than himself. His life went to shit, and he said it was my fault."

No wonder he looked like he'd been to hell and back during the meeting. No wonder he lashed out at Angelica. At him. When Nando is backed into a corner, he's like a viper. Simon should have known that… not that it makes it any easier to swallow.

"Sounds like your friend is on the downward swing," Ciel says, leaning over to grab his coat and slinging it over his shoulders. His beige best looks better after a few million washes, but there are certain stains that will never come out—not to mention the broken buttons and sporadic holes. His bag's fasteners zip shut, and he hoists that up as well. "Sometimes people don't realize how far they're falling until they hit rock bottom. Trust me. Maybe he'll hit the floor, look in the mirror, and decide to pick himself back up again. Either that or he'll stay down, which—believe me—is an option."

Simon watches him travel toward the door and feels a sudden pang. "Are you sure you won't stay?"

"Nah. I've been here longer than I should. The stars are gonna be out tonight. Time for me to keep on truckin' or whatever they say."

He tussles Simon's hair into a floppy mess and drags Angelica into his arms. She complains a bit, but gives in, letting the man wrap around and rock her. "Take care, little one."

"I told you if you called me that, I would stab you with a snapped toothbrush." Though it's said with a little curve to her lips.

Ciel only tucks her head under his chin and squinches harder. "Don't worry. You'll see me again. I'm going to be the first in line to sign up for Simon's program." He tosses him a wink, and Simon feels like falling into a pit of pointed rocks.

"Be good, kiddos," Ciel says, opening the door wide. "And for what it's worth, Simon, you make an excellent chicken soup for the soul."

The door closes softly, a relief after so many being slammed of late, but Simon still wants to cry. What is Ciel going back out to? Did he take enough bottled water so he can take his pills on time? Will he find the two hundred bucks Simon slid into the front pocket of his bag?

If his program doesn't move forward, can Simon ever show his face again?

His eyes water, but no tears fall. He tries to smooth out his hair, but without a reflective surface, it's a useless gesture. It's like straw in his hands. No matter how he pulls at it, it does nothing to ground him. His swirling thoughts leave footprints, scuffing up his neurons and leaving a streaking trail, but it doesn't stop his futile efforts to soothe himself.

"Do you want to do it to me?" Angelica asks softly. She stands beside him, arms wrapped around herself and eyes to the ground. She looks smaller than normal. Frail and delicate. She's usually a ball of fire, but now…

Simon shifts and raises his arm, giving her a wide space to snuggle in beside him, but that doesn't seem to be enough. With a tentative look, she edges forward, sitting on his lap and twisting until she's cradled in his arms, head on his shoulder and lithe legs strewn over his thighs. Her hands rest against his chest, and one threads under his tie, pulling it into a whorl in her fist. The weight of her brings him back into his body, reminding him that he's not alone in his misery. As with so many things of late, they're in this mess together.

One arm wraps around her back and the other slides into her soft mane as he holds her, letting his fingers drift through. Nothing but silk and softness caress him as he cards through her hair, his heart heavy with the weight of his failure.

"I'm sorry," he murmurs. "I feel like I ruined your dream."

She slides her hand to the nape of his neck, petting the skin she finds there, stroking just underneath his collar. It's been so long since she touched him like this, he falls into it, letting his eyes slip closed.

"My dream was to be free. You already gave me that." She tucks in closer, the curve of her rear pressing into him and changing the trajectory of his thoughts.

"I wanted to give you more."

He can hear her smile as she huffs. "You already did that too."

His hand slips down her arm, feeling the tiny hairs on her skin, tracing over the healing wound where her stitches left a mark. Goosebumps raise like braille, and he wants to read every line, his fingerprints gliding back and forth. He peeks at her face, her freckles a starfield of brown stippling, shading the crests of her cheeks and the bridge of her nose. His other arm winds farther around her, resting on her ribs and sinking down to her hip. All it takes is her slight sigh, and his length twitches in his pants.

"I ruined your dream though," she says, nuzzling in. Her sweet touch is enough to make him ache for her.

"You didn't." Her breasts lean against him, plush and supple, and he wants to hold them. Rub his thumbs over the most sensitive parts. He wants to kiss the underside and taste her skin. She shifts her weight, and he can't help the soft sound that hums through him. He's growing hard against her now, the pulse of his blood rushing down his body, seeking her. "Or maybe I just need to find a new dream."

"What would that be?" Her voice is a breathy whisper. God, how he wants to touch her.

The hand resting on her arm trails up and down again, cresting the roundness of her shoulder before sweeping down the inner flesh, grazing the side of her chest and over the wire of her bra. He wants his hands underneath it. His mouth. He wants to swipe his tongue from one peak to the other and dive into the valley between.

His mouth stings as he salivates.

She shifts again, and he feels every millimeter. Choking back a groan, he shifts too, grinding his erection into her. Neither of them says a word, but she clutches him harder, her fingers sinking into his nape. She knows what he has for her. What's begging for her.

Shifting one more time, she straddles him, her skirt rucking up and her core pressing against his clothed length. Her face buries itself in his neck, her lips resting against his thrumming pulse.

If he could feel her, would she be wet?

Her hips roll over him, and he sucks in a short gasp. It seems to egg her on, and she does it again, firmer and slower. His hands rest on the curve of her spine but have minds of their own as they drift down over her skirt, grabbing her rear and pulling her harder onto him.

It's her turn to gasp, and God how the sound does something to him. His head leans back against the top of the sofa, exposing his throat to her mercy. She could kiss him, lick him, bite him. He'd revel in any of it. Yes, and yes, and please.

Her name is on the tip of his tongue as he kneads her, every squeeze making her ride him. Stroke him. Sear him with her warmth.

She lets out a soft mewl, and he's lost. Shooting his hands up, he latches onto her hair and pulls back, giving himself the freedom to stare into her bedroom eyes. Her teeth are pressed into her bottom lip, and he'd like to follow suit. Tilting his head, he moves in…only to have her tug back and stand, leaving him bereft and cold.

"It's been a long day," she says. A lie. They left mid-morning. It's only lunch time. "I need a shower."

His husky tone surprises him. "Can I come?" The double entendre is not lost on either of them.

"Wait your turn. You can come after me." The quirk of her lips is sly, that risqué sentence not lost on them either.

He wants to run his hand over himself. Make her watch him. Make her want him enough to stay. Instead, heat flaring through his cheeks, he lets her go. As soon as she's behind the closed door, though, he palms himself through his pants, finding a slight wet spot where she slid against him.

He curses under his breath, bringing his hand to his mouth and tonguing it, a flat, slick slide of muscle over his heart line. He can't taste her, and it frustrates him. He wants to. The first time didn't count. He wants those tiny gasps. Those little cries. Those honest, sexy truths of her arousal. She wasn't faking it this time. This was all for him.

———

She pulls the shower curtain closed and runs the bath as hot as she can stand it. Her body aches as layers of clothes drop in crumples on the floor. Begging for attention, her insides clench on nothing, empty and lonely for a man to fill her. One specific man.

Simon.

Twirling off the dials, she ducks behind the curtain and into the steam. It clouds in misty wafts that do nothing to soothe her as she eases down with a hiss, water sloshing. It's sensual, the hot splashes echoing against the tiles around her, making her think of everything wet and warm.

This is excruciating.

She ducks her head fully under, unable to deny how tight her nipples are pearled, how her center throbs with the need to be touched. Why she's not giving in to him, she's not sure, but the desire is there. His desire is there. It always has been.

Her lungs burn as she berates herself.

No matter how she tries to bring her thoughts back to purer ground, it doesn't work. Instead, she imagines his cock slipping down her throat as she swallows him. She knows he's as big as one would imagine, given how tall he is, and she'd love to feel that stretch again as he dipped into her.

Coming to the surface, she rests her head back and groans, unsure of what to do with herself...until she is. Her fingers slide to her nipples, flicking them with the tips of her nails before swirling around. They beg for more, singing against her touch. They're so sensitive. So ready for attention. She has to come, or she won't be able to see Simon again without mauling him. Grinding into him so hard he finishes in his pants. Getting to her knees and taking him out, sucking up anything he left behind.

The water shatters around her as one leg lifts. Her heel plants itself on the cool ceramic of the tub's edge, and her knee tilts out at an angle, opening her up. Working her hand down, she dips it between her thighs and tests herself.

Slick. Soaking. This is what he does to her.

She slips up toward her clit and circles it. The liquid around her destroys any friction she can get, which means this will be harder to do. She's going to have to work for it.

She strums and her eyes fall closed, a small cry pulling from her lips. Her clit hardens, ensuring she can find it among the slickness of her folds. She whimpers again as she reaches farther, dipping her finger toward her entrance, not going in, but twirling in circles. Teasing herself. Like he might do before ramming inside.

Her leg tips open wider.

The hand fiddling with her nipple starts again, pinching and stroking. She imagines him sucking on her, his bourbon brown eyes looking up with pink cheeks and desire. It's enough to make her moan and her fingers go faster.

A low voice comes from outside the door. "You're going to kill me."

There's a hushing sound that can only be his hands sliding down the wood grain. "I can hear every sound you make. I think I'm going crazy."

Her adrenaline kicks into overdrive, the thrill of being caught only adding to her need for him.

Without thinking it through, she parts the curtain, just barely, and says, "Come in."

The doorknob twists with a metallic groan and she can see a sliver of him as he enters, eyes locked on the curtain. She knows he can only see her silhouette, but that seems to be enough. He tents his pants and his tie has been torn open, each end lying against his broad chest in crimson stripes. His buttons strain as he breathes too fast for this humid space, and when he finds her gaze, he holds it down with the most alluring look on his face. "Tell me what to do."

Reveling in his baritone, she presses her finger deeper inside. He can't see her do it. All he can see is her face…but maybe that's enough.

"Sit." She glances down to the tile on the floor beside the bath and he matches her.

"Clothes on or off?"

It curls the corners of her mouth before she opens in a gasp. She's found her clit again and strums it like an instrument, her unrelenting rhythm setting her nerve endings ablaze. She wants this. She wants him. His mouth parts as she licks her lips, putting on a show for the man she wishes was inside her.

"On," she sighs, tipping her head back and letting her eyes slip closed. She alternates between pressing in circles, swirling around the edges, and flicking, a delicious combination that would have her shaking any other day. But this is too wet to get her hands on herself properly. She has half a mind to lift herself out, but then she'd beg him to fuck her. She knows it like she knows the sun sets.

When she next flutters her lashes, he's sitting close enough to touch. She can't see below his ribs, just like he can't see beyond her shoulders, but she wants to give him a show. Pull the curtain back and put herself on complete display. Still, something sinful holds her back. Why not create a different kind of memory?

"I want you to touch yourself," she says, sinking her teeth into her lower lip again.

Pink cheeks. How she adores those pink cheeks.

He doesn't argue. He leans forward, and she can hear his belt slither off before his zipper follows suit. He doesn't bother with his pants, leaning back in his business jacket with his first two collar buttons undone and nothing but dark lust in his eyes. His arm flexes in slow movements. He's stroking himself, just like he was told.

"Good boy."

He takes a deep breath and lets it out slow, listing his head back against the wall as he watches her. Her skin sizzles under his regard. Every caress of his gaze lingers, making her taut and needy all over. Her insides throb. She wants him in her cunt. Her ass. Fucking everywhere. He could swallow her whole, and she would die happy.

Another sharp gasp as she hits herself just right, her hand skating from her breast to tuck inside. Fingering. Thrusting. Her hips begin to move, causing slow waves around her, licking their way up her body.

"Tell me what to do," he says again, his tone pleading.

"Go faster."

Obedient, he starts to pant and make soft moans as his fist hits his groin, his arm tensing in pulse after pulse as she keeps him in her peripheral vision. He whimpers her name and electricity shoots up her spine, her toes splaying.

"Say it again, Simon. Make noises for me."

Which is like asking for sweet death. He palms himself even faster. *Thwap, thwap, thwap.* She wishes that sound was him bouncing her off his cock. He grunts and hisses, little gifts for her to wrap around her body as she dances her fingers.

"Simon, you're gonna make me come."

He cries out sweetly. She wants to swallow his sounds. Drown in him.

"I'm getting close." Her voice is high and pitchy. "Are you?"

"Yes. God, yes."

"Come for me, Simon. Be a good boy." She has no idea how his speed can still pick up, but it does. "Are you thinking of me?"

"No one else."

"Do you wish it was me?"

"Always."

It's building up, tensing her belly as her thighs start to shake. "I'm so close."

"Don't stop," he gasps.

She couldn't if she tried.

Teeth clenched, the body-thrumming sensation takes her over and she gasps, arching her back and spilling water over the side.

"Fuck," Simon growls. "I need you."

She mewls through her aftershocks, unable to catch her breath. Simon's throaty moans are pitching up, getting louder.

"Yes," she whispers. "Come on. Do it for me."

His eyes slam shut, his head tipping back as his mouth drops open. His movements pump fast for a second longer and she knows he's spilling into his hand, dripping over his grip, leaving white trails on his skin.

She wishes he could come inside her.

Slowing, he pants through his nose, finding her eyes again. His gaze is intense, as if this has only fueled his lust instead of slaked it. As if he doesn't just want her, he needs her. As if he'd level cities to get to her. Neither seems to know what to say. Instead, they just come down together, lost in each other's eyes.

Long seconds pass by, and a boyish smirk curves his lips. "Do I go or stay?"

Shyness pulls at her, unlike anything she's ever felt. Her smile is giddy as she splashes her leg back down into the bath, and his resounding chuckle is like gold.

"I'll go"—he glances down, clearing his throat and getting red all the way to his ears—"clean up in the kitchen."

Unable to speak through the grin on her face, she just nods, pulling the curtain closed to give him privacy. Giggles come next, her knees locking together and swaying side to side, her hair swimming in a halo around her.

"Maybe this day wasn't a total loss," he murmurs.

She hums a sound of agreement. "Maybe."

And with another amused huff, he escorts himself out.

———

They'd spent the day dancing around each other, knowing smiles on their faces as they did the most mundane of things. Watched TV, her perched on her chair, him splayed on the couch; ate snacks, which she gave up griping about and begrudgingly joined in for; and made dinner, her bland and healthy best to make up for all the salt and sugar he'd shoved into their bodies. Simon made any and every excuse to touch her. His fingertips tingled if he brushed against her hand as they both reached for pretzels. His hips felt zings when they futzed around in the kitchen and bumped by accident. Maybe it was his imagination, but she looked just as smitten, shyly ducking away with little smiles on her face, constantly tucking her hair behind her ear. They both avoided talking about the misery of the morning, the afterglow of the afternoon, and focused on enjoying the now.

But night has come and Simon is lonely in his bed. The full scope of the day catches up to him, and he wallows like a pig in mud, working the horrible truth into every pink wrinkle in his brain. He needs another distraction. Unfortunately, he doesn't have the courage to ask. Angelica might be sleepily nestled in the next room, or she might be spiraling like him, but he doesn't want to intrude upon her space either way. What if that's a step too far? All he wants to do is hold her, be beside her, exist in her orbit, but a "no" at this point would shred him to pieces. So, he lets his heart sink into familiar insecurity and self-recrimination.

He should have realized about Sophia. He should have expected the backlash from Nando. He should have never opened his mouth beyond business in that conference room or inspired his uncle to make such a disgusted face.

He rolls on his stomach, burying his nose in his pillow and sucking in his own carbon dioxide until his lungs beg for mercy. Only then does he curl into a ball, nuzzling in. Swathed in the warmth of his comforter, finding the softest spot possible, he slowly, silently drifts off to—

His cell phone rings and Simon sits up straight, adrenaline spiking in his veins. His addled brain screams out all the questions in rapid succession, the who-what-where-when and whys.

Hand thumping uselessly, he pats down his side table with his eyes closed, ready to mute the shrill ring. Dazed curiosity makes him peek at the screen with one eye.

Lawrence.

He rejects it immediately, letting it go to voicemail. In less than three seconds, it rings again, but a scowling Simon swipes it to voicemail once more.

A text comes through.

> Don't be an ass.

It's probably as appropriate as anything else his uncle could have said at the moment.

The phone rings for the third time and, with his heart in his stomach and a grimace on his face, Simon picks up. "Calling to tell me I'm not CEO?"

There is a long silence before a sigh rings from the other side of the line. "You're not CEO."

"Nando," he states.

"Not him either."

That gives Simon pause. "Why?"

"I ran into a Miss Yang who was in a nightmare fit of tears yesterday afternoon. Stories fell out of her, and I feel like I should either drop *Signore* Armando Ferrante from a bridge or fire him for inappropriate office behavior, given what they did on my desk."

"Never tell me that again."

Lawrence grumbles his agreement. "But I'm not going to hold it against him. Against either of you."

Simon sits up straighter and crisscrosses his legs. "Why?"

A grumbly groan comes from the other end of the line, long lasting and self-indulgent. Then Lawrence, his puritanical, law-abiding uncle, lets out a slew of curses under his breath. Simon knew he got it from somewhere.

"Once upon a time, kid, when I was younger, all I wanted to do was escape my small-town life. That was when I met your dad. He was all energy and mischief back in the day, smuggling me to the city despite my father's begging. That infamous recluse would rather have me work myself to death on our pig farm than visit a big, fancy skyscraper."

"What were you, Amish?" Simon asks.

"Might as well have been. Anyway, your dad and I had to fight to stay in the city. Night classes, crap jobs, but then we met your mother. An heiress, mightier than thou, but she was also someone who demanded respect. Your dad was, well, your dad about it, and despite her best efforts, she fell for him. She wouldn't let him just schlep around anymore, though. She made him get a real job and kicked my ass into doing the same. Your dad started in city hall, but the only job I could get was working under her."

"Nepotism runs in the family."

Lawrence snorts. "Apparently. And then I fell in love with her."

Simon's mind snaps to attention. "You what?"

"After you were born, I was so jealous, I couldn't take it anymore. I kissed her. Believe me when I say she wasn't tempted in the slightest. Woman kicked my teeth in, and the screaming fit she tossed my way nearly castrated me. I thought I'd lose my job at the very least. But you know what your mother told me? She said, 'Your personal life doesn't matter. What matters is your ability to perform.' She kept me on and, when your dad died, the shock reconnected us. We had to cope with the family grief together. Somewhere during all that, she forgave me.

"Today, you reminded me of her. You reminded me of my own mistakes too. I've been thinking a lot in the past twelve hours, kid. You were right when you said every business endeavor you've had was a success. Even now when you're so out of your wheelhouse, you work your tail off, and I see it. No matter what Nando said today, no matter what you have or haven't done, I still believe in you. You've come so far from the little boy who was mad at the world. Now you're a man with a sharp, analytical mind, a heart of gold, and a work ethic that would put anyone else to shame."

The lump in Simon's throat couldn't get any larger. He rubs the heel of one hand over his eyes. "Then why am I not CEO?"

"Eh, I figure I'll keep that job for a while longer. My two best candidates are going to be very busy for the time being. One of them is going to be spear-heading a global reorganization, and the other is going to be integrating a talent acquisition firm into our portfolio."

Simon jumps to his knees, obliterating any tucking in of his sheets. "Are you serious?"

"Besides. I know you've never wanted to be CEO, anyway. You've just wanted to prove yourself. Make your family proud. And you've done that, kid, I promise you. Except for that selling yourself thing. I recommend stopping that immediately."

Simon's grin couldn't get any wider. "Already done. And Angelica?"

"If she's as good as you say she is—and provided she's not doing anything illegal—I see no reason why her past should be any of my business."

Fist pumping, Simon sends his thanks up to heaven for no reason other than habit.

Saying their goodbyes with a newfound fondness, Simon's soul is incandescent, his smile so big his face might split. He claps his hands over his mouth to stifle a girlish giggle, then a tickling titter, then a chuffing chuckle, until he's rolling on his bed, bellowing the word "Yes" and letting off overloud shouts of happiness.

Angelica rushes in like he's gone mental, and he grabs her by the waist, lifting and spinning her in the air until she squeals. He can't make words, only whoops and raucous laughter that puts her guffaws to shame.

He did it. In spite of everything, he fucking did it.

It's time to get to work.

# love

. . .



THE TEXT from Nando takes Simon by surprise as much as it infuriates him. He considers leaving it on read or blocking the goddamn number, but his bitterness gets the better of him.



There are bubbles that go on for eons while Simon scowls at his screen, considering chucking it into the trash, but after several starts and stops, what comes over is two pathetic words.



Asshole. He can take his Sunday and shove it.

Simon's about to click his phone off—not just the screen, but the whole damn device—when two more words catch his eye.

It's stupid how much his heart twinges. He stares at the pixels of those seven little letters and feels the weight of them. Nando never apologizes. Not in the long time he's known him.

> For which part? The part where you stole my idea and passed it off as your own, the part where you came at me like I was an overemotional child, or the part where you destroyed Angelica's reputation?

The memory alone makes him want to strangle this rectangular piece of electronics.

More bubbles start and stop alongside a petulant bout of Simon wanting to delete the thread they've been building for almost ten years, then the message reads:

> All of it.

Damnit. Simon has a horrible habit of forgiving just about anything...but not this. He's not going to give that bastard the satisfaction.

> Please talk to me. Throw your drink in my face, fine, just let me talk to you first. I need to say this.

Because it's all about him, isn't it? His need and his guilt can go straight to hell.

> You deserve to hear me say this.

And that gets Simon's attention. Frowning, he's the one who starts and stops his message this time, deleting unhelpful rants and insults, backspacing phrases where he rolls over and shows his belly, annihilating it when he wants to ask Nando how he's doing with everything that's happened. He lands on:

> What time?

Nando will probably pick something inconvenient. He always does. A time too late to eat and too early to cry off.

> **What works for you?**

Who the hell is this man and what has he done with Simon's frenemy?

> **Six o'clock. One drink.**

Another long pause. One that drags on enough to make Simon concerned. And then:

> Okay.

An uncharacteristic, succinct reaction. Some doppelgänger must have hacked Nando's phone.

It doesn't matter. Either way, now he has a date with the devil. What could Nando possibly have to say? Why is Simon even doing this?

Angelica's gonna be pissed.

———

Why do so many of the pivotal moments in Simon's life happen in this pub?

Inside in the warm yellow light, Nando sits like a lump on the barstool, leaning over with an empty pint glass in front of him, another one half-drank in his hands. A third sits just on the far side, one that is either meant for Simon or a clear indication that this man has plans to get very drunk tonight.

Nando's profile looks like it's aged years in the past few days, tired sacks of prunes drawing purple stains under his eyes. He hunches over his drink like an old man, staring as if imagining the solutions to life are all hiding somewhere at the bottom. Simon tries to stomp down any concern that rises but fails miserably.

Without preamble, he takes his seat to Nando's right and grabs the spare beer, glugging back a few swallows and sucking the foam off his upper lip. "If you've got something to say, say it."

Nando's head hangs lower. "I want you to see things from my perspective."

"What a fantastic apology." Simon goes to stand up, but Nando catches his arm.

"Please." It's spoken soft, but clear as a bell. Nando is one to shout the house down, making even his cohort shake their heads, so this is another tick in the "something's wrong" box.

Flopping down on the barstool, Simon picks up his glass, trying to decide whether to nurse it or toss it back and walk away.

Nando gives a deep, lengthy sigh. "From my perspective, all I saw was my virgin best friend suddenly getting laid, eh? Sounded great. Wonderful even. Fucking celebratory. But it was so much, with so many different women, and you didn't seem to like it. I saw the consultant you were overpaying taking you through the wringer. Then you show up with the shit kicked out of you. A man who keeps his eyes down when he should stand up took the beating of his life, ended up in the emergency room, and he didn't seem to care. Instead, he said he was 'falling in love' with the woman who put him in that situation, ready to forgive because she said a simple 'I'm sorry.'"

"I'm not discussing her with you."

"Try to understand. You were keeping secrets, which you've never done before. Hell, if anything, you're an over-sharer, yes? You were pulling away and angry at me. I get it now, I do—but please see how it scared me. How it made no sense. How I didn't know what to do to protect my best friend."

Simon stares into his glass as well, watching the bubbles fizz. He'd never thought about the optics, too caught up in the whirlwind to see it from outside. What would he have done if the roles were reversed? Not the same thing, but surely something else that would have gone just as terribly wrong.

"I'm surprised you'd still call me 'friend' after what you did. Is that what you think I'll call you?"

Chugging back another gulp, Nando is three-quarters through his drink. "This is where my 'I'm sorrys' start." Setting the glass down with a dull clatter, he flags the waiter, tapping the rim and holding up a finger for one more. Simon wonders how many he had before he got here. "I did some talking with my therapist."

Simon pulls a face. "You have a therapist?"

"As of yesterday. Woman's a saint. She let me rant for two hours and broke it down with me for a third."

"Aren't sessions usually, like, forty-five minutes?"

"Which is why she's a saint."

Simon lifts his glass to the unknown woman.

"You're my only friend," Nando says. "I rag on you for being standoffish and whatever, but I'm just as bad. Too cocky, yeah? Too smug. Fake. *Rompipalle.* Whatever you want to call me. And when I met you, you were all alone. You didn't have a ride-or-die clique you'd been in since elementary school, you were a fish out of water like me. So I scooped you up." His drink gets delivered and he skids his empties to the bartender. "Here's where the therapy comes in. Let's skip the part where it's all about my relationship with my mother. Long and short is I was afraid that you'd abandon me for just being me. So, according to the venerated Miss Alohima, I probably put you down so you'd be too afraid to reach out to other people. I made it so you'd think they wouldn't like you. That only I ever could."

"That doesn't sound toxic at all."

"And I'm sorry. What she says, it makes sense, but if that's true, I don't think I was doing it on purpose. I don't think I looked at you and said, 'How can I keep him under my thumb today,' yeah? You were everything I had. I'm sorry for being such an asshole. I'm sorry for not giving you the benefit of the doubt. And I'm sorry about letting my *meschinità* blow up our friendship to the point where I had to spend half a grand to have someone pick my personality apart."

Simon can't look at him. Instead, he decides to nurse his drink and let this conversation last.

"And you're not the only life I fucked up. Sophia..." He trails off before putting his face in his hands. "I was young and I was stupid."

"You're still stupid," Simon says, and it earns him a half smile.

"That's not nice."

"It's what you would say to me."

There is an unbroken silence as the thought sinks in.

"Do you have Sophia's number?" Nando asks.

"Of course I do. I'm her friggin' emergency contact."

Nando drinks his beer like it's a shot. "Will you text her and ask if it's okay if I have it? I…I found out something. Well, she said something and…"

Saving him the pain of confession, Simon says, "I know. I heard you two had it out when she told you."

Nando steeples his hands in front of his face, his eyes winced shut. "I tried to find her after, but I couldn't."

Because she'd fled the scene and ran into his uncle, apparently. "At least now I know why she took Friday off," Simon says into his drink. He's only got a quarter left.

"I just want to reach out to her."

"More apologies to make?"

Nando's breath is so deep, his shoulders rise and fall. "Do you think I could be a good father?"

It's pained. Vulnerable. Nando's bottom lip trembles and Simon's heart completely thaws. Standing up, he grabs the man into a rough hug and claps him on the back a few times. Pulling away, he keeps his hand on the base of Nando's neck and squeezes. "You can do anything you set your mind to."

"Even making us friends again?"

Simon huffs a laugh. Sitting back at the bar, he signals the bartender once more. "A round of shots, please. Butterball for me and"—he looks at Nando's misery—"straight vodka for him."

"Oh good, get me hammered. I planned on taking this week off, anyway."

"You look like you'd do better taking off a month. What are you going to say to Sophia?" Two glasses slide over the bar top in their direction, and each man picks up their own.

"I want to ask if I can bring…my daughter…to the park or something."

Simon hums in agreement. "That's a good a start."

They clink glasses, hold each other's eyes, and then put the bottoms up. If Lawrence can help them succeed in spite of everything they've done, why can't they do it for each other? They just need to throw all the cards on the table and reset to square one.

Fresh starts all around.

———

"Are you drunk?" Angelica shakes her head in amusement. He'd left three hours ago, only to come back like this.

"Tipsy," Simon says with a firm nod. "But I'm fine. Totally. Totally fine. With it. Gnarly. Righteous. Bussin'. Hip-pah."

Angelica catches him on his feet as he stumbles, the weight of him almost pulling her to the floor. Her calves strain as she maneuvers him up again, leaning him against the door with a clunk as his head bounces off the wood. She has half a mind to thwack him, another half to coddle him until he passes out.

"So, what did that bastard say?"

"A lot of 'I'm sorrys.'"

"Any pointed in my direction?"

"Soooo many." His feet slide on his heels, and he slips down the door, landing on his backside. Pathetic, he whines like an overgrown, raven-haired man-baby. "I think I cracked my ass the wrong way."

That earns him a laugh, no matter how annoyed she is. "I warn you, I hold grudges. I'll forgive that rat bastard around the time Christ returns. But only if the post-apocalyptic world requires human-to-human alliances to survive. Otherwise, a man like that can take his apologies and shove—"

"I love you," he blurts.

Angelica gets down the floor and busies herself with taking off his shoes. "Yeah, yeah."

She finds her hips pawed at until he has a firm grasp on her, tugging back until she lands on him with a hiss. His wallet digs in like a jagged rock.

"No, you don't understand. I love you," he says again, his slur less obvious.

Angelica's heart skips a beat, but she's not going to listen to some drunken, irrational blabber. She wriggles off, earning little groans of either pain or arousal as she scoots away and continues to work on the loops of his shoelaces.

"Angel," he says, firm and soft all at once. His face is serious, his eyes half-lidded and a rose flush covering his cheeks. "I said I love you."

Her skipping heartbeat becomes a hammer.

"And I think you love me too."

A budding tornado whirls. Tingles run from her toes to the tippy-top of her head.

"Am I right?"

Wait.

Wait, wait, wait.

She's gotta be tough or he's going to break down her last defense. She's got very little control when it comes to him. She has to fortify her barriers. Sandbag the ditches. Arm the trebuchets.

"Still can't talk to me?" His smile is lopsided as he shuffles to his knees. "Let me ask you more questions then. I like playing this game." Lifting her necklace, he rubs the green stone in slow strokes. "Number one: Do you like it when you see me?"

She makes her mouth a straight line.

He leans closer, pressing his lips to the faux green gem. "Number two: Are you happy to hang around with me all the time?"

Chest rising and falling too fast, Angelica's resolve begins to crumble, leaving the hatches unbattened.

He nuzzles her jawbone, a soft hum rumbling inside him. It makes her tummy flutter, butterflies doing swoops. Leaning up, his thumbs caress her cheeks as he presses soft kisses to each one. "Three: Do you like it when I hold you?"

There's only one answer.

"When I say nice things to you?"

Like he so often does.

"When I make you laugh?"

Which he does every day.

Pulling back and running the pad of his thumb over her bottom lip, he watches the motion with fascination. "When I want to kiss you?"

Her body trembles. "Do you want to kiss me, Simon?"

His hum becomes a growl. "Absolutely."

The press of him against her lips is anything but soft. It's hungry, fast, and firm. Before she knows it, she's on her back with her arms held over her head, his chest heavy against hers. She arches and gets nowhere, pinned by his weight. He's got her right where he wants her. Trapped, vulnerable, and unable to escape.

Good.

His tongue doesn't ask politely, it sweeps in without asking, taking her breath away. He tastes like sweet liquor and smells uniquely *him*. Something special and so utterly Simon that it makes her melt beneath him. She matches his pace, stroke for slick stroke until he purrs for her. It's so low, she can feel it thrum, her heartbeat skyrocketing as she lets out a soft cry. He responds by taking her lower lip between his and suckling.

"I want you. Can I please have you?" He tips his groin against her core, and she can feel how hard he is. His rutting draws a searing line over her, hot and thick, and she has never wanted any man more in her life. This was worth waiting for. She'd never dared dream of a feeling like this, never believed it could exist in what was left of her heart, but can she truly be in love? Is that what this volcanic eruption is within her? This letting go she can't control? This heady heat making trails of fire in her veins?

She threads her fingers through his hair. "Your room or mine?"

———

He's going to die for how fast his heart is beating. "Yours." Simon never wants to take her in his room again if he can help it. The memories there are too raw. Too sad. There's no room for that now.

That tipsy feeling makes his head light, and he smiles wide. Even after all his experience, he feels childishly giddy, wanting to giggle at being in her arms. She returns his grin and bops his nose before leaning up to kiss it. Then his mouth. Again. And again. Then her tongue delves and swirls, bringing him back to the moment. To the heat of her beneath him. The softness of her breasts and the column of her throat as he slides his hand down to cup it. His thumb caresses straight down the middle, feeling her pulse flutter.

*Mine,* he thinks, delirious and drunk on her. His hips swivel of their own accord, seeking the firm angle of her hip as he pivots against it. He wants to be inside her, feel how wet she is. How wet he made her. He wants her to scream for him.

"Simon," she murmurs against his lips. "Bed. Now."

He doesn't need to be told twice. Lifting, he takes her hand, guiding her up and placing a kiss on her knuckles. He's Noah. He's not Noah. He's Simon. He's more than Simon, and he wants her. No matter what part of him is bubbling up, he accepts it, walking her backward with his hands sliding up her waist as he keeps his mouth locked on hers. When he flattens her against the wall, he takes full advantage, pinning her and diving down to suckle her neck. He pushes her hips so she rides his thigh again. She liked that before, he knows, and her soft cry says she likes it now too.

He doesn't let them stay. The lady gave him a request, after all. Tucking his hands under her rear, he lifts, and when her legs wrap around him, she grinds against his length, making him gasp into her mouth.

*Please, let this be real. I need this time to be real.*

He lays her down like she's made of glass. Her fingers work his shirt buttons, dragging the fabric over his shoulders and pulling her nails back along his skin in slow drags.

"How can I want you so much?" he pants. Her only answer is to pull him down atop her as she grabs the hair at the nape of his neck, tugging until his nerve endings ache with pleasure-pain. "Tell me you want it too."

"I want everything." Her hands travel down and push at him until he raises on his hands and knees. Her deft fingers undo his trousers in moments and slide them down, taking his boxers along with them. He can't help his loud, throaty moan when she palms him for the first time, but her playful smile makes it all right. Yet playful isn't how she should look right now. She should be desperate, like him.

"Turn over for me?" he asks.

She obeys, lifting up until her rear rides him and her back is flush to his chest. Clutching one hand around her stomach, he arcs his bare skin against the silken texture of her teasingly tight skirt. It slips and slides against him, cooler than the rest of her body, but he wants warmth. Heat. Fire.

Sliding down, he grabs the hem and yanks it higher over her curves until her black, lacy panties are on display. They weave a pattern against her, their design artful and sensual, but he wants them off. He wants to feel her. Needs it.

He moves the gusset of her panties to the side and slips his fingers along her entrance. She lets out a deep murmur he can't decipher as he swirls around the wetness he finds there. He's rock-hard, knowing she wants him. Finally.

He slides the black fabric down over her thighs, pressing kisses between her shoulder blades. Her jet-black hair is swept aside, and he marvels at the arch of her back as she presents herself to him, full and unashamed.

"Tell me," he says, nipping her bra strap through her shirt and tugging it, careful not to bite her. "Tell me to touch you."

She pushes back against him, coating his erection in her sweet slickness as she slides their bodies together. "Put yourself inside me."

His voice falls into reverence. "Absolutely."

Her giggle is cut off by a little moan as he pushes in. He's not slow, not with how much he aches. She grips him in small, mind-melting clenches, and he bites into her bra strap again, if only to stifle his own moan. His mouthing makes her white cotton blouse turn translucent, showing off another outline of black lace. She's so sexy. So perfect.

If he moves, he's going to come too soon.

Leaning back, he takes a good eyeful of her shape impaled on him. He sees where they connect, where he ends and she begins, and sets the image in stone in his mind. She tries to move, tries to pull forward, but he holds her tight, gritting his teeth. "Stay still."

She tightens inside and he bites his bottom lip as she squeezes him. His body begs him to take her. To pound into her. But this moment is more than that.

His broad hands push her shirt up, and he traces his fingers over her spine, touching her soft skin. He begins to knead it, working the muscles of her back in slow circles. She tries to pull forward again, but he clamps onto her hips, hushing her before going back to his slow strokes. He could stay like this forever, locked inside her, keeping her at his mercy as he tries to give her pleasure in every way he can.

Breathy, she says, "I think we finally found your kink. It's cockwar—"

"I don't need to know what it's called." His fingers swirl across her ribs, digging in and moving upward. "I nevvver need to know what it's called."

"I like this," she whispers.

He can't help but buck a little. He bottoms out with a grunt as she mewls beneath him.

"Do it again," she commands.

"I can't. It will be over too soon. I've wanted this for too long."

She rams back against him this time, taking him by surprise, and the wet sound between them makes his eyes flutter closed.

"Then we'll do it a second time. And a third."

"I'll never get enough," he manages through grit teeth.

"Then I'll never stop giving it to you."

His resolve breaks. Strengthening his grip, he guides her, sharp and fast as he snaps his hips forward. Her quiet whine is all the encouragement he needs. Again, and faster, he hits the deepest part of her, clenching his jaw to keep from exploding.

"More."

He loves it when she tells him what to do. A cold thrill travels from his bottom to his top as he starts a rhythm. Simon isn't a slow lover. The women he'd been with wanted it fast and hard, and it seems his dark angel is no different. He bounces her off his body, the sound of their skin colliding its own sensual song as her noises drive him mad. He's going to melt into her.

He's never been this hard. It's never felt this good. She's taking him so well, every inch he has to give her, and he wishes he could lick her everywhere. He wants to feel her come on his tongue. He wants to feel her come now.

"Touch yourself," he demands.

He sees her hand snake down and disappear between her thighs.

This is a fantasy. This is a dream. Especially when she starts panting and letting out those little cries.

"That's right. Just like that."

Tension builds up through his groin. His balls are heavy as they slap against her. He can feel her fingers as she circles herself, and he imagines it's his mouth in their place, licking and flicking and sucking.

*Slap, slap, slap,* their skin collides. He's huffing now, watching himself split her in two as she starts to tremble. He's dying. He can't hold it back.

"Come for me, sweetheart. I need it. Give it to me. Fucking come."

His filthy words seem to break her, and she shatters around him. She's so tight he can barely move, and it's perfect. She flutters and he fucks, slamming until she's screaming, crying out his name, and pleading for him to make her his. She *is* his. For now and for fucking-ever.

He sees stars as he explodes, his head dropping back in an open-mouthed moan. Still, he keeps going, riding out his high until she's wailing beneath him, arms sprawled and clutching her blankets so hard her knuckles whiten.

Perfect. She's so perfect.

Spent, he crashes down on top of her, inside but unmoving, kissing every part he can reach. "I love you," he says again. "I love you. And someday, when it's real, I want you to love me too."

———

Those words play in Angelica's mind as he leans to the side, flopping down and taking her in his arms. Her shirt and skirt are up at half-mast and her underwear is around her thighs. His shirt is off, but his pants and boxers are at his knees. They're a mess. Tell that to him, though. He acts as if they're in the world's comfiest pajamas as he runs his fingers through her hair, once, twice, before he seems to drift off, holding her like a teddy bear. His face is flushed, whether from their actions or alcohol, she's not sure, but she adores it, either way.

She does love him. She must. Her heart burns with it. Part of her wants to scream it from a rooftop and part of her wants to run far away. But here, in his arms, she's never felt more safe. More needed. More at home. She never had a home, not really. Not until now, in this moment with this man.

His soft breaths deepen, and he twitches the little muscle-flickers of sleep, making her grin, pressing deeper into his chest.

*I do love you, Simon.*

*And someday, I promise, I'll tell you.*

# sweet resolutions

. . .

"WELL, Pezner used to be in marketing before he went down the drain. Maybe he can do some basic training around that," Joe says, gesturing to the monitor on the wall as Ciel, Simon, Lawrence, and Mrs. Jennings from the talent acquisition firm look at the roster of teachers on the screen.

"Does he have a degree?" she asks. "We should only hire qualified people."

Ciel leans back in his chair, throwing an arm over the top, looking like he belongs in this space. He owns the conference room like he's been here for years, his new suit fitting him impeccably. Cleaned up and shiny, the only thing he refused was to cut his braid. He said he'll keep it 'til the day he dies. "If you ask him, he says he has a bachelor's, but we should check his references. Make sure he didn't just get some online certificate."

"What's wrong with online certificates?" Simon asks.

Mrs. Jennings and Ciel just look at him. "A certification is not a degree, Mr. Javik."

"And sometimes, you don't even have to work hard to get one," Ciel agrees. "I got a certificate for party planning from the library computer the other day and learned jack shit."

"Party planning?" Joe narrows his eyes in disbelief.

"I'm always in for a good time."

Lawrence snickers at the other end of the table before tapping his fingers off the polished wood and turning inward, pensive. "Can we handle the influx of new people?"

Mrs. Jennings flicks some papers back and forth. "We need to start slow, but we can take on another twenty trainees in the accounting program. If Mr....Pezner?...can put together a training program in a quarter, we'll be able to take on another twenty to forty depending on the hours he's willing to work. Imagine them all training for three-month periods, then we can place them in entry-level roles."

"Will the state still pay unemployment if they're not actively looking for work?" Simon asks.

"We have connections. Working with us counts as active search. We can place them early if they do well enough."

"Are you talking about testing?" Joe asks, futzing with the buttons on the polo shirt he hates. "Some of us suck at tests. Better with hands-on."

"Our tests are hands-on," Mrs. Jennings assures. "Except for GEDs. Many of our ladies failed SATs and GMATs, but we do well getting them high school equivalency. That's a bar we can't drop."

Lawrence nods, leaning back. "How long until we start turning a profit after the cost of building that housing unit?"

"Six months," Simon says. "Sooner if Nando can consolidate the shared functions. We're nixing our low-performing staff in IT and HR and replacing them with Mrs. Jenning's best."

"Call me Mary, please," she says with a gracious smile. He returns her expression.

"Only if you call me Simon."

———

"Yes!" Angelica hears Simon shout across the bar, fist pumping and obviously annoying Dr. Tyler Knight. He points a dart at Simon in a half-assed threat.

"Javik, I'm taking you down."

Simon flaps toward the bull's-eye. "I just hit two of those in a row. You and your skin knitting can't do that, no matter how 'precise' you claim to be."

"Who are you and what have you done with my Simi?" Nando grumbles. Ginger sits in his lap, playing with his phone, clicking together little colored jewels that jingle and disappear.

Simon raises a finger and points. "You're next." Nando rolls his eyes.

"Didn't know he had a competitive streak, did you?" Angelica asks, leaning back and sipping her martini.

"I knew he had one, I just didn't know it applied to bar games."

"Don't be so bitter." Sophia *tsks*. "All he did was kick your butt at pool. If it makes you feel better, he kicked mine too."

"This man is a bar game maniac," Tyler calls, closing one eye, aiming at the dartboard, and getting slightly off center with a curse. "How he never coerced you into losing before is a wonder. He's been hustling in places like this since he got his fake ID at fifteen."

They all go wide-eyed, looking at Simon with gaping mouths. Grinning, he only crosses his arms and shrugs.

Angelica nods down at the munchkin in Nando's lap. "Surprised they let her in here. This place is a den of vice and sin."

"I know the owner," Sophia says. "I bring her here all the time. As long as I'm not dipping her juice straw in vodka, we're fine."

Nando sours, bouncing Ginger on his knee a little and making her giggle. "Well, as long as she gets to bed on time, yes? Yes, *bella*? Are you tired now, huh?"

Snorting, Sophia takes her little one back. "First off, daycare will let her take naps if she gets cranky. Second, I'm the one putting her to bed, not you."

"And third," Angelica chimes in, "you're not in line for Daddy of the Year yet. Keep your shirt on."

He scowls but says nothing. Angelica revels in their tense relationship, but even she has to admit it's more like annoyed grumbles than her railing at him of late. He's been taking her abuse like a champ, only complaining to his therapist, according to Simon.

"Give her back," Nando grumps, raising his arms and waving

forward. Ginger reaches toward him and squiggles until Sophia hands her over with a sweet smile. They're not together, not by a long shot, but Sophia still glows with joy. Angelica is happy to see her friend like this. It took a little while to get here, but she said it was worth all the while.

Her phone buzzes, and she takes it out. It's the unmarked number... That can only mean Maxine.

Angelica swallows and sets down her drink.

> How's my little bird doing?

She doesn't know whether to respond. How to respond. But looking at the crowd of people around her, something in her heart speaks for her.

> I'm happy.

There is a pause, and then:

> Well, would you look at that, I just felt something akin to pride. Odd. Seems I must have been rooting for you after all.

> Good luck then, Sadie.

> Make every moment worth it.

Little tears prick Angelica's eyes, and she blinks them back.

> I will.

She waits to see if any more will be said, staring blankly with a lump in her throat, but when Sophia asks, "Who are you texting with?" she only smiles, shakes her head, and tucks her phone in her pocket.

The past is gone. It's time to move forward.

———

Angelica watches Simon mutter over his dough. His massage therapist told him there are other ways to relieve stress, and he decided making bread was it. Thank God people from the office eat it, because Angelica will never touch that carb-riddled crap with a ten-foot pole.

Except when she does.

But Simon pretends not to notice.

"What are you abusing this time?" she asks.

He picks it up, flips it over, and smashes it back down with a *thwack*. Flour dusts the space like either fresh snow or a small fortune's worth of cocaine. "Pizza dough, can't you tell?"

"It all looks the same to me. Except when you make banana bread."

"That doesn't count."

Speckles of flour grace his face with freckles like hers, only powder white. Giggling, she ducks under his arms, putting herself between him and the counter and fluffing him off with little pats that make clouds in the air. He *pffts*, his eyes cinched as his head shakes, barely avoiding a sneeze.

"What are you doing to me, woman?" he gripes.

"Preparing to kiss you."

He peeks out of one eye, his smile blooming. Always ready for attention, this one. "I told you you love me."

She waggles her head back and forth as if in contemplation. "I'm not sure. How would I know?"

His smile becomes a slow grin. "Hmm, let's see… Are you happy to come home to me every day?"

She slides her hands over his cheeks and leans closer. "Maybe."

"When I make love to you?"

"When we fuck like rabbits, you mean."

He chuckles, ducking his head down until their foreheads touch. "Can you ever picture yourself leaving me?"

She shakes her head, letting her eyes slip closed. "Nuh-uh."

"Then you love me."

"Yeah. I guess I do."

Their kiss is soft and slow. He wraps his hands around, getting flour all over her, but she couldn't care less. Scooting back, she hikes herself onto the counter to get a better angle, swooping in on him with a beautiful, heart throbbing ache in her chest. "I think I've loved you for a long time."

Tucking into her neck, he smiles against her. "I knew it."

She chuckles and kisses the crown of his head. "Is this where our happily ever after starts then?"

"No." He nuzzles in. "I think it started the minute you first laid eyes on me."

The kitchen is quiet except for the sound of their contented breath as they hold each other, no secrets, no lies, no tricks between them. Open and honest with hearts entwined. Shared home, shared friends, shared lives.

Angelica never wants to leave.

Bee would be so proud.

# ILLUSTRATIONS

Angelica
Simon

Sniff

I'm not scared of you...
I HAVE A BIG STICK

I'm not...
I'm not...

Zzzzz

# acknowledgments

Ahh, my lovely readers, thank you so much for taking a chance on this book. *Selling Simon* is so incredibly special to me, not only because I love Simon, Angelica and the rest of our cast, but also because this book has resonated with a broader, contemporary audience. I love writing Dark Omegaverse Romance and Horror, but this story—for all it's sharp edges—is the most lighthearted novel I've ever written.

I'd like to thank the Reylo fandom. Its authors, illustrators, and voice actors have inspired me to go for my dreams knowing that—if two idiots on opposite sides of the war in a galaxy far, far away had the opportunity to fall in love—nothing is impossible.

I should be flogged with a stick if I forgot to mention the "321...Write!" authors group on Discord. Together, we bat around story ideas, beta read for each other, and hold each other accountable for our goals. Everyone in that space is welcoming, talented, and enthusiastic, and I love how we help each other keep our eyes on the prize. Though everyone is precious to me, I'd like to specifically call out a few who are essential in helping me walk the author's journey. Mari, the one person I say "I love you" to more than my husband and son combined; Maude, whose expertise and diligence makes her a bedrock of inspiration; Ashley, whose stories keep me on my toes; and Liana and Tristen, for launching and nurturing this space, giving us authors a place to call home.

Thank you to everyone. I appreciate you. I admire you. I adore you. See you in the next book.

XO

Nix

# about the author

From the Boston area, Nichol is a fan of all things art. Known for her uniqueness and general snarkasm, she works to captivate her audience through engaging stories with a twist, hoping to take her readers for a good ride.

She loves tea with honey, indulging once a week on Saturday. Specifically, Saturday. If it's not Saturday, tea shall not happen.

————

STAY IN TOUCH WITH NICHOL:

nixcomix.com
Facebook, X, Bluesky & TikTok: Nixcomix
Instagram & Tumblr: NixComix1